Praise

'A t

'A must-read for our times – a story that entertains, challenges, and ultimately leaves you feeling hopeful'
Sunday Mail

'Clever and astute, I'd expect nothing less from the author of *The Change*, which was a cracking read'
The Belfast Telegraph

'Powerful . . . bewitching and satisfying'
i

'A brave, resonant novel'
Woman's Own

'Powerful . . . A feminist thriller for our times'
Nina Pottell, *Prima*

'Kirsten Miller has that rare ability to take a serious subject and make it very, very funny. I enjoyed this novel and you will too'
James Patterson

'A roar of rage, a pacy page-turner, I loved it with all my broken heart. Read it. You'll love it'
Marian Keyes

'A fantasy that feels true. A story that's as furious as it is tender. A look at where justice fits in a world that shows women so little mercy'
Emily Henry

'A brilliant book. Thrilling, fast paced and original. I couldn't stop reading'
Sarah Morgan

Kirsten Miller grew up in a small town in the mountains of North Carolina. At seventeen, she hit the road and moved to New York City, where she lives to this day. Kirsten's first adult novel, *The Change*, is a feel-good feminist revenge fantasy and was selected by the *Guardian*, *Prima*, and *Woman & Home* in their 'Books of the Year' round ups. It has been optioned for a film by Made Up Stories.

Lula Dean's Little Library of Banned Books is her second adult novel, and explores book banning and those brave enough to stand up against censorship.

Follow Kirsten Miller on Instagram @kirstenmillerbooks

Also by Kirsten Miller

The Change

Lula Dean's
Little
LIBRARY *of*
BANNED
BOOKS

KIRSTEN MILLER

ONE PLACE. MANY STORIES

HQ
An imprint of HarperCollins*Publishers* Ltd
1 London Bridge Street
London SE1 9GF

www.harpercollins.co.uk

HarperCollins*Publishers*
Macken House, 39/40 Mayor Street Upper,
Dublin 1, D01 C9W8, Ireland
This paperback edition 2025

1
First published in Great Britain by
HQ, an imprint of HarperCollins*Publishers* Ltd 2024

ISBN: 978-0-00-865430-6

For all the good people down south

CHAPTER 1

FOOD OF THE GODS

Ronnie Childers was tripping his balls off in Jackson Square when an angel of the Lord appeared before him. She was a glorious vision, dressed in black gym leggings and a Bikini Kill T-shirt, her golden hair twisted into a messy knot on the top of her head. She looked a lot like a girl he used to get stoned with back in high school.

The angel hovered over his park bench, the streetlight casting a halo behind her head. "What the hell are you doing, Ronnie?" she asked.

"Am I that fucked up or is it really you?"

The angel snorted. "Both," she told him.

Tears of pure joy sprang to Ronnie's eyes. "Hallelujah," he said. The Lord sure did work in mysterious ways.

"You've been out in the cow pasture again, haven't you?"

Ronnie giggled. "You got me." He opened his hand and presented a little brown mushroom as an offering.

The angel plucked the mushroom out of his palm and slipped it into her bra for safekeeping. "You realize it's two o'clock in the morning?"

"Then the night is young." Ronnie patted a spot on the bench. When the angel didn't plop down beside him, he swept an arm across the square. "I ain't making a move. I'm just asking you to take a moment to appreciate all this fucking beauty."

Sometimes Ronnie wondered how he'd never noticed it before. He'd spent half his life in Troy's town square, under the branches of its giant oaks and magnolias. As his mama cleaned the floors at the DMV, he'd whiled away the hours turning the fountain's water bloodred with Rit dye or vandalizing the Confederate general's statue with beautifully drawn penises. Those days were long gone, but the square was still Ronnie's favorite spot. He'd discovered its true beauty on nights like this—when the world was quiet and peaceful and no one was arguing about book bans and butt plugs and all the other bullshit that got the people of Troy riled up these days.

"You know, this could be a pretty nice place." Ronnie sighed.

The angel, staring out across the darkness, seemed to see the same thing. "Yeah," she agreed. "Hey, if you're free right now I could use a hand. You think you can walk?"

Ronnie looked down at his ripped jeans and work boots. His right leg kicked out when he willed it to move. "Looks as if. Where we heading?" For the first time he noticed the giant suitcase she'd been wheeling behind her.

"To cause some trouble," the angel told him.

"Fuck yeah." Ronnie stood up and shook out his lanky limbs. "That's rule number one in the Ronnie Childers playbook—never turn your nose up at trouble."

It really didn't get any better than this, Ronnie thought. High as hell and traveling through the night with an angel on a mission. He'd have to be at work at the Piggly Wiggly in a few short hours, but that was just to pay the bills. This was the sort of experience that fed the soul. Ronnie was absolutely certain that the world would be a much better place if more folks stepped out of the boxes they'd come packed in and opened their minds to the mysteries of the universe.

It wasn't until the angel stopped in front of a house that reminded Ronnie of a prissy white wedding cake that he started his slow descent from the heavens.

"You know Lula Dean lives here." He figured the angel ought to know. Most people in their right minds did their best to avoid Lula.

The angel turned and lifted a finger to her lips. She wheeled the suitcase over to a little purple cabinet fixed to the top of a post just inside Lula's front yard. Shaped like a house and hand-painted with flowers, it held two short shelves crammed with books. *Lula's Little Library* was written in cursive below the front eave.

The angel opened the glass door. "Take everything out," she whispered. "Stack all the books in a pile."

Ronnie pulled a thick tome off the top shelf. "*The Southern Belle's Guide to Etiquette*. Where the hell does she find this stuff?"

The angel was too busy opening her suitcase to respond. Packed inside were at least two dozen books.

Ronnie whistled softly. "Those what I think they are?" he asked.

The angel looked up with narrowed eyes. "I thought you were high."

"I ain't so high that I can't recognize contraband," Ronnie told her, returning to the job she'd given him. "No worries, your holiness. I won't interfere with the Lord's work."

Once there were two stacks of books standing side by side, Ronnie stepped back.

"What now?" he asked.

"Switch the covers," the angel ordered. "Put Lula's dust jackets on the books I brought. Then put those books in her library. Lula's books will go into the suitcase."

Ronnie paused. "Just so you know, I'm not one hundred percent convinced of the legality of this operation," he told her. He'd had more than a few run-ins with the law during his two decades on earth. If he weren't a convicted felon, he might have made a good lawyer.

"That gonna be a problem?" the angel asked.

"No, ma'am." Ronnie shook his head.

When they finished swapping the books, the little library looked exactly as they'd found it.

"Good work," the angel told Ronnie. "Come on. I'll walk your stoned ass home."

HOW LONG HAD IT BEEN since they'd spent time together like this? At least two years, Ronnie figured. It felt just as right as it always had.

"So is that what counts for fun in Troy now? Eating shrooms and sitting in the square?" the angel asked as they strolled back through the park.

"Naw. Most folks round here prefer Oxy or meth."

The angel didn't laugh. "You're better than all this, you know."

"Yeah, well, still not good enough to come up with the cash for college," Ronnie said. "Plus, I got felony possession on my record now, so I reckon I'm fucked. I know this is gonna sound crazy, but if it weren't for the shrooms, I think I might have fallen down a deep, dark hole and never come out."

"It doesn't sound crazy at all. They've been using mushrooms to treat depression. Psilocybin may be schedule one here in Georgia, but it's considered medicine in other parts of the country."

"Maybe I should move to one of those parts," Ronnie said. "'Cause finding shrooms and using them are the only two things I've ever been really good at."

"That's bullshit and we both know it. But maybe you can find a use for those skills. Help people and make bank all at the same time—sounds like a good combination to me."

They stopped at Ronnie's front porch. He could still remember the first time they'd sat on the swing together—back in the days when neither of them knew that Lindsay was rich and Ronnie was poor, and they couldn't imagine a day when their paths would no longer run parallel.

"I love you," Ronnie told the angel. "I always have."

"And I love you right back," she said. "But as we both know, I'm pretty damn gay."

"Just my luck," Ronnie said with a shrug. "So how long you in town for?"

"I'm heading out tomorrow," she said.

Ronnie laughed. "You went to all that trouble tonight and you ain't gonna

4

stay to watch the shit hit the fan? That fancy-ass school hasn't changed you at all. You're one bad bitch, Lindsay Underwood."

"I came down to help my mom, but she doesn't want me to stay." Then a devilish grin spread across Lindsay's face. "Don't worry, though. I have a feeling I'll be back in town before long."

CHAPTER 2

LORD OF THE FLIES

Beverly Underwood just wanted life to go back to normal. You wouldn't think that would be such a controversial position, but you couldn't predict how people were going to react these days. Seemed like everyone was always itching to fight.

"I'm touched that you came down from college, sweetheart, but I can handle this. I really don't think it's worth you missing any more school."

Beverly didn't like to see her daughter scowling. Beauty like Lindsay's was a gift from God, and it felt like a sin to hide it.

"Is it true you don't need any help?" Lindsay shot back. "Or are you worried your gay kid will get in the way?"

Beverly slid forward on the couch cushion and grasped Lindsay's hand. "Oh, good gracious, no! How could you say such a thing?" Her daughter may have been twenty-one years old, but she was still Mama's baby, and Beverly couldn't have been any prouder. "Your father and I have given you our full support since that Barbie incident back in first grade. You being gay has never made one bit of difference to us."

"Then why are you telling me to get lost?"

Beverly gasped. "You think that's what we're saying?" She turned to her husband for support. "Trip, did you hear that?"

"I'm sorry?" Trip Underwood looked up from his crossword puzzle. "What did you say?"

Beverly fixed her frown before she turned back to her daughter. "Lindsay, that is *not* what we're saying. You will always be welcome in this house. All I'm asking now is that you finish out your semester while I try to put all this unpleasantness behind us."

Lindsay studied her mother and shook her head. "I can't believe it," she finally announced. "You're terrified of Lula Dean."

Once upon a time, Beverly would have laughed at the suggestion. Now she knew better. Truth was, Lula Dean was scary as hell.

LULA NEVER COULD GET ENOUGH attention. Beverly had diagnosed the disorder all the way back in high school. Even then, Lula had been desperate for people to see her—and she'd been blessed with all the gifts that caught others' eyes. Trouble was, most people never stuck around for a second look. Until her senior year of high school, Beverly couldn't have put a finger on what it was that scared everyone off. Then she'd found how far Lula was willing to go for the recognition she craved—and just how much she believed she deserved it.

After graduation, Beverly had planned to leave town and cede Troy to Lula. Of course, that's not how things turned out. For the past twenty-five years, the two of them had lived in houses half a mile apart. They both attended the First Baptist Church. They belonged to the booster club and baked mountains of cookies for the PTA. An outsider could be forgiven for thinking two women who shared so much in common might lead similar lives. But Beverly, now head of the school board, had long been seen as a pillar of the Troy community. Until recently, Lula Dean had been known as the town crank.

As usual, Lula had brought it all on herself. After her husband died and her kids left town, a lot of folks took pity on her. She could have taken the opportunity to mend some fences. Instead Lula seemed dead set on using her time and energy to punish the world for ignoring her in the first place.

Most of her efforts never paid off. Nobody gave a damn if Walmart sold butt plugs—or if the gift shop on Main Street carried cards for gay dads. Then Lula discovered pornography in the baking section of the local library. Within a month, she was famous throughout the state.

It didn't matter that a thirteen-year-old delinquent confessed to slipping the erotic cake cookbook onto the library's shelves as a prank. Lula had found her calling. Having successfully rebranded herself as a righteous crusader, she got right to work. The children of Troy were in terrible danger, Lula announced on Facebook. Within weeks, she'd recruited a group of like-minded residents. Together, Lula's Concerned Parents Committee assembled a list of books they believed had no place in a God-fearing town. Beverly found an identical list online, but Lula claimed it wasn't plagiarism—just proof they'd picked all the right ones.

Beverly could have kicked herself for refusing to take Lula more seriously. But over her forty-four years, she'd watched countless panics flare up and fade away. A while back, every store in town kept the laundry detergent under lock and key. Now no one worried about kids nibbling on April Fresh Tide pods, and Beverly expected Lula's crusade to share the same fate. Then, on the first of May, she received a frantic call from the high school's librarian. The principal had allowed six members of the CPC into the library, and they were yanking books off the shelves. By the time Beverly made it over to the high school, the Concerned Parents Committee had already moved on to Troy's middle school. The elementary school and the public library were ransacked before the end of the day.

As head of the school board, Beverly convened an emergency session. But her fellow members weren't eager to act. The CPC would be holding a press conference the following afternoon, and they wanted to hear what Lula Dean had to say. Stunned by her unexpected defeat, Beverly logged on to Facebook, where Lula had posted pictures of the books they'd confiscated from the town's four libraries. What should we do with this filth? Lula asked her followers. Beverly scrolled down through the replies. The most common response appeared to be: Burn it!!!

Beverly sat back and stared at all those exclamation points. She could sense the excitement. There were people in Troy who thought burning books would be fun.

WHEN LINDSAY GOT WIND OF the latest developments, she'd hopped in her car and driven five hours to Troy—even though her junior-year finals at Duke were just around the corner.

"You can't let them burn those books, Mom," Lindsay announced the second she set foot through the door.

"Honey, I'm not *letting* them do anything," Beverly told her, unwilling to admit that the situation wasn't under control. She'd just heard that the principal of the high school had lent the Concerned Parents Committee the school auditorium for its press conference. Beverly could sense the tide turning against her.

The next afternoon, Beverly and Lindsay were sitting side by side in the front row of the high school auditorium. Beverly counted thirty boxes of books stacked on the stage. The crowd went silent when Lula sashayed out to the microphone. Twelve members of the Concerned Parents Committee filed out behind her. Some—like the high school valedictorian's father—were people Beverly would never have expected to see. One of them was the mayor's wife.

Beverly was so shaken she barely heard Lula's speech. But when it came time for questions, she was the first to rise to her feet. "How did you decide which books should be removed?" Beverly asked. "Have you read them?"

"Do I look like a person who'd read this kind of smut?" Lula asked, holding up a copy of *Anne Frank: The Diary of a Young Girl.*

Lindsay let out a startled laugh, and Beverly saw Lula's eyes land on her daughter.

"Looks like somebody thinks all this is funny." Lula was not amused. "Lord only knows what damage these books have done to the youth of this town. While we weren't paying attention, we may have lost an entire

9

generation. And who's been taking our children? Hold tight and I'll show you. It's not like he's been hiding. He's been sitting right here on our library shelves."

Lula left the mic, marched over to the nearest box, and plucked a book off the top of the pile. The red, black, and yellow cover showed a terrified boy, his body licked by flames.

"Recognize this?" Lula called out. "Y'all know who the Lord of the Flies is, don't you? You think it's a coincidence this book's named after the devil? He's been right here in Troy, and he's opened the door to a whole slew of demons. Anarchists and pedophiles and socialized health care. He's the reason your children complain about going to church. He's why your doors have to be locked when you leave the house. Without the Lord of the Flies, kids wouldn't be getting kidnapped or groomed or given double mastectomies."

Lula paused to catch her breath, and Beverly saw a flash of uncertainty. For a moment, even Lula seemed to wonder if she'd gone too far. Beverly glanced over her shoulder at the audience. The faces she saw all appeared fearful. But it was impossible to know what exactly had scared them.

Lula went back to the mic and held the book against her ample chest. "This is how the Lord of the Flies gets into your homes," she said in a voice that sounded somber, even reasonable. "Through books that encourage our children to use drugs, have sex, and pursue the homosexual lifestyle. The CPC has brought these books to your attention. Now the people of this town must decide what to do with them before it's too late."

"Bonfire!" shouted a man on the committee.

"No." Beverly finally recovered her voice. "The school board will look into the matter."

"And how many children will we lose while the board takes its time deliberating?" Lula demanded.

"Mom!" Beverly heard Lindsay whisper behind her. "You have to make them put the books back!"

Beverly ignored her daughter. "Until we issue a ruling, the books will be stored in a secure location."

After the citizens of Troy filed out of the auditorium, Beverly and Lindsay silently loaded the boxes into their Highlander and stacked them all in the Underwoods' basement.

BEVERLY WENT TO BED THAT night knowing Lindsay thought she was a coward. And she was. She should have fought harder to keep the books on the shelves. She should have stood up to Lula Dean. The truth was, Beverly wasn't scared for herself. She didn't mind being in Lula's crosshairs. But she knew where Lula was heading with her talk about the "homosexual lifestyle," and she wasn't going to let that woman go after her daughter. Lindsay had a right to lead her life without little-minded monsters like Lula taking shots at her.

In the morning, the paper announced that Lula Dean was considering a run against Beverly for her seat on the Troy school board. "Do we really feel comfortable reelecting a woman who keeps pornography and communist propaganda in her house?" Lula had asked the reporter. The picture that accompanied the article showed Lula in her front yard. A cabinet shaped like a little house was fixed to a pole by her white picket fence. Lula had painted it lavender, decorated it with pink and white flowers, and filled its three shelves with only the most wholesome books.

"I've heard people think I don't read, and that's just not true!" Lula was quoted as saying. "I want to share the books that helped me become who I am. So, I'm making my own little library available to everyone!"

THAT DAY, EVERYONE IN TROY stopped by Lula Dean's library. When Lindsay visited in late afternoon, there wasn't a gap on the shelves. Not a single book had been borrowed. She couldn't understand how the townsfolk had all passed up classics like *The Southern Belle's Guide to Etiquette*, *Buffy Halliday Goes to Europe!*, and *101 Cakes to Bake for Your Family*. Some people claimed Lula had filled the shelves with books she'd bought for twenty-five cents a pop at a Goodwill store. But Lindsay wasn't so cynical. She didn't have any trouble believing that books like these had made Lula Dean the woman she was.

As she walked home that day, Lindsay had never been more grateful she'd been born an Underwood. Though it would have come as a surprise to Beverly, she had never considered her mother a coward. Beverly had been a wife by twenty-two and a mom eight months later. She hadn't had a chance to figure out what she wanted, so she'd made the best of what she got. Some people might have resented being stuck in a small town, but Beverly had worked hard to make Troy a better place. Maybe she didn't always use the right words—and it wasn't uncommon for her foot to get lodged in her mouth. But Beverly had the biggest heart of anyone Lindsay had ever met—and more guts than everyone in Troy put together.

When her mom said she could handle Lula Dean, Lindsay knew it was true. She'd watched her mother kick ass a hundred times, starting with the now famous Barbie incident back in the first grade.

"At lunch today, Lindsay was making the Barbies kiss." Mrs. O'Connor had called Beverly in for a conference, certain she'd be scandalized. People often looked at Lindsay's mother and saw someone she wasn't.

"And what did you do?" Beverly sat across from the teacher, prim and proper as ever.

"I took the Barbies away and put Lindsay in time-out."

"So you embarrassed a six-year-old child and put her in time-out for having dolls kiss?"

That was the moment when Mrs. O'Connor realized things weren't going as planned. "It wasn't a peck-on-the-cheek kind of kiss."

The disgust on Beverly's pretty face made it clear who she thought the true pervert in the room was. "So?"

"Well, it's not natural."

Lindsay still remembered how her mother smiled as she leaned forward to deliver the coup de grâce. "My child is exactly how the good Lord made her. And any adult who suggests there's something wrong with her can go straight to hell," Beverly had informed Mrs. O'Connor. "You ever embarrass Lindsay again, and I swear to God, I will send you there myself." Next election, Beverly had run for the school board.

Lindsay wanted to sic that badass on Lula Dean. It was what the town of Troy desperately needed. But when she sat down to say so, her mom asked her to leave. Though Beverly Underwood would never admit it, Lindsay knew she was treading lightly to protect her gay daughter. That's when her daughter decided to take matters into her own hands.

Before she headed back to school, Lindsay stopped by Ronnie Childers's house. She'd found a copy of *Food of the Gods* among the banned books, and she'd slid it into his mailbox. Then she couldn't resist swinging by Lula Dean's house for one last look at the library. Lindsay was admiring her handiwork when Bella Cummings jogged past. Lindsay had known Bella for years—first as her babysitter and later as a friend.

"Hey there!" Lindsay waved Bella over and handed her a book. "I found something for you."

Bella looked down at it. *The Southern Belle's Guide to Etiquette.* "Is this a joke?" she asked.

"Nope." Lindsay tapped the cover. "I want you to read it. This is the book that made me who I am."

CHAPTER 3

101 CAKES TO BAKE
FOR YOUR FAMILY

t was round about her eightieth birthday that Wilma Jean Cummings noticed a change. She was still the same, of course. It was everybody else in the family who'd lost their damn minds. They leaned in so close when they spoke that she could read their breath like a Chick-fil-A menu. Then their voices would go soft and sweet as marshmallow fluff, and they'd avoid any words with more than two syllables. At first, she wondered if they'd been licking the paint. But her children seemed perfectly normal when they talked to one another. Or at least as normal as they'd ever been, which—truth be told—wasn't saying so much. That's when Wilma Jean realized it was all for her sake.

"Why are y'all talking to me like I'm some kind of idiot?" she asked her oldest son.

"Aww, Mama," he'd crooned, bending down to kiss her cheek. "Nobody thinks you're dumb." One whiff and she knew he'd had Taco Bell for breakfast—three months and two days after open-heart surgery. And somehow *she* was the one they all thought was touched.

"Well, look at you!" Her daughter Cissy clapped like a trained seal one evening after Wilma Jean completed a phrase on *Wheel of Fortune* with only two *T*'s and an *F* on the board. Cissy's expression was the same she'd been wearing the first time her son squeezed out a poop on the potty.

"You know I used to be the district attorney," Wilma Jean reminded her.

"'Course you did, Mama," Cissy said.

Wilma Jean had to get up and shuffle back to her home office to make sure she hadn't dreamed it. But there on the wall were her fancy diplomas and her favorite photo with her least favorite governor. It had been taken just as the governor's hand cupped her ass—and a millisecond before her stiletto heel broke his toe. The memory, fresh as ever, still brought a smile.

Over the course of her eighty-four years, Wilma Jean had raised six children, buried three husbands, made a fortune as a lawyer, sent hundreds of feral hogs to meet their maker, and brought an infamous serial killer to justice. One might say she knew a thing or two. And if anyone had thought to ask, Wilma Jean could have spilled top-quality dirt on everyone in town. But instead of acknowledging their matriarch as a paragon of wisdom, her family acted like her brains had gone mushy.

"Mama, how would you like to go see that swanky assisted living facility they just put up down on Orchard?" her son Dean had the gall to ask her.

"How would you like to kiss my ass?" she replied.

Dean looked up at his brother and cackled. "Oooh boy, Mama sure is ornery today. You reckon she's constipated?"

After that, Wilma Jean stopped answering stupid questions. She figured that would teach 'em. Instead they all assumed she'd lost her hearing along with her marbles. Once she'd reputedly gone deaf, the revelations never stopped coming. Her children didn't think twice about bickering over their inheritance while she was sitting in the same room, trying to enjoy a bowl of butter pecan and catch up on *Mindhunter*. One night all six of them showed up in a pack and took an unsanctioned tour of the house, divvying up her possessions among them. There was a vicious fight over the antique wardrobe where Wilma Jean's church dresses were hanging. Later, she listened in while they argued about which broker in town could get the best price for the house. *Her* goddamned house. The one she'd bought at auction after she'd bankrupted the rich bastard who'd called her daddy trash. The one that had hosted all three wakes for her husbands. The one that had kept the rain off her head for forty years and had borne witness to her heartbreaks and triumphs.

Wilma Jean knew she should have said something, but she didn't. Somewhere along the way, she'd lost the will to fight.

After the tour, the children began showing up every night to sit watch, worried their siblings might abscond with the butt-ugly china that Wilma Jean's second mother-in-law had pawned off on her—or shove a pearl necklace down their pants. With all of them crowded into her living room, Wilma Jean was reminded of a video one of the great-grandbabies had shared with her. Filmed in the murky darkness at the bottom of the ocean, it showed hundreds of writhing white creatures feasting on the carcass of a massive whale. The existential horror of the video had haunted Wilma Jean for years. She couldn't have imagined a less dignified fate. Now she marveled at how limited her imagination had once been.

She told the children they were just being paranoid about things getting snatched. Their family had more than its share of morons, but she hadn't raised any goddamned thieves. The very next morning, Wilma Jean spotted a dark patch on the wall where a frame had been hanging for nearly forty years. Missing was a portrait of Wilma Jean that her second husband had commissioned from a young Alabama artist who'd gone on to great fame and fortune. The night of the tour, two of the children had come to fisticuffs over who deserved it. Neither of them had any intention of passing the portrait down to their offspring. To them, the painting was nothing more than money on the wall. Now one of her heirs had snuck inside during the night and made off with Wilma Jean's most prized possession. She called upon the piece of her soul that the artist had captured to curse all whose eyes ever gazed upon it. When that didn't prove satisfying, Wilma Jean called her attorney in Atlanta and secretly changed her will. She wanted every damn cent she had to go straight to saving the whales.

And yet, even after all that, Wilma Jean didn't have the heart to banish her family entirely. Problem was, it got lonely when no one else was around. Wilma Jean had no friends left to visit. Her three spouses were just ghosts she'd encounter in the rooms they'd once favored. From time to time, she'd try talking to Malcolm, the love of her life. But she never could get his voice quite right and the conversations always felt sad and one-sided. The truth was, he'd abandoned her, along with everyone else she'd picked to be in her life. One at a time, they'd all dropped dead. The only folks she had left were the ones fate had given her. Wilma Jean loved her six children, she really did. But she often wondered what in God's name she'd done to deserve them.

THREE MONTHS BEFORE WILMA JEAN turned eighty-five, she woke up in the middle of the night covered in sweat and filled with dread. For decades her family had gathered at the house on her birthday. And every year, Wilma Jean would bake herself a glorious seven-tier cake. It was meant to be fun. No one was ever obliged to come. On an average year, she handed out cake to two dozen guests. This year she hadn't even sent out an invite and the RSVPs were already rolling in. She had six children, twenty-four grand-children, and forty great-grandbabies. It was looking like every last one of them would be paying their respects. Add spouses and that meant upward of one hundred people showing up at her door in May—each and every one determined to brownnose their way into her will.

Come May, Wilma Jean had decided to cancel the whole affair. She was sick to death of her family. It seemed like there wasn't a single one of them who hadn't shown their ass at some point over the previous months. Then her grandson's wife, Britney, rolled up in the drive at nine o'clock on a Thursday and perp-walked their teenage daughter up Wilma Jean's front steps and through the front door. Britney looked angry and flustered, but the girl appeared perfectly composed. It wasn't easy to keep track of forty great-grandbabies who never stopped growing, but Wilma Jean recognized this one straightaway. Bella's face was always showing up in the local paper. It was a particularly attractive face, with a perky nose, long lashes, and perfectly rouged cheeks. Head of the cheerleading squad and prom queen, Bella was small-town royalty. Wilma Jean immediately suspected a plot. The girl was there for her money.

"Hey, Meemaw!" Britney yelled across the room. "I'd come in and say hi,

17

but I'm in a rush. You mind if Bella stays here with you while I head to the hairdresser? She's been suspended from school, and her daddy doesn't want her home by herself."

The girl rolled her eyes. "Grandma can hear you. You don't have to shout," she said.

Wilma Jean did a double take and Bella winked at her. She wished the girl would tell Britney she hated being called Meemaw as well.

"Come again, missy?" Britney turned on her daughter. "I'd mind your manners, if I was you. You're in trouble enough already."

Wilma Jean fixed her gaze on Bella. *What'd you do, princess?* She hadn't been in the mood for company, but now she was dying to know.

"Fine," she said. "Bella can stay."

Britney pressed her palms together and thanked the Lord. Wilma Jean didn't blame her. Those grays really did need a touch-up. "I appreciate it, Meemaw. By the way, your birthday's just round the corner. You up for making your famous cake again this year?" The smile on her face froze while she waited. "Meemaw?"

Wilma Jean's mind was already occupied with far more interesting thoughts. Bella didn't strike her as a junkie or a brawler. Probably hadn't thrown a punch in her life. Petty theft, Wilma Jean figured. She'd prosecuted a few sticky-fingered beauty queens back in the day.

"Meemaw?"

"What?" Wilma Jean snapped.

"I was just gonna say, if you're not up for making your birthday cake, just give me the recipe and I'll be happy to bake it."

Wilma Jean had stolen the recipe off the back of a box of Betty Crocker cake mix back in 1972, but everyone in the family was convinced she was a culinary genius. "No," she said. "I'm baking the damn cake like I always do."

Britney was in too big a rush to argue. "Alright then! Well, y'all watch out for each other today. Bella, I'm warning you. You better be on your best behavior."

The door slammed and Wilma Jean and her great-granddaughter were suddenly alone. Most of the other great-grandchildren were timid in Wilma Jean's presence. They'd read all the fairy tales about old ladies who poisoned apples and gnawed on little-kid bones. Wilma Jean wondered if the tales had been invented by old ladies who'd already raised their own damn children and just wanted to live the rest of their lives in peace. But this girl wasn't intimidated.

"So I was right. You can hear," she said, coming closer. She held a thick book against her chest.

"How'd you know?" Wilma Jean asked.

The girl shrugged. "Just a hunch. I wish I could ignore our family, too."

"I *pretend* to be deaf, Bella. I still have to hear them."

"At least they don't expect a response." The girl plopped down in a plush chair across from the sofa. "By the way, I'm thinking of changing my name to Lilith."

Wilma Jean lifted an eyebrow. "Is that right?"

"It's fine if you want to stick with Bella. The preacher told Mama that Lilith's a demon and I might be a Satanist. She's convinced I have 666 tattooed somewhere on my body."

"That's ridiculous," Wilma Jean scoffed. "Maybe your mother should do her own research instead of swallowing everything she's told."

"I offered to let her read my book," the girl said. "There's a whole section on Lilith, but Mama told me she didn't have time."

The girl held up the book she'd brought, and Wilma Jean recognized it at once. *The Southern Belle's Guide to Etiquette*. The cover showed three blond girls in dainty white dresses sipping afternoon tea. In the fifties, all the rich girls in town had owned a copy. Back then, Wilma Jean's family had been too poor to give a damn about books, tea, or etiquette. She'd perused the handbook once or twice and couldn't recall a section on Lilith. She wondered what on earth *The Southern Belle's Guide to Etiquette* had to say about a two-thousand-year-old feminist icon who'd been written out of the Bible.

"Your mother has time to check you for Satan's mark, but she can't be bothered to read a damn book." Wilma Jean sighed. "Sounds about right. Welp, you're in my house now. And here, we all get to be who we want to be. So how 'bout this? I'll call you Lilith today if you swear you won't call me Meemaw."

Bella seemed thrilled by the victory. "Easy-peasy. What do you want to be called?"

No one had ever asked her that before. Not once in her entire life had Wilma Jean Cummings been given the option to choose her own name. She took a second to think it over. "How 'bout Wilma?" She'd never much cared for the Jean.

Bella reached across to shake her great-grandmother's hand. "Deal," she said.

"I was just fixing to make some coffee. Would you care to join me?" Wilma hadn't asked anyone to have coffee in twenty years.

"Sure!" Bella said, so Wilma led her back to the kitchen, where the girl slid into the breakfast nook. The second Wilma was occupied with the coffee, Bella immediately tucked back into *The Southern Belle's Guide to Etiquette* like it was the greatest book ever written.

"In case you were wondering, there is an upside to spending time with old ladies." Wilma tried to catch a glimpse of the text as she set a plate down in front of her great-granddaughter, but Bella closed the book. "We buy people's love with pie."

"Then you're going to have a hard time getting rid of me." The girl took a bite and closed her eyes as she savored the strawberry rhubarb. "This is great. I'm so glad Mama's not baking the cake for your birthday. I look forward to yours every year."

Wilma brought their coffee over and took a seat. "I was thinking I might do something different this time," she confessed. "People seem to think I've gone daffy. I need to prove that my brain is still functioning."

Bella's smile slipped away. She set down her fork and touched her napkin to the corner of her mouth like a perfectly trained Southern belle. "That's a good idea. I was going to tell you before I left today. Mom says they're

20

planning to put you in a home. Your children are going to convince a judge that you can't care for yourself anymore."

"You don't say?" It didn't surprise Wilma one bit. She could have seen that news coming a mile away. And now that it was finally here, she wanted to beat it to death with a lead pipe. "Then I guess I'll just have to show those traitors what I can do."

Bella clearly approved of the plan. "I know you won't need my help, but I'm happy to give it."

"Thank you, Lilith. I'll keep that in mind." Wilma sipped her coffee and studied the creature across the table. Just when you thought you'd seen it all, life could still surprise you. She'd known there were a few good genes in the Cummings DNA, but until that moment, she wasn't sure where they'd gone. "Now, Lilith. I don't mean to pry but—"

"You want to know why I was suspended."

"I'll admit, I'm awful curious."

Bella leaned in as if sharing a scandalous secret. "I wore a tank top to school on Monday."

Wilma blinked. "That's it? That's why you're under house arrest? Were your lady bits exposed or something?"

"Nope. All my lady bits were perfectly covered. But the dress code says girls can't show their shoulders, so they sent me home. I went back Tuesday wearing a top with spaghetti straps, and they sent me home again. Then I showed up yesterday in leggings, which are *strictly* forbidden. The high school has a three-strikes policy, so I finally got suspended."

"And that's what you wanted?"

"I figured it was the least I could do to show my support. A girl in tenth grade got sent home last week for wearing a tank top. There was a boy in her class wearing the very same shirt, but he got to stay. The girls were confused, so I looked up the dress code and found out it only applies to us."

It had been the same when Wilma attended the local high school seven decades earlier. She felt a hot blast of shame remembering the day she was sent home after a shirt she'd worn without comment at twelve was deemed pornographic by a male teacher shortly after she turned thirteen. Wilma recalled her mother frantically scrounging to come up with money to buy clothes that disguised Wilma's growing breasts. Seventy goddamned years later, and absolutely nothing had changed.

"So you decided to protest the dress code?"

"Not right away," Bella told her. "First I went to see the principal to tell him the code was old-fashioned and unfair. He said dress codes are necessary because if girls are allowed to wear what we want, the boys won't be able to focus. I said why not let the girls dress comfortably and send the boys home until they can show self-control?"

"That's an excellent argument." The girl should go to law school, Wilma thought. "What was the principal's response?"

"He said it's easier for girls to dress modestly than for boys to behave. And so I told him I wasn't interested in following rules that make life harder for girls so it can be easier for boys. Until the rules change, they'll just have to make do without their head cheerleader."

"What's in it for you?" Wilma asked.

"Justice," Bella said as if it was the only reason that mattered.

Damn. Wilma knew that feeling. That burning desire to balance the scales had sent her to law school all those years back. The need to fight injustice, right wrongs, kick ass, and prevent the strong from screwing the weak.

"Most girls in our family have gone to that school. You're the first to stand up and challenge those stupid rules. I'm impressed."

"I got the idea from this book." Once again, Bella held up *The Southern Belle's Guide to Etiquette.*

"May I see that?"

Bella passed the book across the table, and Wilma opened it up to a random page and found herself confronted by a jewel-colored illustration of female genitalia. Convinced she couldn't be seeing things right, Wilma squinted and brought the book close to her face. She'd been alive for eighty-four years. She'd had three husbands and six children. And yet until that very moment, Wilma had been laboring under the misconception that her urethral opening was in a different spot. She was suddenly jealous of the rich girls who'd owned copies of *The Southern Belle's Guide to Etiquette*. What else had they known that she didn't? Then a light went on in Wilma's brain. She closed the book and opened it back up at the title page. Someone had slipped the dust cover of *The Southern Belle's Guide to Etiquette* over *A Girl's Guide to the Revolution*.

Wilma was familiar with that title, too. She'd seen it in the paper on the town's list of banned books.

"Where did you say you found this?" she asked her great-granddaughter.

"Lula Dean's little library," Bella said, without mentioning a word about Lindsay.

Wilma wouldn't have thought Lula had it in her. "Hop up," she ordered her great-granddaughter. "You and I are going for a walk."

"Where are we going? You're not mad about the library, are you?"

"Hell no, child. We're going to your school," Wilma said. "You ever hear of Title IX?"

Bella nodded. "There's a chapter about it in my book, but I haven't gotten to it yet."

"Title IX is a federal law that forbids sex-based discrimination in schools. That means your school can't have one set of rules for girls and another for boys. The dress code as it's written is illegal."

"That's right!" Bella exclaimed. "Mama said you used to be a lawyer."

"I'm still a goddamned lawyer," Wilma told her.

IT HAD BEEN AGES SINCE Wilma had taken a stroll through town. It wasn't that she was feeble, like her family assumed. She'd simply lost interest in life. Maybe that was what her children had picked up on. Her body had been functioning, but her heart wasn't in it. The woman who'd broken the governor's toe had slipped away. That's why they'd treated her like she was half dead. For all intents and purposes she had been.

On the way to the school, Wilma and Bella stopped in front of the Dean house. A post rose above the white pickets of Lula's fence. Fixed to the top was a wooden hutch in the shape of a house, its walls lavender and decorated with hand-painted flowers. The cabinet's door was a glass window through which three shelves of titles could be browsed.

"You sure this is where you got the book?"

"That's it," Bella confirmed.

The remaining books seemed ridiculous. Wilma spotted *Chicken Soup for the Soul* and *Buffy Halliday Goes to Europe!*

"Look, here's one for you!" Bella opened the library and pulled out a copy of *101 Cakes to Bake for Your Family* and handed it to her great-grandmother. "Didn't you say you wanted to try something new for the party?"

Wilma opened it and staggered back a step before recovering. Bella let out a whoop.

"Yep," Wilma said, snapping the book shut. "You were right, sweetie. This one will do perfectly."

LATER IN MAY, THE ENTIRE Cummings family gathered in the backyard at Wilma's house. Once again, Wilma had baked herself a giant birthday cake. Unlike previous years, this cake remained carefully concealed behind a folding screen until everyone who'd RSVP'd had arrived.

The hidden cake was the cause for much speculation—most of which Wilma, still presumed to be hard of hearing, was able to enjoy. The screen hid a disaster, the guests had concluded. She simply couldn't have pulled it off again this year. This would almost certainly be the last celebration of this sort, they said. The old girl didn't have it in her anymore.

When the time came, Bella (who'd decided to stick with her given name) was the one who got everyone's attention.

"Wilma wants me to thank you for coming! She made this year's birthday cake from scratch and she'd like to dedicate it to all y'all. But before we get started, I'll need all the great-grandchildren to follow me inside for a special surprise!"

Once the kids were safe in the house, Wilma stepped forward and opened the screen. Behind it stood a four-foot-tall penis cake rising from a base of two hairy balls.

Cissy looked like she might faint.

"We really should get this on camera for court," Dean muttered.

"Poor thing has lost her mind," one of his daughters whispered.

"I've lost my mind, have I?" Wilma demanded, demonstrating her excellent hearing. "I think it expresses my feelings perfectly. Y'all have been a bunch of pricks lately. By the way, I'd like you to meet my representative, Ms. Dorinda James from the Atlanta firm James, Jackson and Monroe."

Ms. James stepped up. She was a six-foot-two Amazon with a degree from Yale and a Ms. Olympia title.

"Now, Ms. James, some members of my family have been questioning my mental fitness, so I figured this cake might settle things. It's a red velvet cake with beige buttercream icing. I used dowels to ensure the structure stayed nice and rigid. The testicles are chocolate cake baked in a hemisphere cake pan and covered with fondant and coconut shavings. They're not just beautiful. They're functional, too."

Wilma hit a switch and whipped cream sprayed out the top of the cake and fell like snow on the crowd. Some of the family froze in horror, unable to pull their eyes away from the eruption. A few ran for the house to avoid getting stains on their clothes. The ones she'd always liked best stayed put and stuck out their tongues.

"Y'all seen enough or should I show you what else it can do?" Wilma lifted up the table skirt to reveal a motor underneath.

Struggling to keep a straight face, Ms. James spoke for the crowd. "I think we've seen more than enough, Ms. Cummings."

"Then let me make something clear to my family, once and for all. I ain't dead, I ain't demented, and I want my goddamned picture back."

CHAPTER 4

BUFFY HALLIDAY
GOES TO EUROPE!

Dawn Dugan had never been one for history. That was her husband's area of expertise. Nathan had a whole room in the basement dedicated to the memorabilia he collected. Once a week, he hosted a group of men who shared his passion. He'd send Dawn down to his man cave to dust the frames and display cases before his friends came over. When they left, she'd gather up all the beer cans and dirty dishes. Nathan locked the door after she was done. He didn't like anyone messing with his collection. He'd caught Dawn flipping through a book back before they got married. Judging by his reaction, you'd have thought she'd ripped out the pages and lit them on fire. He made sure it wasn't a mistake she repeated.

History wasn't her thing anyway. She didn't see any point in reading about stuff that had happened long before she was born. She wanted to look forward, not back. That's why she loved books that were written for young people with their lives still ahead of them. She'd been one of them a long time ago. But now she was thirty and her path had been chosen. She wasn't always sure it was the one she'd have picked for herself. It had gotten off to a rocky start, with an unplanned pregnancy, but now she was on the straight and narrow. Nathan owned his own roofing business and made a good living. She stayed home and took care of Nathan and their thirteen-year-old son.

That son, Nate Dugan, was the light of her life. He'd been born with her black hair and dark eyes, so she'd named him after his father. They both knew it was like naming a house cat Tiger. You can call somebody whatever you want. It won't change who they really are. And for the first twelve years of his life, that boy had been hers and hers alone. Small and shy, Nate had clung to her whenever his dad was around. It disgusted his father, but Dawn was grateful. She wasn't sure she'd have made it through without him.

Then, in the space of one year, Nate had grown half a foot. By thirteen, he was five inches taller than his mother, with the end of his growth spurt nowhere in sight. His shoulders broadened and his frame filled out. Dawn still remembered the first time she saw his father hesitate before smacking him. She secretly cheered the day Nate caught his dad's hand in midair.

For as long as they'd been together, Nathan had collected what he called strays—young men in need of direction. He'd lavished time on them, but he'd never shown any interest in Nate. Suddenly, he was dedicated to bringing his boy up right. They'd vanish into Nathan's inner sanctum for hours at a time. Dawn was thrilled to see Nathan sharing his interests with their son. Nate, for his part, had never seemed happier. When the two of them talked at the dinner table, Dawn usually took care not to interrupt.

"Mr. Bartlett said the Reichstag fire was a false-flag operation," Nate told his father one evening.

Dawn thought she might need to explain that Mr. Bartlett was Nate's social studies teacher, but it seemed that Nathan already knew.

"Yes, 'cause that's what they've trained teachers like Mr. Bartlett to think. The Jews bought up all the newspapers and publishers and Hollywood studios back in the day because they knew if you control the media, you control the message. Once you have all three of those, you can control people's minds. That's why it's so important that we refuse to let our schools spread their propaganda."

"Isn't Mr. Stempel Jewish?" Dawn didn't know why she asked. Everyone in town knew he was.

"What's your point, Dawn?" Nathan had responded in the tone that told her to tread carefully.

"Nothing." She kept her own voice bright as sunshine. "He was just always real nice to me. You remember Mr. Stempel, don't you, Nate?"

After Dawn's daddy died when she was seven, her mother had gone to work for Mr. Stempel at his clothing store downtown. For a year, the bus had dropped Dawn off at the shop every day after school. Only when she was older did she realize most employers wouldn't have looked kindly on a little kid running around their place of business. But Mr. Stempel called Dawn the store's spokesmodel and let her pass out flyers and help with the window displays. Never once had she felt unwelcome. Her mother had to quit after she married Dawn's stepfather. Dawn couldn't recall ever feeling wanted in her own home again.

When Nate was little, she'd stop in to see Mr. Stempel every few months. Her parents were both gone by then, and it felt good to have someone gush over her baby. After Mr. Stempel's wife died, she took him two frozen casseroles and sat with him for a while in his living room.

Nathan was still glaring at her. "I'm waiting for the point."

"All I'm saying is that Mr. Stempel doesn't seem to control any media. Not that I can tell, anyways." Humiliated, she turned back to her chicken. Sometimes she didn't know when to stop.

"Your mother's not a serious person," she heard Nathan tell his son. "She doesn't know much about anything."

It stung because it was true. She wasn't a serious person. When Nathan put on the TV, she'd find something else to do. Dawn just couldn't handle the doom and gloom. It was too hard keeping track of everyone who was out to destroy America. Even when she tried, she couldn't tell folks apart. She'd end up feeling bad for somebody sleeping out on the street, only to find out from Nathan that they'd been there by choice. It didn't make any sense, but as Nathan always said, you could fill the Grand Canyon with all the shit Dawn didn't understand.

The year Nate started kindergarten, Dawn thought about going back to school part-time. She'd given birth to her son second semester of her senior year and she'd been too busy after that to focus on learning. But once Nate was in school six hours a day, she figured she had time to get her GED and take a few classes at the community college. When she read through the course catalog, everything looked interesting. But Nathan didn't think it was a good investment. So Dawn had gone to the library and checked out some books for free. The next morning, he'd returned them all without asking.

"You already got a job," he told her when he got home that evening. "Why don't you focus on doing *that* right for once?"

Usually his word was law, but this time Dawn had pleaded with him. He always switched off the Wi-Fi in the morning when he left for work. Now that Nate was gone most of the day, once Dawn's chores were finished, there was nothing for her to do but sit and stare at the walls.

"Fine," he'd finally agreed. "You can check out books. But you pass them by me before you start reading. You have no idea what kind of damage the wrong books will do to a weak mind."

Nathan was a serious person and there was nothing he took more seriously than books. He'd been a fierce supporter of the effort to rid the libraries of communist propaganda. He even helped Lula Dean draw up the list of books to be banned. But he couldn't get rid of everything objectionable, and it took Dawn a while to get good at choosing books he wouldn't take back. Pastel-colored covers, she discovered, barely got a glance. Loopy letters and illustrations of teenage girls usually—but not always—ensured a book was safe.

The day she visited Lula's library Dawn felt like she'd hit the jackpot. Here were books handpicked by the lady Nathan was advising. Dawn had to stop herself from taking them all. The one she chose showed a pretty girl in a fifties-style poodle skirt and twinset standing on a bridge that spanned a canal. A handsome boy waved to her from a boat below. *Buffy Halliday Goes to Europe!*

Dawn started reading as soon as she got home. It wasn't quite what she'd been expecting. The book's narrator seemed a lot younger than the girl pictured on the cover. But she was smart and funny. She had parents who loved her, an older sister and friends. All the things Dawn used to pray for. As it turned out, her name was Anne. She lived in Amsterdam. And she was Jewish. Nobody in the book was named Buffy Halliday.

"What is that?" Nathan asked when he got home, snatching the book out of her hands.

Dawn held her breath while he studied the cover. She was enjoying the book more than anything she'd read in quite a while. "This looks like it's a hundred years old."

"I think it might be. I got it from Lula's library."

He set the book down on the counter with a grunt. "It's Friday night. The boys are coming. You got the den ready?"

"I'll do it right now," she said, taking her book with her when she left the room. Before she headed downstairs, she slipped it behind the dresser in her bedroom. Just to be safe.

DAWN AND NATE USUALLY PLAYED Life on Friday nights. She got the game set up and made some popcorn. She was just about to take her first spin of the wheel when a shadow fell across the board. Nathan's latest stray, Logan Walsh, had come up from the basement with a message for Nate.

"Your dad says it's time for you to join us," he told Dawn's boy.

Nate rose from his seat as though he'd been summoned by God. Dawn didn't want him to leave. She didn't want his father to have him. But she could feel Logan's eyes boring a hole through her, so she said nothing. He was young, and most women would have called him handsome, with sandy blond curls that reminded her of a fairy-tale prince. She'd heard Nathan say he'd inherited a fortune. The men in her husband's group were all a bit scary, but Logan was the one who made her squirm. She sensed something desperate about him. Like he was searching for something, but he didn't know what. Whenever he looked at her, she could imagine him cutting her open to find it.

As soon as he was gone, Dawn took the popcorn to the bedroom, locked the door, and pulled her new book out of its secret spot.

That night, the tale took a very dark turn. Anne and her family had gone into hiding and were forced to stay indoors at all times. If the Nazis discovered the family, they would all be arrested. Much later, they heard that many of their friends had been loaded on trains and sent to concentration camps. Rumor had it, they'd all been gassed. Which meant executed. But that couldn't be true, Dawn told herself. Why would the Nazis kill children? Maybe adults who could fight against them. But kids? It just didn't make sense.

Shortly after eleven, Dawn heard boots on the stairs. Her husband's friends were leaving. Heart racing, Dawn immediately slipped the book behind the dresser. Then she hurried down to the basement to clean up after the meeting. Usually, she paid no attention to the books on the shelves or the weapons in the cabinet. The blandly handsome mannequin who wore a black uniform and clutched an old pistol was in the same corner he'd stood in for years. But this time, Dawn felt him watching her as she gathered beer cans and picked stray potato chips off the carpet. She jumped out of her skin at the sound of someone bounding down the stairs. Seconds later, her son rushed into the room. He paused for a moment when he found Dawn frozen in terror. Then he grabbed a book off the couch and disappeared up the stairs to his room.

SUNDAY MORNING, WHILE NATHAN WAS off fishing, Dawn went to church and prayed for Anne's family and her own. After the service, she stopped by the grocery store. When she arrived home an unfamiliar car pulled in the drive after her. She was surprised to see Mr. Stempel behind the wheel. When she waved, he didn't budge. He seemed uncertain of what to do next, so she left the groceries in the back of her car and walked round to greet him.

"Mr. Stempel," she said when he finally opened his door. "It's so good to see you!"

As he got out, Dawn was struck by how old he looked. His hair was no longer gray but white, and his shoulders curved inward.

"It's nice to see you, too, Dawn," he said. "Or do you prefer Mrs. Dugan now?"

She couldn't understand why he was being so formal. "It'll always be Dawn for you," she told him.

"Thank you." He sounded relieved. "Well, Dawn, I wish I was here for a friendly visit, but I'm afraid I'm the bearer of bad news. I woke up this morning to find the front door of my house had been vandalized."

"Oh no!" Dawn cried. "I'm so sorry to hear that!"

"May I show you a picture?' He pulled out his phone and scrolled through photos until he found the one he was looking for. Then he passed the phone to Dawn.

"That's a swastika," Dawn said. She'd seen the same symbol every week for the past fourteen years. She'd shaken dust from flags that bore it—and wiped off black-and-white pictures of men saluting it. She'd cleaned cases filled with hats and medals and documents with the very same icon. Dawn wasn't dumb. She knew the Nazis were bad. But they were villains from a story so far removed from her own life that it might as well have been *Star Wars*.

But now she knew what that sign meant and what it could do. And she knew why it had been drawn on Mr. Stempel's front door—to hurt an old man who had been nothing but kind to her. And when she looked in his face and saw he was scared, she felt her heart break because she felt very certain she knew the person who'd done it.

"It is a swastika," Mr. Stempel confirmed. "I'll admit, it's been a while since I saw one in person. I was hoping I never would again."

"Do you know who did this?"

"I do. And that's why I came here instead of going to the police."

Dawn braced herself. It had to be one of her husband's friends. At that moment, she knew in her heart it was Logan Walsh.

"One of my security cameras recorded the person responsible." Mr. Stempel clicked on a video and passed the phone back to her. The film was so grainy it looked like it had been shot in a snowstorm. A male in a black hoodie approached the house. His hand emerged from the hoodie with a spray can. Five seconds later, he was sprinting back across the lawn.

Dawn hadn't braced well enough. She felt her knees buckle. "Dear Lord. That's my son."

"I know," Mr. Stempel said sadly.

She started to cry because it was all her fault. She should never have mentioned Mr. Stempel's name at dinner.

"I am so sorry," she told him.

"I am, too," he said.

"What should I do?" It wasn't fair to ask him. Dawn knew that. But there was no one else she could turn to.

"I can't say," Mr. Stempel said. "I don't know your son well. But I do know you, and I trust you. That's why I'm deleting this video."

She wiped her eyes on her shirtsleeve. The tears had already stopped. Now a rage was bubbling up inside her. "Thank you, Mr. Stempel," she told the old man.

"It's Joel," he said, putting his hand on her arm.

AS DAWN MARCHED TOWARD THE house, she could see Nate standing at the living room window. He tried at first to stare her down the way his dad always did. To prove her emotions meant nothing to him—that she wasn't

33

worth a response. But he was still her boy, and he broke before she burst through the door.

"I'm sorry, Mama," he said, backing away.

"Why would you do that?" she demanded. "Why would *my son* be the kind of person who hurts someone for no reason?"

"They control the world! We have to fight back!"

She might not have been a genius, but that was the dumbest crap she'd ever heard. "Mr. Stempel controls the world? A sixty-nine-year-old man who lives here in Nowhere, Georgia. You're telling me he controls the world?"

"His people do."

"His people?" she was yelling now. "*What* people? His wife died two years ago and his son lives in Austin. *We* are his people! The people who live in this town are his people!"

"He's a Jew, Mom. He's not one of us. You don't know anything!"

She pushed him against the wall. Her son, who was big enough to hurt her. Another kid might have. But Nate didn't, and that meant something. "I know one thing for sure. That old man just did you the biggest favor anyone has ever done you. His security cameras caught you on tape. He could have sent you to jail. You're going to go over to Mr. Stempel's house right now and clean that nasty mark off his door."

"No, Mama." Nate shook his head. He was terrified. But it wasn't of her. "Please don't make me. I can't."

"Why not?"

He opened his mouth but no words emerged.

"I asked you a question!"

"Because Dad's just starting to like me." Then he started to cry.

That destroyed her. Because she knew just how he felt. For years, she would have done anything for the slightest sign of affection from Nathan. She'd let her little boy see her scrape and grovel. He'd watched as she let Nathan train her to be the obedient servant he wanted—because she was too scared to think for herself. Nate was only following her lead. It was all her fault.

34

DAWN DIDN'T GO TO BED that night. By the time she finished reading her book, the sun was up. Before her husband could rise and demand his breakfast, Dawn headed out to the hardware store, where she bought a paintbrush and paint.

"I'm here to clean up your door," she told Mr. Stempel when he answered the bell. The Stempel house was right on Main Street. Everyone in Troy would see Dawn at work. And that's exactly what she wanted. She'd pay dearly for it later, but it was the right thing to do.

"I was hoping your son would come," Mr. Stempel said.

"Nate's got school this morning," Dawn told him. "And I didn't think this should wait any longer."

"I see." He didn't sound satisfied.

"Also, I've been reading this book, and I had a question I was hoping I could ask you." She reached into her bag and fished it out.

"*Buffy Halliday Goes to Europe!?*" he asked. "I have to admit, I've never heard of it."

"Sorry, I should have mentioned—that's just the cover. There's a different book on the inside."

Mr. Stempel opened the book. "*Anne Frank: The Diary of a Young Girl.* Isn't this on the banned book list?"

"Have you read it?"

"Oh yes," he said.

"Lula Dean called it smut at her press conference. But all girls think the kind of stuff that Anne did. I don't know why we pretend that they don't."

"I was never a girl, so I'll have to take your word for it," Mr. Stempel said. "You said you have a question?"

"Yes." Dawn cleared her throat. "Do you know what happened to her? The book just ended without saying."

Mr. Stempel's forehead furrowed as though he thought he might be the butt of a very bad joke. Then, slowly, his eyebrows lifted high in surprise. "You really don't know, do you?"

"No."

"Anne died. They murdered her."

Dawn shook her head. That couldn't be right. Why would they do that? "But she was the hero."

"I'm sorry," Mr. Stempel told her. "I thought everyone knew."

"But she didn't do anything!" Dawn argued passionately, as though reason could save a girl who'd been dead for decades.

"None of them did," Mr. Stempel said. "My uncles and aunts didn't do anything, either."

"The Nazis killed them?"

"Their children, too. The youngest was an infant. They were murdered at Bergen-Belsen. The same place Anne died." He paused. "You've really never heard of it?" He seemed horrified.

"I didn't finish school. But I'll look it up," she said, but that didn't feel like enough. "I promise."

Mr. Stempel stepped back into the house, but Dawn couldn't let it end there. She needed him to know that she was on his side, not theirs.

"The Nazis were monsters to kill little girls."

"I know that's what people say," Mr. Stempel told her. "But most of them weren't. They were just ordinary people. That's what makes them so terrifying. Monsters you can fight. But when the people who come for you in the night are your neighbors and coworkers and classmates . . . When you never know who's sick and who's not . . ." He shrugged.

"Sick?"

"Hate is a disease, Dawn."

Dawn felt her stomach heave. She put a hand to her mouth for fear she might vomit. "I think my son has it," she whispered when she could.

Mr. Stempel nodded. "For how long?"

"A few months. Since his birthday."

"Then there may still be time to help him."

"There's a cure?"

"Yes, and you have it," Mr. Stempel said. "It's the truth. It won't work on everyone. But maybe your son isn't too far gone."

DAWN GOT HOME JUST AFTER noon. It took less than a minute to kick open the door of the room in the basement. Now that she wanted in, a flimsy lock couldn't keep her out. Item by item, she dragged her husband's "memorabilia" up the stairs. Then she re-created Nathan's museum best she could on the front yard of their house.

"What are you doing?" a passerby asked. Then the wind caught a flag and unfurled it.

"Sharing the truth about my husband," Dawn called out as the woman hurried away. "I want everyone in Troy to see just who he is."

She was done by two-fifteen. Then she drove to the school and picked up her son. After a stop at the bank, they left town, just the two of them. She handed her son the only thing she'd packed. A copy of *Buffy Halliday Goes to Europe!*

CHAPTER 5

OUR CONFEDERATE HEROES

Everybody in town was talking about the Nazi like they never saw it coming. If they didn't, it was only because they hadn't bothered to look. Delvin Crump saw everything. He knew what was what.

Six days a week, he walked the same route through Troy. Never once in twenty years had he met with trouble. Most folks smiled and said hello when they saw him. Some weren't all that personable, but hardly any were rude. If you'd followed Delvin around for a day, you'd have come away convinced that the people of Troy were the nicest on earth. As long as you didn't look at their mail.

He'd had Nathan Dugan's number for years. He didn't need to see the packages from Relics of the Reich to know there was something wrong with the man. Dugan's wife and kid, both nice enough, were skittish as two beat dogs. On several occasions, Delvin had spotted Dugan glaring at him through the living room window when he dropped off the mail on Saturday afternoons. Dugan never greeted him at the door. Delvin said a prayer for Mrs. Dugan and her boy. People said the two of them had fled town. He hoped like hell they were gone for good.

But it wasn't the sick motherfuckers like Dugan who got to you. If you were sane, you knew those types were out there. It was all the little surprises that did you in. The pimple-faced teenager who'd started getting mail from a white nationalist organization. The Confederate flag you glimpsed hanging over the living room couch of a local lawman when he opened the door for a package. It was the woman you'd been friendly with back in high school who kept a Curious George doll in her front window throughout the Obama presidency.

The hatred hung in the air like a virus. Occasionally, you'd get a blast of it from the news playing on the television set of some sweet old lady. Half the county was hooked on opioids or meth, but the big story was always crime 150 miles away in Atlanta and the perpetrators were always Black. Twice a day, Delvin walked past the monument in front of the courthouse that didn't honor the three generations of *his* family who'd fought for America—but instead commemorated a Confederate general who'd done his damnedest to destroy it.

Everywhere Delvin went—whether a football game or the grocery store—he'd spot the infected. It got to the point where he didn't know if he could go another day without calling folks out. He started staying home so much that his wife and kids called him a hermit. He didn't explain. He didn't want them to know what he knew. More and more he just kept to himself.

IT WAS SHEER LUCK THAT he happened to glance at Lula Dean's library as he passed. Lula was one of the people Delvin went out of his way to avoid. She'd greet him at the door on a hot day. Offer him lemonade and yammer on about the weather. Meanwhile she was making lists of books that Delvin's kids shouldn't be allowed to read. When you have everything, the only luxury left is taking things away from others. It was an indulgence that Lula Dean certainly seemed to relish.

Delvin wished he could make her listen to *his* story. He'd start with his great-great-great-grandfather, who had broken the law when he taught himself how to read. Remind her that when the public library was built back in the fifties, no one in *his* family had been allowed inside. Show her the newsreel of his father, age ten, being spit on by his classmates the year Troy's grade school was integrated. And maybe then she'd understand why Delvin didn't want *any* books taken away. His family had fought like hell for the right to read them. In the Crump house, the written word was sacred. There wasn't a week that went by without his daughters checking out books from the library. His oldest girl, Jasmine, was reading *Their Eyes Were Watching God*. Nahla, the youngest, had started *The Hate U Give*.

If those two books hadn't been at his house, Delvin had a hunch they would have been yanked off the library shelves. Lula Dean and her goons had banned *Anne Frank,* and now she was offering up *The Art of Crochet* in its place. How do you improve yourself without challenging your mind? How do you leave a better world for your children? Delvin wondered. Then he remembered that was the point. People like Lula didn't want change. They were perfectly happy with the way things were. He skimmed the titles on the top shelf of Lula's little library. Then he came to an abrupt stop at the second from the right on the bottom. *Our Confederate Heroes*.

Not *Leaders of the Confederacy* or even *Confederate Heroes*. Those would have been bad enough. No, this book to which Lula Dean had given her stamp of approval was about our heroes. *Ours. Not yours, Delvin Crump. How dare you ever think you were one of us?* it asked him. *Sure, your family has lived on this land as long as anyone else's. And yeah, y'all fought for us. But everyone knows you don't really belong here.*

Not once in his life had Delvin Crump ever contemplated burning a book. When he'd joined the army, he had taken an oath to defend the Constitution, which gave all Americans the right to free speech, including the backward-ass bastard who'd written *Our Confederate Heroes*. But it was time to take this piece of shit out of circulation.

Delvin dropped the book into his mailbag. That night, when his wife and kids went out to the movies, he fired up the grill. As the coals were getting hot, he opened the book to page one.

124 was spiteful.

Delvin stopped. He knew that first line. The second, too.

Full of a baby's venom.

Carefully, reverently, he unwrapped the book from the dust jacket.

There, emblazoned in gold on a bloodred background, was the book's true title. *Beloved*.

Someone here did that, Delvin marveled. Someone in Troy, Georgia, had smuggled a story about the dark legacy of slavery into Lula Dean's pretty purple library. Maybe some folks in town were supervillains in disguise. But somewhere out there, at least one person was fighting for good. And that was a fight Delvin Crump had been looking for all of his life.

CHAPTER 6

THE RULES: TIME-TESTED SECRETS FOR CAPTURING THE HEART OF MR. RIGHT

Crystal Moore had a schedule, and she stuck to it every day of the week. She locked up her classroom at Troy Elementary at four-thirty and was home by five. Between five and five-thirty, she took off her work clothes and folded laundry or tidied the house. At five-thirty she started dinner, which was always on the table when Russell pulled into the drive precisely one hour later.

Thursday was chicken parmesan night. Russell's favorite. But it was seven o'clock and he still wasn't home.

Crystal hated to bug her husband at work. Russell managed the Piggly Wiggly on 441 right outside Troy. He always said it was like running his own country, and the Piggly Wiggly couldn't have asked for a better king. No one loved produce like Russell Moore. He could pluck a perfectly ripe cantaloupe out of a pile with his eyes closed. He was a master of meat, who chose the very best cuts for his own barbecues and would often wax eloquent on the subject of marbling. And every Saturday, he liked to greet kids at the store entrance dressed as the Piggly Wiggly mascot, Mr. Pig. Each year around September, Crystal's second-grade students would discover her secret identity as Mrs. Pig and pandemonium would briefly ensue.

Crystal and Russell had been married for twenty-five years, and she could count on one hand the number of times he'd been late for dinner.

"Hey, honey." Russell sounded winded when he answered the phone. That alone was unusual. Managing the Piggly Wiggly might have been mentally taxing, but it didn't require much in the way of physical exertion. "I just saw the time."

"Everything okay?" she asked.

"Yeah, yeah. The supply chain is still all kinds of screwed up. We got a bunch of shipments in all at once. Gonna take us a bit to sort through them. You okay there?"

"'Course." Crystal watched the cheese congeal on top of her chicken.

"Alright then," Russell said. "I'll be home when I can."

THE NEXT MORNING AT BREAKFAST, Russell looked bleary-eyed.

"What time did you get home last night?" she asked as she set a plate of biscuits down in front of him.

"Round eleven, I think," he told her. Crystal was always asleep by ten.

"That late?" She'd heard him come in at one-thirty. She felt her pulse pick up speed. Russell had never lied before.

"'Fraid so." Russell kept his eyes on his plate as he dug into his food.

Crystal's heart was pounding like a pile driver, and she could feel the earth opening up beneath her. "Do you think you'll be late again tonight?"

"Not sure yet," he said. "I'll let you know."

HE DID *NOT* LET HER know. So at seven that evening, Crystal slapped some foil over the skirt steak and potatoes that had grown cold on the stove and drove across town to the Piggly Wiggly. She pulled in next to Russell's truck and walked across the lot toward the brightly lit windows, which were already decorated with Fourth of July bunting. She could see her tall, handsome husband in his white short-sleeve dress shirt and red tie, hair graying just a smidge at his temples, waist just as trim as the day she'd met him. He was standing by one of the checkouts, and chatting with Janelle

43

Hopkins. Crystal slowed at the sight of his smile—that wide toothy grin she'd fallen in love with. Then a customer showed up and started slapping packages of ground chuck onto the conveyor belt, and Janelle reluctantly turned back to her register. Crystal was ten feet from the windows when she witnessed Russell reach out a hand and knead Janelle's shoulder. Crystal stopped like she'd rammed into a wall. Her feet refused to move and her lungs wouldn't breathe as she watched the cashier lean her head back and nuzzle her husband's arm. It lasted two seconds tops, but it told Crystal everything she needed to know. As soon as Janelle's customer stepped forward to pay, Russell let go of her shoulder and moved on.

Crystal sat in her car and wondered how it had all gone so wrong. She had followed the rules. She'd done everything that had been asked of her. She saved herself for marriage, despite the best efforts of her senior-year boyfriend. She'd worked like a demon to get good grades. She won a scholarship to Emory, but chose a good Christian college instead. There she met Russell and fell madly in love. They were married before God and raised three beautiful children. Two were now upstanding citizens and the third was trying his best. Aside from the month Crystal spent in the hospital after her youngest was born, she'd never missed a Sunday at church.

And now Russell was fucking a cashier at the Piggly Wiggly.

On her way home, Crystal stopped off at the package store, bought a nine-dollar bottle of rosé, and drank every last drop on an empty stomach. She cried herself to sleep and woke at ten the next morning, reeking of vomit and filled with shame. Having never suffered a hangover before, she took it as a sign of God's displeasure. In the face of adversity, Crystal had crumbled. She promised the Lord it wouldn't happen again and crawled out of bed to find her husband. All wasn't lost. There had to be *some* way to make everything right. But Russell, she soon discovered, was not in the house. In fact, there was no sign that he'd come home the previous night. So she slipped on her shoes and set out to hunt down his cheating ass.

When Crystal reached Janelle Hopkins's house, Russell's truck wasn't in the drive. She might have banged on the front door, but Janelle's twin boys were wrestling in the front yard, their shrieks of pain alternating with peals of laughter. The Hopkins boys had been in her class two years earlier, and by the spring semester, they'd had Crystal questioning her calling.

"Look, look! It's Mrs. Pig!" Daniel shouted, pushing his nose up into a snout. Cute, charismatic, and completely evil, Danny had the makings of a successful salesman or serial killer.

"Hey there, Mrs. Pig!" Brian waved with both hands. He'd either be president or in prison by age forty, Crystal was certain. Both boys followed their greeting with a chorus of snorts and oinks.

Her cover blown, Crystal waved back and picked up her pace, frantically searching for something to explain her presence on the Hopkins's side of town. She found it just up the street at Lula Dean's house.

She'd been meaning to stop by Lula's lending library since she'd read about it in the paper. She was curious to see what kind of books the town bully thought they all should be reading. Crystal had no respect for anyone who'd ban books—much less burn them. Her daddy had been a man of God. He'd even handled a snake or two in his youth, but he'd never censored his children's reading material. As far as he was concerned, if your faith was shaken by foul words or sex scenes, then you must not have had very much to begin with. Back in high school, Crystal had dedicated her spare hours to reading every Stephen King novel ever written. Those books were filled with f-bombs, blow jobs, and beheadings. She slept with the lights on for years, but none of it ever made her any less Christian.

Crystal browsed Lula's silly library, trying to pretend that was what she'd walked across town to do. The selection seemed to have been thoroughly picked over. The few titles left on the shelves looked like castoffs from the local library. *The Art of Crochet*, *Contract with America*, *Manhood*, and *A Caledonian Fling* appeared to be the best Lula's library had to offer. Then Crystal's eyes landed on a book partially hidden from view in the upper left corner. She pulled it out and examined the cover, remembering the fuss that had accompanied its launch thirty years earlier, back when she was in college. All her friends had bought copies and read them cover to cover, but Crystal hadn't bothered. She hadn't felt any need. She'd already met Russell.

Now God had sent her *The Rules: Time-tested Secrets for Capturing the Heart of Mr. Right*. Clearly, it was a message. She still had a lot to learn. And with her rival for Russell's heart just a little ways down the street, she certainly didn't want to leave the book where it might fall into Janelle Hopkins's home-wrecking hands. So Crystal hurried away with *The Rules* tucked under her arm.

Once she was safely home, Crystal took a seat at her breakfast bar and cracked the book open in the middle to the strangest recipe she'd ever encountered. Confused, she flipped back a page to find a chapter heading: *Make a Blazing Heart Burn Only for You*. Right below the heading was a warning:

If you ignored the rest of the book and flipped straight to the love spells, please return to the beginning. Witchcraft is a spiritual practice and a worldview. It is not to be dabbled in lightly. If you are in a rush and won't listen to reason, please read Chapter Three at the very least.

Crystal immediately stole a glance over her shoulder to make sure no one was watching. It sure felt like the warning had been meant just for her. *Witchcraft?* She sat back and let the word tumble around in her brain. She couldn't recall any of her old college friends dabbling in the dark arts. At a Christian school like theirs, the thought alone could have led to expulsion. And hadn't *The Rules* author been on *Oprah* back in the day? Sure, she'd cursed the world with Dr. Phil, but would Oprah really have welcomed a witch?

Always a stickler for doing things right, Crystal closed the book and started again at the beginning. According to the title page, it wasn't *The Rules* after all. Lula must have mixed up the dust jackets. The book's true title was *All Women Are Witches: Find Your Power and Put It to Use*. Well, that certainly explained Lula's rise to prominence, Crystal thought. The self-righteous ones were always the biggest hypocrites.

Crystal turned the page and found the table of contents. Chapter One was titled *No, You Won't Be Summoning Satan.* That came as quite a relief. Crystal was willing to do a lot to keep her husband, but she had no interest in selling her soul. Chapter Two was even more on the nose. *Yes, Witches Can Believe in Jesus.* Crystal stopped for another quick glance behind her. To be honest, it was getting a little creepy how the book kept reading her mind. The third and absolutely essential chapter, *The Chapter You Must Read Before You Begin,* started on page twenty-seven.

Before you can cast an effective spell, you must set your intention. In order to do so, you must know what you want and be able to articulate your desires. This may sound simple. Sometimes it is. More often it's not.

Easy enough, Crystal thought. It wasn't as if she hadn't daydreamed about it for years. She wanted to go back in time. Preferably to June 3, 1996, the day she and Russell first met. She wanted to relive the first ten years of their relationship and fix all the mistakes she'd made along the way.

What you want must obey the laws of physics.

Well, that didn't seem terribly magical. Fine, so no going back in time. Then let's keep it simple, Crystal bargained with the universe. Just keep Janelle Hopkins and her giant boobs away from my husband.

Be sure to consider any unforeseen consequences.

The old Monkey's Paw dilemma. Janelle gets run over by a brush hog (a fantasy Crystal had been gleefully entertaining), but Russell ends up grieving his lost love for the rest of his days. Whatever, Crystal decided, just make him fall back in love with me.

And ask yourself if you really want to interfere with another's free will.

Dammit! If deciding what you wanted was this hard, no wonder people ended up summoning Satan. Crystal would just have to figure it out later. There was no time to lose. Russell may have been gone that morning, but he would be back at some point, and Crystal wanted to be ready. She returned to the love spell and jotted down a list of ingredients. Matches, an iron pot, fresh water from an unsullied spring, DNA of the beloved (preferably blood), honey, hot sauce, chocolate, the pollen of a wildflower, and a lock of her own hair.

Crystal loaded a tote with all the ingredients she had on hand—including a Band-Aid that Russell had left in the bathroom wastebasket—and hurried through her back door to find the others. For twenty-five years, she'd washed dishes at a kitchen window that looked out at the edge of a forest. Only a handful of times had she bothered to cross the moat of mulch and petunias that separated her tidy world from the one beyond. When they were little, her kids would disappear into the wilderness for hours at a time. They'd return for dinner filthy as pigs and happy as clams. She'd heard them talk about a spring somewhere out there—and the trail they'd forged to reach it. When Crystal looked, there it was. Her kids had been out of the house for a while now, but somehow the path remained clear. It was almost as if it had been waiting for her to find it. She set off into the forest, relieved to be taking matters into her own hands.

Once Crystal was well on her way, her mind returned to the question she hadn't been able to answer. *What is it you want?* What she really wanted more than anything, Crystal realized to her surprise, was to scream. She'd never thought of herself as an angry person. In fact, she'd spent two decades teaching seven-year-olds how to cope with their feelings. But she hadn't bothered to deal with her own. She'd been stuffing her rage down deep inside of her until every cell in her body was smoldering. It seemed safer to keep it there. The last thing she wanted to do was offend someone. But in the woods, there were no neighbors to frighten. No church ladies to scandalize. No children to hear—and later repeat—all the terrible things she desperately needed to say. Crystal stopped on the path and let it all out in a great gushing torrent of profanity and heartbreak and rage.

"Fuuuuuuuck! Fuck you, Russell, for breaking your vows. And fuck you, Janelle, and your fucking cleavage. Fuck me for believing in happily ever after. And fuck you, Mama, for not telling me how things really are. And fuck Lula Dean and her book banning posse! Fuck that fucking Nazi! Fuck

48

Mr. Pig! Fuck my kids for not calling every week after I worked my ass off to raise them! Fuck all you fucking fuckity fuckers!!!"

The moment it was all out of her, the wind swept it away. The trees whispered their reassurances, their voices the soothing sound of rustling leaves. A hawk screeched its support and a dove cooed in sympathy. The smell of rich earth and green chlorophyll surrounded and sedated her. The dappled sun danced on the leaves. Emptied of her rage and resentment, Crystal kept going, feeling lighter than she had in years.

The path disappeared at points and reappeared later. She couldn't tell how far she'd traveled and it never occurred to her to check the GPS on her phone. The sun was directly overhead when she found the spring—its crystal-clear waters collected inside a bowl it had carved into a boulder. She stood in shock at the edge of the water. A magical fairy-tale oasis had been out here all along and she'd never even suspected. *What do you want?* The question popped back into her head, and this time she had a different answer. She wanted a fucking swim. Without a second thought, Crystal stripped out of her clothing and jumped in buck naked. How many years had it been since she had gone swimming? How many hours had she wasted worrying about stretch marks and cellulite? The only thing that mattered now was that the water was cold and the sun hot and *damn,* her boobs felt amazing now that they were out of that bra.

When she emerged, she lay naked on the boulder until the sun dried her off. She thought, perhaps, she should get to work on the spell. But she didn't want to. She ate the chocolate bar and opened the book she'd brought.

There is no need to make *magic. There is magic all around us. We need only to recognize it and make use of what is already there.*

Crystal's old self would have rolled her eyes. Now she could see it. The seeds with their perfectly formed wings twirling down from above. The oak sapling rising in the last spot of sunlight. A tree trunk, which had stood for hundreds of years, carved and carbonized by a bolt of lightning. The pollen that sprinkled the boulder like fairy dust. Every patch of ground was a world of its own. Every life-form inside it was thriving, dying, or transforming. And all these years, she'd been trying so hard to keep things the same.

What do you want? The sun was heading west, and she still couldn't answer the question. She found it much easier to list all the things she *didn't* want. Arguments seemed pointless. Accusations the same. But going back to the way things had been simply wasn't an option. She realized there were no rules for her to follow now, and that was totally fine. Crystal no longer believed in them anyway. And if she ever saw another plate of chicken parmesan, she planned to fling the fucking thing at the nearest wall.

The ping of a text message brought her back to the world. She rooted through her discarded clothing until she found the phone. Russell was announcing he'd be home for dinner. The clock informed Crystal it was almost four-thirty. She needed to get going if she planned to have dinner on the table by six. Crystal picked up a nearby rock and smashed the phone. That was what she wanted to do. She had no desire to go back yet.

She lay by the edge of the pool and watched the sun set and the moon rise. The light made her flesh appear to glow. She slept and woke in the morning to the sound of birds chattering in the trees all around her. When she opened her eyes, she knew her marriage was over—that it had been for years. It surprised her to realize she had no desire to blame Russell. He'd been an excellent husband and father. Perhaps things hadn't ended as neatly as Crystal would have liked. And Russell could do a lot better than Janelle freaking Hopkins. But Crystal cherished the memory of their first decade together, and she did not want to resent the man who had made her so happy—even if he no longer could.

AT DUSK A HUNTING DOG bounded out from between the trees and practically pounced on her. Crystal was wearing a shirt at that point, but little else. A camo-clad man in his mid-twenties soon emerged. A dirty blond beard covered most of his face. The little that was left was obscured by a baseball cap or concealed behind sunglasses. He held a rifle to his chest, which was dressed in a hunting vest with orange safety patches.

When the man reached the clearing, he froze, as though he'd stumbled upon an exotic beast—and he was trying to determine whether to shoot it or run.

"You Crystal Moore?" He hadn't let down his guard. He still had the rifle in a ready-carry hold, as though he might have to use it.

"Yes," she told him. She kept her voice neutral—her answer merely a statement of fact. She was alone in the woods with a man holding a gun. His dog was stationed three feet away from her, awaiting its owner's command. She kept her eyes on the man, sensing what might happen if she dared look away.

Finally, he pulled a walkie-talkie out of a holster and held it up to his mouth. "Got 'er." Then he let it drop. "You get lost out here? Your husband's got the whole county looking for you."

If he was looking for her, why bring a gun? "I'm not lost," Crystal said. "I just needed some time to myself."

She saw the man's head turn toward the book she'd been reading. She'd left the dust jacket back at the house, and the gold-embossed title on the cover shone in the sun. When the man returned his attention to her, she could sense his hatred and fear. There was no telling what he might have done if he hadn't already radioed the search party.

"You know what the Bible says about witches, don't you?"

Crystal smiled. He wanted to scare her back into submission. That's how men like him kept women in their place.

Who the fuck cares what he thinks? Crystal asked herself. What do *you* want? A hot bath and a sandwich, she thought. "I haven't eaten in ages. Would you mind calling Russell and asking him to make me a PB&J?"

"You want your *husband* to make *you* a sandwich?" the man sneered.

"He won't mind," Crystal said. "He's a better man than most."

RUSSELL WAS IN THE BACKYARD, waiting to greet her with a PB&J when she and the hunter emerged from the woods.

"She's fine. But if I were you, I'd keep a better eye on her in the future," the man told Russell. He handed her husband the book, as though it could explain the whole episode.

"If he were *you,* every woman he met would run away screaming," Crystal said with a mouth full of peanut butter.

The hunter took a step in her direction and Russell rushed to smooth things over.

"My wife gets cranky when she's hungry," he explained, putting a hand on the younger man's shoulder. "We're both real grateful for all your help, Logan." Once the hunter moved on, Russell glanced down at the book, then made sure no one else was in earshot. "Everyone's going to say you're a witch now," he whispered, sounding relieved and amused.

"I don't care what anyone says," Crystal told him.

"Were you really out in the woods casting spells?"

"I considered it, but then I realized I don't need a spell to get what I want."

"And what's that?" Russell asked.

"I just want us both to be happy now," she said. "Our marriage was a complete success."

CHAPTER 7

CHICKEN SOUP FOR THE SOUL

Elijah Wright was bored out of his ever-lovin' mind, but he wasn't about to budge. He'd been hanging out on a bench in Jackson Square for three hours, waiting for the beautiful Bella Cummings to jog by. Elijah didn't know if he could survive the weekend without seeing her. He wondered if she knew how cruel it was to disappear from his life for two whole days in a row.

He'd had to suffer even longer than the week Bella got suspended from Troy High. People were saying she'd started some kind of rebellion just by wearing spaghetti straps. Elijah definitely wouldn't put it past her. Bella was smart as hell and she could do a split better than anyone he'd ever seen. He had to bite his lip just thinking about it. *Damn*, that girl made him crazy. So what if there were a few years between them? Maybe in high school three years made a difference, but when they were older, wouldn't nobody blink an eye. Of course by then he'd be filthy rich and famous from playing in the NFL. Girls would be throwing themselves at him right and left. He'd be swimming in so much cooch he'd need a snorkel. But he would never love anyone the way he loved Bella Cummings.

Even back in middle school, he'd been besotted. That's what his older brother, Isaac, called it. Elijah had looked up the word to make sure it fit—and damn, if it didn't. Isaac and Bella had been best friends since kindergarten, and soon they'd both be graduating and heading off to college. Elijah had always wondered why Isaac never made a move. Bella liked guys who were book smart—and everybody said his brother was the town genius. When Elijah had found out why Isaac wasn't interested, his first reaction had been sheer relief. He didn't need any more competition. As far as Elijah was concerned, it was as simple as that. Since then, things had gotten a lot more complicated.

Now Elijah was sitting on a park bench with a book he'd borrowed from Lula Dean's library. Isaac would be pissed as hell if he heard that Elijah had gone anywhere near the crazy lady's house. The shelves at the high school library were half empty now, thanks to that "book-burning barbarian," as Isaac called her. Elijah wasn't quite as quick to condemn Lula Dean. He supposed she thought she was protecting them all by hiding the books about sex and such. It was kinda sad and a little bit funny, truth be told. She and her crew seemed really concerned that kids might learn about butt plugs. Like every other boy he knew, Elijah had been secretly watching internet porn since the sixth grade. If Lula Dean had seen even *half* the stuff he had by age twelve, butt plugs would have been the least of her worries.

If they were planning to refill the shelves with books like the ones in Lula's library, they might as well ban reading altogether. Elijah had stood in front of it for a full fifteen minutes. He needed a book to read so Bella wouldn't think he'd been sitting in the park just waiting for her to run by. But Bella was never gonna believe he'd pick up a book by some pasty politician named *Newt*. He skimmed the back cover of *The Art of Crochet* before he put that back, too. Everybody at school knew he'd flunked art class. It almost got him kicked off the football team. Finally, he pulled out a copy of *Chicken Soup for the Soul*. It promised inspiration and everyday miracles, and the whole Wright family was desperate for a bit of both.

By noon, it was hotter than hell, and Elijah had pretty much given up on Bella running by. Still, he stayed put on the bench he'd come to think of as his own. He hadn't slept well the previous night, he'd left his wallet on his dresser, and all his friends had taken off for the lake. There was nowhere for him to head but home, and that was the last place Elijah wanted to be, even if he would have killed for a nap. It seemed like his mother had been crying for three weeks straight. His father never shed any tears. He just sat on the back porch and fumed in silence. The preacher was there half the time, talking in hushed whispers with one of Elijah's parents or attempting to counsel his older brother, who was polite as ever, but showed zero interest in the man's advice.

"I am exactly as God made me," Elijah heard Isaac inform the preacher. "I will not question God's wisdom and neither should you."

Elijah hadn't been the only one eavesdropping when he said it. Their mother let out a sob when she heard and locked herself in her room for the rest of the day.

At first, he figured his parents were pissed 'cause Isaac was everyone's favorite. Their hopes and dreams had always been pinned to his brother's perfectly ironed sleeves. They probably thought Isaac would grow up to be a rocket scientist, marry a supermodel brain surgeon, buy them a vacation home somewhere with mangoes, and give them lots of bougie grandbabies. Now that Isaac was gay, they'd just have to be happy with Elijah and Bella's kids. And they weren't gonna be some crappy consolation prize, either, dammit. They would be gorgeous badass geniuses. There wasn't a doubt in his mind.

Then the preacher pulled Elijah to the side, and he learned that being gay was far more dangerous than he'd ever imagined from watching Felix and Will make out on *The Walking Dead*. The gay lifestyle could lead to disease, drug addiction, and debauchery. Elijah figured that, along with the butt sex, could ensure Isaac spent eternity in hell. No wonder his mom wouldn't stop crying. She had to know all the misery that was waiting for her oldest son. And to be honest, Elijah hadn't slept well after his chat with the preacher, either. There had been quite a few nights when he'd lain awake imagining Isaac burning when he would have much rather been thinking about Bella Cummings. He joined his parents in begging his brother to get some help for his condition. The preacher said there were programs specially designed for kids like him. Isaac refused to consider the option. You couldn't cure being gay any more than you could cure being white, Black, or Brown, he argued.

"There is no gay in my DNA," their father said. "You chose this for yourself."

"Was that Mr. Minter involved?" their mother whispered once when their father wasn't around. Mr. Minter was a beloved music teacher at the high school who'd been fired after someone from Troy saw him exiting a gay bar in Atlanta. "Did he recruit you before he left town?"

"It isn't the army, Mom," Isaac had replied. "No one gets *recruited*. By the way, why hasn't anybody asked how Mr. *Concerned Citizen* just *happened* to be in the parking lot of a gay club at three o'clock in the morning when Mr. Minter came out?"

Their mother had gasped, one hand to her chest. "I don't even want to think about what you might be suggesting."

"Sounds to me you don't want to think at all. You just want to believe everything you're told. 'Cause if you sat down and thought it through, you'd know that I'm right. I haven't changed one bit since the day I was born."

But their parents refused to believe it was providence. At night, as he lay in bed sleepless, Elijah listened to them speculate about the cause of Isaac's condition. Their father, a fan of talk radio who'd long leaned a little to the right, threw out Isaac's soy milk and had the water tested. Then Lula Dean discovered the dirty cake book that Elijah's friend Mack had slipped into the library. She and her committee showed up at the high school library a few days later and started yanking books off the shelves. Turned out a few of them had "homosexual themes." Elijah's mom recognized one of the covers. Isaac had brought the book home at the start of the school year. Finally, their dad had his answer. He knew why his son was gay.

Isaac and their parents stopped speaking after their dad began spending time with the book-banning buffoons. Only a few months earlier, their house had been one of the happiest in town. Now family dinners were silent aside from their mother's sniffling. Their father spent most evenings with Lula's committee. Isaac joined the small group of protesters dedicated to fighting them. And Elijah was tortured by dreams of his beloved brother burning in hell. It was hard to believe it was all happening just because Isaac liked dudes. For the two thousandth time, he closed his eyes and let God know he'd do anything—anything—to bring his family back together.

IT WAS SO HOT ON the park bench that Elijah couldn't find the energy to open his eyes when the prayer was over. He nodded off for a second and *Chicken Soup for the Soul* slipped off his lap and landed open on the ground beside him. As he bent over to grab it, a single word caught his eye.

Penis.

Elijah snapped back up and left the book spread open on the cobblestones. Of all the words in the world, why had his eyes landed on *that* one? Is this how it started? Was this the slippery slope? Eventually curiosity overtook his fear and Elijah leaned over again and scanned the page for the word. Maybe it had been used in some harmless, personal hygiene kind of way. *He took Jaylen's penis into his mouth.*

Elijah sat bolt upright, eyes wide. His whole body was burning. Were the flames he felt licking him a preview of what was to come? A mysterious figure appeared on the other side of the park, and Elijah knew for a fact that God was reaching out to him at that moment when he recognized Lula Dean and her dog. She was prancing straight toward him, a pink cupcake of a woman with a dollop of marshmallow fluff trotting beside her. Elijah reached down, snatched the book off the ground, and held it open in front of his face, hoping she'd walk on by.

Instead, Lula stopped right in front of Elijah, the fumes from her perfume wrapping his head in a choke hold. "Elijah Wright. Did you get that out of my library?" she demanded to know.

"Yes, ma'am," Elijah replied, knowing he'd just been outed.

"Such a wonderful book, isn't it?" Lula practically glowed with excitement. "I know your family is going through a rough spell. I sure hope you find what you're looking for."

She moved on, leaving Elijah frozen in terror. What the hell did Lula Dean know? What was she trying to tell him?

Elijah turned back to the book and found himself staring right at the title page. *Rivals and Lovers.* It wasn't *Chicken Soup for the Soul.* It was that book Isaac had brought home from the library. God was speaking to Elijah through Lula Dean. He swiveled around in his seat and watched the woman stroll out of the park.

When Elijah looked back down at the book in his lap, he saw it for what it was: a test. It had to be. He'd just told God he'd do anything to bring his family together. Now the Lord was calling his bluff. He wanted Elijah to put his money where his mouth was. *Fine,* Elijah told God. If reading *Rivals and Lovers* was what it would take, then so be it. He closed his eyes and took a moment to remember Bella's spaghetti straps. Then Elijah Wright flipped to page one, knowing deep down in his soul that by the end of the day, he'd be homosexual.

THE HEROES OF *RIVALS AND LOVERS* were two dudes named Jaylen and Julio who met their junior year of high school in Brooklyn. Captains of opposing debate teams, they hated each other at first sight. Jaylen was out and proud, while Julio was still stuck in the closet. Then one night after a particularly heated debate on the subject of capital gains taxes, they shared a secret kiss in the subway.

Damn, this is boring, Elijah thought. They should add an alien invasion or something.

But he couldn't stop reading—and he didn't really want to. Sure, Jaylen and Julio were dorks, but the whole thing was still kinda sweet. He wondered if Isaac was making out with any guys at school. He fucking *hoped* not. Nobody in Troy was good enough for his brother.

The heroes end up going to Columbia University, where Jaylen is super popular and getting busy in secret with the captain of the basketball team. Julio focuses on his work and pines for the boy he kissed back in high school.

Ho-ly shit. Get to the drugs and debauchery already, would you? Elijah checked his phone. It was two o'clock and he was about to keel over from hunger. As soon as his boys hooked up, he'd head home and eat everything in the fridge.

They finally got busy on page 122. That's when the penises came out. After all that workup, it was a bit of a disappointment, to be honest. I mean, he was happy for them and all. But the penis-in-the-mouth bit was as raunchy as it got. There weren't even any butt plugs involved. If this was someone's idea of debauchery, he sure hoped they never typed *cream pie* into Google. Elijah flipped forward to page 212, hoping the story would get a bit saucier.

Jaylen and Julio now shared a fabulous apartment in Manhattan. Julio was stressed out from his pediatrics residency and Jaylen, who designed athletic wear for a European luxury brand, worried their relationship might be losing its spice. He knew there was a handsome doctor on the staff at the hospital who had his eye on Julio. So, one night, over an excellent bottle of Falanghina, he surprised Julio with a dream vacation to the Amalfi Coast. The reveal did not go as planned.

You've got to be kidding me, Elijah chided Julio. *It's the Amalfi Coast! Take a week off and focus on your relationship!*

Annoyed by the character's lack of gratitude, Elijah flipped forward another fifty pages. Jaylen had forgiven Julio for his brief dalliance with a coworker. *What? I can't believe I skipped that part.* Now the two were married. They were searching for a surrogate to carry their second child, but they still hadn't settled on whose sperm to use.

Oh my God. This is going to be an absolute nightmare. Jaylen made the first kid, Julio should make the next!

"HEY THERE. WHATCHA READING?"

It was like an angel had spoken right in his ear. Elijah shrieked and fumbled the book, which slipped out of its cover and fell to the ground. When Bella Cummings picked it up, he knew his life was over.

"*Rivals and Lovers*. I think your brother read this, too."

The sun was setting but it was still hot, and Bella was sweaty from running. It drove him crazy when she wore her hair in a ponytail.

"I know," Elijah said. "My parents think it turned him gay." *Damn, that came out wrong.*

Bella cocked her head and grinned at him. "Interesting," she said. "Did it just make you gay?"

Elijah checked. "No." His heart was pounding, his stomach fluttering, and his body tingling. He was just as besotted with Bella Cummings as he'd ever been.

"Figured," Bella said. "Books don't work that way. Where'd you get it?"

He pointed across the park. "Lula Dean's library."

Bella snickered. "That Lula. Spreading tolerance and understanding right here in Troy, Georgia." When she took a seat beside Elijah on the bench, he closed his eyes and savored the moment. This was quickly becoming the best day of his life. "Well, what did you think?"

I think I love you even more than Jaylen loves Julio. I swear I will treat you like the goddess you are. And someday when I'm quarterback for the Falcons, I'm gonna buy you a trip to the Amalfi Coast. Wherever the fuck that is.

"What did you think of the book?" Bella clarified, as though she sensed some confusion.

"Honestly?"

"Of course."

"It's boring as hell. Even worse than *Old Yeller*." He flipped through the pages. "Is this really what it's like to be gay? I mean, there's like a single blow job before they get married and start popping out kids."

"I guess it's one way to be gay," Bella said.

Elijah nodded. For the first time in weeks, he felt something like hope. "Then I absolutely loved it," he informed her.

Bella laughed. "You just said it was boring!"

"Yeah, but nobody's going to hell for anything in this dumb book. I don't understand why the committee would even bother to ban it."

That cracked Bella up. "You really think Lula Dean read *Rivals and Lovers?*" she asked. "Or any of the other books on her list?"

"You're telling me she didn't?" The second the words came out of his mouth, Elijah realized how stupid they sounded. "Holy shit. She's been lying to everyone, hasn't she?"

"I bet Lula hasn't read a book in thirty years. She just wants to scare people. She's figured out that's how to get their attention."

"Damn. That's *diabolical.*" Elijah had spent fourteen years living in the same town as a supervillain, and he'd never even realized it.

"Yeah, well, don't give her too much credit. She didn't invent it. Using fear to control people is about as old as time."

Elijah thought of his mother. "What if you showed them there's nothing to be scared about?"

"You could do that," Bella said. "But first you have to get them to read a book."

Elijah knew who needed to read *Rivals and Lovers* next.

CHAPTER 8

IT'S NEVER TOO LATE: FINDING HEALTH, WEALTH, AND HAPPINESS IN MIDDLE AGE

ula wished Beverly Underwood could have been there to see her interacting with that Wright boy. Just a few weeks earlier he'd have been with those degenerate friends of his, smoking dope and sneaking pornography into the public library. Now there he was, sitting in the park like a perfect gentleman, reading *Chicken Soup for the Soul*. Lula had never read it herself, but the lady at the Goodwill in Macon swore up and down that the book had set her on the right path. Lula could see that her fifty-cent investment had changed that boy's life for the better. If only she could have gotten to his older brother in time. She never would have guessed Isaac Wright would announce to the whole world he was gay. Lula knew the boys' mama well—and their father was on the committee. For years, the Wrights had set a wonderful example for their people. It was a shame a selfish child could destroy a whole legacy.

Just the thought drove Lula crazy. It wasn't like that boy didn't know any better. He'd been raised in the church. Not *her* church, of course, but he knew what the rules were. God had made them perfectly clear. You do not kill. You do not covet. You honor your parents. And men who diddle other men go straight to hell. Somehow Isaac Wright had come to believe those rules didn't apply to him. And nothing got Lula all fired up like people who thought they were above the law.

What on earth had given people the notion they were free to do what they want? Half the town was divorced, the other half sleeping around. The kids were giving themselves new names, lopping off their penises, and walking around with butt plugs. Just the other day, the young man carrying her groceries at the Piggly Wiggly was wearing mascara and eyeliner. Someone had to let him know that he looked ridiculous, so Lula did her duty. That boy had the nerve to tell her to mind her own business. Of course she took her business straight to the manager. But that spineless Russell Moore just hemmed and hawed and never did a thing. Whatever spells that witchy estranged wife of his was casting out in the woods must have turned Russell into a eunuch.

Back when Lula was a teenager, folks knew how things were supposed to work. God gave you a lot in life and you made the best of it. Was she happy that her once wealthy family was forced to endure reduced circumstances? *No, sir.* Would she have liked to marry a man like Trip Underwood? *Absolutely.* But neither of those things had been in God's plan for her. Lula had walked the line for forty-three years, and now at long last, she was getting somewhere.

Once Winky had her wee in the park, Lula headed back to the frilly white Victorian she'd lived in alone since her husband had tragically passed ten years earlier. As she rounded the corner onto Peach Street, she ran into the postman returning two books to her little free library. One, she could see, was *Our Confederate Heroes*. It had made Lula's day to discover a copy at Goodwill. Her granddaddy once owned hundreds of books on the subject, but the collection had been lost along with the family home. There hadn't been room enough for a library in the modest house in which Lula had been raised. According to Lambert family legend, her father had offered to sell the books to the evil lawyer woman who'd snatched up their house at auction, but she wasn't interested.

"I don't need any books about the so-called Lost Cause. Unlike y'all, I learn from the past," Wilma Jean Cummings had told Lula's daddy. "I have no desire to relive it."

"If I was descended from dirt farmers, I suppose I'd feel the same way," Lula's daddy had famously responded. He donated the books to the local library. Lula had always meant to stop by and look for them on the shelves, but she didn't get to the library all that often.

Lula chuckled over her daddy's quip every time she walked by the old family house. Folks in town said Wilma Jean was demented, which gave Lula immense satisfaction. In her prayers, she thanked Jesus that the woman's wicked ways were finally being punished.

"AFTERNOON, MRS. DEAN."

The postman was staring right at her, just waiting for her to come closer. In the past, whenever Lula had tried to strike up a conversation, Delvin Crump would get all squirrely and slip away. Lula supposed she couldn't blame him. They came from two different worlds. A generation back, his whole family had likely worked for hers. It had been forty years since the mill had been stolen out from under her father, but the old divisions still remained, and most folks weren't brave enough to bridge them. But once again, Lula's little library had worked a miracle. Today, the postman seemed thrilled to talk to her.

"Pleasure to see you, Mr. Crump. You been doing some reading?"

"As a matter of fact, I've been making good use of your wonderful library. I was hoping you wouldn't mind if I added a book of my own." He held up a copy of *The Art of the Deal*.

Lula beamed. She'd started a movement! "Of course I don't mind! And may I say, you have excellent taste in literature."

"As do you, Mrs. Dean. And thank you so much for what you've done for the community. We booklovers need to stick together!"

Thank you for what you've done for our community. Lula clutched those words close to her heart for the rest of the day. So much was happening and Lula's only regret was that Beverly Underwood wasn't there to see all of it. She wondered if she could get Delvin Crump to film a testimonial for her campaign's Instagram account. Finally, people in Troy were recognizing what she had to offer. Snooty Beverly Underwood's reign would soon be over.

THEY'D BEEN FRIENDLY ONCE, BACK in high school. Not *best* friends, of course. Lula was a year younger. But good acquaintances who smiled when they passed each other in the hall. Both had been cheerleaders since their peewee football days, and by her senior year, Beverly was captain of the varsity squad.

Up until then, five spaces opened up on the squad every year. But Beverly had already gone and offered spots to two seniors—both Black girls—she thought had been unfairly denied a place on the team. That meant there were only three openings left on varsity that year. But Lula knew she was destined for one of them.

She'd spent weeks practicing her hurdlers and herkies. Two of the open spots were likely to go to the captain and cocaptain of the junior varsity squad. But the third was up for grabs. Lula's only competition was Darlene Cagle, who lived in a double-wide with a lawn decorated with rusting auto parts. Everyone said she was cute. Lula guessed they were right. Personally, she couldn't get past Darlene's knockoff Keds and frizzy home perm. But being poor wasn't what made the girl unsuitable for Troy's three-time-state-champion cheerleading squad.

After church the Sunday before tryouts, Lula had done her best to warn Beverly. She'd caught up with her in the parking lot of the First Baptist Church, right before Beverly slid into Trip Underwood's Mustang.

"May I speak to you for a moment?" she'd asked.

"Sure," Beverly answered a bit coldly. "As long as it's not about tryouts. I have to maintain the appearance of objectivity."

If Lula hadn't been so nervous, she might have laughed right in Beverly's face. *The appearance of objectivity.* Talk about uppity. Who did she think she was? Sandra Day O'Connor?

"There's just something I really think you should know," Lula said. "I hate to be the one to tell you, but it's going to get around sooner or later if it hasn't already."

Lula recalled Beverly looked perfect that day. Her mama could afford to buy her the most beautiful dresses from Laura Ashley. And nobody could curl her bangs as high. Even though she was two inches shorter than Lula, it always felt like Beverly was looking down at her. That moment was no exception. She hadn't even answered straightaway. Her nose twitched like she'd caught a whiff of something nasty on the wind.

"I suppose if it's serious, I ought to know. Cheerleading doesn't get enough respect as it is. We have a reputation to uphold."

"I'd say it's pretty serious." Of that, Lula was certain. "Darlene Cagle got fall-down drunk at Kevin Marshall's lake house at the beginning of the summer and slept with three guys at the same time."

Nearly thirty years later, Lula could still feel the weight of Beverly's stare.

"How do you know?" Beverly's voice had been flat and emotionless, like a doctor asking you to open wide.

"Because I was there!" Lula replied. "I saw them take her into the bedroom." It wasn't a rumor, it was firsthand knowledge.

"Who were the guys?"

"Skeeter Sykes, Brian Frizzell, and Jason Johnson."

"And you thought you should tell me because—?"

"Because, like you just said, cheerleaders need to be taken seriously. Everybody's going to know Darlene is a slut, and that won't make us look good."

She recalled Beverly had nodded, and for a second Lula thought she'd triumphed. "So, let me get this straight. A girl who was fall-down drunk was taken advantage of by three guys. You knew, but did nothing to stop it. And you want to use this information to get yourself a spot on my squad?"

Lula hadn't found the words to respond. While her jaw dangled, Beverly stepped closer until Lula could smell her Eternity perfume. For the rest of Lula's life, even a whiff of the scent would make her break into a flop sweat.

"Let me tell you what's important to me, Lula. When you're on the squad, your teammates are your sisters. When you do stunts, you put your lives into each other's hands. You rely on your teammates to support you and to keep you safe. You know everything about them. You do not spy on each other. You do not tell tales. And you always have your sisters' backs. Do you understand?"

At that point, Lula knew she'd stepped in it. She hung her head and prayed she'd get off with nothing more than a stern lecture. "Yes."

"Getting that drunk is a mistake, but it's forgivable. And I am of the opinion that it's nobody's business who a girl chooses to have sex with. But if the girl doesn't *get* to choose, it's not sex. It's *rape*. If you knew a girl was raped, and you didn't try to stop it—*that's* unforgivable. I won't have anyone like you on my squad. In fact, I don't think I ever want to be in the same *room* with you again. Do you understand?"

Adding insult to injury, Lula's banishment took place within earshot of Trip Underwood. The captain of the football team and the subject of Lula's every daydream since the third grade looked ready to vomit.

"Should we go to the police?" Lula heard Trip ask as she slunk away.

"That's Darlene's decision," Beverly said. "I'll have a word with her."

FOR MONTHS, LULA LIVED IN fear that the police would come knocking on her door. But they never did. Randy ("Skeeter") Sykes, Brian Frizzell, and Jason Johnson were cut from the football team, which no one noticed since they hardly ever took the field in the first place. All three of them got their butts kicked by linemen on a fairly regular basis, but even that wasn't all that remarkable. They spent the two years till graduation keeping pretty much to themselves.

But at least they had each other. Lula was left with no one. She watched from afar as Darlene Cagle took her spot on the squad. The girls won the state championship that year. Darlene was named captain the next. She dated Trip's best friend, Matt Honeywell, and they both got athletic scholarships to Chapel Hill. Now they lived in a beautiful house in Savannah, drove Range Rovers, and took trips to France. The Cagles' old trailer had been hauled off to the dump years ago, and the lot was empty. But if you looked, you could see a rusting truck camper and a stack of old tires peeking above the tall grass. Darlene might have fancy clothes and five-hundred-dollar highlights, but underneath it all, she was still trash.

Before the cake book came along, Lula had to remind herself every day that Darlene Honeywell hadn't stolen her life. God had a plan, and he'd kept Lula off the squad for a reason. Lula knew her calling would be important, and she'd kept the faith all those years. She'd married John Dean and given birth to twins. She'd gone to church every Sunday at ten. They'd never had enough money to keep up with any Joneses, but after John died unexpectedly at forty-five, the insurance payout made Lula a wealthy woman. Then her kids left Troy and abandoned their poor mother. After all she'd done for them, those ingrates wouldn't even give her their phone number. The last few years had been a vast, lonely desert to wander. The only thing that kept her going was her hatred of Beverly Underwood.

That and doing the Lord's work, of course. The powers that be were too lazy or corrupt to enforce the rules, so Lula was often forced to take matters into her own hands. Everyone knew that music teacher, Mr. Minter, was light in his loafers. People had whispered about it for years. But she was the one who finally got the goods on him. She saw him coming out of that gay bar at three o'clock in the morning, and she sent in the anonymous tip, along with a picture and links to his social media pages. And when the parks department started offering those baby yoga classes, she'd made sure everyone in town knew it was anti-Christian. Unfortunately, they were still grooming infants to be Hindus down at the rec center. That Indian doctor who'd recently moved to Troy was probably behind it all. Even Lula couldn't win every battle.

Then she'd pulled out that book of erotic cakes. At first, she was merely annoyed that she couldn't find a decent recipe for popovers because the library—always pushing the homosexual agenda—seemed to think penis cakes were more important. Then she'd realized what kind of treasure she held in her hand. Now it was *her* face on the front page of the paper—not Beverly Underwood's. *She* was the one everybody was talking about. *She* was the woman they all wanted to please. Some people loved her. Other people loathed her. But she could feel the fear radiating from all of them. They knew she could make their lives miserable if the fancy struck her. For the first time in her life, Lula had the power she deserved.

Some people, like Beverly Underwood, were early bloomers. They peaked in high school and everything went downhill from there. Thanks to Beverly, Lula's youth had been blighted. But Lula had been right about God's plan for her. She wasn't a dud. She was just a late bloomer. Lula had lived by the rules and done everything that had been asked of her. Now, at last, she was being rewarded.

CHAPTER 9

THE CLUE IN THE DIARY

Back in the nineties, rapes were committed by men wearing masks. If a stranger jumped out from a bush and forced himself on you, the police might show some sympathy. If your rapists were three boys who sat behind you in chemistry, you didn't go to the cops. If you were drunk when it happened, with only hazy memories of what had been done to you, you kept your mouth shut altogether. It didn't even occur to you to seek retribution. You were the one responsible.

Darlene Cagle's mother believed her daughter was to blame. She said as much the night of the party—or to be perfectly accurate, early the following morning. Darlene had walked home barefoot from the lake, hiding behind trees every time a car passed. She hadn't been able to locate her bra. All she'd wanted was to get in the shower and wash the night off her. After three hours of walking, she'd reached the trailer she shared with her mother, only to find the front door locked for the first time in her life.

She'd banged on the fake wood. Louder and louder, her panic building as though everything she'd left back at the lake was bound to catch up with her. Finally, she heard her mother's slippers shuffling across the living room floor. The door swung open and her mother stood there wearing her latest boyfriend's boxer shorts and a Mickey Mouse tank top.

Her mom's mouth had opened to deliver the lecture she'd been waiting half the night to deliver. Then she stopped as her eyes took the terrible journey from her daughter's head to her toes. Hair in knots. Mascara running in streaks down her face. Bra missing. Breasts visible through the gaping holes left by three missing shirt buttons. No shoes—only socks.

For a moment, it could have gone either way. Darlene thought about that moment a lot. So much had been decided in that five-second interval. Now that she was older, she knew that her mother had likely been on the opposite side of that threshold at some point in her life. She must have known exactly what Darlene needed to hear in a moment like that. But no one had shown her any kindness, so she chose not to offer any to her daughter. Instead, she dragged Darlene down into the muck she'd been trapped in for sixteen years. That, more than anything else that had happened to Darlene, was the thing that came closest to killing her.

"Do you have any idea what time it is?"

"No."

She didn't know how to tell her mother what had happened. She didn't even know what words to use.

"You've been drinking, haven't you?" her mother had demanded, as if that were all that mattered.

"Yes." She had been. There was no point in denying it. Darlene could smell it oozing from every one of her pores. No one had forced her to fill her Solo cup with the stuff they called Green Goddamns. No one had poured it down her throat. But then again, no one had told her that even a little would be too much. Or that someone who'd only had three beers in her life had no business consuming a mixture of grain alcohol and green Kool-Aid.

"I thought you were supposed to be better than all this."

"Mama—" Darlene hadn't cried all night, but now she started.

"I'm not interested," her mother said. "You made your bed, now you'll lie in it."

IT WAS JUST THE TWO of them. Darlene's father lived in ritzy Cashiers, North Carolina, with his real family. He and Darlene's mom had hooked up in high school. Or at least that's what he'd called it after the results of the paternity test had come in. He'd been away at college when his daughter was born. It was ridiculous to think a boy with such potential would embrace fatherhood at nineteen, so no one had bothered to ask him. His folks hadn't wanted much to do with Darlene or her mother, but they'd picked up some of the bills for a while. They'd both died in a car crash when Darlene was in the sixth grade. Their son had never come back to Troy. Not even for their funeral.

Her mother didn't talk about the years before Darlene was born. It was as if she'd skipped high school altogether and gone straight from eighth grade to working at the Stop & Shop. Darlene's grandfather had been the local postmaster. Her grandmother ran the high school cafeteria. The Cagles weren't rich like the Lamberts, Wainwrights, or Underwoods. But no one would have called them trash. Darlene had been ignorant of her role in her mother's fall from grace until she was eight years old and the police dropped her off at her grandparents' house after her mother's first arrest for possession.

"You know, she could have done something with her life if it hadn't been for you," Darlene's grandmother informed her.

That came as a surprise to Darlene. It seemed like such a strange thing to say. But the poison oozing from her grandmother's voice told her there had to be truth in it. She lived with her grandparents for two months while her mother got clean. That was long enough to find the boxes in the basement filled with books, spelling bee trophies, science fair blue ribbons, and straight-A report cards—mementos pointing to a life her mom had never had a chance to lead. Two months was also more than enough time to figure out why her mother never showed any desire to visit her parents.

DARLENE TOOK THREE SHOWERS AND two baths the day after the lake. When her mother got home from work that evening, Darlene went straight to her bedroom and barricaded the sole means of entry. Her room had one tiny window too small for a human to squeeze through. As long as the dresser was shoved in front of her door, Darlene felt safe. She stopped going to her summer job at the ice cream parlor. She wouldn't pick up the phone or answer the door.

When her period came, she spent the whole day thanking God, though deep in her heart she was furious at him as well. She had made one mistake and paid a terrible price for it. It didn't feel like something a loving God would do to a sixteen-year-old girl.

WHEN HER MOTHER NOTICED THE pads in the trash, she seemed angry that Darlene hadn't been properly punished.

"So you got away with it, did you?" she said. "Next time you might not be so lucky."

Determined to avoid a next time, Darlene hardly left her house for the rest of the summer. Only during the day, while her mom was working, would she emerge from her room. There was no television. The library books on her nightstand—*Flowers in the Attic*, *It*, and *The Giver*—had all been read and were long overdue. There was nothing to do but practice cheerleading jumps in the backyard—never too far away from the trailer to run inside if a car turned into the drive. The jumps were the only thing that cleared her head. So she practiced them for eight hours every day. Over and over again. Nothing else on her mind.

Her mom would return home after dark. By that time, Darlene had already been locked in her bedroom for hours. Sometimes Darlene would hear her mom talking. Sometimes a man would respond. But never once did anyone knock on Darlene's door. Not even when Darlene woke up screaming in the middle of the night.

School started in August as always. Darlene kept her head down, hoping everyone had forgotten her. Judging by the number of boys who went out of their way to say hello, they hadn't. Darlene wouldn't have bothered with varsity cheerleading tryouts if the girls' coach hadn't caught her on her way out the door and insisted she return to the gym.

Darlene performed her favorite drill—the same one she'd practiced 315 times over the summer. Afterward, she hadn't stuck around to hear the results. She'd seen Lula Lambert's routine. It was good—not as good as hers, but good enough to make the cheerleading captain, Beverly Wainwright, feel comfortable giving the last spot to one of her own. Darlene knew how things worked in Troy. Rich girls stuck together. Poor girls fended for themselves.

She slipped out of the gym and made her way home. When she got there, she went straight to her room. There was no point in practicing anymore. The idea of cheering in front of a crowd squeezed the breath from her lungs. The last thing she wanted was to be conspicuous. There was no way she could perform knowing Randy and the others would be watching.

THAT AFTERNOON, WHEN SHE HEARD the sound of the car in the drive, she ignored it. When the knock on the door came, she pulled the covers over her head. When she heard Beverly's voice calling her name, she threw the sheets back.

"I know you're in there! I'm not leaving until you come talk to me."

Darlene lay there, prepared to test Beverly's resolve. But Beverly's resolve appeared to be superhuman. She launched into a routine of show tunes, country songs, and stupid jokes that lasted until Darlene appeared at the front door ten minutes later.

"I was in the shower," Darlene said by way of explanation.

Beverly gave her a once-over. Darlene was still in the clothes she'd worn to tryouts. "We announced the new varsity squad. Why weren't you there?"

"Didn't think I stood much of a chance. We both know how things work around here. There are people who matter in Troy, and I'm not one of them."

Beverly didn't even try to deny it. "What if I told you I was planning to change things?"

Darlene snorted. "Then I'd wish you the best of luck."

"You don't think I can do it?" Beverly appeared more than willing to accept any challenge. Darlene had known who she was since grade school, but her assumptions about the girl were, one by one, proving to be incorrect.

"I suppose if anyone can, it's you," Darlene told her. "Where are you planning to start?"

"I'm going to start by giving the last spot on the squad to the person who deserves it the most." Beverly seemed to wait for an answer that wasn't coming. "In case you're wondering, that would be you."

The panic surged, leaving Darlene lightheaded and sweating. "Thanks," she managed. "But I don't have time for cheerleading this year."

"I know you were raped at the lake this summer," Beverly blurted out. "I heard yesterday from a girl at church. I looked all over for you today."

Darlene wasn't sure what to say. The bluntness of the word *rape* had caught her off guard. There was an honesty to it. It seemed like people in Troy were always trying to pretty things up. People weren't mentally ill, they were *touched*. They didn't die, they *went to a better place*. They stepped politely around uncomfortable subjects—and the people who inspired them. "I was drinking that night."

"What difference does that make?" Beverly demanded.

"It makes a lot of difference to a lot of people," Darlene told her.

Beverly shook her head emphatically. "Not to me," she said. "Not to God."

"Well then, it's too bad neither of you is my mama."

Darlene hadn't cried since the night she'd come home from the party. She hadn't even considered it. But Beverly threw her arms around her and squeezed Darlene until the tears came out, bringing something that almost felt like relief.

"If you want to go to the police, I'll go with you," Beverly said when she finally pulled back. Her eyes were wet with tears, too. "I know there's at least one witness. There could be more. You'd have a strong case."

"Do you even know who I am?" Darlene gestured to the run-down trailer behind her. "Do you see where I live? Do you know who my mother is? Or how many times she's been arrested? Do you think for one second they'll ever believe me?"

Beverly hung her head. "No," she said. "I suppose not."

"When bad things happen to girls like me, we're expected to tuck our tail between our legs and slink away."

Beverly looked up. "Then don't."

"*Don't?*"

"Don't slink away and give them the satisfaction. Be there in front of them. Make them look at you. If not every day, then at least every Friday night."

The horror of the thought left Darlene weak in the knees.

"Don't let this fucking town win," Beverly said, and Darlene marveled at how dainty she made the word *fucking* sound. "Do not let it stop you from being the person you're meant to be."

"What if the boys tell everyone? What if they do it again? What if all the parents find out?"

"It will be okay because you aren't alone anymore. You have nine sisters now, and whatever happens, we will be right there by your side."

No one else had ever gone out of their way for Darlene. She didn't know how much to believe. "Really?"

"Really," Beverly said, as though there were no other answer. She hugged Darlene again. "But I do need to ask you for one teensy little favor."

"What?" Darlene asked.

"Well, the guys who attacked you can't go unpunished. I respect your decision, and I understand why you don't want to go to the police. But would you allow me to make sure they think twice before raping another girl?"

THE TEN TROY HIGH SCHOOL cheerleaders stood side by side at the game that Friday, in front of the entire town. Only three people were missing from the stadium. Randy Sykes, Brian Frizzell, and Jason Johnson. They'd been warned by the captain of the football team himself that their presence that Friday—or any other—would not be tolerated. For the rest of the year, they slunk through the halls and avoided all parties, hiding from the cheerleaders, who made their life hell, and the linemen, who kicked their asses for sport.

Darlene and Matt's first date had been a double date with Trip and Beverly. Then Beverly got her father to recommend Darlene for a summer job at the courthouse that paid three times what the ice cream shop did. When Darlene needed recommendation letters for colleges, Beverly and her mother called in a dozen favors. With the help of the Wainwrights, Matt and Darlene both won scholarships to Chapel Hill. Darlene went on to medical school, where she studied psychiatry. She and Matt lived in a lovely house in Savannah with their gorgeous twin girls.

The sad irony was, Darlene made it out of Troy, but Beverly never did. Her mother was diagnosed with cervical cancer, and Beverly dropped out of college to nurse her. Three years later, her mother died and Beverly called Darlene to say she was pregnant. After she and Trip married, Beverly took care of baby Lindsay while her husband went to law school. When he graduated, they settled in Troy, where Beverly spent her days organizing bake sales, fundraisers, and luncheons for the town's charities.

Beverly didn't change Troy. There was only so much one person could do, even if they were Beverly Underwood. But there was no doubt at all that she had saved Darlene's life. And though she had never—not once—asked for anything in return, Darlene had been waiting nearly thirty years for an opportunity to pay her back.

DARLENE'S TWIN GIRLS, ELEANOR AND Julia, were now the age she had been that night at the lake. She'd never told them what had happened. She knew she wasn't protecting them by hiding the truth, but she just hadn't been able to find the words. She discovered them on a family trip to Troy.

Her mother died a year after Darlene graduated from college, but Matt's mother still lived in the house where he and his brother grew up. Darlene and her brood visited several times a year. Ordinarily, these were peaceful trips. Darlene adored her mother-in-law, Margaret, who'd been the nurse at the elementary school for four decades. But this year, sweet eighty-year-old Margaret Honeywell, who was still in possession of *almost* all of her marbles, could hardly sit still, she was so consumed with rage. One of the very worst children she'd ever had the misfortune to know was plundering the local libraries and making off with important books.

It took Darlene a moment to realize that the "child" to whom Margaret was referring was, in fact, forty-three-year-old Lula Dean. It took a bit longer to explain to Margaret why she was laughing.

"I'm not kidding around. She is awful," Margaret told them. "I hate to say such things about a child, I really do. But I worked with a lot of tough kids. Thieves and liars and bullies and malingerers. I tried my best to love every one of them. But I couldn't find it in my heart to love Lula Dean. That child is Satan's seed."

Darlene didn't know much about Lula—only that Beverly Underwood had never cared for her, either. The year they cheered together, Beverly wouldn't let Lula anywhere near her. Darlene couldn't recall Beverly ever mentioning what had inspired such hatred, and Darlene had never bothered to ask. As far as Lula's personality was concerned, it seemed like there were plenty of loathsome qualities to choose from.

Margaret Honeywell's greatest disdain had been reserved for Lula's library. "That fool went and bought a bunch of crap at a used bookstore, shoved it into a cabinet, and is passing herself off as a great philanthropist. You know what I saw in there? *The Southern Belle's Guide to Etiquette.* Can you believe it? My generation had to fight like hell to get rid of gloves, hats, and pantyhose, and now Lula Dean wants to bring it all back? I am not giving up pants. I don't care what that horrible woman says!"

Following the rant, Margaret's two granddaughters immediately set out across town to see what all the fuss was about. When they returned, they brought a book with them.

"Mom," Julia said. "We went to that Lula lady's little library. The Southern belle book was gone, so Eleanor picked this one."

She held up a copy of a book, *The Clue in the Diary*. On the cover, titian-haired Nancy Drew ran from a burning building while a man hid in the bushes.

"Yes, I'm sure Lula thinks all fifteen-year-old girls should stick to reading books written a hundred years ago," Darlene said. "Though I don't remember ever seeing *her* touch a book back in the day."

"I don't think she touched this one, either." Julia handed her mother *The Clue in the Diary*. "When we opened it up, there was another book inside. We think it's one of the books on the banned book list Grandma showed us."

"We *know* it was banned," Eleanor corrected her sister. "We found a clip online where Lula Dean called it pornographic."

"Really?" Darlene took off the dust jacket. The title of the book was emblazoned on the front. *Speak*. She recognized the title. Troy wasn't the first town to have banned the young-adult book about a girl who'd been raped. "Do you mind if I look through this?" she asked her daughters. "I'll give it back to you as soon as I'm done."

"You don't need to," Julia said. "We've already read it."

When Darlene finished, she was glad they had. She'd never censored her conversations with her girls, but she hadn't been able to prepare them for the reality of rape. The worst thing you could do as a parent, she thought, was to shield young women from the ugliness of the world—then blame them when they did not see it coming. Darlene knew the time had come. She needed to tell her girls everything.

THE NEXT DAY, DARLENE SAT down and wrote her own story. She left nothing out but the names of individuals. But she included all the details people in Troy would need to identify those responsible for hurting her. No villains were spared, not even her mother. No detail was too minor. Everything Darlene remembered went down on the page. And when she was done, Darlene posted the story on her Facebook account. Then she walked to the kitchen, poured herself a giant glass of red wine, and guzzled it. Then she poured herself another.

By the time she got back to the computer, the post had blown up. Her phone, which she'd left on the desk, was ringing. She wasn't surprised. Two years earlier, Randy Sykes had been elected Troy's mayor. Jason Johnson owned a successful software company in Memphis, and Brian Frizzell was dead of an opioid overdose.

Darlene ignored the first three calls. Then Beverly's number appeared on the screen.

"You did it," she said when Darlene answered. "I'm so proud of you."

"I was worried it might be too late to make any difference."

"It's never too late," Beverly said.

"For you, either," Darlene reminded her.

CHAPTER 10

SECRET KEEPER GIRL

You didn't need to be a kid detective to know something big was going down. Beau Sykes was at his bedroom window when he heard the front door slam. That alone would have been *extremely* suspicious. Slamming doors was forbidden in the Sykes house. He set his binoculars aside and looked down to see his mother heading for her car. She was in a rush, though she was trying hard not to look like it. A second later, his father raced across the lawn after her. When he reached the driver's side, he grabbed the door handle. There was only time to try it once before Melody Sykes sped off down the street, almost taking her husband's hand with her.

Beau took a step back from the window and grinned. There was nothing he loved more than seeing something he wasn't meant to see. Everyone in Troy thought his parents were perfect. Only Beau and his brother knew any different. He'd been keeping tabs on them for almost eleven years, taking note of all the things they tried to keep hidden. Like the bottle his mother had stashed away behind the beans in the pantry. Or the time his father slapped his mom for sticking her nose in his business. But when Beau heard the sound of a car firing up in the driveway, he knew what had just happened was bigger than the other stuff. Beau returned to the window and watched his father scrape the paint off the mailbox post as he backed out of the drive. Beau couldn't believe his good luck. They'd left him all alone.

It might be his only chance. He couldn't miss it. There was no telling when he might get another. Beau lifted his binoculars and trained them at the target—Lula Dean's house. He could see the lady in her kitchen, talking on the phone as usual. His mother's friends whispered about her like she was some kind of monster, but Lula never seemed to run out of people to talk to. Beau's mom had hauled him over for a visit at least once a week since Lula started her committee. If you stayed quiet and kept your ears open at Lula Dean's house, you could hear secrets about everyone in Troy. It was too bad Beau still had no idea what most of them meant.

"What's a hysterectomy?" he'd asked his mother after he heard Lula fake whisper that Beverly Underwood had gotten one.

"It's a lady thing," his mom had responded. Then she'd looked worried. "Don't say that word in front of your father. He doesn't want that kind of talk in his house."

Beau's father had a lot of rules, and Beau was always discovering new things they couldn't discuss in their house. He tried his best to be careful, but only days later, he had a question he just couldn't keep to himself. "So if a woman has a baby, but she doesn't have a husband, does that mean her baby came from God?"

His mother spray-painted a wall with a mouthful of sweet tea. He'd patted her on the back while she coughed up what she'd inhaled.

"Where on earth are you getting these ideas?" his mother demanded once she'd wiped down the wall with a wet paper towel. "Has Peter been telling you things?"

Peter was Beau's teenage brother and an endless font of information. But like all the best secrets, that one had come straight from Lula Dean. Beau figured it was best not to tell his mom he'd heard Mrs. Dean talking about someone in town. A detective never reveals his sources. So Beau shrugged and said he didn't know where his ideas came from.

He kept quiet for a long time after that. But then, one day, he was reading in the living room while his mother chatted on the phone with a friend and he picked up on a snippet that scared him to death. "Mama, I heard you say you were bleeding like a stuck pig. Are you okay?"

He couldn't understand why that question got him marched across the kitchen and sent straight up to his room.

"It's something gross that happens to women," Peter had confided later that evening. "Their cooters bleed for a few days every month."

Beau wasn't 100 percent sure what a cooter was. But if it was anything close to what he imagined, the idea was ridiculous. "*What?* Why? No, you're kidding. Stop joking around!"

"No joke," said Peter, clearly delighted to have shocked his brother so badly.

"Where does the blood come from? Does it hurt? Does is spurt out or just ooze? Do they have to wear Band-Aids on their butts?" Beau had so many questions, but his brother didn't have any answers.

"Hey," Peter whispered. "Have you ever seen a naked lady?"

Beau shut up and shook his head. He figured it must have something to do with all his questions. Why else would Peter ask?

Peter pulled out his phone and scrolled through his saved pictures. Most were selfies, with a few group shots of Peter's equally dumb friends. Then he stopped at a photo he'd swiped off the internet and turned the phone to face Beau. A woman in a fur coat and boots stood beside a snowman with a huge pecker. Beneath the coat she was completely naked. "What does this make you feel?"

Beau stared at the picture. He felt a lot of things. Fear, fascination, and concern that the lady might freeze. He'd never made a snowman before, and he wondered if it was normal to give one a penis. "What do you mean? What am I supposed to feel?"

"You'll find out soon. Unless you're gay. Then Dad's gonna kill you. Don't tell anyone that I showed you."

"Okay, but what about the blood?"

"Oh, right. That." Peter didn't seem keen to return to the subject. "Part of them falls out every month. If you don't believe me, just look under the bathroom sink. That's where Mom hides her bandages."

That night, Beau quietly locked the door as his bath ran. Then he crouched down and carefully opened the cabinet beneath the sink. His brother hadn't told him what to look for. He figured it probably wasn't bleach or drain cleaner. Then he spotted a pink plastic bag toward the back, partially hidden behind rolls of toilet paper. Pink was the lady color. Boys were supposed to avoid it. He'd hit the jackpot.

Beau reached in and pulled the bag out, careful not to knock anything over. The writing on the front said, *Soft, Breathable, 100% Protection.*

Protection from what? Beau wondered. He opened the bag and removed a thick pad of cottony material with stickers on one side. He couldn't imagine what it might protect someone from, but it had to be bad if it was making them bleed *that* much.

Beau wrapped one of the pads up in his dirty clothes. After his bath, he planned to continue his investigations. But as he walked back toward his room, the pad slipped out of his bundle of laundry. It made no sound at all when it landed on the hallway carpet. Beau hadn't even realized he'd lost it.

"Excuse me, what is this?"

Beau turned to see his father. He had the personality of a giant if not the stature. He held the pad pinched between two fingers—like something revolting that he'd rather not touch.

"I don't know what that is," Beau said, and that was the truth. No one in the family would have dared lie or talk back to Randy Sykes when his face was that red. "It was in the cabinet."

"Why was it mixed up in your clothes just now?"

Beau felt the blood draining out of his face. "I was going to do some research."

"Research on what? Being a girl?"

"Yeah." The word flipped a switch. Beau saw his father was about to explode. "No—on why they need those things," he added quickly. "I don't want to be a girl."

"I would hope to hell not. You should thank God every day you weren't born one of them. And be glad you don't need to know what these nasty things are."

AFTER THAT, THE PAD HAUNTED him. Until then, Beau hadn't spent much time thinking about girls and women. He knew they were different from boys and men. Women had babies and took care of the house. Men went to work and shot things on the weekend. Women smelled better and had less body hair. Men had penises and could pee wherever they wanted.

He knew men and women were different. That much was obvious. But it hadn't occurred to him that the females he knew might all be hiding a horrible secret. Something so awful that even his dad—the mayor of Troy—couldn't bear to discuss it. Beau asked around at school. A lot of boys wouldn't go anywhere near the subject. His friends, with varying degrees of reluctance, shared what they knew. The blood came out of women's vaginas. They called it a period. It meant a female was ready to make babies. That was the most terrifying thing of all. Beau did not want any babies. He started keeping his distance from girls.

But try as he might, Beau couldn't avoid them all. He had to sit next to girls in class. They flirted with him at recess. They grabbed french fries off his tray at lunch. In the past, he'd enjoyed the attention. He liked all the girls in his class, aside from Tiffany, who was mean as a copperhead. Now he couldn't stop thinking about what they were hiding.

Then one day he was turning in a math quiz, when he accidentally knocked his teacher's handbag off her desk. As they both scrambled to collect the contents that lay scattered across the floor, Beau came across a little white cotton bullet in a clear plastic wrapper.

He snatched it up and handed it straight to Ms. Throgmorton. Beau was convinced that he was her favorite. And he knew for a fact that she was his.

"Is this protection?" he whispered. "Are you all right?"

The teacher laughed and blushed. For the first time, he wondered if the secret might not be that bad. "It is. But I'm fine. Thank you, Beau."

Beau stood there. He couldn't waste the opportunity. "I've never seen one of those before. What is it?"

"Your mom and dad haven't told you?" She was still smiling.

"No," he said. "We don't talk about stuff like that in our house."

That was when Ms. Throgmorton's face got all serious. "Then I'm afraid I can't, either." She must have seen how disappointed he was. "I'm sorry. It's against the rules for me to discuss these things without your parents' permission. I could lose my job."

Beau turned and headed for his chair. If the secret was awful enough to make a teacher lose her job, he wasn't sure he wanted to continue his investigations.

"But hey." Ms. Throgmorton waved him back. "You know there's a place you can go with all your questions. The public library. That's what it's for."

"I'm not sure if I want to know any more."

Ms. Throgmorton leaned closer. "The truth isn't as bad as you think," she whispered. "It's just human biology."

After school, Beau headed for the library, but people from the television station were blocking the front steps. Someone had found something terrible in the baking section. An eighth grader watching from the sidewalk was telling everyone it had to be a book about cannibalism. What else could be so bad?

When Beau got home and switched on the TV, he found out it had been a book about dirty cakes. When the cover flashed quickly on the screen, Beau thought it looked a lot like something one of Peter's friends had brought over.

The library was shut down for two days after that. Not that it mattered, anyway. Beau was no longer allowed to go to the library by himself. He could only use the family computer when his parents were in the room, so that was another dead end. And then, one day, God smiled on him. Lula Dean opened a library right across from his house.

RIGHT FROM THE START, BEAU knew there was something unusual about Lula's library. People liked to visit at strange times. The postman often added books instead of taking them out. And then, a little over a week after the library opened, Beau was sitting on the window seat in his room one night when Bella Cummings stopped by. He watched her look around all sneaky-like and slip a book onto the shelves. He couldn't read the title from a distance, but he could see the spine was pink. The next morning, he set off for school thirty minutes early. He needed to see the book before anyone else could get their hands on it. When he laid eyes on the title, he knew his prayers had been answered. *Secret Keeper Girl,* it was called.

"Did you find something you like?" a woman called just as Beau began to reach out. Lula was standing on her front porch in her speed-walking gear.

Beau had shrieked and sprinted for school.

The book sat there for the next twenty-four hours, taunting Beau from across the street. He had never wanted anything so bad in all his life. But someone had always seemed to be watching him. Until now.

MOMENTS AFTER HIS PARENTS SPED off in their cars, Beau was down the stairs and out the door. He stopped on the stairs and ran back inside to get a plastic bag. Then he casually walked around the side of the house, whis-tling a peppy tune. He made a point of looking both ways before he crossed the street. As he stood in front of the little library, he heard Lula pass by an open window, talking on the phone.

"They're saying what happened back in high school was an open secret, but I swear to you, Jemma, no one ever told me!"

Beau opened the library door, took out the bright pink book, and dropped it into his plastic bag.

His heart was racing as he walked back to his own front door. Only when he was inside and the door closed behind him did Beau breathe easy. He took a moment to recover, then he raced up the stairs and into his room.

Secret Keeper Girl. This was it. Beau took a deep breath. No matter how disgusting it was, he promised God he'd always be nice to his mama. And

Ms. Throgmorton. *Especially* Ms. Throgmorton. He turned to the first page and began to read.

Are you there, God? It's me, Margaret.

Oh no, Beau thought. It's only page one and she's already asking God for help.

But he summoned his courage and kept reading. A few chapters in, he let down his guard. There'd been no gory bits so far. It was just a book about a girl getting her period, which turned out to be a normal thing. In fact, he was a little ashamed that he'd been so freaked out by it. The story was pretty good, though, and the girls in it were funny.

More than anything, Beau was thankful he had something to read, because he hadn't been allowed downstairs since his dad had returned. Randy Sykes and a bunch of men were sitting around the dining room table. His mom had come home, too, but she hadn't made dinner. He could hear her crying in her room. He would have gone to comfort her, but he had a feeling that was not what she wanted.

It was after dark when he heard his brother bounding up the stairs. Then his door swung open. Peter ducked inside, a bag of ranch-flavored Doritos in his hand. He closed the door and stood there with his back against it, as though he'd just made a narrow escape.

"Holy shit," he said.

"Oh!" Beau had forgotten about the bright pink book in his lap. "I swear. I was just curious!"

"What?" Peter saw the book. "Dude, I don't give a shit if you're gay. Dad just resigned as mayor."

88

CHAPTER 11

THIS BLOOD AND SOIL

The plate-glass windows of Val's Beauty Spa on Main Street looked out on Jackson Square. The downtown park was the reason Troy had been named one of the prettiest small towns in the South ten years running. Oaks and magnolias lined walks that all led to a moss-covered marble fountain right smack dab in the center that sprayed cool jets of water into the air eight months out of the year. Every summer, pranksters would dump a bottle of Dawn dish detergent into the water and a magical dome of glistening bubbles would rise up to the heavens. In front of the fountain stood the handsome, mustachioed statue of Augustus Wainwright, the general in the Confederate Army who'd owned Avalon, an enormous plantation on the outskirts of town. Sherman had marched out of his way to burn the mansion, sparing the town of Troy from his wrath. Temporarily bankrupted, Wainwright had risen again, becoming one of the wealthiest men in the United States less than five years after he signed his oath of allegiance. On the far side of Jackson Square stood the county courthouse he'd built—the pride of Troy, if not all of Georgia. A giant brick layer cake of a building, complete with Doric columns, Juliet balconies, and topped with a gleaming golden cupola. In private, Wainwright had called it his personal *fuck you* to Ulysses S. Grant.

Growing up, Beverly Wainwright Underwood had heard the courthouse story told a thousand different ways. It was meant to make her feel proud of her heritage, her town, and her state. And it had—until she started to learn what it all really meant. But that revelation had taken young Beverly a while to reach. When she was a child, she'd been taught things were simple. The War of Northern Aggression had been a barbaric invasion—an attack on the Southern way of life. Before everything went wrong, all the rich families who'd settled the land had been lifted up by God himself, who'd blessed them with good brains, excellent breeding, and a Puritan work ethic. The Black folks who'd toiled in their homes and on their farms—first for free, then for next to nothing—were every one of them lucky to be there. They were all so happy they danced and sang in the fields. Meanwhile, the poor whites who drank and stole and spread venereal diseases only had themselves to blame for their misfortunes.

These ideas had been hammered into Beverly's head from the time she was old enough to listen. There hadn't been anyone around who could set her straight—or was even the slightest bit interested in doing so. In school, she'd learned her ancestors had fought for states' rights. No one mentioned that the "right" they were so keen to defend was the institution of slavery. The historical markers around town recalled the heroism of Confederate soldiers defending their homeland. She attended parties thrown on the lawns of old plantations where girls dressed in hoop skirts and floppy Georgiana hats that tied in velvet bows under their chins. She'd followed tour guides through magnificent old houses and never noticed the humble shacks out back. She'd listened to the older generations tell stories passed down about the years before the war and come away enchanted by a South that was Camelot, Eden, and Tara all rolled into one.

And even if none of that had made an impression—even if she'd slept through history class and skipped all the parties—the inscription etched beneath the statue of Augustus Wainwright would have been impossible to miss. People believed the man had composed it himself, and every citizen of Troy knew it by heart. They set it to music. They recited it before football games. They had it hammered into the granite that marked their own graves.

BOW NOT BEFORE TYRANTS
FIGHT FOR YOUR FREEDOM
SACRIFICE ALL BUT HONOR
AND DIE WITH DIGNITY

This, she'd always been told, is what it meant to be a citizen of Troy. It was a way of life—a dedication to honor—that her ancestors had given everything to defend. What was there to argue with in those four simple lines? Beverly might have gone to her grave none the wiser if her mama hadn't gotten sick.

When the diagnosis was first made, Beverly took a leave of absence from Vanderbilt. It was first semester of her freshman year, and she assumed she'd be back after Christmas break. By then, however, the cancer had infiltrated her mother's lymph nodes. Trip told her there was no rush—she could return to school whenever she was ready. But Beverly had known there would be no going back. Her mother needed her in Troy. If she was going to expand her mind, she'd just have to educate herself.

Of course in those days there were no bookstores near Troy. No Amazon to deliver. No streaming documentaries to watch. So Beverly turned to the local library. The librarian back then had been a woman named Jeanette Newman. She never wore a spot of makeup or ironed out her natural curls. These eccentricities, along with a degree from some school in Vermont and the kudzu-eating goats the librarian kept in her backyard, inspired many of the town's fancier types to refer to her as *that hippie*.

"Don't let that hippie try to sell you any reefer," Beverly's mother ordered when Beverly mentioned she was walking over to check out some books.

"Oh, I won't, Mama," Beverly promised. Correcting her mother was out of the question. It just wasn't done. "I only take reefer if it's free."

"Beverly!"

"Don't worry, Mama. If I get some, I'll be sure to share with you."

Her mother shook her head, but Beverly could tell she was struggling to stifle a laugh. Beverly had always gotten away with saying things no one else would have dared. Everyone knew a girl with dimples and perfect white teeth and a blond ponytail with the ends curled just so could never do any wrong. Beverly sometimes wondered if anyone other than Trip could see the real her.

That was before she got to know Jeanette Newman.

The librarian had three number-two pencils stuck in her hair that morning. Beverly couldn't tell if they were there on purpose or how long they'd been there.

"Well, I wasn't expecting to see you today," the librarian said as Beverly approached the desk. "Aren't you supposed to be off at school?"

"God had another plan for me," Beverly told Jeanette. "Looks like I'm gonna need to educate myself."

Nothing seemed to surprise Jeanette. She'd heard it all over the years. "I'm happy to help. What interests you these days?" she asked.

"Everything," Beverly told her. "That's the problem. I don't even know where to begin." Then her eyes landed on a book that was lying on the counter. *This Blood and Soil*. "What's that?"

She'd seen the way Jeanette took her measure before she spoke. Years later, Beverly remained amazed that the librarian had decided to trust her. Ms. Newman had seen something in her that few people had ever bothered to look for.

"It's a book about the plantations of Georgia. It won all kinds of awards when it came out last year, but it's not what you'd call a lighthearted read. It's history as seen through the eyes of the enslaved. You might learn a few things about your ancestors that aren't all that flattering."

"Are they true?"

"Yes," Jeanette told her. "They're true."

"Then I'll take it."

WHEN SHE FINISHED THE BOOK, Beverly finally understood the phrase *ignorance is bliss*. Her world was different. It was shattered, it was sullied. It was turned upside down. She saw things now that no one had shown her. The vastness of the fields outside of town. The mortar between the bricks in her family home—mixed and spread by enslaved human beings. The hand-hewn tombstones huddled together at the edge of the woods, miles away from the perfectly manicured cemeteries where Troy's Confederate veterans were laid to rest.

And when she reread the inscription below Augustus Wainwright's statue, she was overcome by shame at her family's role in it all. The audacity of a man like her ancestor—claiming words like *freedom, honor,* and *dignity* when he'd deprived so many people of those very things.

Beverly walked through this new world in a daze. She had no idea what to do with the information she'd gleaned. She wondered how anyone could live with the knowledge that their forefathers had enslaved other people. That they'd beaten them. Raped the women. Stolen children from their mothers and sold them. How did you live with the fact that the descendants of the people who'd suffered still lived all around you? That you likely shared DNA with many of them? And finally Beverly realized you *couldn't* make peace with it. She knew why so many who'd gotten a glimpse of the horrible truth had chosen to turn away.

Beverly didn't know what to do. She wasn't sure what to fix—or if fixing was possible. But she knew she wouldn't flinch. She took the book back to the library.

"What did you think?" Jeanette asked her when Beverly slid it across the desk.

"I'm not sure who I am anymore," Beverly confessed. "I was always proud of being a Wainwright. Now I know I'm descended from monsters."

"Every human being has their share of monsters lurking in their family tree. Millions of people around the world can trace a family line back to Genghis Khan."

"I'd rather be one of them."

"Augustus Wainwright was your great-great-great-grandfather?" Jeanette asked.

"Four greats," Beverly said.

"Well, you have sixty-four great-great-great-great-grandparents," Jeanette told her. "I promise you, they weren't all monsters." Then she leaned forward across the counter. "You get to choose whose footsteps you'll follow. Find a set that went in the right direction. Somewhere out there, you have an ancestor who made the world better. Whoever they are, decide to take after *them*."

"Where do I look?"

"Does the Wainwright Bible have a family tree in it? Maybe start there. Or ask your parents what they know. There are sure to be plenty of folks in your history who've been waiting to step out of Augustus Wainwright's shadow."

"Seems like I should be doing a whole lot more."

"The first thing you need to do, Beverly, is keep learning. There are people in this town who are stuck. There are some that insist on going backward. You want to make up for what your ancestor did? Learn everything you can and do your best to lead the way forward."

That day, Beverly went home with three new books.

NOW BEVERLY SAT IN THE chair in Val's salon, staring out the window at Jackson Square and the statue of Augustus Wainwright as she got her blowout. By the 1860s, Wainwright had purchased and sold thousands of souls. Those who toiled in his fields were beaten, tortured, and worked to death. In 1860, he joined the Confederate Army and fought a war to keep the enslaved in shackles. After he recovered his fortune, he toiled day and night to prevent Black citizens from exercising their hard-won rights. Before he expired, he commissioned a statue of himself. The young man atop the pedestal was far more regal than Augustus had ever been—and bore no resemblance to the disease-ridden drunkard he'd become in late life. When the statue was erected, it was common knowledge he'd stolen the epitaph off a monument to Revolutionary War heroes. But no one remembered that anymore.

A van with a satellite dish on top and a giant blue 4 painted on the side pulled up across the street, blocking Beverly's view of the statue and the courthouse behind it. Val switched off the blow dryer that had been howling in Beverly's ear for the past twenty minutes and began fluffing her creation with a comb. "You suppose they're here about Skeeter?"

"Can't imagine who else," Beverly said just as a second van arrived and parked behind the first.

Less than twenty-four hours had passed since Darlene Honeywell had published her post on Facebook. For legal purposes, she hadn't named any names. But everyone in Troy knew exactly who she was accusing. And more than a few of them knew it was true. Randy Sykes had resigned as mayor the previous evening. Now it seemed all the local news stations had picked up on the story, too.

"Better late than never, I guess," Wanda Crump piped up from the chair beside Beverly's.

Beverly tried to look over without moving her head. Yvette Jones was still at work touching up Wanda's grays. "Sure was looking like it was gonna be *never*," Yvette said. "You know that rat bastard thought he wouldn't have to answer for what he did."

"'Course he thought he'd get away with it," Val said. "Rape was hardly even a crime back then."

"Well, 'least we did what we could to put him on a righteous path," Yvette said. "We showed him hell our senior year."

"I see the man every day," Wanda added. "He still can't look me in the eye."

Val cackled. "Like they say—don't fuck with cheerleaders."

"Nobody ever says that," Beverly told them.

"Well, they should!" Val insisted.

Of the ten girls on the cheerleading squad that Beverly Underwood had captained, only four had stayed in Troy. Val inherited the salon from her mother (Big Val), and Yvette rented a booth from Val on Tuesdays and Thursdays. She specialized in braids and extensions, though she was just as gifted when it came to color and nails. Wanda worked for the registrar of deeds over at the courthouse. Beverly and Wanda had standing appointments with Val and Yvette every three weeks—whether their hair needed a touch-up or not.

"I heard that Bella Cummings has picked up our torch."

"Umm-hmm." Yvette's second job was assistant cheerleading coach. "Girl is kicking butt and taking names. And she's got the best pike I've ever seen."

"So what was it made Darlene go public after all these years?" Wanda brought the conversation back around. In high school, Wanda had encouraged Darlene to go to the cops. A white girl might see some justice, she'd argued. But Darlene had refused. To people in uniforms, trailer trash was still trash, no matter what shade their skin was.

"She told me she was inspired by a book," Beverly said. "Something her girls found while they were visiting town over the weekend."

Yvette yelped when Wanda unexpectedly spun her chair around. "What do you mean, *a book*?"

"A book," Beverly repeated, surprised to find herself the subject of Wanda's laser-like focus. "What's so strange about that?"

"Where'd the girls get it?"

Beverly shrugged. "I don't know," she said.

"Was it Lula Dean's library?" Wanda asked.

"Naw," Val chimed in. "Couldn't have been. I looked on Saturday. Only books in Lula's library are about cakes and Newt Gingrich. I don't know how she manages to be evil *and* boring, but damn, if Lula ain't killing it."

"I dunno." Wanda wasn't satisfied. "Something's up in this town. I can feel it. Delvin borrowed a book from Lula's library and that man hasn't been himself since. Keeps talking in his sleep about fighting the forces of evil like he's Black Panther or something. I mean, I ain't complaining. It's got him out of the funk he's been in, but I'm telling you, it's weird."

Yvette lifted an eyebrow. "Delvin Crump—your hermit husband—borrowed a book from Lula Dean? What's he going to do next? Put in an application for the Daughters of the Confederacy?"

"Who the hell knows!" Wanda cried. "This is the same Delvin Crump who once called Lula a boil on the ass of humanity. Now he's swapping books with that bitch."

"You know what? I hadn't thought about it before now, but you're right," said Val. "This town hasn't been the same since Lula's library went up. First that Nazi gets dragged out of the closet, then Darlene spills the beans. Shit that's stayed settled for decades is getting all stirred up."

She was right, Beverly thought. Things hadn't been the same. "What was the book Delvin borrowed from Lula?" she asked.

"Something called *Our Confederate Heroes*."

Yvette snorted. "Yep, that sounds like a Lula Dean book."

"I know, but it sure put a bee in Delvin's bonnet. Now he's even talking about trying to get the Confederate statue pulled down," Wanda said.

"Delvin wants to demolish old Augustus?" Val pointed out the window with a roller brush. "Good luck with that."

"He says it's an affront to every person who's ever served in the United States military."

"Not to mention every Black person in the state of Georgia," Yvette added.

All eyes turned to Beverly. "No offense," Wanda said. "I know y'all are related."

"And I've spent the last twenty-five years wishing I wasn't," Beverly said. "Hell, I'd have that damn thing knocked down tomorrow if I could. Unfortunately, the school board doesn't decide which statues get to stay."

"Who does?" Yvette asked.

"The mayor," Wanda replied.

The room may have gone quiet, but their thoughts couldn't have screamed any louder.

"You know, it's a funny thing," Val said, savoring every syllable as she whipped the black salon cape off Beverly with a flourish. "I think this town might be in the market for a new one of those."

Beverly looked in the mirror and saw them all grinning back at her. "No, no, no." She slid out of her chair, adjusted her pearls, and straightened her pink oxford shirt. "I got more than enough on my plate right now. If I let Lula Dean take my seat on the school board, the only things left to read in this town will be the Bible, *Green Eggs and Ham,* and *Our Confederate Heroes.*"

"You think Lula's going to let *Green Eggs and Ham* stay on the shelves? It's got a dog driving a train," Yvette said. "We can't let dogs drive trains. That's goddamned dangerous!"

"Betcha the mayor could do something to stop her," Wanda said. "You want me to look into it?"

"This town has never had a woman mayor," Beverly argued. "That office has been passed down from one good old boy to another for the last two centuries. Hell, Skeeter's uncle was mayor for thirty-five years!"

"Mmm-hmmm. You'll be the first woman mayor." Wanda was already acting like it was a done deal. Once she got an idea lodged in her head, there wasn't anything short of brain surgery that could get it back out again.

"The timing sure seems to be right," Yvette offered, "considering the last mayor turned out to be a rapist and all. I think some ladies round here might be ready for a bit of a change."

"Think of everything you could do for this town," Val said.

"Bet your daughter would be proud to know her mama was a force for good."

Damn, Beverly thought. Of course it was Wanda who had to bring out the big guns.

BEVERLY WALKED UP TO THE mirror and freshened her lipstick. She wished she were just a little bit taller—and that she'd chosen an outfit that lent her a little more gravitas. She looked like a forty-four-year-old former stay-at-home mom, which on most days was exactly what she was. She'd never dreamed of holding any office higher than school board—and she wasn't sure she was qualified. Though a lack of qualifications certainly hadn't stopped Skeeter or any of the men who'd held the office before him. But her friends were right. An opportunity had presented itself—a chance to bring real change to Troy. Maybe she'd fail. But she had to give it a try.

"If you don't run, you can bet your butt Lula will," Wanda said.

"Fine." Beverly turned around. "I'll do it."

"Great. Then let's make it official." Val headed straight for the door.

Beverly rushed after her. "What? *Now*?"

"You just got your hair and nails done. You look gorgeous, and there are three television crews right outside waiting to ambush the slimeball who just resigned as mayor. And you think there could be a better time to announce your candidacy?"

Val threw open the front door of the salon and stood on the threshold. With two fingers in her mouth, she whistled at the crowd across the street. "Y'all come on over and meet our next mayor!" she shouted.

No one took her up on the offer.

"She's gonna battle the book banners!"

A few people turned around, but none of them bothered to head across the street.

"And she's gonna pull down that damn statue!"

Suddenly they were all looking. But they still weren't moving.

"Did I mention the statue is her great-great-great-great-granddaddy!"

All at once they were rushing toward the salon. Reporters, camerapeople, and assorted hangers-on.

"Well?" one shouted. "Where is she?"

"*Who* is she?" asked another.

"Ladies and gentlemen," Val called out to the growing crowd. "I give you Troy's next mayor, Beverly Wainwright Underwood!"

CHAPTER 12

THE ART OF THE DEAL

You ain't got nothing bigger? My granny wouldn't be caught dead in this pussy mobile."

Mitch Sweeney was sixty years old and both his grandmas had been dead for decades, but that wasn't the point. The point was, he needed to make an impression and this shit wouldn't fly.

When the Hertz attendant shook his head, his floppy blond hair looked like something out of a shampoo commercial. Mitch had already noticed a trace of polish on his thumbnail. He wondered how anyone in their right mind could argue the crap the government put in the water wasn't turning men's grapes into raisins.

"The Toyota Tacoma is the largest model we have on the airport lot today. I could call round to our other Atlanta locations if you like. You have a specific vehicle in mind?"

"RAM 3500 or Ford F-450. A Hummer might work in a pinch." Back in LA he drove a Mercedes-Benz G-Class, but in Georgia, only American-built would do.

"Alright then, why don't you come on back to the office and we'll see what we can find for you." The attendant paused and his eyes narrowed as he took Mitch in. "You know, you look awful familiar."

"Mmm-hmmm." Mitch refused to engage. Usually he loved being recognized, but today he had shit to do.

"You ever work down at the Pep Boys on Peachtree?"

"Fuck no, soy boy," Mitch said. "I'm an international movie star."

"Of course," the attendant said with the distant smile of someone forced to take abuse for a living. "That must be it."

It was times like these when Mitch wished he was just a regular Joe who could kick the shit out of a loser and not make the news.

"Are you kidding me? I was Roy in *American Spirit*."

"Right. Haven't seen that one yet," the attendant admitted. "I was a little too young when it came out."

"Guess you never snuck into an R-rated movie?" Mitch said with his signature sneer.

"No, sir. Not back in preschool," the attendant told him.

WHEN HE FINALLY SLID BEHIND the wheel of a silver RAM 3500, Mitch did a quick check in the rearview mirror. A quick check was all he could stomach these days. He'd left Georgia in '86, a lean mean six-three and 180 pounds, with a chiseled jaw and a head full of chestnut-brown hair. Last he checked, he was still six-three, but that was where the similarities with his former self ended. The head he saw in the mirror had been shaved clean to camouflage male-pattern baldness, and his once steely jawline had melted into a set of jowls.

Not that Hollywood cared. Mitch still got as much work as he ever had. He'd simply transitioned from playing one set of villains to portraying another. There were always plenty of roles for actors with authentic Southern drawls. Evil state troopers. Evil sheriffs. Evil overseers. Evil army generals. Evil hillbillies. Evil corporate types. Evil grand wizards. Evil coaches. Evil cartoon characters. When he'd first moved to California, he'd done everything he could think of to break out of the bad guy rut. But the very few Southern romantic leads all went to pretty boy Matthew McConaughey and the Oscar bait crap to Billy Bob Thornton.

"You look like an asshole," a casting director had told him. "And you sound like one, too. It's a gift. Make good use of it."

It didn't feel like a gift, though. An actor should be able to disappear into any role. That was impossible when people had you pegged the second they heard your voice. Dumb, angry, and racist, they figured. But when he tried ditching his accent, he just ended up blending into the crowd. Actors who blended in didn't make bank. So at some point, Mitch stopped fighting and became the man they wanted him to be. That's when he started to go viral.

It began one night in 2016. He'd been lying in bed, performing his daily Google search of his name, when he stumbled across a tweet by some Ivy League activist who'd described the men at a Trump rally as "mouth-breathing, gay-bashing, white nationalist Mitch Sweeney types." Until that point, Mitch had never made a public comment about anything political. Hell, he wasn't even registered to vote. But there was something that made it okay to go after him—and everyone knew what it was.

Mitch had talked about the discovery a million times since. Though he loved to embellish his origin story, he never revealed how he'd truly felt at that moment. A little bit hurt and a whole lot scared shitless. He'd typed out his subtweet and turned out the lights, but he hadn't fallen asleep for hours.

White. Southern. Male. Straight. I was born this way. What the fuck is wrong with that?

The next morning, he woke up to a hundred thousand likes and a voice-mail from the host of the biggest news show in the country.

"I didn't choose to be a straight white man," he told the host on TV later that day. "I didn't choose to be born in Georgia. I don't discriminate against anyone, and I sure as hell have never owned any slaves. So I don't understand why anyone would want me to feel bad about shit I can't help. I'm trying to get through the day just like everyone else. I will not accept blame for things that happened before I was born, and I am not going to apologize for who I am. I have a right to be proud. All of us do."

For a few hours after that first interview, Mitch had fretted that his use of foul language might have been a mistake. But his willingness to defy the censors only served to convince viewers of his sincerity. Within a few months, he had two million followers on Twitter and over a million on Instagram. He was a regular on *Alex Jones, Rush Limbaugh,* and *Joe Rogan.* When Donald J. Trump *himself* asked Mitch to join him onstage at a rally, Mitch was honored to oblige. He didn't know much about Trump's policies back then, but he knew Hillary Clinton was an uptight cunt, and he wasn't afraid to say so. It was Trump who pulled Mitch aside and told him he ought to consider a career in politics. The world needed more men who called things like they saw 'em.

What Mitch was seeing by that point was his own glorious future. He'd finally landed the perfect role—one that would attract millions of adoring fans and require minimal acting on his part. Of course, there were plenty of haters, too. You couldn't say a word in support of white men without every virtue signaling asshole coming right for your throat. And when those #MeToo bitches crawled out of the woodwork, Mitch had to postpone his plans while the lawyers dealt with a couple of ghosts from his past. But two personal assistants who couldn't handle seeing a grown man naked weren't going to stop Mitch Sweeney from going hard against the libs.

Feminists won't be satisfied until white men surrender our guns, our rights, and our balls.

That tweet got five hundred fifteen *thousand* likes.

"You better be careful," his brother, Jeb, had told him. It was the first time they'd spoken in months. Years earlier, Mitch had bailed out the family farm, where his brother still lived, but Jeb wasn't big on phone calls or gratitude. "You're starting to sound like a Nazi with all this white men shit."

"You know I'm not a Nazi," Mitch said. "I've worked with a million gays and Jews. Liked almost all of them."

"The Nazis sure think you're a Nazi," Jeb replied.

"So?" Mitch demanded. "What am I supposed to do about that? I can't tell them who to like."

"You're kidding," Jeb had responded, like the self-righteous asshole he was.

"Fuck you. This is war," Mitch told him. "It's time to choose sides, and I'll take all the help I can get."

Jeb did not choose Mitch's side. It stung a bit, but looking back, his brother had always been a fucking libtard. Mitch tried not to hold it against him. He knew it must have been hard for Jeb growing up in his shadow. The only way for Jeb to stand out was to be as different from his brother as possible. So he'd been the sensitive child. The smart one. Then he went to vet school and started saving sweet little kittens and everyone loved him and thought he was the greatest thing since sliced fucking bread even though Mitch was talented and famous and had millions of followers.

HALFWAY BETWEEN ATLANTA AND TROY, Mitch pulled over for gas. A cuck at the next pump kept sneaking peeks over his shoulder.

"For fuck's sake, just ask," Mitch told him. Nothing annoyed him more than a man with no 'nads.

"Okay. What's it cost to drive that beast all the way from New York?"

"What?" Mitch looked down at his jeans and boots. He'd worn them home after his last day of playing a good old boy type. The costume manager was one of the best in the business. He had to appear authentic. "Do I *look* like I'm from fucking New York?"

"You got New York plates."

Mitch left the pump in the fuel filler and stomped around to the front of the rental truck. "Moth-er-fucker!"

He kicked the front tire three times with each foot. If there'd been time to turn back, he probably would have. But he needed to get to Troy straightaway.

Just like God told him to tweet back in 2016, he'd had Mitch switch on his favorite news show the previous night. The first thing he saw on the screen was his hometown's hero, Augustus Wainwright, in all his glory.

"Mayor Randy Sykes resigned yesterday evening and candidates are already lining up to take his place," said a voice-over. "School board member Beverly Underwood was the first to announce a run, and she's already making big promises." The video cut to some prissy-looking blond woman standing in front of Val's salon across the street from the square.

"Just as book banning has no place in a democracy, a slaveholding Confederate officer should not be honored in the United States of America," the lady announced. "I am a direct descendant of Augustus Wainwright, and if I'm elected mayor, I will have my great-great-great-great-grandfather's statue removed from Jackson Square."

The camera cut to the show's host, jaw dangling like the bitch had slapped him right across the face. Mitch thought it was sad that his new best buddy didn't get credit for being one of the finest actors around.

"That statue of General Wainwright has stood on the same spot in Georgia for over one hundred and fifty years—a tribute to the philanthropist who built the county courthouse. Now one woman thinks she has the right to blow a town's history to smithereens. This!" The host pointed up to a graphic of the statue exploding. "This is what we can expect if we let liberal feminists gain the power they want—to see our heritage and way of life destroyed."

It wasn't the host's heritage, of course. He'd grown up in Greenwich, Connecticut. But Mitch had ancestors who'd fought side by side with Augustus Wainwright.

"Not in my fucking town." Mitch picked up his phone and dialed the host at his studio in New York City.

For a few hours, Mitch toyed with the idea of running for mayor until he was reminded it would mean actually living in Troy. Besides, his friends in the news business thought he should set his sights higher. There were several statewide contests coming up in the next couple of years—and that might give him just enough time to convince his ex-wife not to open the door for any nosy reporters. What Mitch needed right now was to build his profile. So he'd thrown his support behind the feminazi's opponent. This one was a female, too, but nobody's perfect. Lula Dean had made a name for herself around Georgia by ridding the local libraries of propaganda and pornography. Woman or not, she was exactly the kind of politician his people loved—the kind that got liberal panties all in a twist.

Just found out my hometown's being threatened by the liberal elite, he posted. Only two people can save it. Me and @luladeanformayor. Heading down tomorrow to kick some ass.

Lula was suitably thrilled. They agreed to meet at her house the next afternoon when he got to Troy. As soon as Mitch set foot in the place, he started to worry he'd hitched his star to the wrong broad. The lady's home was done up like the inside of a vagina. Everything was decorated in shades of pink and the furniture upholstered in silk or velvet. The place made Mitch feel itchy and claustrophobic. First thing he did was walk to the windows and check to make sure no one could see in. Having his picture snapped in a room like this would destroy his credibility. Plus, he was sweating like a motherfucker.

"I see you have a flair for decorating, Mrs. Dean." He brought out the charm while he wedged his manly ass into an armchair. "Does your husband love pink as much as you do?"

"Oh dear Lord, no," Lula said. "When John was alive, we had our living room done up in tartan with walnut trim. After he passed, just the sight of Black Watch made me burst into tears. I had to go pink for the sake of my sanity. Can I tempt you?" She'd picked up a plate and paused with an unnecessarily large knife poised over a pie in the center of the coffee table.

"Yes, thank you," Mitch said. "Is that apple?"

"Peach," Lula said. "I can't live without peach pie, so my girl and I spend all summer canning them."

"It's hard to find a woman who knows her way around a kitchen these days. The feminine arts seem to be dying out." Mitch took a bite of the pie and forced himself to swallow. He washed it down with a mouthful of coffee and let the plate rest on his knee for a second while he waited to see how Lula would respond.

"Mmmm," she said, savoring her creation. "And my mama said I couldn't bake. Can you believe that?"

"Madness!" Mitch offered. He could still taste the grit in his mouth. The peaches were weird and flavorless, and if he hadn't known any better, he'd have guessed the crust was made of that kinetic sand shit you used to see at the airport.

Lula set her plate down and folded her hands in her lap. "Now, am I to believe that an international movie star has flown all this way to support little ole me in my bid for mayor?"

"Yes, ma'am," he said with a chivalrous bow of the head.

"No, I'm afraid I was being serious just now." The saccharine-sweet smile was gone and Mitch realized he'd walked into an ambush. "Why should I believe you're really here to help me?"

"Excuse me?"

"Your brother, Jeb, has been a massive pain in my rear end lately. Every time I hold a press conference, he's always right there holding a silly sign. Last time it was some nonsense about burning books leading to burning humans. Made me sound like a horrible person."

Mitch took a second look at Lula. When he'd first laid eyes on her, he'd seen an aging belle with a Botoxed forehead and orange hair that matched her Lilly Pulitzer tunic. She looked like all the bored rich ladies who opened boutiques on Main Street, and he'd assumed she would be easy to manipulate. But now he'd met the real Lula Dean and Mitch realized she wasn't the woman who'd greeted him at the door. He'd fallen for an act, just as he had with his ex-wife. Women like Lula made you feel like a king until they got you where they wanted you. Then the claws would come out.

Also, *fuck Jeb*. That woke asshole had been a thorn in Mitch's side since grade school.

"Jeb and I don't always see eye to eye, but I assure you I can find a way to make him stop harassing you."

"That would be greatly appreciated." Lula was smiling again. This time, Mitch found it troubling. There was something unnatural about this woman. "But let's not pretend you're here for me. You say you want to help? What's in it for you?"

He didn't dare lie. He was starting to suspect Lula could see straight into his soul. "Visibility. I want to run for statewide office someday and I need to start making a name for myself in politics."

"Here—or back in California, where you've lived for the past forty years?"

The lady wasn't fucking around. "*Here*. This is my home. There were Sweeneys on this land before there was even a town."

Lula seemed to approve of that answer. "And why would someone want to vote for you? Aside from a willingness to film full frontal nudity, what exactly do you stand for?"

Ho-ly shit. Lula Dean had just informed him that she'd seen his penis. That was one hell of a power move. Respect was due. "Loyalty," Mitch said. "I always stand by the people who are loyal to me. I will not turn on them or let them down, no matter what the coastal elites say or who tries to cancel them."

"You mean the people who are loyal to you—or the people who do what you tell them to do?"

Mitch snorted. "Same thing, ain't it?" he asked.

"Close enough," Lula agreed.

As Lula took another bite of her nasty pie, her eyes never left Mitch's face. The bitch was seriously hard-core.

"What about you?" He couldn't let her just run him right over. "What do you stand for, Mrs. Dean?"

"You drive past that run-down brick building out by the highway on your way into town?" she asked.

"You mean the old Lambert mill?"

"That's the one. My maiden name is Lambert, and my daddy was the last person in my family to run that mill. His great-grandfather built it, and before there was a mill, my great-great-grandfather ran a gin on that site. If I'm not mistaken, your family's fields supplied a lot of the cotton that went through their machines."

"I'm sure that's right," Mitch confirmed. "The Sweeneys made a pretty good living back in the day."

"A fortune, I'd bet. Just like the Lamberts. We built a big house. We turned out judges and congressmen and even a senator. But then things started to change. When I was a little girl, the district attorney brought a case against my father for paying the workers the way they'd always been paid. Nobody was complaining, but she called it wage theft. We lost everything. Your family fare any better in the past fifty years?"

Mitch stifled a yawn. Was he supposed to wish the Sweeneys were still farmers? Did Lula want to be running a fucking cotton mill? All this good-old-days bullshit was holding folks back.

"There wasn't any money left in growing cotton. There hasn't been a farmer in the family for three generations."

"What about that land the Sweeneys were living on before Troy was a town?"

"'Fraid most of that's gone, too."

"Along with the respect that went with it. Being a Sweeney isn't quite what it used to be, is it? Not much to separate y'all from the riffraff these days. Is that why you hurried off to Hollywood? To get the respect and attention you deserved? The attention you'd been denied all the years you were here?"

This time, Mitch didn't feel any need to respond. The woman was clearly obsessed.

"Look, I'm not trying to get at you," she continued. "I would have done the same thing if I'd had any talent. Instead, while all y'all moved away, I stayed here and watched everything go to seed. Didn't seem like there was anything I could do to stop it. Truth is, I didn't figure out what I'm good at until recently. You know what my gift is?"

"I can't wait to find out." What he really wanted to know was why was he sitting inside a giant vagina discussing this woman's gifts when he honestly couldn't give a fuck.

"I'm very good at finding people who are just as frustrated as I am. Folks whose fortunes have fallen and those who worry their circumstances will be reduced. I know how to talk to them. I know how to rally them to the cause. You know how I do it?"

Now they were getting somewhere. "How?"

"By saying the things they've been afraid to say and doing the things they've been afraid to do. You asked what I stand for and it's real simple. I believe that we're at a crossroads. People like my opponent want us to give up everything we've always held sacred. Our values, our history, our place in this world. If she wins and this town follows her, men like you are going to be tossed on the scrap heap of history right next to Augustus Wainwright."

"And if *you* win?"

"I will follow the lead of the two white men who built this town— Augustus Wainwright and Jesus Christ. And if you'll join us, Mitch, I truly believe we will make Troy great again."

He liked the sound of that. "Then count me in."

"Wonderful. But before we can do anything, we need to destroy Beverly Underwood."

"Remind me who that is again?" Mitch Sweeney asked.

OUTSIDE, REPORTERS HAD GATHERED. MITCH and Lula stood together outside her picket fence. Red, white, and blue Lula for Mayor! signs called out from the yard behind them.

"Thank y'all for being here today," Mitch addressed them. "I came down to Georgia because things have gone way too far. The radical left has pushed its agenda into our schools and our libraries. I hear they've got our kids baking dirty cakes and learning how to use butt plugs. Now they're out to destroy our statues and what's left of our great heritage. If we don't rise up and stop them now, I promise you, there will not be another opportunity. If we want to return to the way things were—to a time when our way of life was honored and respected—we have to defeat these libs for good. That's why I urge everyone here in Troy to vote for Lula Dean!"

"Thank you, Mitch," Lula cooed as she accepted the microphone. "I gotta say, I'm just tickled pink that an international movie star like Mitch Sweeney would come all this way to lend me his support. I think it shows how much good we've done so far. People are tired of being pushed around. Life used to be simple in towns like Troy, and I'm convinced that it can be again."

"Let's get a shot of you both with Lula's little library," a reporter from the *Herald* called out.

Mitch and Lula posed on either side of the purple book-filled cabinet.

"You should take a book." It sounded more like an order than a question. Lula reached in and pulled out a book and thrust it into Mitch's hand.

"Well, how about that? I didn't know you stocked the classics," Mitch joked. "This here's my favorite book." He held *The Art of the Deal* up for the reporters to see, offering them his widest grin. "I think we've all got a lot to learn from the master."

CHAPTER 13

YOU CAN'T GO HOME AGAIN

Jeb Sweeney sat on his front porch wearing blood-spattered camo and drinking a cold Bud Light. In the distance, a truck pulled up at the end of his drive. Jeb raised his rifle and put the sight to his eye. His older brother slid out of a 3500 and rattled the locked gate. Jeb kept him in the crosshairs as Mitch paced back and forth in frustration before hoisting his ample form up the four-foot-high cattle guard. He made it over the top, lost his footing on the other side, and fell backward onto the gravel.

"No stunt doubles down here, son," Jeb muttered, setting the gun aside and taking another sip of his beer. He picked up his phone and opened his brother's favorite app. The first thing that popped up in his feed was Mitch's response to a post by Lula Dean welcoming Troy's prodigal international movie star back to town. Jeb put his beer down and began to type.

Well how 'bout that. @mitchsweeney has set foot in Georgia for the first time in 10 years. #fakesoutherners #hollywoodelites #igotyournumber motherfucker

Jeb picked up the gun again and watched his brother pull out his phone and type like mad. Mitch had clearly set up an alert. Jeb was almost touched.

When I find you I'm going to rip off youre head off and shit down your throat.

Jeb came a hair short of snorting beer out his nose.

Good luck with that dumbass. #igotyournumbermotherfucker

Jeb didn't bother to hide the phone as his brother approached. He'd been trolling Mitch online for years. The accounts changed as soon as he got blocked. But the hashtag remained the same. *#igotyournumbermotherfucker* was Jeb's anonymous calling card. Mitch still hadn't figured it out. He'd never been the brightest bulb on the tree.

"Hey," Mitch said. "Almost didn't see you there."

"Was that a camo joke?" Jeb asked. "Y'all find that sort of shit funny out in California?"

Mitch stopped in front of him. "Ten seconds in and you're busting my balls. That how you say hello to your only living relative?"

"My only living relative? You mean aside from my wife and kids?" Jeb asked. Then he grinned. "Hey, Mitch, want a beer?" He pointed to the cooler sitting between the porch chairs and watched his brother grimace at the blood-covered lid.

"Feral hogs," Jeb explained, leaning down to open the cooler for Mitch. "Gotta keep the numbers down. They've been tearing up the orchard out back."

"You got anything other than this gay shit?" Mitch asked, peering into the cooler.

"Beer can't be gay," Jeb explained. "It's a liquid."

Mitch looked disgusted but not enough to turn down a cold beer. He opened the can and took a long swig.

"You feeling the urge to belt out any show tunes?" Jeb asked. "As I seem to recall, you used to do a great 'Hello, Dolly!'"

"Shut the fuck up," Mitch replied. "Don't you wanna know why I'm here?"

Jeb didn't bother to point out to his brother that announcing every movement on social media lost you the element of surprise. "I'll admit,

I'm curious as hell. What brings an international movie star to our Podunk neck of the woods?"

"I'm thinking of running for office in Georgia."

"Are you, now."

"Don't sound so excited," Mitch said.

"I was under the impression that anyone representing the state of Georgia was required to inhabit the state of Georgia."

Mitch shooed away the thought like a bothersome fly. "I'm fixing to buy a house while I'm here. Besides, won't be for a while. I got a lot of work to do."

Jeb drained what was left of his beer and opened another as he stared out at the vast yard that doubled as a pasture. Sometimes his patients needed a close eye kept on them, so he let them graze in front of the house. Most of the time the patients were horses, but he'd also boarded alpacas, an ibex, and three capybaras. His kids had loved it when they were little, but his wife still missed her flower beds.

Maybe this was an opportunity, he wanted to convince himself. Jeb always tried to look on the bright side, even when his brother's antics threatened to block out all light. He'd long since given up on waiting for Mitch to mature. At sixty, his brother was just as hungry for glory as he'd been at sixteen. And Jeb had witnessed the lengths he'd go to in order to get it. You'd think Mitch had grown up neglected, but that hadn't been the case. Their parents had been loving. One might even say *doting*. They'd done everything possible to give Mitch what he needed. But no two human beings could fill that bottomless pit. Mitch took everything they had and still wanted more.

But maybe this time he had something to give back. Raging narcissist or not, Mitch did have a public profile. If he really was open to helping his hometown, he could bring nationwide attention to their part of the state, maybe even cut through all the red/blue bullshit that kept anything meaningful from getting done.

"I could help you understand the issues if you're interested," he told his brother. "We got a whole slew of problems down here that nobody's talking about."

"I know. I can't believe they're letting that boy in Clarkesville swim on the girls' team."

Jeb breathed in deep, knowing full well that if he took the bait, the conversation would go around in circles for hours. "I don't see fourteen-year-olds as much of a threat to my health, wealth, or happiness. I'm thinking more along the lines of groundwater and stream pollution. There's hardly a trout left in this county that's safe to eat."

Mitch wasn't interested. "What about all the crime? Who's doing anything about that?"

"The crime we have around here is largely drug-related," Jeb said. "It's a hard nut to crack."

"I thought so," Mitch said. "Dealers coming down from Atlanta and fentanyl streaming across the border."

"We don't import all of our problems. Most of them started with doctors prescribing too many opioids and locals figuring out how to cook meth in their kitchens."

Jeb had been a member of the volunteer fire department for two decades. He couldn't even count the number of lab fires they'd had to put out. A few years back, two of his best buddies had died in the line of duty when a trailer exploded.

"'Least the cops know who to pick up when shit gets stolen. You just go round up all the junkies."

"What's a junkie look like?" Jeb asked.

Mitch snickered. "You know," he said.

Jeb took his cap off and ran a hand through his hair. "Gimme a description."

"I don't have to," Mitch said.

"No, you don't," Jeb said. "Every firefighter carries Narcan these days. More often than not, we're the first ones to respond to medical emergencies, so I see a lot of junkies. Last one was twenty-four years old. Good kid. Injured his knee playing football first year of college. Coach got the doctor to give him Oxy. Told him it was totally safe. When the season ended, he couldn't stop taking it. And when the prescription ran out, he turned to heroin. He died, in case you were wondering. We got there too late to save him."

"That's too bad. Maybe his people should have done more to help him."

"His people? The kid was white, not that it matters, you ignorant ass. Opioids are equal-opportunity killers. I've seen people of every description taken down. By the way, if you're really interested in helping the state of Georgia, you should know that forty percent of us ain't white."

"I only need fifty-one percent to win."

"Welp," Jeb said. Once again, he'd tried to get his brother to act decent and he'd failed miserably. "If that's how you see it, I'm afraid I won't be one of them."

Mitch laughed hard. "I didn't come here for your vote, you woke-ass motherfucker. I came here to tell you to stop tormenting Lula Dean."

"By *tormenting* Lula Dean, you mean protesting her book bans? Aside from the fact that people should be free to read whatever they like, can't you see how fucking *stupid* this shit makes us look? Weren't you the one who used to bitch and moan about Southerners being typecast? She's just proving those assholes right. The rest of the world thinks we're all Cletus the Slack-Jawed Yokel."

Mitch sighed. "I see I haven't made myself clear," he said, adjusting his waistband. "What I meant to say is stop making your cute little signs or I'll sell the farm."

Mitch had him pinned. There was nothing left to do now but say uncle. That was how it had always worked for the two of them. Older by five years, Mitch had used his size advantage to whup his little brother on a regular basis for fourteen years. For another two years after that, he'd relied on his willingness to cheat.

Now he'd done it again. When their mother passed, she'd left the family farm to the both of them. Mitch had already been in LA for years. Jeb was newly married and just out of vet school. He wanted to live on the farm,

116

but he couldn't afford the upkeep. Mitch bought Jeb out and let him stay on as caretaker. Since then, Jeb had offered a thousand times to buy it, but Mitch had told him it wasn't necessary. The farm would always stay in the family. After all, Mitch's only heirs were his niece and nephew. It was a lie, of course. Mitch didn't give a fuck about the farm. It had never been anything to him but leverage.

"So you're joining forces with Lula Dean?" There was no point in arguing. Mitch had Jeb's balls in a vise and he wasn't afraid to squeeze.

"Yep. I'm all about protecting kids from communist pedo predators."

"You know Lula doesn't care about any of that. She only wants the attention. She'd let this whole town burn to the ground if it got her on the goddamned news."

"Long as I get what I'm after, I'll strike the damn match."

Jeb nodded. "At least you're honest. You planning to stay here on the farm while you're in town?"

Mitch seemed amused by the suggestion. "No offense, but the farm's a bit rustic for my taste. A fan saw I was coming and offered to set me up in his swanky guesthouse." Mitch checked his watch. "Matter of fact, I need to get moving. I told him I'd be there by five."

"I'll walk you back to your truck," Jeb said, half-heartedly wondering if the local cops were capable of solving a homicide—and if the feral hogs out back were up for eating a body.

"So who's this fan of yours?" he asked. "You sure this isn't going to end up one of those *Misery* situations?"

"Name's Walsh."

Jeb stopped. "Logan Walsh? Lives out on Holcombe Road?"

"That's the one." Mitch kept going.

"You don't want to get involved with him and his friends." Jeb hustled to catch up. "I know you talk tough, but those assholes are bad news."

A MONTH EARLIER, HE'D BEEN called out to Logan Walsh's house to treat a sick horse. It wasn't an unusual request. He made house calls all the time, and he'd known Logan years earlier when he was coach of the kid's Little League team. Jeb remembered him as a shy boy with a great arm and a father with a penchant for punching umpires. The dad was a rich muckety-muck in the county—a state supreme court judge who sat in the same seat his father and grandfather had held. Jeb never got to know the man. He'd yanked Logan out of Little League after the umpire incident. About six years later, Jeb saw on the news that Judge Walsh had been killed in a tragic hunting accident. The bullet, which sailed straight through his neck and into a neighboring tree, had come from a gun fired by his only son. Jeb heard all the gossip about what had happened between the two Walshes that day, but he reserved judgment. And he didn't lose a minute's sleep over the older man's passing.

Now Logan Walsh was in his mid-twenties, with a compound way out in the boonies. First things Jeb had seen as he made his way toward the barn were a fleet of ATVs, a fishing boat that inspired some serious envy, and a shooting range where the targets had celebrities' faces pinned to them. Most of the faces belonged to liberal politicians. More than half were Black.

The sick horse would have died without medical intervention, so Jeb went ahead and treated it. Wasn't the animal's fault that a racist asshole owned it. When he'd finished working, Walsh had invited him inside to write him a check—and to show off the arsenal he kept behind glass in his den. That was nothing new. Pretty much everyone around Troy owned guns. Back then, Jeb didn't know of anyone else who also collected Gestapo and SS flags.

"You live here by yourself?" Jeb remembered asking.

"For the moment," Logan told him as he filled out a check for Jeb's veterinary services. "I'm working on fixing that."

"Not sure how many women would appreciate your style of decorating."

Logan found that funny. "Any woman I invite here will know her place."

Jeb pitied the woman naive enough to mistake a rich psychopath's posturing for real strength.

"Do *you* like the display?" Logan asked.

"No," Jeb had told him. "I don't. Aside from what they did in Europe, my grandfather fought a war against those bastards and came home crippled."

"It's just history." Logan finished signing the check and handed it to Jeb with a smile. There was disappointment in the younger man's eyes, and Jeb realized he'd failed a test. "We got a lot of history buffs around these parts."

That made it clear. His interest wasn't a hobby, and it wasn't a game. And Jeb knew that incident in the woods had not been an accident. Logan Walsh was fucking dangerous.

"WHAT DO YOU MEAN I *talk* tough?" Mitch sneered.

"Forget that," Jeb said. He couldn't have Mitch getting all distracted. "Just listen to what I'm trying to tell you. There's a man in Troy named Nathan Dugan. His wife just fled town with their son, and before she did, she emptied out a secret room he'd been keeping in the basement. It was filled with Nazi memorabilia. Ask around. Everyone in town knows about it."

Mitch shrugged. "You've obviously never been in a prop house," he said. "They got Nazi everything and nobody's worshipping Hitler."

"You're not listening. Logan Walsh is buddies with Dugan. He's got the same shit in his den. They aren't filming movies or doing some cosplay shit. They *are* fucking Nazis."

Mitch rolled his eyes. "You don't know that," he said.

"And you haven't lived in the real world for a very long time. There have always been people who kept a swastika or two hidden away in a drawer. I don't know if there are more sympathizers these days, but I will tell you this—our generation's Nazis aren't quite as shy."

"I don't give a shit what people keep in their drawers. This is a free country. They can think whatever they want."

"It's a slippery slope between tolerating Nazis and becoming one, Mitch. Ask anyone who lived in 1930s Germany."

Mitch reached the gate. "I can't. They're all dead."

119

"And that's a big part of the problem."

"Open the fucking gate, Jeb."

"So you're just going to leave? I'm telling you your new friends are dangerous."

"You're making me uncomfortable, so I'm getting the hell out of here. Which is exactly what you should do if you think you're surrounded by terrible people. Just pack up your bags and head for Manhattan like all the other libs."

As Jeb opened the gate, he realized his brother was onto something. Too many people hadn't stuck around. Most of those who remained couldn't afford a fight.

Mitch got into the truck and turned over the ignition. "Here." He motioned for Jeb to come to the window. "I brought you a present," he said, reaching an arm out. Clenched in his hand was a hardcover book. "Lula's not so bad. She's been giving out free books in that little library of hers."

Jeb took the book. It was *The Art of the Deal*.

"If you want to get ready for the future, you better start reading that."

Mitch peeled off, leaving his brother in a cloud of dust. Jeb walked back to his porch and took out another Bud Light. He stared at Donald Trump's smirking face on the cover. Then he cracked open the book. Inside was a cartoon panel with two men—one older, one younger—wearing mouse masks.

People haven't changed . . . Maybe they need a newer, bigger Holocaust.

The image was instantly familiar, but it took Jeb a moment to realize what he was looking at. He pulled back the dust jacket. The book inside was *Maus* by Art Spiegelman. Jeb wondered who could have switched the covers—and what it all meant. He didn't reach any conclusions or compose a list of suspects. Still, there was no doubt in his mind. It was a sign shit was gonna get ugly. But Jeb Sweeney was staying put.

CHAPTER 14

A FIELD GUIDE TO THE
MUSHROOMS OF GEORGIA

The door to Mara Ocumma's office swung open just as she turned a page of the latest Stephen King novel and took a giant bite of her roast beef sandwich with homegrown horseradish and wild greens.

"Sorry to bother you on your lunch break, Mara," Natalie whispered. "I thought you should know. Mrs. Sykes is here."

Mara held up a finger while she finished chewing. "She come alone?"

Natalie nervously checked over her shoulder. They were all on edge these days. "Looks like it."

Not long ago, the head librarian of the Troy Public Library would have dropped everything to greet the mayor's wife at the door. Now such measures no longer seemed necessary. "Then it's fine," Mara assured the assistant librarian. "Given everything that's going on with the Sykes family, I doubt Melody's here to hunt for propaganda or pornography."

Melody Sykes was a founding member of Lula Dean's book banning posse, but Mara doubted her heart had been in it. She'd stood by Lula at all the rallies and press conferences, staring sweetly into space and batting those big brown eyes in a way that made her appear a bit bovine. But Mara knew for a fact that Melody Sykes was a lot smarter than she chose to look. She just ran in circles that didn't always see intelligence as a desirable feminine trait.

Before the infamous erotic cake incident, Melody had been one of the library's very best patrons. She and her youngest son checked out books every week. Melody was partial to the works of Tana French, but would read any good true crime or procedural, while Beau preferred Captain Underpants. Mara suspected the mayor's wife was one of the few members of Lula's posse who'd actually read any of the titles they pulled off the shelves. During Lula's first raid, Mara had hoped Melody might step forward to talk some sense into the crowd. When the mayor's wife remained silent, Mara felt betrayed. Since then, she'd faced so many disappointments that Melody Sykes's hypocrisy barely registered.

In retrospect, she was sure Mayor Sykes had insisted his wife lend her support to Lula. But now Randy was no longer mayor, and given the circumstances under which he'd resigned, Mara wondered if Melody would be doing her husband many favors for the foreseeable future.

"Mrs. Sykes isn't here to ban anything," Natalie said, her face grim. "She's sitting at the plotter's desk. She's got one of your blue moon books."

In the north corner of the Troy Public Library, hidden from view by three of the least visited shelves, sat a single small wooden table. It was a dreary spot, lit by a flickering fluorescent light that lent it a horror-movie ambience. Most library patrons were likely unaware of the desk's existence. Those who stumbled across it rarely chose to sit. Over the fifteen years that Mara Ocumma had worked at the library, the sad, lonesome desk had rarely been used. More often than not, the people who chose it were teenagers with racy novels tucked into their textbooks. In those cases, Mara looked the other way. It was the adults who sat at the desk that concerned her. She called them the plotters because all of them had one—and only one—thing in common. They were definitely up to something.

Mara set down her sandwich. "Did you see what Melody is reading?" she asked.

"Looks like *A Field Guide to the Mushrooms of Georgia*."

"Oh shit." Mara wiped the horseradish off her hands and scooted her chair back. "That *is* serious."

A Field Guide to the Mushrooms of Georgia was on Mara's blue moon list, along with titles like *A is for Arsenic: The Poisons of Agatha Christie* and the

Pocket Guide to Field Dressing Big Game. Most people who sought out the list's titles were genuinely interested in mushrooms, murder mysteries, or deer hunting. But once in a blue moon, a person in crisis would arrive at the library, pluck a book off the shelves, and carry it back to the plotter's desk without checking it out. There was no way of knowing what they planned to do with the information they gathered, but there was also no doubt they were serious. Otherwise they would have stayed at home and gone online. For whatever reason, they were at the library to avoid leaving a trail of digital breadcrumbs.

Mara kept a special book in her top desk drawer for such occasions. She'd only had to use it a handful of times, and she never would have predicted she'd one day have to offer it to Melody Sykes. But after fifteen years at the Troy Public Library, and five as the town's head librarian, it was getting damn near impossible to surprise Mara Ocumma anymore.

She tucked the book under her arm and made her way through the stacks to the plotter's desk.

"Thinking of doing some mushroom hunting?"

Melody Sykes froze with her index finger on the entry for *Amanita phalloides,* and her giant brown eyes rolled up to meet the librarian's. Mara could tell she hadn't been sleeping, nor had she put on any makeup that morning. Women like Melody wouldn't leave the house to give birth unless their hair was blown out and their eyeshadow perfect. Her pasty skin and ponytail were a sure sign that she was on the verge of homicide.

"There's another guide I recommend to people with a newfound interest in fungi. Thought you might want a look at it." Mara set the book down on the table. The cover was black, with the image of a giant gold fingerprint beneath the title: *FBI Handbook of Crime Scene Forensics.*

Melody's eyes shot down to the cover then rolled back up to Mara. "Just say what you want to say, Mara. I'm done playing games."

Mara didn't blame her. "Fine. You feed Randy death caps and he'll be dead in three days. As soon as your husband dies, they will perform an autopsy. There's a good chance they will determine that he died of amatoxin poisoning, and the first thing they'll do is come here. They'll check that field guide for fingerprints and interview all the librarians. I'd say your secret is safe with me, but I'm afraid I'm not the only person who's seen you reading it."

Melody shut the book and sat back with her arms crossed. "Are you going to turn me in?"

"For what?" Mara asked. "Nobody's dead yet, and last I checked, it wasn't illegal to read. Besides, you think you're the only woman who's had a good look at that book? Come with me to my office, and let's find what you really need."

IT WAS ALMOST FUNNY, MARA thought. Every woman with a hankering to kill someone went straight for the mushroom book, when there was more than enough poison in the flower beds outside the library to dispose of every enemy they'd made since third grade. But they assumed the flowers were harmless because they were out in the open. White people were convinced that real dangers, like death caps, dirty books, witches, and Satanists, needed to be hunted down and rooted out. Which is exactly what their forefathers had done to Mara's people.

For thousands of years, the Cherokee were among the tribes that lived in what was now called Georgia. In the early nineteenth century, US troops rounded them up and forced them all to march on foot to Oklahoma. Countless men, women, and children perished along the way. Fewer than a thousand Cherokee managed to stay behind in their homeland. Mara's ancestors had been among them. Most twenty-first-century citizens assumed Jackson Square, in the center of Troy, had been named for General Stonewall Jackson. But the park was older than the Confederacy, and the man it honored was Andrew Jackson, the president of the United States who'd ordered the removal of all Native Americans east of the Mississippi—without a doubt one of the greatest crimes in American history.

As a child, Mara had spent summers with her grandmother in a ramshackle house set deep in an Appalachian hollow. There, she heard stories about how their people had hidden in the forest when the government came for them. Their understanding of the land was key to their survival, and that knowledge was something her grandmother was determined to pass down.

The old woman knew everything that lived or grew on the Cherokee reservation. It was not unusual for people to show up at her door with a basket of wild mushrooms, asking for help sorting out the deadly ones. Others would arrive hoping for help with an ailment. Mara's grandmother didn't take patients, but if she liked you, she might make you something that would lower your blood pressure or soothe your sore throat. Mara was far more interested in trawling the creeks for crawdads and hellbenders than in studying toadstools or foul-smelling herbs, but her grandmother insisted she learn.

"This wisdom is who we are. For hundreds of years, they tried to steal it or outlaw it. But we never let it go. It has fed us and healed us. We are the only ones who possess the knowledge, and we must pass it down. If we lose it for good, a part of ourselves will disappear, too."

And so Mara studied what her grandmother wanted to teach her. The first thing she learned was that few things in this world are wicked. The very same herbs that might poison one person could save another. The trick was knowing what was right for each individual. When Mara was twelve, her grandmother was diagnosed with cancer and Mara saw that wisdom put into practice. Some folks were surprised when the old woman turned to Western medicine to treat her tumor.

"The medication I'm getting originally came from a yew tree," Mara's grandmother told her as they sat together in the chemotherapy center. "But that's not what's important. What matters is never letting people tell you what to think. Don't let them convince you that one way is right and another way wrong. Gather as much knowledge as you can, because information is power. And choosing how to use it is freedom. The more you know, the freer you will be."

On the morning Mara's father told her that her grandmother had died, Mara found a mushroom growing in her yard. It wasn't one she recognized. This specimen was native to her hot, humid home in south Georgia, not the cool, misty Smoky Mountains. She hopped on her bike and rode across town to the local library to look up a field guide to mushrooms. She'd been there a million times before and thought nothing of it. But this time, when she stepped through the doors, Mara knew her grandmother had sent her. She didn't see books and magazines and newspapers. She saw the answers to every question that had ever been asked—and a woman with wild hair behind the counter who knew just where to find them.

MARA CLOSED THE OFFICE DOOR and pulled out a chair for her guest.

"Since we're being frank with each other, Melody, why don't you tell me why you want to poison your husband."

"Did you read Darlene Honeywell's post?" Melody sat with her legs crossed at the ankle and her hands balled into fists in her lap.

"Yes," Mara admitted as she made her way around the desk. "But it seems to me like there are a number of ways to deal with the situation that don't involve murder."

"People keep calling me, telling me Darlene is exaggerating. That it was a long time ago and it wasn't that bad and why is she dragging this stuff out now." Melody stopped. An index finger popped out of her fist and she wagged it at Mara. "You know what that means? It means they all knew! This whole time they knew and nobody told me."

Mara would have murdered the bastard, too, but she wasn't about to say that. Melody was teetering on the edge and she didn't need anyone giving her an excuse to jump.

"If that's true, I'm sorry," Mara said instead. "If I were in your shoes, I suppose I'd be reading up on mushrooms, too."

"This is not what I signed up for! I did not leave college early and move here from Texas so I could end up a pariah in a little hick town in the middle of Georgia."

Mara felt her sympathy drain away. "Still, you have two kids here who need you. I don't think poison's the answer."

Melody's jaw clenched. "Then there is no answer," she said through gritted teeth.

"What about a divorce? My friend Crystal Moore just—"

"A *divorce*? Where would I go? My parents are dead. I've never worked outside the home. I can't leave my boys, and if I take them with me, we'll be poor as church mice."

"Get a good lawyer, and I'm sure you'll be able to keep the house and the kids."

That suggestion only appeared to increase the woman's frustration. "Where am I going to find a lawyer around here? Besides, Randy has my phone password and he keeps an eye on the family computer. He says he wants to know where the boys go on the internet." Melody took in a deep breath. "I always figured he was watching me, too. I just didn't think it would be a problem."

"We have computers here," Mara told her. "You can use them all you like and your husband will never find out what you're researching. That's why libraries exist—to make sure people always have access to the information they need. Every day, we help people find answers to questions that they're terrified to ask."

"What if somebody sees me searching for divorce lawyers and tells Randy?"

"You can use my computer for the next couple of hours," Mara offered. It meant she'd need to stay late to get her own work done, but that seemed a small sacrifice to prevent a murder. "Is there anything else I can help you with?"

Melody started to shake her head. Then she stopped. "Actually, yes. There is. Darlene mentioned a book in her Facebook post," Melody said. "If you have it, I'd like to read it." Melody didn't seem aware of the irony of her request, but it certainly wasn't lost on Mara.

"*Speak* is one of the books your committee confiscated. I believe it's being stored in Beverly Underwood's basement until this town comes to its senses and stops letting Lula Dean tell us what we can and can't read."

Melody seemed to realize she'd just stumbled across a trip wire. "If that book was on the committee's list, a lot of other people must have found it offensive, too."

"*Speak* is about a girl who's been *raped*." Mara heard her voice building and she paused for a moment to regain control. "The things the book talks about need to be said because there are people like Darlene who desperately need to hear them."

Melody's eyes glazed over and Mara knew the former mayor's wife was about to repeat the party line. "We just want to shield our children until they're ready for more mature material."

"Children?" Mara shot back. "You mean like a high school kid who's been raped by classmates and has nowhere to turn?"

This time, Melody offered no defense.

"When people like Lula hide all the books about rape, who do you suppose they're really protecting?" Mara demanded. "Do you want to go back to the days when we never talked about rape? When women like Darlene kept their mouths shut and the men who assaulted them went on to be mayor?"

Melody's face turned scarlet, but she refused to admit defeat. "See, you're talking about older readers," she argued. "As far as I'm concerned, they can do what they want. I'm just concerned about the little children—"

"Okay, so let's focus on younger kids," Mara pressed on. She hadn't planned to get into a debate, but she wasn't going to let Melody off easy. "What exactly do you think books will do to them?"

Melody threw up her arms. "Scare them, for starters!"

"That's funny, 'cause I didn't see you pulling any horror books off the shelves. Most of the books you took were about Black history, the Holocaust, and LGBTQ subjects. A few of the YA novels you banned were a bit raunchy in parts, but I noticed the romance section remains untouched."

"There was that pornographic cake book in the baking section!"

"Which a teenager snuck onto the shelves. But I fail to see how a book of penis cakes could do anyone irreparable harm."

"Maybe that's 'cause you're not one of us," Melody said.

Mara couldn't believe her ears. "Excuse me?"

"I didn't mean white!" Melody hastened to add. "I meant Christian!"

Six of one, half a dozen of the other, thought Mara. "For your information, I was raised Methodist, and unlike many of your fellow holier-than-thou types, I do my best to follow the teachings of Jesus."

"I, I . . ." Melody fumbled for the right words.

Mara sighed. It wasn't her first time at the racist rodeo. "You know what I think, Melody? I think you're scared that your children are going to open a book and discover the truth. They'll realize that the Holocaust happened and that slavery was worse than they ever imagined. They'll find out that both men and women like sex and that gay and trans folks are just regular people. These seem to be the things you're trying so hard to hide from them. Why is that?"

Melody straightened her spine. "They just aren't in keeping with our way of life."

"So you're worried your children will be lured off the righteous path?"

Melody smiled with relief. The conversation could end now. "Exactly."

"But isn't the whole point that each person *chooses* the right path in life, instead of being tricked into taking it?" Mara asked. "Why not give your kids the freedom to make their own decisions?"

"When they're adults, they can make any decisions they like. Until then, we're their parents and it's *our* decision what they check out at the library."

"But you have no right whatsoever to make those decisions for other people's children," Mara pointed out. "And that's what you've done by taking books off the shelves. You're denying your neighbors their freedom to raise *their* kids as they see fit."

"If children are in danger, someone needs to step in."

They were going around in circles. Mara could see Melody wasn't going to stray from her talking points. Whether she was brainwashed or stubborn, Mara couldn't say for sure. "Before I go and leave you to your research, let me ask one more question—what should I do with the mushroom guide you were reading?"

Melody's brow furrowed. "I don't understand," she said.

"Well, you came in today planning to use that book to commit murder. I'm thinking maybe we need to take *A Field Guide to the Mushrooms of Georgia* off the shelves."

"That's ridiculous," Melody said.

"Is it?" Mara asked. "If we hadn't spotted you reading it, that book could have killed a man. Who knows what horrible things would happen if a kid ever got their hands on that guide."

"Oh, I see what you're doing." Melody wasn't stupid.

"Do you?" Mara wanted her to say it out loud.

"Without that field guide, people could end up eating poisonous mushrooms. It needs to stay in the library."

"But if it could make a good Christian woman like you kill her husband—"

Melody rolled her eyes. "The book didn't make me want to kill my husband."

"It didn't lure you off the righteous path?" Mara asked.

"No."

"Are you sure?" Mara pressed her. "The book didn't have anything to do with it?"

"I said no," Melody replied bluntly.

"So do you think there's a chance that some of the books *you've* labeled dangerous might actually be able to help some people?"

Melody glared at her. "Maybe," she finally conceded.

"Just checking," Mara said. She got up and stood at the door of her office. "The computer password is *NancyPearl*. I hope you find a good attorney."

Mara left the mayor's soon-to-be-ex-wife sitting at her desk and returned *A Field Guide to the Mushrooms of Georgia* to its rightful place on the shelf.

CHAPTER 15

ALL THAT SHE CARRIED

Betsy Wright was all cried out. So she didn't shed a tear as she stood in front of Lula Dean's house, where the yard bristled with campaign signs.

MAKE TROY GREAT AGAIN. VOTE LULA DEAN.

LULA LOVES LIBRARIES!

FEAR GOD, PRAISE JESUS, VOTE LULA!

Lula was running for mayor against Beverly Underwood. That's what you got in Troy—a choice between a rich blond white lady and a rich white lady with orange hair. Some would say it was progress to have two women in the race. Betsy wasn't fooled. Those ladies belonged to the same group who'd always run the place. Maybe they were slapping lipstick on their pigs now, but that was the only thing that had changed. And right there was the proof, on a banner fixed to the street-facing side of Lula's white picket fence.

RALLY IN SUPPORT OF TROY'S CONFEDERATE HEROES!

JACKSON SQUARE, 6 P.M.

TONIGHT!

Betsy read it twice over, her heart breaking for her husband, James. She'd warned him time and again not to place so much faith in Lula Dean.

Betsy knew Lula better than most people in town—and she knew Lula loved novels that wouldn't make it past any censors. Lula leading a crusade against dirty books was like Colonel Sanders waging a war against chicken. But James had believed in his heart that Lula's cause was righteous. Even though she'd predicted he'd end up disappointed, Betsy hated to see herself proven right.

Confronted by the hateful sign, she almost turned around and walked away. But she'd brought something that belonged to Lula, and she was determined to return it. Betsy opened her pocketbook and pulled out the book her son Elijah had given her. *Rivals and Lovers* had no place in a little library where young children might find it, so Betsy slid it into Lula's mailbox and raised the red flag. Before she left, she closed her eyes and prayed that would be the very last contact her family would ever have with Lula Dean.

AS SHE PASSED THROUGH THE town square, the courthouse clock told Betsy there was time left on her lunch hour. The florist shop where she'd worked for thirty years was less than three blocks away. She had a few minutes to sit and think. She'd started at Fairview Florist right out of school, cleaning the floors and plucking faded petals off all the roses. When the owner retired, she'd bought the place from him. She was the boss now, but she'd never forgotten how hard her father, who'd worked at the mill from the age of sixteen, had fought for the right to eat lunch in peace. So Betsy took a sixty-minute break every day in his honor. She rarely ate much of anything, but not even the Queen of England could persuade Betsy Wright to fill an order between the hours of one and two.

Instead, she often came to Jackson Square to sit, and she always chose the same bench near the fountain in the center of the park. When her boys were little, she'd brought them here to run wild and get the silliness out of their systems before she took them home to their father. She did so *because* of that statue that loomed over the square, not despite it. She wanted Augustus Wainwright to see her sons enjoying their birthright—the beautiful park that had been bought and built with the blood, sweat, and tears of their people. Few things delighted her as much as imagining that bastard rolling around in his grave.

A flock of starlings took flight, and Betsy saw Isaac and Elijah chasing after them. In her mind, the boys were still little. In her heart, they would never grow up. Isaac was seventeen years old and well over six feet, but just a week back, she'd caught herself reaching out for him as they crossed a street. Elijah was big enough now to pick Betsy up and toss her into the air. But he still needed a kiss from his mama before he went to sleep every night.

In the old days, it was Elijah who'd worried Betsy, not his brother. The boy had been born without filters or restraints. Whatever he was feeling spilled right out of his mouth. Every impulse that hit him got indulged. He sang when he felt like it. He petted every dog and chased every squirrel. Once, at the Piggly Wiggly, he'd run up to Mr. Pig and jumped right into his arms. Russell Moore was a good man, so Elijah had gotten a hug and an apple in return. Betsy made sure her son knew that others around town might not be so kind, but Elijah couldn't conceive of an enemy. He'd never met anyone who wasn't a friend. And though everyone liked to pretend times were different, that zest for life could still get a Black child killed.

Betsy had thanked the Lord every day that Elijah had Isaac to keep him safe. As an infant, Isaac rarely cried, but he was naturally cautious. When he took everything in with those big beautiful eyes, you could almost see the gears in his mind whirling as he studied the situation and calculated the risks. As a boy, he'd never stopped his brother from reveling in life, but he was always there, waiting to step in if necessary. When Elijah danced too close to a campfire, Isaac yanked him back. If a pit bull decided it didn't want to be nuzzled, Isaac would distract it while Elijah escaped. And on the many occasions when his motormouth brother got himself sent to the principal, Isaac would show up to act as his counsel.

Isaac reminded Betsy so much of her father, who'd died long before her boys were born. When she was a girl, her father made sure she knew the history of their town—and the unacknowledged role their family had played in it. Betsy was proud to learn that her father had been one of the workers who'd fought for fair treatment at the mill—and surprised when he admitted how scared he'd been. Over time, though, she realized what he'd described was *bravery*. Her father had known just how high the stakes were at the time. Other families had been run out of town—or worse—for protesting. But her father wouldn't let those in power use his fear to control him.

Elijah may have been fearless, but his brother was the brave one. Betsy had seen it when Isaac told them all he was gay. He'd announced it at dinner, with no preamble or explanation. Looking back, she was sorry she'd burst into tears. But Isaac didn't know the world the way she did. For once, her brilliant, brave boy had miscalculated the risks. He hadn't anticipated his father's reaction. He hadn't consulted the pastor or the Bible. And he certainly hadn't considered how hard life could be for a young man in the South who was Black *and* homosexual. But the truth was, Betsy didn't fault Isaac. She cried—and kept crying—because *she* was to blame. A mother's most important role is to prepare her children for the day when she's no longer there to protect them. When Isaac insisted he was the same person he'd always been, she knew he was right. She'd been too blinded by pride to set her boy on the right path from the very beginning. She was the one who'd let him go astray.

For three weeks, she'd watched in despair as the revelation ripped her family apart. James needed something to blame, and Lula Dean stepped in with a scapegoat. Betsy knew that a book hadn't turned their son gay any more than the romance novels she'd once loved had made her a harlot. Betsy wasn't convinced the Concerned Parents Committee even cared about books. She pointed out that some of the members—like that Walsh boy—seemed downright sketchy. Even James's faith wavered after Nathan Dugan was exposed as a Nazi. But Lula swore she hadn't really known

Dugan at all. The committee was open to the public. She had no control over who showed up at the meetings.

Betsy knew why James was so willing to believe her. He'd always been one of the most conservative members of their community. Family and faith were the bedrock of his existence. Finding out he'd raised a gay son had shaken both. Joining the CPC had given him a sense of control. James couldn't stand feeling helpless—and Betsy loved him too much to tell him there was nothing he could do. The die had been cast. Their son was not going to change.

Betsy saw her husband flail while her eldest son pulled away, and she felt helpless to prevent the disaster she saw hurtling toward them. Then Elijah came to her with a book—the same book James believed had ruined their eldest son. The boy was convinced that *Rivals and Lovers* would change her mind about his brother's fate.

"You really read this?" Holding the three-hundred-page book in her hand, Betsy couldn't help but be skeptical. Elijah had many fine qualities, but he'd never had the attention span for reading. It had taken him two months just to finish *Old Yeller*.

"Yes, ma'am," Elijah confirmed. "But don't worry! I still like girls. Well, *one* girl. Anyways, it didn't make me gay."

Betsy merely nodded at that. It was not the time to speak her mind on the subject of Bella Cummings.

"You read the whole thing?"

"Yes, ma'am. This afternoon," Elijah told her. "It's really boring. All they do is drink wine and have babies. I think you should read it, too."

"You're asking me to read a boring book about gay men drinking wine?"

"Not for me, Mom. For Isaac. Please?"

It wasn't what Elijah said. It was the way he said it. It sounded like he was pleading for the person he loved most in the world. Bringing their family back together was all that mattered to her youngest son. And in a moment of perfect clarity, Betsy realized it was the only thing that mattered to her, too.

"I know you're worried about Isaac's soul, but we're going to lose him while we're here on earth," Elijah told her. "And I really don't think hell could be any worse."

Out of the mouth of babes came the truth. Pure and simple and unmistakable. "Okay, honey," Betsy promised him. "I'll read it."

Elijah's face lit up with a joy so pure it had to be heavenly. That's when Betsy began to wonder if maybe the Lord wasn't sending a message. Then Elijah told her where he'd found the book, and she almost dropped to her knees. "God talks to people all the time," Betsy's father used to say, "but most of us never listen." This time, Betsy heard him loud and clear.

IT HAD BEEN A GOOD five years since Betsy and Lula had exchanged more than a brief hello as they passed each other in the grocery store. Lula quit work at the florist after her husband died unexpectedly and the insurance made her rich. Before that, she and Betsy had worked side by side for almost fifteen years. Lula had hated every minute of it. She felt the work was beneath her and wasn't afraid to say so. Betsy had to ask Jesus for patience whenever Lula rambled on about the Lambert mill—or talked about how much respect she had for "you folks." Both subjects came up almost daily.

Mostly, though, she felt sorry for Lula, who kept careful track of where everyone stood on the town's social ladder. When they lost the mill, her family had slipped several rungs, and Lula spent most of her waking hours trying to work her way back up. Lula didn't consider her coworker competition, and Betsy had no desire to play the white women's game. But that didn't make it any less fascinating to hear Lula's tales of treachery, betrayal, and backhanded compliments. The ladies of Troy had devised a secret language just to put one another down. You could insult someone's whole family by bringing the wrong dish to a potluck. They used words like *nice* and *sweet* as their daggers and would stab you right in the heart with a *cute*. And heaven forbid anyone ever said you *mean well*.

Lula knew the language, and she was a talented storyteller. Betsy told her as much, though she was convinced Lula's flair for drama could have been put to much better use. The tales Lula told always left her agitated or enraged or somewhere in between. For reasons that remained shrouded in mystery, Lula was obsessed with Beverly Underwood. None of it made sense to Betsy. Here was a woman who had a kind husband, a comfortable home, and two children she adored. Lula had everything she needed to be blissfully happy. Instead, she insisted on taking part in a game that made her life miserable. It never occurred to her that she did not have to play.

After Lula's husband died, Lord knows what might have become of her if it hadn't been for the twins. Taylor and Talia were babies when Lula came to work at the florist shop, and Betsy got to know them both over the years. They were pretty little things—so well-behaved and polite. Lula was right to be proud of them. Her devotion to those children was a marvel to behold. She often arrived at work exhausted, having worked half the night making them the beautiful clothes she couldn't afford but thought they deserved. Whenever one of the twins starred in a school play or musical, Lula would tape a poster in the florist's front window and pass out flyers to anyone who stopped by. She devoted her weekends to the pageant circuit, and crafted extravagant costumes to distract the judges from Talia's stage fright.

Then, the day they graduated from high school, Lula's children up and vanished. Betsy saw Lula at the Piggly Wiggly later that summer and noticed how much she'd changed. She was still a young woman, but it was like the life had gone out of her. She told Betsy the twins were at Ole Miss and left it at that. She didn't brag about their grades, accomplishments, or countless charms. Later, Betsy heard she'd been telling people they were both at Tulane. Now she claimed the twins were living in Birmingham, "doing the Lord's work." Whatever *that* meant. But one thing was for certain. In the years since they'd been gone, neither one of Lula's children had paid their mother a visit. And in those years, Lula Dean had lost her mind.

Betsy understood. Lula was all alone. Few knew how her husband's death had shaken her. All they saw was the money. People whispered she'd killed him, and Betsy couldn't imagine how much that hurt. Lula must have known then that no matter how hard she tried, they'd never let her fit in. When her kids skipped town, it probably felt like she had nothing left. There she was, all by herself in that frilly pink house, with no one to give her the attention she coveted or the respect she desired. So she did whatever it took to get it.

Lula spent two weeks in front of the rec center informing parents that yoga could turn their babies Hindu. She wrote passionate Facebook posts complaining about the pornographic swimsuits being worn to the local pool. She bought three boxes of Samoas from a Girl Scout troop in Jackson Square—then called 911 to complain they were running a business on public property. Her behavior made Lula a local joke. Most folks went out of their way to avoid her. People who knew Talia and Taylor claimed she'd driven them nuts. Then Lula had found a book filled with dirty cakes—and with it came all the attention she'd ever craved.

WHEN BETSY TOOK *RIVALS AND LOVERS* back, she'd planned to pay Lula a visit. She wished she'd done so years ago. Maybe she could have worked the conversation around to Taylor and Talia. See if she could find out if there was anything she could do. That woman needed her children just as much as Betsy needed hers. Then Lula had to go and plan a rally for Augustus Wainwright.

"Passed your boy on Main Street a few minutes ago."

Betsy opened her eyes to see Delvin Crump coming toward her. He nodded at the statue. "Suppose I'll be seeing you and James here at the rally this evening?"

"Excuse me?" Her husband had known Delvin Crump since grade

school. Despite their political differences, they'd always been friends. Betsy had assumed Delvin was solid. But the postman was clearly on drugs. "You're going to celebrate this town's Confederate heroes?"

Delvin's forehead furrowed like she'd just spoken gibberish. "I'd rather eat glass than celebrate the Confederacy. I want to see what Isaac has planned."

Betsy pressed one hand to her heart. "*My* Isaac?"

Delvin reached into his postal bag and pulled out a flyer, which he passed to Betsy.

JOIN US IN JACKSON SQUARE AT 6 P.M.

AND LEARN THE TRUTH ABOUT

TROY'S CONFEDERATE HERO

Betsy stared at the piece of paper. *The truth about Troy's Confederate hero.* Dear Lord, she asked herself, what has Isaac discovered?

"Isaac and Bella Cummings were passing them out. You didn't know?"

"All I know is that Cummings girl has Isaac putting himself in harm's way and Elijah swooning like a lovesick fool. She's trouble for both my boys, that one."

"So I'm guessing the protest didn't get your stamp of approval," Delvin noted.

"Isaac should know better. If there's a price to pay, he's the one who'll be paying it. That pretty little prom queen's got nothing to lose. Nobody's going to shoot *her* or drive *her* car off the road. Things are different for Isaac. Those men hunted down Ahmaud Arbery, and all he did was set foot on a building site. *He* didn't demand they pull down a statue. Imagine what they'll do to protect their damn heroes."

Delvin wasn't smiling after that. He knew every word she said was true. "I don't think the protest was Bella's idea."

"Probably not." Betsy knew she'd been uncharitable. "That boy gets more like his granddaddy every day."

139

"Well, for what it's worth, I'm grateful. That statue needs to be sent straight to the scrapyard, and Isaac is brave for saying what needs to be said. You and James did a wonderful job bringing that boy up. I'm happy to help y'all watch out for him."

The jury was still out on her parenting, but Delvin was right about Isaac. If only the world would see him the way she did. "You know he's gay, don't you?" She hadn't meant to say it. The words just slipped out. She whispered it like a secret, even though the whole town must have heard.

Betsy was shocked to see the postman shrug like it meant nothing. "That's what they're saying, but I'm not sure why it should make any difference," Delvin said. "Books are being banned in this town. Nazis are hiding in basements. Lula Dean is running for mayor, and folks are worried about kids being gay?"

"The pastor says Isaac's soul is in jeopardy."

"Oh, come on," Delvin said gently. "You really believe that?"

Betsy didn't know what she believed anymore. "The Bible says men lying with men is an abomination."

"The Bible's got about a million words and that's the only quote people can ever come up with to prove God frowns on gay folks. It's from the Old Testament, which also says pigs are unclean and shouldn't be touched. I don't recall the pastor turning his nose up at any barbecue."

Betsy laughed at the thought. "Last time he was at our house for dinner, I was pretty sure he was going to eat a whole pig."

"Even if he did, he'd only be guilty of gluttony," Delvin declared. "Once Jesus arrived on the scene, all those Old Testament laws no longer applied. The New Testament tells us we're supposed to follow Christ, not the old ways. And as far as I know, Jesus never said a damn thing about gay folks *or* barbecue. But he sure did talk a lot about love."

Those words lingered in Betsy's mind for the rest of the workday.

She had been blessed with two wonderful sons who had brought her immeasurable happiness. Why in God's name would she want to change them? Why would she think for one second that was what the Lord wanted?

The book Elijah found was a message, that much was certain. It was God's way of warning her not to share Lula's fate. Her duty was to keep her family together and love them with all of her heart.

That was something Betsy knew she could do.

WHEN SHE ARRIVED HOME THAT evening, Betsy found her husband sitting on the screened-in back porch. The ice in the tea beside him had melted, leaving a layer of clear water floating atop the dark liquid. The back porch was where he came to fume or sulk. He stared out at the pokeweed forest that grew every summer on their neighbor's property and dripped purple poison berries into their yard.

"I walked by Lula Dean's house this afternoon," Betsy told him.

"I'm through with all that," James told her.

Betsy said nothing, just pulled up a chair beside him. They'd survived so many disappointments over the years—watched so many people reveal their true selves. But even now, after all they'd been through, Betsy couldn't bear to know he'd been hurt. She felt James's pain more intensely than she felt her own.

"I'm sorry," she said.

"I thought she had changed. I was sure she was a righteous woman now." He turned to his wife. "Can you believe she had the gall to ask me to attend that rally and stand on the stage next to her and Mitch Sweeney? She wanted a Black face up there so she can claim she's not racist."

Betsy had no trouble believing it. "Lula's a troubled soul," she told him. "No doubt. But we have bigger fish to fry right now. Isaac is staging a counterprotest at the rally. I think maybe he knows about Augustus."

CHAPTER 16

THE BIG REVEAL

ooks like Lula's running for mayor," Talia said.

"I thought we had an agreement. You can hoover up all the hometown gossip you want. But do not talk to me about Lula Lambert Dean." Taylor resumed bedazzling her nails.

"She's all over Facebook. There's no escape." Talia's hand suddenly flew to her mouth. "Oh Lord, Taylor. You're not going to believe this."

"What?"

"I just clicked on her profile. She's got fifty thousand followers."

It took Taylor a moment to recover. Then she shook the thought right out of her pretty head. "You know she must have bought them. There aren't fifty thousand people in that whole county. Why are you telling me all of this anyway?"

"She's holding some kind of rally in the square tonight." Talia gasped. "It's in support of 'our Confederate heroes.'"

Taylor held her hand out for the phone. "When did Lula start caring about any of that Lost Cause crap? I bet she thinks Manassas is something that happens if you don't eat enough fiber."

Talia kept the phone and didn't answer. Her eyes widened as she scrolled back in time. "She formed a book-banning committee. They've been pulling books out of the libraries."

"What?" Taylor cringed at the thought. "Some nerve that woman's got—

telling people they can't read dirty books. She was dipping into monster erotica before we left."

"She's banning more than dirty stuff. Lula posted a list of the banned books. I see *Anne Frank* and *Beloved* up top."

The twins looked up and locked eyes.

"She's lost her damn mind," Taylor said.

"We both knew it was bound to happen."

Taylor shook her head and leaned toward the mirror to touch up her eyeliner. "Nothing we can do about it right now," she said. "We're booked up here in Florida till the end of the week."

"You know what she's capable of," Talia warned. "She's ruined people's lives. We should have been keeping a closer eye on her."

"Don't act like we've been spending all our time at the beauty salon," Taylor argued. "We've been busy doing the Lord's work. The people down here need us, too."

"Yeah but—"

"But what?" Taylor demanded.

"I feel like she's our responsibility," Talia said.

"After everything she did? Why is that bitch our burden to bear?"

"Because we're the only ones who can stop her."

Taylor stood up and checked herself in the mirror. Her diadem gleamed and ebony curls spilled over her shoulders. A golden lasso of truth hung from her spandex-clad hips. In her knee-high red boots, she towered over her sister.

"How am I supposed to help you with your cape when you put on your boots first?" Talia asked.

"Sorry." Taylor plopped back down in her seat.

Talia attached the cape to Taylor's uniform and used a steamer to rid the garment of wrinkles.

"Alright, let's see it," Talia said.

It always felt like a sacred moment. That first glimpse of her full uniform never failed to remind Taylor why she'd squeezed into it in the first place. Her mission was to fight back the darkness and act as a force for good in the universe.

As Taylor rose from her seat, the white satin cape unfurled down the full length of her back. Written in cursive in sparkling golden sequins was *MOXIE!*

Talia may have been dressed in her usual jeans and T-shirt, but the two of them shared the same mission. They had always been a team.

"Alright," Taylor said. "As soon as we're finished here in Tallahassee, let's go home and take care of Mama."

CHAPTER 17

GONE WITH THE WIND

D id I tell you I saw your brother reading *Rivals and Lovers* in Jackson Square the other day?" Bella Cummings asked her best friend.

"*Rivals and Lovers?*" For a moment, Isaac Wright couldn't quite place the title.

Bella grinned at him from her grandma's front porch swing. "It's about a gay couple in New York. I remember you checked it out from the library a while back."

"Right." Isaac returned to his work. "Unusual choice for Elijah, don't you think?"

"He was reading it because your parents think that's the book that turned you gay."

Isaac looked back up at her. "You're pulling my leg."

"Nope," Bella said and burst out laughing.

For more than a minute, Isaac couldn't catch his breath he was howling so loud. Finally he rolled up in a ball on the porch, clutching his aching stomach. Of all the books Isaac had read that year—including the gorgeous *All Boys Aren't Blue* and *Giovanni's Room* by James Baldwin—his family had decided a silly romance between two bougie Brown boys had lured him to the gay side.

"Elijah read every word of that book, and he did it for you," Bella said once Isaac dragged himself off the floor and resumed his work. "Have you ever heard of anything so sweet? He was worried you might be going to hell. I think *Rivals and Lovers* really helped him."

Isaac chuckled. "Then I'm glad he found it. I love that kid. I don't know what I'd do without him." He finished the last few letters on his banner and sat back on his haunches to let the paint dry. "What do you think?"

"You gonna tell your parents what we're doing?"

The smile slipped off Isaac's face. "They'll find out soon enough."

"So you really haven't told them anything about your discovery?"

"I shared one secret with them," Isaac reminded her. "Didn't do anyone any good."

"You don't think this is different?"

They'd had this conversation three times already, and Isaac hoped this would be the last. "You really think they're going to welcome this news? They didn't take the last batch very well."

"Your parents grew up hearing from everyone that gay people were hell-bound. That's what their parents told them, it's what the preacher told them. I'm sure they heard it in school. They need to get past forty years of brainwashing. That doesn't happen overnight."

Bella may have been right, but she didn't have to live with James and Betsy.

"I understand they need time," Isaac said. "That doesn't mean I have to feel good about it."

ISAAC'S PARENTS WANTED TO GO back to the way things were. He knew this because his mother had told him so every day for the past three weeks. She bawled her eyes out talking about what a perfect child he'd once been. How he'd stayed by her side after Elijah was born and the demon of depression had done its best to kill her. How he'd stunned the preacher by reciting Psalms from memory at the age of four. How he'd won every academic award they gave out in the eighth grade—and how proud she'd been to see him walk up to claim them, looking like a little bitty president in his tan summer suit.

"What happened to my baby boy?" his mother would sob. "Where did I go wrong?"

"You never went wrong," Isaac assured her. "I had a wonderful childhood." He wouldn't have said so if it hadn't been true. That was the promise Isaac had made to himself—he wasn't going to lie anymore. Not to himself. Not to anyone else.

When his mother reached to clutch his hands, her fingers were wet with tears. "Why can't we be like that again?"

"I was always this way, Mama," he tried to tell her. "What do you want to go back to? The days when I was hiding myself from you? When I was pretending to be someone I'm not?"

"You can't tell me that tiny boy in that sweet little suit was a homosexual."

"That little boy didn't know the first thing about sex. But I promise you, he was the very same person who's sitting here today."

When the conversation was over, Isaac's father had stopped him on the way out the door. James Wright hadn't spoken directly to his son in ages.

"You're killing your mother," he told Isaac, his face a mixture of fury and grief.

It was almost more than Isaac could bear to see his parents suffering. They were good people. They'd spent their lives working to give him and Elijah every advantage they could. Their approval meant everything to their sons. But Isaac couldn't change who he was to appease them.

"I'm not the one hurting you and Mom," Isaac told him. That, too, was the truth. He could only hope that one day, they'd see that.

A TRUCK ROARED BY THE Cummings porch, a cloud of black smoke billowing from its tailpipe and a Confederate battle flag slapped on its bumper. Everywhere Isaac looked, people wanted to go back. Back to a time when people like him either didn't exist—or kept their damn mouths shut. Back to a time when there were plenty of confirmed bachelors, but nobody was gay. Back to a time when Black kids didn't go to school with white children, and if they did, they weren't valedictorian and they *sure* as hell weren't best friends with the prom queen.

When it was announced that Isaac would be Troy High School's vale-dictorian, there had been anonymous calls for a recount. Some parents just couldn't believe it was possible that a Black kid could come out on top. They blamed everything from affirmative action to BLM. It was the students who'd eventually convinced their elders that there'd been no mistake. No one who'd ever seen Isaac in class would have doubted how hard he worked—or what he was able to accomplish. Still, even those who accepted the truth treated him like some rare bird—a flamingo that had flown off course and landed in their pond. Some were clearly worried that there were more on the way.

Isaac knew what those people saw when he walked down the street. They saw a future that scared them—a future where everyone had a chance (just a chance!) to be their best selves. If you were smart and worked hard, you might rise to the top. You could love who you wanted and dress as you liked. It was hard to argue with any of that in a country that proclaimed everyone to be free. So they had to turn ordinary people into villains. Black folks were criminals, their news channels shouted. Gay men debauched. Feminists were man-haters. Drag queens were groomers. Democrats were pedophiles. And all good Americans should take up arms against them.

Fighting the forces of evil—whether Black, gay, feminist, or fabulous—would take drastic measures, the hate-mongers told their followers. Books would need to be banned and laws broken. Some parts of the Constitution might no longer apply to everyone. And there were sections of the Bible they'd have to ignore, starting with *love thy neighbor.*

They didn't care if lives were ruined in the process. People like Mr. Minter, the high school's musical director, would pay. Since he'd been run out of town for imaginary crimes, the school hadn't put on a decent pro-duction. But for people like Lula Dean, that was a reasonable price. They had to do whatever it took to keep future generations from living lives more fulfilling than their own.

Instead of an equitable future, they preached a return to a glorious past. They walked around with Technicolor pictures in their heads—ideas planted by Hollywood of what the fabled South had been like. They dreamed of a *Gone with the Wind* Georgia that had never existed. Of white mansions with fluted columns and women in crinolines. Of mint juleps on the verandah and cotillion waltzes. Of happy Black folks tending the fields and benevolent slave masters introducing the heathen to Jesus. Of strapping young white men in gray uniforms marching off to fight for a cause that may have been lost but was no less noble.

The historical reality would have sickened them. Literally. After a month in the old South they would have been suffering from malaria, cholera, or yellow fever. The people they met during their travels would be dystopian versions of the characters from their favorite movies. Real-life Mammy would have spent her fertile years nursing white babies while her own were sold off to the highest bidder. Ashley Wilkes, the ideal Southern gentleman, would own a plantation designed to turn human flesh into dollars. The soldiers nursed by saintly Melanie would reck of gangrene after losing limbs to a cause whose origins eluded them. Pretty Scarlett would do her business in a chamber pot she kept under the bed.

This glorious antebellum South they yearned for never featured any of the ugly realities of the past—body odor, hookworm, rape, cesspools, death, disease, and whippings, not to mention the unrelenting poverty of the folks called white trash. Anyone who tried to open their eyes was ignored or vilified. They made heroes of sadists like Augustus Wainwright. They went around waving a flag they claimed was all about heritage. The flag for which their poor ancestors had fought and died, while the rich slaveholders who'd started the war were exempted from service by Jefferson Davis himself.

But there were uglier truths still—rabbit holes so horrifying even the most intrepid explorers of the past went out of their way to avoid them. Not long after his mind had been blown by *The Hemingses of Monticello,* Isaac had stumbled across a passage in a Civil War–era diary written by Mary Chesnut, the wife of a high-ranking Confederate in Charleston, South Carolina:

The mulattos one sees in every family . . . resemble the white children. Any lady is ready to tell you who is the father of all the mulatto children in everybody's household but her own. Those, she seems to think, drop from the clouds.

No three lines he'd ever read had left such an indelible mark. Isaac couldn't help but remember a comment an uncle had made at a cookout years earlier about a rich, white ancestor way back in the past. When Isaac had asked his father, he was told the uncle in question was a prankster who liked to tell tall tales whenever he drank. Now Isaac wondered if the story might not have some truth to it. On a hunch, he had used a bit of Christmas money to purchase a DNA kit. When the results came back, he wasn't surprised to find that he was of African, European, and Native American ancestry. Then Isaac linked his DNA results to the digital family tree he'd created using names pulled from his family Bible. His parents had both come from large families, and hundreds of matches began to appear—a web of cousins all over the state of Georgia. Some he knew. Others he'd heard of in passing. Most names were completely unfamiliar. One name was Beverly Underwood.

Isaac recognized a single name on Beverly Underwood's family tree. When he entered that name into a blank space on his own, the DNA matched and the site accepted the man as an ancestor. The forefather he and Beverly Underwood shared was the man who'd "saved" Troy, Confederate general Augustus Wainwright.

Isaac spent hours following the Wainwright branch of his tree back in time—first to Jamestown and Plymouth, then hundreds of years back into Europe and Britain. None of the other branches on his tree went back further than 1830. As much as it amused him that he was now eligible for membership in the Mayflower Society, Sons of the American Revolution, and Sons of the Confederacy, it made Isaac furious to think that so much of his family's history had been stolen—erased by the very people who had so carefully documented their own. But it was one empty space that haunted Isaac more than the others—the one right beside *Augustus Wainwright*. The unnamed Black woman who was the matriarch of their family.

Who was she? Where had she been born and where had she gone? How did she come to give birth to a Confederate general's child? How many more had she had? Isaac thought of Sally Hemings, whose relationship with Thomas Jefferson was often whitewashed as romance. How do you fully consent to sex with a man who owns you? When saying no isn't an option, how can it ever be anything other than rape? And yet Augustus Wainwright's blood flowed through his veins. Isaac looked for something to redeem him. Some sign that the man had given the world something other than a gaudy gold courthouse and a statue of himself.

Isaac's search was in vain. Months of study uncovered nothing to suggest that Augustus Wainwright had been anything but a monster. He found plenty written about Wainwright's plantation, known as Avalon, with its beautiful big house that some historians argued was the inspiration for Tara. And Wainwright had been a handsome man in his youth—everyone agreed on that. But the rest read like a horror novel. Augustus Wainwright made most of his money trading slaves, not cotton. It was said that many of those slaves were likely his own children. During his time in the Confederate Army, he had personally ordered the massacre of fifty Black Union soldiers who had been forced to surrender. After the war, he'd rebuilt his fortune by exploiting newly freed people who had nowhere to go. At least part of that fortune was used to fund the local branch of the Ku Klux Klan. He paid almost nothing for the courthouse that was built in the center of Troy, having cheated his suppliers and forced Black laborers to work for a pittance. By the time he died, most of his money had gone toward gambling and prostitutes. His one legitimate son had hated Wainwright so much that he was known to get sloppy and piss on his father's statue every year when the old man's birthday rolled around.

Over time, that piss-stained statue became a touchstone for the town—a monument to a past that had never existed. Just as Wainwright knew it would. The general may have been a sociopath, but he wasn't stupid. Far from it. He'd learned his history better than most. He knew that the people history remembers are those who build monuments out of marble. And he knew that an image carved into stone would be the only thing later generations would ever see—and the words etched beneath would one day be accepted as fact.

Yet history is full of unintended consequences. When commissioning his statue, Augustus Wainwright inadvertently did one good thing. He stole an inscription for his monument that would inspire a town. Wainwright himself hadn't lived by it—and he certainly hadn't died by it. Letters between family members suggest he stumbled drunk into an outhouse behind a brothel and drowned in the cesspit. But long before he knew anything about him, Augustus Wainwright's great-great-great-great-great-grandson had taken those words to heart. Isaac Wright refused to bow before tyrants.

The day he decided on a course of action was the very same day Isaac told his family he was gay. He'd had no doubts about his sexuality since middle school, but he'd always figured it would be prudent to wait until college to come out. He hadn't applied to any schools south of the Mason-Dixon Line. He wanted to put some distance between him and Georgia. But whenever he looked at that blank space next to Augustus Wainwright's name, *safe* simply didn't feel like an option. The truth had waited long enough.

"THAT THE BANNER?" ELIJAH HAD just arrived at the Cumming house. Usually he only had eyes for Bella whenever she was near, but this time was different.

"Yep," Isaac said.

"I can't believe you just dropped this shit on me today. Is there anything else I need to know?"

"You should know that what we're about to do could put us both in serious danger," Isaac informed his brother.

"If you aren't up for it, I'll help Isaac with the banner," Bella offered.

"Nope," Elijah told her. "My brother and I need to do it."

CHAPTER 18

THE SOUND AND THE FURY

Everything was coming together. All the years of struggle were finally paying off. Lula Dean and Mitch Sweeney stood side by side on a wooden stage at the center of Jackson Square, with Augustus Wainwright behind them. Lula had on a cute coral dress from Ann Taylor that she'd seen the lady senator from Tennessee wear on TV. The members of the Concerned Parents Committee flanked the statue. The only person missing was James Wright, even though Lula had sent him a personal note just that morning inviting him *again* to stand next to her and Mitch. A representative from Troy's Black community would have gone a long ways toward keeping the woke crowd quiet. It was disappointing that James had chosen to abandon Lula in her time of need, but she couldn't let that get her down. Melody Sykes had made up for it by baking hundreds of cupcakes and decorating them with miniature Confederate and American flags. Her husband, Randy, was holed up at his family's cabin in the mountains, but letting his wife attend the rally sent a clear message to his supporters: Lula Dean was his pick for mayor.

As the people of Troy trickled into the square, television crews set up their equipment at the front of the stage. Not only was every network in attendance, they'd all sent their name-brand reporters. Photographers from newspapers and websites roamed the crowd, catching folks just as they bit into their Dixie cupcakes. Everyone who was anyone in Troy was there. Even Beverly and Trip Underwood had arrived to watch. Lula couldn't wait to see that snooty woman's face when she realized what a terrible mistake she'd made. Beverly had forgotten she lived in the South. Down here, you didn't mess with history and heritage.

Lula was thrilled to find more of her foes in attendance. The librarian lady, Jeb Sweeney, and that witch Logan Walsh rescued in the woods—they were all there. Nathan had phoned to let Lula know he'd caught wind of a protest, and he'd sent Logan to keep an eye on things. Lula hadn't thought it was necessary, but Nathan wasn't a man who liked to hear the word *no*. He referred to Logan as his "eyes and ears" and expected the younger man to take his place on the Concerned Parents Committee until all the Nazi business blew over. Whenever Lula seemed unhappy with the arrangement, Nathan reminded her of all the work he'd done to get the CPC up and running. None of this would be possible without him, and she owed him a debt of gratitude.

Still, Lula had been planning to beg Nathan to please send someone other than Logan to the next meeting. His protégé hadn't been blessed with social skills. James Wright had never been comfortable around him, and Logan had scared a few ladies on the committee when he'd referred to Beverly as a feminist whore.

"He can't go around town calling people *feminists,*" Melody Sykes had said afterward. Lula promised she'd have a talk with him, but she still hadn't found the time.

Lula glanced over her shoulder. Logan was positioned right behind her and Mitch, standing there like some kind of undercover Secret Service agent, with his sunglasses on, his legs apart, and his hands clasped in front of his privates. She couldn't tell if he was looking at her or not, but she smiled just in case.

"Boy ain't right," Mitch had informed her when he showed up to the rally looking a bit ragged. "I slept with one eye open."

"What'd he do?" Lula wasn't sure she wanted to hear the answer.

"Asked me to join him for target practice," Mitch said and wouldn't say any more.

Lula snuck another peek at Logan Walsh. At least he was on their side, not the liberals'. Then the church bells began to toll the six o'clock hour, and Lula set all her worries aside, closed her eyes, and took a moment to thank the Lord. She'd found the one thing her life had been missing—a calling. *This* is what she was made for.

"HOW Y'ALL DOING TODAY!" MITCH shouted into the mic to kick things off.

A light smattering of applause and a few half-hearted whoops from the crowd followed.

"Oh, come on now, I didn't drive all the way to Georgia for a greeting like that. Gimme some Southern hospitality!"

The response was only slightly more enthusiastic, but Mitch didn't seem to notice.

"So looks like there's gonna be a mayor's race soon," Mitch said. "And my good friend Lula Dean is fixing to win it. But we're not here today to ask for your vote. We've gathered in this square to show our support for someone who's under attack and can no longer defend himself. General Augustus Wainwright."

Mitch paused and stepped to one side to gaze up at the statue with a perfect rendition of reverence and respect. Lula couldn't have done it any better. Mitch may have been an idiot, but he was a damn fine actor.

"This man right here fought against Northern invaders to preserve our unique way of life. Sherman marched out of his way to burn Augustus Wainwright's home to the ground. As a result, the town of Troy was saved from destruction. After the war, Wainwright *personally* financed the building of our world-famous courthouse. And how do some folks want to thank him in the twenty-first century? By tearing down the statue that has stood on this spot for one hundred and fifty years."

Mitch shook his head sadly. "Fortunately, a hero has stepped forward to defend the general, just as he defended this town all those years ago. And let me tell you, Augustus Wainwright could not ask for a better champion. As

I'm sure y'all know, Lula Dean is one tough cookie. She's already taken on the pornographers, perverts, and propagandists, and now she's going after all the folks who want to send our beloved general to the county dump!"

The applause echoed through the square.

"Y'all give it up for Lula Dean!"

The photographers surged forward as Lula took the mic. This was her moment.

"Can you believe it? An introduction like that from the great Mitch Sweeney? I wish I could go back to 1990 and tell nine-year-old Lula this day is coming!"

She fluttered her eyelids at Mitch and the crowd loved it.

"While we're back in time, I want y'all to remember what it was like. Just think about the way things used to be right here in this square. Wasn't that long ago, but it feels like forever. I remember Fourth of July parades, Confederate Memorial Day picnics, and family reunions with Augustus looking on. Remember how wonderful that was? Remember how safe you felt? Our mamas and daddies could let us pick out books at the library without worrying we'd accidentally come home with some piece of filth that would rot our minds. And we could play outside until sundown without anyone ever worrying we'd end up kidnapped and trafficked. Y'all remember that?"

They were eating it up! Lula nodded along with them.

"Mmm-hmm, I knew you did. People didn't fight and argue as much back then. There was no CRT or BLM to get folks riled up. Everybody used the same two pronouns. Divorce was something that was frowned upon. If married folks had a problem, they went to the Lord with it, not to the courthouse. You taught your children what you saw fit—and you did it in keeping with your family values. You weren't told to hand over their education to folks with agendas. We revered our ancestors and were grateful for the sacrifices they made. Everybody got treated fairly, no matter who they were or what they looked like. Men were allowed to be strong and women feminine and nobody took pride in being a victim. Y'all remember those days? Feels like a million years ago, doesn't it?"

156

She waited forever for the crowd to stop clapping. She'd hit the right nerve.

"Then what do you say we bring those days back. Let's stop letting the forces of evil tear our communities apart! Let's stop letting them label us all racists or bigots just because we won't do what we're told! And for heaven's sake, let's stop them from tearing down our monuments and our statues!"

That's when she spotted the Wright brothers making their way through the crowd toward the front of the stage. They were dressed nice in chinos and button-downs, and they both looked so wonderfully serious. Lula's heart swelled to see them. James Wright hadn't let her down after all.

"Looks like we have a few latecomers rolling in. Y'all make way for the Wright boys. Their daddy was one of the earliest members of our Concerned Parents Committee. Now he's sent his sons as his representatives. You two come on up."

Lula wasn't thrilled to see them bring that Bella Cummings onstage with them. But she supposed it wouldn't hurt for the photographers to get pictures of Troy's pretty prom queen supporting the cause.

Without saying a word to her or anyone else, the Wright boys positioned themselves at either end of the stage front, unfurling a banner between them. After a loud gasp, the crowd fell utterly silent. Suddenly, every hand held a smartphone aloft.

"How do you know?" a reporter shouted.

"Do you have proof?" another called out.

"Wait just a second," Lula demanded. "What's the sign say?" She walked around to a spot where she could see what was written.

We are descendants of the rapist Augustus Wainwright, the banner read. *We want him removed from Jackson Square.*

"How dare you!" Lula exclaimed. "You can't make things up like that!"

In his left hand, the older boy raised a rolled-up document. "I have a printout of our family tree. The man who commissioned this statue of himself had a child with one of the women he enslaved, who was in no position to give her consent. The woman he raped was our ancestor. I have the DNA results to prove it. And so, it disgusts me to say, the slaveholding tyrant Lula Dean and her supporters have come here to celebrate is our great-great-great-great-great-grandfather."

Suddenly everyone in the crowd was talking at once. The reporters were all pushing their way toward the two boys. Every camera had turned in their direction.

WHY DID SHE DO WHAT she did at that moment? It was a question that Lula would have to ponder. What would have happened if she hadn't said anything? Would things have turned out for the better or worse? First, Lula looked over at Mitch, who seemed utterly confused. Then her head turned just a smidge more, and she witnessed Logan Walsh drop to one knee and hitch up a pant leg. She saw the metallic glint of a gun in an ankle holster.

"Mitch!" Lula screamed. "Stop him!"

Jolted out of a trance, Mitch responded. But he hadn't seen Logan. With the growl of a furious bear, he charged forward toward the boys with the banner instead. Halfway across the stage, his foot caught the mic cord, and in the mayhem that followed, Lula lost sight of Logan.

Mitch lurched forward, slamming right into Bella Cummings. Lula watched the girl sail into the air and off the platform. The crowd screamed and parted. Then Bella vanished from sight as she plunged to the earth and landed with a dull thump on the cobblestones. Lula ran to the edge of the stage. Bella was lying on her back five feet into the audience. The older Wright boy leaped into the crowd and knelt by the girl's side.

"You motherfucker!" someone shouted.

Lula swiveled and saw the younger Wright brother, the football star, barrel into Mitch Sweeney, who'd just struggled back to his feet and was bleeding profusely from a long, jagged head wound. Within an instant, the movie star was on the ground again with a furious football star astride him.

"Get off!" Lula grabbed the boy's shirt and tried to pull him away. No one else stepped forward to help, not even Mitch's useless brother, who seemed perfectly content seeing her guest star get whupped by a teenager.

Then a voice rose above the commotion. "What the hell are you doing?" the older Wright boy shouted. His little brother looked up and everyone else turned around. "We have to get Bella to a doctor! She needs help right away."

AND THAT WAS THE END of Lula's glorious rally. After such a wonderful start, it had concluded in the worst way possible, with her guest star bleeding from a head wound and the sheriff ordering everyone to get the hell out of Jackson Square. Melody's cupcakes had been smooshed into the ground, including the two that Lula had set aside to take home with her. All of her enemies left with their prayers answered, and Beverly Underwood had the *nerve* to ask if she needed help cleaning things up. Lula marched right off without saying a word.

The phone kept ringing, but for the rest of the evening, Lula was too heartbroken to talk to anyone. It wasn't until she was soaking in a hot, rose-scented bath that she remembered the glint of metal on Logan Walsh's ankle. What on earth had that idiot been thinking? Was he planning to shoot the Wright boys there on her stage? What did he think that would achieve—other than getting Lula canceled and ending her bid for mayor? First thing in the morning, she was going to call Nathan Dugan and tell him Logan Walsh was no longer welcome on the Concerned Parents Committee.

CHAPTER 19

A CALEDONIAN FLING

The first of Bernice Hutton's two regrets in life was that she'd ever given a good goddamn what anyone thought. Now she was old—very old—and she could see just how little their opinions really meant. Sometimes she imagined herself standing on top of Troy's big gaudy court-house, looking down at the townsfolk scrambling around trying to outdo one another. All of them thinking the differences between them were important. Believing anyone would give a damn in a hundred years what model car they drove or who their granddaddy was. When they reached her age, and gained the perspective it offered, they'd come to know what she'd found out. The only thing that matters is who you've loved. Once they knew that simple truth, they'd wish to God, just like she did, that they'd figured it out while their life was ahead of them.

When you're very old, people want to know—what's the secret to a good, long life? Bernice would tell them: live and let live. Be true to yourself and let others do the same. It was good advice, but people never seemed to listen, which Bernice found depressing. That lesson hadn't come easily, and she wanted to spare them the suffering she'd endured. But that's not how humans work, she'd realized. We all have to find out the hard way for ourselves.

Bernice's second regret, by far the biggest, was that she hadn't run away with Samuel Yates when she had the chance. It was a complicated dream to lose herself in completely. Because if she had followed her heart back then, she wouldn't have her children or grandchildren, and she loved them all very much. But when she looked at Sam now and felt her pulse surge just like it had when they were eighteen years old, she couldn't help but think how wonderful it would be to go back in time and spend sixty years with him.

She still remembered with heartbreaking clarity the last time she'd seen him as a young man, standing below her window and telling her he had to leave. He'd begged her to come with him. They'd head up north, where things weren't perfect but they might be a bit easier. Bernice had stayed in Troy for the very worst reasons. She was scared of the people in this pissant little town—of what they might think of her and what they might say to her father. Bernice's cowardice cost her happiness. It had been a terrible price to pay.

In those days, the town's eyes had been glued to them every time they spoke. Aside from the Lambert mill, the streets were the only spaces in Troy where white and Black folks ever mingled. The movie theater was off-limits to Sam. The soda fountain, too. Bernice and Sam went for walks in the woods, hoping they didn't run into hikers or hunters. Even though they never did anything but hold hands, both knew all too well what could happen if they were ever discovered. They were only a couple of years younger than that boy, Emmett Till, who'd been brutally murdered at age fourteen after a white woman lied and claimed he'd whistled at her.

These days, Bernice and Samuel were old and no one gave a damn what they did. They could walk around arm in arm, invisible to all. Bernice's husband died in 2019. Sam's wife passed on Christmas Day a couple years later. Six months after that, once he'd put his affairs in order, Sam had driven eighteen hours to Troy from Milwaukee. He didn't know where Bernice lived and he didn't dare ask—for her sake, not for his. A lot of things had changed down south, but he wasn't sure exactly which ones. So he sat on a bench in Jackson Square for hours each day, waiting for her to pass by. When she finally saw him, it was like they'd never been apart.

They talked about getting married, but decided against it. They'd both had the experience and felt no desire to repeat it. And neither of them had any use for another toaster. All they wanted or needed was each other. So they splurged on a cruise around the world instead of a wedding. Six months later, they settled down together in Troy.

Every evening (weather permitting) they returned to the bench where they'd been reunited. But on this night, it wasn't a thunderstorm that kept them from observing their ritual. They found Jackson Square looking like Sherman himself had just marched through it. Someone had constructed a wooden stage right in front of the statue, but it now stood abandoned. A banner made from a painter's drop cloth and two long dowels lay draped over a bench. Only two words written in red paint—*descendants of*—could be read. Cupcakes smashed into the cobblestones bore the shoe prints of a frenzied mob. But there was no sign of the crowd. Only a single woman remained in the square—a petite blond in a pretty summer dress. She was picking up litter and stuffing it into a kitchen bag.

"Beverly?" Bernice called out, and the younger woman looked up.

"Evening, Bernice." Beverly Underwood pulled off one of her rubber gloves and walked over to offer a hand to Bernice's companion. "You must be Sam. I'm Beverly. Welcome back to Georgia. I sure have heard a lot about you."

Sam shot Bernice a droll side-eye as he shook Beverly's hand.

"We both get our hair done at Val's," Bernice told him.

"Well, that explains it," Sam said. "What happened out here tonight?"

Beverly sighed. "Lula Dean held a rally in support of the Confederate statue. I'd like to see it go—and apparently I'm not the only one who feels that way. Some young people came to protest and things got out of hand. Bella Cummings was injured."

"Wilma Jean's granddaughter?" Bernice asked. "She gonna be all right?"

"I think so. They took her to see Dr. Chokshi. I'm just cleaning up a little and then I'm going to head over to check on her." Beverly paused for a moment while a question seemed to form in her mind. "Y'all notice anything different about Troy in the past couple of weeks?"

162

Bernice took in the state of Jackson Square. "Sure does seem like there's something strange in the air."

Beverly nodded. "I was talking to Wanda Crump, and she thinks that little library Lula opened might have something to do with all the things that keep happening," she said.

"I wouldn't be shocked," Bernice said. "That woman's an agent of chaos, God love her."

"Well, would you mind taking a peek for me? Lula and I are both running for mayor, and I can't really be seen loitering outside her house."

"May I ask?" Sam spoke up. "Who's this Lula Dean who's been holding rallies and opening libraries?"

"Her maiden name is Lambert," Bernice told him. "She's Leonard's daughter."

"Y'all knew Lula's father?" Beverly asked.

"Oh yes," Sam told her. "The Lamberts were the reason my family had to leave town."

SIXTY YEARS EARLIER, THERE HAD been another gathering in Jackson Square. On that day, Sam's father had been at the front of the crowd. He wasn't there to defend Augustus Wainwright, but to rally a group of mill workers—many of them descendants of the men and women who'd worked in the Wainwright fields. The Emancipation Proclamation was one hundred years old, but the area's Black folks had never been fully free. Many felt like they'd gone straight from one form of slavery to another. The jobs at the mill were supposed to pay the minimum wage, but the checks they took home from the mill never added up. The days lasted sunup to sundown, just as they had before the war. They were expected to arrive early and leave late. There were no breaks or vacations. You prayed you never got sick. Those who were injured on the job were let go. Whole families could starve if a father broke an arm.

For over one hundred years, this was the way things were done. Exploiting the Black people in town—preventing them from ever getting ahead—well, that was as much a tradition as cornbread and greens. Samuel's father had tried to change that. All he'd asked for was the same basic rights that workers in other places were given. For his impertinence, their house had been burned to the ground after the rally. A mob was searching for Samuel and his father the night he begged Bernice to leave. There was no point in calling the police for help. Some of the men hunting them worked for the local sheriff. The entire Yates family was forced to flee Troy, hidden in the back of a delivery truck.

For twenty years after that, things went back to the way they'd always been. Then a local lawyer sued the mill on behalf of the workers. Wilma Jean Cummings's father had once worked for Leonard Lambert, and she knew exactly what kind of man he was. When she and the workers prevailed in court, Lambert was bankrupted. He'd been forced to sell the mill to an outside company. The new owners would never have been mistaken for socialists, but at least they let the workers take lunch breaks and paid them what they were owed.

It was a small step forward. But for many, the damage had already been done. Lives had been sacrificed. Others, like Bernice's and Sam's, had been ripped apart. Progress had arrived at last, but it had come at a terrible price.

BERNICE'S EYES SKIMMED DOWN THE line from *The Art of Crochet* to *Manhood*. It had to be the most ridiculous selection of titles she'd ever encountered.

"These are the books your friend thinks might be changing the town?" Sam asked.

"Oh Lord," Bernice said. "Look at this one." She pulled out *A Caledonian Fling*. The cover showed a handsome Highlander in a kilt wooing a lass in a tartan dress while a herd of sheep looked on. "I haven't seen this book since I was in grade school. I nicked it from my mother thinking it might be naughty. Damn thing bored me to tears."

Sam reached out for the book and she passed it to him. He flipped to a random page and read.

"'My secret vices are no longer secret and I no longer have to be clandestine or to hide the covers of the books.'"

"What?" Bernice said. "I don't remember that part."

Sam turned to another random passage. "'We had one rhythm from the beginning. We didn't need to practice, or tune our instruments. He would be astonished and proclaim his astonishment. I wouldn't have time to share in his proclamations. My time was dedicated wholly to pleasure. I would fall silent. I would cling to his body and bury my face beneath his armpit and breathe his smell deeply into my chest.'"

Sam paused and whistled softly. "You were one jaded schoolgirl. This is some good stuff!"

Bernice playfully swatted Sam on the arm. "You're making it all up!"

Sam laughed. "I wish I was capable. I'm just reading what's right here on the page."

"Lemme see," Bernice demanded, and Sam turned the book to face her. She studied it for a moment. "Oh!" She peeled off the cover and stuck it back in Lula's library. "There's a different book inside."

"'*The Proof of the Honey,*'" Sam read from the book's spine. Then he grinned. "Someone's gone and switched Lula's books."

"You suppose this one's real dirty?" Bernice asked.

"Only if we're lucky," Sam said, tucking the book under his arm and offering the love of his life his hand.

CHAPTER 20

HOW THE WORD IS PASSED

Keith Kelly was rolling up his sleeve for the tetanus shot when the office's front door slammed against the wall and someone shouted for Dr. Chokshi. He and the doctor hurried out of the exam room to find two teenage boys in the reception area. A burly, athletic kid was carrying Bella Cummings, her body limp and eyelids fluttering. His tall, terrified brother brought the doctor up to speed.

"Mitch Sweeney knocked her off a stage in Jackson Square five minutes ago. She was unconscious for just under two minutes. She's been disoriented since she woke up."

"Bring her in," Dr. Chokshi ordered. "I'm sorry, Keith—"

"No worries." Keith raised his hands and hopped out of the way on his good foot.

It went without saying that girls with head injuries took precedence, but the truth was, Keith was more than happy to wait. As much as he loved his family, he was in no rush to get back to them. In the three days since he'd come home from college, he'd endured a constant barrage of death, destruction, and drag queens. The minute his parents got up in the morning, the news came on—and it didn't go off until the two older Kellys went to bed around ten. He felt like he'd wandered into a war zone. The territory in dispute was his brain.

That afternoon, Keith had escaped for a walk. He strolled down Main Street, bought a pair of salmon-colored shorts at a boutique, and browsed the books in a purple little library. He'd chosen *Contract with America* by Newt Gingrich and carried it to a bench in Jackson Square. The book inside didn't match the dust jacket, but Keith would have read almost anything. By the end of the first two chapters, he was hooked. That's when a group of townspeople appeared and began to construct a stage around the statue of Augustus Wainwright in Jackson Square. Then a crowd began to gather, and Keith got up to leave. On his way out, he stepped on a dropped nail that had landed sharp side up between two cobblestones.

There was a doctor's office on the other side of the square. It wasn't much trouble to hop there. Only one thing bothered Keith, and it wasn't the pain. Now, with an injured foot, he'd be stuck at home. The next two days were going to be hell. The exam door closed, Keith Kelly drew in a breath and relished the silence.

"TURN UP THE TV, WOULD you, sweetheart?" Ken Kelly called out to his beloved wife of twenty-two years. He was still in the kitchen, fixing their after-dinner smoothies.

When Glenda and Alan Johnston purchased their split-level ranch in 1985, they thought they were buying peace of mind. Their suburb outside of Baltimore was known for its good schools, friendly neighbors, and low crime rate. But over the years, Baltimore descended into chaos, and the criminal element began to stretch its tendrils out of the inner city and into the suburbs. As crime gained a stranglehold on their beloved neighborhood, Glenda and Alan refused their children's pleas to move. Then one night, just as the couple were preparing for bed, there came a knock at the door. On the other side was a young man, who told them he'd been in an accident. The Johnstons' doorbell camera caught Alan and Glenda stepping outside to help. It was the last time the elderly couple was seen alive. Their mangled bodies were discovered—

"Oh dear Lord!" Kari Kelly hoisted herself out of the La-Z-Boy and hustled to the front door. She jiggled the knob to make sure it was locked. When she was satisfied, she pulled the curtains on the front window aside and peeked out into the yard. She'd bought the brightest bulbs she could find, but the porch light still couldn't fight back the darkness beyond the front steps. Anything could be out there. "What is this world coming to?" she asked her husband.

Ken Kelly came into the living room, shaking his head in despair. "The good folks in this country let their guard down. We can't let it happen again," he said solemnly as he handed his wife her smoothie. "Don't worry, we're covered." Ken took a seat and patted the drawer of the side table that stood next to his chair. Inside was his handgun. There was another upstairs in the nightstand on his side of the bed and a shotgun tucked out of sight in the linen closet.

Kari moved to a window on the other end of the room. "What's keeping Keith so long? It's been *hours*. He just stepped on a nail, for goodness' sake! You'd think he sawed off his whole leg."

"That ruckus downtown must be keeping Dr. Chokshi pretty busy. He's a good doctor. I'm sure he'll get to our boy soon."

"What did Keith say last time you texted him?"

Ken grimaced. He'd hold back the truth in certain circumstances, but he refused to lie to the woman he married. "He hasn't texted me back."

"*What?*" Kari screeched. "Why didn't you say so?"

"Because it's all okay, Mama," Ken consoled her. "I can see his location. He's at the doctor's office. And I know he's your son, but technically he *is* a grown man. Sit down and enjoy your smoothie. I promise Keith will be home as quick as he can."

Kari took one more peek out the window and reluctantly returned to her chair.

Baltimore is not the only city that's crumbling. Every city in America has seen a major uptick in crime. Those with Democratic mayors have witnessed skyrocketing rates of violence. Murderers and rapists roam the streets with impunity in places like New York and Philadelphia. Vagrants and addicts have taken over entire neighborhoods in San Francisco and Los Angeles. In Atlanta—

The volume shut off.

"What on earth are you doing?" Kari demanded. "We need to hear that!"

"Now is not the time, Mama," Ken said. "When Keith's home safe—"

"Kenneth Monroe Kelly, you were the one who let our only child enroll at Georgia Tech—right there in the middle of that cesspool of a city."

"Woman, have you lost your mind? *I* let him go to Atlanta? I did everything I could to stop him! The boy was eighteen years old. He got a full scholarship! We both know I didn't have a say in the matter."

As much as Kari wished her husband had laid down the law back then, the truth was their son had been free to do as he wished. Even now, a year and a half after Keith made his decision, it was a hard pill to swallow. Every night, Kari watched the news. And every night, she prayed for her little boy's safety. She wished that his world could be the same one she'd grown up in—a world where faith, kindness, and hard work were all that mattered. A world where looters didn't run rampant in the Lenox Mall, pedophiles couldn't hold public office, and little kids with wild imaginations weren't prescribed hormones.

The idea that her son was out there all alone could leave her sobbing. But tonight, Kari knew she needed to hold it together and wait for Keith to get home. In the morning, she'd talk to him one more time. She'd try to convince him to stay closer to Troy. Ken could use a partner to help grow his septic tank business. *Kelly and Son* did have a wonderful ring to it.

As the grandfather clock struck eight, the volume on the television began to rise once more.

A virus is spreading across college campuses. But this one doesn't infect the lungs—instead it makes its home in young people's brains. It's called critical race theory, and it's being injected into everything from history courses to calculus. Some minds are strong enough to resist it, but others quickly fall prey. The signs and symptoms are easy to spot but difficult to treat—a growing contempt for church and country; a conviction that society's problems all boil down to race; and a belief that white men are always to blame.

Kari felt tears well in her eyes, and she couldn't help but let out a sniffle. All she'd wanted was what was best for her son.

"Sweetheart, were you listening? He just said some minds are strong enough to resist it," Ken pointed out. "Keith was raised right. He'll be able to see straight through that hogwash. It's people like Keith who will fight back against it."

Kari nodded and tried to stay quiet while the tears trickled down her cheeks. It was too much of a burden for one young man's shoulders.

KEITH KNEW HIS PARENTS MEANT well. He'd tried his best to keep them from worrying so much, but every time he visited, he found himself fielding a new set of urgent questions.

No, Mom, I don't care who uses the men's room. Nobody goes there to make friends.

Yeah, I'm sure people hate me, but it's not 'cause I'm white. It's 'cause I'm so awesome.

No, I'm not trying to make you feel better. None of my friends have ever been mugged.

I'm registered Independent, not Democrat. And no, we're not gonna discuss how I vote.

Just 'cause I haven't brought a girl home from school doesn't mean I've "gone gay."

Why would I bring a girl home if you're just gonna ask her questions like these?

Yes, I did have a wonderful childhood, and yes, I do love you both very much.

Sitting in the waiting room at the clinic had felt like a vacation. Shooting the shit with the Wright brothers (who confirmed that they *had* heard that joke) was the best time he'd had in days. They'd been sent out to the reception area while the doctor finished up with Bella Cummings, and once they knew she was going to be fine, the brothers spun the craziest story he'd ever heard. Keith told Isaac—who turned out to be some kind of genius—that it would make a great book.

"I mean, it's got everything," he'd marveled. "A beauty queen, a star football player, a famous general, a backward-ass little Southern town's gay Black valedictorian, and to top it all off, an international movie star with a giant gash on his head who's waiting in the parking lot for a doctor to finish treating the prom queen he knocked cold."

And *just* as Keith finished saying it, in walked the Wright brothers' fancy-pants new cousin and right behind her was an old woman who looked pissed as hell.

"May I speak with you two alone for a moment?" Beverly Underwood asked the Wright brothers while Keith sat there spellbound. "Pardon the interruption," she told him. "These gentlemen and I have matters to discuss."

Isaac looked like he might pass out.

"I'd like to see Bella first," Elijah insisted. Keith was impressed. If the kid could postpone *that* plot twist, he *had* to be crazy in love.

"Don't you worry. I'll wait here for Bella," said the old lady, who turned out to be Bella's great-grandmother. "But before you go, which one of you two took Mitch Sweeney down?"

"That was me, ma'am." Elijah held up his hand.

The old lady kissed him on the cheek. "You need anything in the future—don't matter if it's a lawyer, a new car, or a piece of pie—you come see me, you hear?"

"I will," said Elijah, who was not at all shy.

Then the exam room door opened, and out came Bella Cummings, looking totally lucid and holding an ice pack to the back of her head. While everyone asked her all kinds of questions, the doctor gestured to Keith. He hobbled into the room, the door closed, and suddenly everything was silent again.

"*Dude.*" For a minute, that was all Keith could say.

"I concur," said the doctor, who was much younger and cooler than the last physician. "*Dude.*"

"So Bella told you the whole story?"

"She did. Very sorry it took so long to get to you. I wasn't sure at first if Miss Cummings was hallucinating."

"*Dude.*"

This time the doctor laughed. "You're Ken and Kari's boy, am I right?"

"That is correct," said Keith.

The doctor began preparing the shot. "Your parents are sweet people. They're always worried to death whenever I head home to New York. I wonder what they're going to think about all the excitement here in Troy this evening."

"Probably lock me in my bedroom for the rest of my life. They're already nervous as hell about me going back to Atlanta."

"Were they always so anxious?" The doctor lifted Keith's shirtsleeve and swabbed a patch of his skin with iodine.

"Nope," Keith said. "They keep saying the world's changed. But I'm pretty sure it's them. I don't remember them being so scared when I was a kid."

AFTER HIS SHOT WAS ADMINISTERED and his wound cleaned and wrapped, Keith hobbled out of the exam room to find three men sitting side by side in the reception area. One was the county sheriff. One was an international movie star. The third was a younger man with blond hair and a beard who couldn't have been more than a few years older than him. He was holding the book that Keith had brought with him.

"Mind if I grab that?" Keith said. "I forgot it out here when I went in for my shot."

He held out his hand, but the man didn't pass the book to him.

"You know this ain't *Contract for America*." The man took off the dust jacket and held up the spine for Keith to read.

"Excuse me?" Keith replied. "What do you care what it is?"

"Your parents know you're reading this CRT crap?" the man demanded.

Keith glanced over at Sheriff Bradley, a well-weathered man of fifty with granite-colored hair and cold eyes. He folded his arms and said nothing.

"Last I checked, this was the United States of America," Keith said, snatching the book from the man's hands. "I can read whatever the hell I want."

As he pushed through the door, he heard the doctor come into the reception area. "Mr. Walsh, you have no business here," Dr. Chokshi said. "Please wait outside until I've finished."

There is nothing these people want more than to take your rights away. They don't give a damn about the Constitution. All they care about is having their way with you. They'll tell you they don't want your hunting rifles or handguns. They'll tell you they just want to keep weapons out of the hands of minors and the mentally ill. But what they really want is to get the snowball rolling. One day you're going to look up and it will be rolling down the hill, and it won't just be taking your AR-15s with it. It's going to take your means of protection and your most fundamental rights. And then, when you're at your most vulnerable, it's going to come for everything else you hold sacred.

"They'll have to pry my gun out of my cold, dead hands," Ken assured the television.

"Don't say that!" Kari cried.

"That's what it could come to," Ken told her. "These people are evil. Don't kid yourself."

Just then, they heard someone stomping up the front porch stairs. Heart pounding, Ken slid open the side table drawer and took out the handgun he always kept loaded for moments like this.

While Kari hid in the coat closet, Ken took his position beside the front door with his gun locked and loaded. The doorknob jiggled and he aimed at head height. As soon as the bastard got through the door, he'd be in for one hell of a surprise. Then he heard a key slide into the lock.

"It's Keith!" Kari screeched.

Within a split second, Ken's gun was back in the drawer and their son was limping into the living room with a book in his hand.

"I'm so glad you're safe!" Kari burst out of the closet, pulled her boy into a hug, and began to cry. His chest was so broad that she could barely wrap her arms all the way around him.

"Damn, Mom." He laughed. "I just stepped on a nail."

Ken cleared his throat and hoped he'd be able to talk. It wasn't every day that you nearly shot your own son. "You know how she worries," he managed to croak. "Kari? You okay, hon?"

Kari pulled back and wiped her eyes on the collar of her shirt. "What kept you so long?"

"Bella Cummings got knocked out by Mitch Sweeney and me and the Wright brothers sat and talked while they waited for her."

Ken blinked three times. "Come again?" he asked.

Keith sat down and told them the whole story.

"So that's what all the fuss was about?" Ken asked. "The statue?"

"I can't believe those Wright boys would get mixed up in something like that," Kari said. "I always thought they were such a nice family."

"They *are* a nice family," Keith told her.

"Then why would they want to destroy a symbol of our history and heritage?"

"Because it's theirs, too, Mom. In fact, as it turns out, it's a lot more theirs than ours. Don't you think they should get a say?"

"Hold on a sec. We need to see this." Kari turned up the volume on the TV.

Mark my words, they are going to steal every vote they can. They do not care about the sanctity of the electoral process. They will be stuffing

174

ballot boxes and hacking voting machines and registering their pets to vote. If we don't stop this now, there will never be another fair election in the history of this country. And those of us who work hard and love America will find ourselves under the heel of those who want to bleed us all dry.

"Why do they keep showing Black people?" Keith asked. He hadn't watched the news like this since he left for school. Is this how it had always been?

"What are you talking about?" Ken had always prided himself on his tolerance.

"Well, watch!" Keith grabbed the remote and rewound the program. "The guy talking is white, but everybody they show in the footage is Black."

"Because they're Democrats, and that's who's trying to fix the election."

"Naw, that's bullshit," Keith said.

Ken and Kari wheeled around in unison.

Keith shrugged as if he'd said nothing outlandish. "It is. If anything it's the other way around. You know they closed down polling places in Black neighborhoods in Atlanta right before the last election? They had people waiting eight, ten hours just to vote. Meanwhile in fancy-pants Buckhead, it took about fifteen minutes."

"What's your source?" Ken demanded.

"My *source*?" Keith laughed. "How 'bout my own eyes?"

"Sweetheart, your dad and I watch the news every night. And you would not believe some of the things they're doing. Voting for dead relatives. Taking names off of tombstones. They have to cheat in order to keep the pedophiles in office."

"Wait—what pedophiles?" Keith asked. "Do you know how crazy that sounds?"

Ken's face went as red as a candy apple. "Boy, are you calling your mother crazy?"

"No!" Keith insisted. "But—"

"I did not raise you to talk back!" Ken bellowed.

In the seconds that followed, Keith let the silence stretch out. Then he nodded. "You're right. Good night, folks. I got an early day tomorrow. I'm going to bed."

Ken kept an eye on his son's door. When it closed, he reached for the book that Keith had left behind on the couch. He flipped through the pages and stopped at a random passage.

The Lost Cause is a movement that gained traction in the late nineteenth century that attempted to recast the Confederacy as something predicated on family, honor and heritage rather than what it was, a traitorous effort to extend and expand the bondage of Black people.

"I knew it!" he whispered. Then he passed the open book to his wife. "This is some of that CRT stuff. Our boy's been brainwashed."

Ken leaned over his wife's shoulder as she traced another selection from the book. "This can't be true, can it?" she asked.

"It's mind poison," Ken said. "We are not sending our child back to that school."

"I'm not a child."

Keith was there, holding out his hand.

Ken reluctantly handed the book over. "We'll be talking about this in the morning."

"We're having an intervention!" Kari announced.

"Y'all can have whatever you want," Keith said. "I sure as hell won't be here."

KEITH GOT DOWN ON HIS knees by the side of the bed and prayed for his mom and dad. Back when he was younger and his parents were busy with things like Little League and PTA meetings, life had been different. With the television off, all they'd had to guide them was common sense and good hearts. No one told them to be scared, so they weren't. No one told them who their enemies were, so they didn't have any. No one warned them to avoid dangerous books, so they read whatever called out to them—mostly

John Grisham. And maybe he was wrong—maybe he'd just been a little kid—but everything had seemed perfectly fine. Keith prayed they could return to *those* days.

And when he finished, he lay down on his bed, opened the book he'd brought home, and started to read.

CHAPTER 21

OUTLAW

D r. Chokshi was not looking forward to the next patient. The man was sitting in the reception area between Logan Walsh and Sheriff Bradley, a bloody bandage wrapped around his head. He'd need stitches, which meant they'd soon be spending some quality time together. When he'd moved to Troy eighteen months earlier, the doctor had never anticipated he'd find himself treating an injured international movie star.

The doctor added that to the long list of things he'd experienced in Georgia that he'd never expected. He'd been shocked by just how different a homegrown peach could taste. Delighted by the old lady who paid him in produce and insisted on making him his first tomato and mayonnaise sandwich. After that, he'd eaten one every day and mourned for weeks when tomato season came to an end. He'd been touched by how thoughtful people could be, inviting him to their homes, churches, and cookouts—and introducing him to their local cuisine, one remarkable dish at a time. Brunswick stew—always with peas—hoecakes, succotash, and an astounding amount of fried chicken.

Then there had been the less pleasant bombshells. Like being called a terrorist in the Walmart parking lot by the douchebag motherfucker sitting to the right of Mitch Sweeney.

Dr. Chokshi waited until his previous patient was out the door. Then he stepped into the reception area.

"Mr. Walsh, you have no business here. Please wait outside until I've finished."

"Why?" Walsh shot back.

"I'm not stitching anyone up till he's gone," Dr. Chokshi told the sheriff. "You want to sit here all night?"

"Son, just do it," the sheriff told Walsh. He'd clearly had enough.

"COME ON IN, MR. SWEENEY." Dr. Chokshi held the door open.

Once, while kayaking in Alaska, he'd encountered an orca. It swam beside him for a second or two, but that was long enough to be humbled by its size. He was reminded of the experience as Mitch marched into the exam room. He'd seen the man in a dozen movies. On-screen, he was an imposing presence. In person, Mitch was fucking enormous. The doctor almost considered leaving the door open. He didn't relish the thought of being alone with a giant who'd just knocked a prom queen cold and traveled with a Nazi escort. But he took a deep breath and closed the door.

"How are you this evening, Mr. Sweeney?" What else did you say? Back home you could be brusque. Here, there was protocol to observe.

"She gonna be okay?"

"Excuse me?"

"Bella Cummings. Is she gonna be okay?"

He looked just as ashamed as he should have. This was a whole new role for Mitch Sweeney.

"I can't really discuss other patients," Dr. Chokshi said. "But I wouldn't have let her go home if I thought she was in any danger."

Mitch nodded his head and stared at the floor. "It was an accident. I didn't mean to tackle the girl."

"No," the doctor replied. "From what I've heard, you were attempting to take down the seventeen-year-old high school valedictorian." Guys like Mitch were too used to people letting them off easy. He wasn't going to get away with that shit in Dr. Chokshi's exam room.

"Yeah," Mitch said, but he didn't sound proud.

The doctor turned to the sink to wash his hands. "And this was all over a statue?"

"It's not just a *statue*." The word was like a match to a pilot light. Mitch's famously volatile personality flared up. "It's about our heritage and our history. You're not from here. You wouldn't understand."

"You're absolutely right." Dr. Chokshi pulled on his rubber gloves. "Heritage and history mean *nothing* where I come from." As he began unwrapping the bandage around the movie star's forehead, he could feel the man twitching. There was something Mitch desperately wanted to ask. The doctor was surprised he was holding back.

"Where *do* you come from?"

Dr. Chokshi smiled. Mitch knew better, but he'd gone ahead anyway. Over the past few months, the doctor had heard the same question a hundred times. Sometimes the way it was phrased was clearly hostile. But Mitch sounded genuinely curious. "Queens," the doctor answered. "It's in New York City."

"I know that," Mitch said. "I meant *originally*."

"I'm from Jackson Heights, Queens. Born and raised. I attended Queens High School for the Sciences and I will root for the Mets till the day I die."

"Humpf." There was always a *humpf.* "Where are your parents from?"

"Queens," Dr. Chokshi said. "Also born and raised. If you're inquiring about my ancestry, my ancestors lived in India. What about yours?"

"Ireland, mostly," said Mitch. "That's where the Sweeney name comes from, anyways. Got some Scots in the mix as well."

"Yeah, and when did they come over?" One of the surprising things Dr. Chokshi had discovered during his time in Troy was how much white people *loved* being asked that question. Talk to one shortly after their 23andMe results had come in, and the conversation could go on for hours.

"They all made their way here at different times. Some branches go way back in America. Got a lot of people who came over during the potato famine."

"What an amazing country this is, am I right?" Dr. Chokshi said. "Do you think our ancestors could have imagined that the two of us would meet in the middle of Georgia?"

Mitch snorted. "Probably not," he said.

And he'd been doing so well, the doctor thought as he revealed the wound. "Quite a gash you got here. I need to clean you up a bit, but looks like you're going to need about a dozen stitches and a tetanus shot. Do you know if you're allergic to lidocaine?"

"Doubt it," Mitch said. "These are hardly the first stitches I've ever got."

"Well then, you know it's probably a good idea to drive up to Atlanta tomorrow and get a plastic surgeon to take a look."

"You thinking I'll have a scar?"

"Most likely," Dr. Chokshi told him. "Though a plastic surgeon—"

"Nope." Mitch cut him off short. "Happy to take a scar. It'll be good for business."

"As long as no one finds out how you got it," the doctor said.

In the tense silence that followed, the words hovered between them. Guys like Mitch weren't used to people calling them out. Maybe they'd get "canceled" by Twitter. But few people had the balls to tell a man Mitch's size what they really thought to his face.

"I bet you're wondering why someone like me moved to your hometown." Dr. Chokshi waited, but Mitch wouldn't take the bait. "No? Well, your friend Mr. Walsh didn't hesitate to ask. He seemed to think I came here to bomb the Walmart. I assured him that I didn't leave the Empire State Building behind so I could blow up a fucking discount store in south Georgia."

"What the *hell*?" Mitch responded with unfeigned surprise. "Logan called you a terrorist? Shit, I'm sorry to hear that. I just met him yesterday, and it is quickly becoming apparent that the little fucker ain't right. For the record, I did not ask where you're from 'cause I think you're a terrorist. I happen to love Indian food."

"Yeah? What's your favorite dish?"

"I've been to India a few times. Never ate a single shitty thing while I was there. But if you want to know my favorite, it was probably the kosha mangsho in West Bengal."

"Sure it wasn't the tikka masala?"

"You're fucking with me, aren't you? That shit's British. Just because I'm from here doesn't mean I'm a moron."

"So I guess you got this gash on your head by acting like an intelligent, fair-minded adult."

"I *told* you I was protecting my heritage. By the way, if you got a problem with people like me, I got news for you. This town is full of us."

Dr. Chokshi had been waiting for the conversation to return to Troy. "Which brings us back to the reason I'm here. I moved to this lovely town because one of the last GPs in Troy died of old age two and a half years ago, and they couldn't find a single person to take his job. Not a *single one*. His former patients weren't getting the care they needed. A couple of old folks died needlessly. It got so bad that an organization offered to pay off a new doctor's student loans if they took over the old guy's practice. For a long time, there were no takers."

"Why wouldn't anyone take the job?"

"Well, first, it pays shit. Though believe it or not, there are doctors out there who aren't in this line of work for the money. But the do-gooder types didn't want the job, either. You know why?"

"No."

"Because of that statue you were fighting for—and what it represents."

"What it *represents*? We look at that statue and see our forefathers who died fighting an invading army. We see bravery and honor. That's what it represents."

"Okay. Let's say that's one hundred percent true. Now let me tell you what the rest of the world sees. We see the statue of a man who owned hundreds of human beings and fought a war to keep them. And we see people living almost two hundred years later who want *that man* standing outside their county courthouse. The courthouse where every American is supposed to be treated equally. So I guess you could say the rest of the world sees that statue as a message, which, if you've ever read anything about Augustus Wainwright, you'd know is *exactly* what he intended it to be. Wainwright put it there so the Black people who actually *built* the courthouse would know they'd never be given a fair shake in this town. And so people who look like me would know we're not welcome."

Mitch crossed his arms and winced while the doctor administered the lidocaine. "Well, I am sorry if that's what y'all think. But we don't have to give up our history because it makes you feel uncomfortable."

"And I'm sorry that when I'm gone, your town might just have to make do without a doctor because nobody outside of Troy can read your fucking minds and see that all your thoughts are peaceful and pure and full of love for the illustrious Augustus Wainwright, who you claim wasn't a terrible person despite the fact that he bought and sold human beings."

As Mitch sulked, Dr. Chokshi began the stiches. He'd sealed up half of the gash before Mitch spoke again.

"So you came down here to live with all us backward racists just to pay off your student loans?"

"Wait, *you* live here?" the doctor shot back. "Thought I read somewhere that you make your home in the Hollywood Hills."

"The ex got the house in the divorce," Mitch grumbled. "I'm buying a place while I'm here."

"Wonderful! Let me be the first to welcome you to the community." Dr. Chokshi was starting to enjoy himself. "I know it's been a while since you lived down south, but you can't believe what people say about us. Aside from a few notable exceptions, one of whom was just sitting in my waiting room, most people here are friendly and welcoming. Just like my dad told me they'd be."

Mitch kept his head still while he rolled his eyes upward to meet the doctor's. "I thought you said your dad lives in Queens."

"He does. But when he was a young obstetrician, he spent three years working in a town like Troy. I grew up hearing all about it and wishing I could have the same kind of experience. Good works are a big part of our religion. Plus my whole family loves country music."

"Oh yeah?" Mitch sounded skeptical. "Who's your favorite?"

"Johnny Cash."

"He's the man," Mitch said.

"Waylon and Willie, too. I like the Outlaws. My dad's into the wholesome early stuff. The Carters. Jimmie Rodgers." The doctor paused. "You know—that's what really gets me. There are a million great Southerners who'd make a better statue than the one you've got."

"Who would you pick?"

"From this state? Probably Little Richard—the Georgian who singlehandedly invented rock and roll. Or maybe Brenda Lee? Alice Walker or Erskine Caldwell if you're feeling fancy? André 3000? Whoever came up with the recipe for the fried chicken at Chester's? The South's greatest gift to the world is its culture. Half the music people listen to these days has its origins here. Hell, the South gave the world *barbecue* and you want to honor a slaveholding asshole who lost a war in the middle of the nineteenth century? You know what, I bet there are a ton of great actors from around here, too."

"Julia Roberts—"

"Julia Roberts! And you're out there fighting to protect a statue of *Augustus Wainwright*? What the hell is wrong with you people?"

Mitch laughed.

"Who knows, Mitch, maybe one day they'll put up a statue of you. But first you better get on the right side of history. Stop hanging out with book burners and racist assholes. Take a lesson from Johnny Cash and try to make the world a better place. Besides, don't you think playing against type could get you a lot more attention?"

It was the last sentence that seemed to make an impact on Mitch. "You know what? You may be right."

"Well, if you're going to make a change, you'd better do it fast. Sounds like everything that happened at the rally was caught on camera. And if

I were you, I wouldn't be caught dead hanging around with a Nazi." Dr. Chokshi stood back to admire his work. "I think we're done here."

Mitch pulled out his phone. "I'm gonna need to arrange a different ride home. You mind if I hang out for a moment and call my brother to come get me?"

"Go right ahead."

"Thank you, Doctor."

Dr. Chokshi put out a hand. "When I was born, my parents tossed a coin to see who got to name me. My father won. You can call me Hank."

CHAPTER 22

MANHOOD: THE MASCULINE VIRTUES AMERICA NEEDS

I t was three years earlier—four years after his father died—that Logan Walsh met the man who would change his life. In those days, he preferred to keep his own company. Even though he'd been cleared of wrongdoing, people had a way of scattering when he made an appearance, like rabbits at first sight of a wolf. But the groceries still needed to be purchased and the tank filled up. So there he was, pumping gas at eleven o'clock in the evening when a man in a RAM 1500 pulled up behind him.

Logan was used to people sneaking peeks when they thought he wasn't looking, but this man stared straight at him without blinking. When Logan returned the gaze, there was no fear in the man's eyes, only recognition. Aside from the eyes, he was a regular-looking dude. Not tall or short. Fit but not ripped. Strong chin, thin lips, a few freckles here and there. But you could tell he was someone when he didn't look away.

"You know the history of that symbol?" The man gestured at a sticker on Logan's back bumper. The way he asked made it seem like he knew something Logan didn't.

"It's the Celtic cross," Logan replied. "Saint Patrick brought together the cross with a symbol of the sun to help convert the pagan Celts to Christianity."

"That all?" When the man asked, it felt like a test. Logan hated to be tested.

"I'm Irish," he said, turning back to the pump. "That's the story that matters to me."

"You're white," the man replied. "It should mean a lot more."

He'd felt a jolt—an electric shock that set every atom in his body in motion. "Oh yeah? Like what?" He'd wanted to sound casual, but his *oh* shook.

"You know about Stormfront?"

The pump clicked off and Logan replaced the gas nozzle. "Sure. I've checked out the site." He'd scrolled through it once and hadn't gone back.

"That's a good start. I host a weekly discussion group if you're interested. My name is Nathan Dugan."

"Is this some kind of gay shit?" Logan cringed when he heard those words coming out of his mouth. He'd forgotten how to engage with people. He couldn't even recall the last conversation he'd had.

"Naw, son," Nathan responded. "And talk like that tells me how much you need us."

BEFORE NATHAN, HE'D LIVED MOSTLY online. He'd get sucked into games and lose a few days at a time. When he emerged from a world, he'd relax with a little YouTube or Pornhub. Sometimes when a migraine would keep him away from screens, he'd head out to his deer blind and drink beer until he saw something to shoot. It was a largely human-free existence.

Two days after he met Nathan, Logan swallowed the red pill and entered a different world, with new friends and a mission. He hadn't bought into it all just yet. He didn't know any Jews aside from the old man who owned the shop downtown. And he'd gone to school with plenty of Black kids who seemed okay. But that didn't mean he wasn't proud of his people. No matter what all the libtards claimed, defending the white race didn't mean attacking anyone else. And what could be wrong with preserving masculine values? God wouldn't have made men and women different if he'd wanted everyone to be the same.

In the past, Logan hadn't spent much time on such topics. Soon, he realized just how much he'd been missing. After a meeting at Nathan's, he always drove off feeling like he was king of the world. For the next few days, his muddy view of life always seemed to clear. He knew who the enemies were. He knew why he, Logan Walsh, had been put on the planet. He had a reason to get his ass out of bed every morning.

All week, Logan looked forward to the meeting in Nathan's basement. He'd been alone for so long that he hadn't even realized he was lonely. Now that he belonged to a group, he took his duties seriously. When Nathan gave him something to read, he read it. When Nathan offered advice, he took it. And in the moments in between, he studied his mentor's perfect life. Like the rest of the men in the group, Logan was fascinated by Nathan's woman. All he had to do was shout upstairs, and Dawn would be down in minutes with sandwiches or beer. Even more impressive, there was never a complaint. In Logan's experience, the pretty ones were rarely so eager to please.

"It's like training a dog. You have to get them young," Nathan told them. "You teach them early who's boss and give them a clear set of rules. Keep 'em focused on what's important. Women's minds aren't as powerful as ours. They'll get distracted from their duties if you don't keep them in line."

Who'd have thought that bitch would end up ruining it all?

And just when everything had been going so well, too. The group had moved past discussions and started putting plans into action. Nathan had given Lula Dean a list of books that contained antiwhite propaganda. She'd made sure they were removed from the town's libraries. No one else on the book committee had asked any questions. They were too busy making sure all the gay books were pulled. It was a major victory for the cause. Troy's children did not need to be told that white people were evil—or that they were responsible for something that happened a hundred and fifty years before they were born.

Then Nathan's son joined the group. At first, Logan worried Nate might come between them. Then he realized it was an opportunity. If he befriended the kid, he could be more than Nathan's protégé. He might just feel like a member of the family. So Logan volunteered to show young Nate the ropes. He was the one who'd encouraged the boy to paint a swastika on the Jew's front door.

Never in a million years would he have suspected Nathan's wife knew the old man—or that she'd choose him over her husband. For years Logan had complained to the group that he couldn't find anyone like Dawn Dugan. Logan had even started to wonder if he might be to blame. But after Dawn betrayed Nathan, it was clear the problem was with the female species. None of them could be trusted to keep their word. They were too fucking simple to understand concepts like loyalty or honor.

The day Dawn stabbed her husband in the back, Nathan came home from work and found everything all gone. The bitch had kidnapped his son and dragged his most treasured possessions out onto the lawn. After that, Nathan lost his biggest roofing contracts, even though many of his best clients were sympathetic to the cause. Lula Dean had called to say it was best if he didn't attend Concerned Parents Committee gatherings until things died down. All this in America, where you're supposed to be free. If that had ever been true, it sure as hell wasn't now. Even the weekly meetings had come to an end. Logan was the only member who'd stayed by Nathan's side.

It was hard to believe that one woman could ruin so many lives. Dawn Dugan had been on Logan's mind when he found that bitch in the forest. Days had passed and Logan couldn't stop thinking about Crystal Moore. A woman that age letting half the county search for her while she hid out in the woods? She should be ashamed of herself. It was disgraceful how she'd embarrassed her husband. When Logan saw that witchcraft book she was reading, he almost shot her right there on the spot. The Bible says you shouldn't suffer a witch to live, and he'd had an unregistered handgun with him. He could have buried the cunt in the forest and no one would have known the difference. Logan promised himself he'd seize the day if he ever got another chance.

She was hardly the only person in town who deserved a bullet in the

189

head. When Logan was done with her, the doctor was next. That mother-fucker had some balls mouthing off to him like that. Telling him to leave the office when Logan was just looking out for Mitch Sweeney. Nathan always said people didn't know their fucking place anymore. All these ass-holes coming over from shitty countries, taking advantage of everything real Americans had worked so hard to build, then bitching and moaning about how they deserved so much more than they got.

Now that he thought of it, he might just go back a bit later and teach that bastard a lesson or two. Logan had woken up with a hunch something would go wrong at the rally, so he'd strapped a gun into his ankle holster. Nathan told him not to, but somebody had to protect the innocent. Those two little thugs with their bullshit banner were lucky he'd never had a clear shot. But it wasn't too late to punish the doctor for taking care of a CRT-loving mama's boy before he even bothered having a look at Mitch's head wound.

AFTER LOGAN GOT KICKED OUT of the clinic, he'd taken a walk to burn off the rage. It didn't work. It never did. Now he found himself alone in the darkness, looking up at the statue of Augustus Wainwright.

"That right there is what a real man looks like," Logan's father once told him. "He gave everything he had to protect what he loved. Soon, there won't be any men like him left in this world."

Logan couldn't have been more than ten at the time, but even then it went without saying that his father was one of those men. Everyone in town would have agreed. Hollis Walsh could have led a life of leisure, but he'd chosen a life of service instead. For twenty years, he'd served as a superior court judge, overseeing the county's most important cases and ensuring justice was served. For a time, he'd been the most powerful man in Troy. No terrorist immigrant from some backward country would have *dared* ask Hollis Walsh to leave a waiting room. And any sheriff who'd sided against him would have paid dearly for the mistake.

Hollis Walsh never believed for one second that Logan would grow into a real man. He'd always said his son was soft and weak, just like his mama. He'd been wrong about that, even if he'd been right about everything else.

Logan took a breath. At moments like this, he knew his father would be glad he'd died when he did. He would be horrified to see what was happening to the town he loved. It was up to Logan to fix things—to show his father he'd been mistaken about his only son. Logan bowed his head and closed his eyes. "Dear Lord," he said. "I need you here with me now. Things are falling apart, and I have to do something. Please give me the strength, vision, and wisdom to see that thy will is done. Amen."

When he opened his eyes again, they were staring straight at the inscription he'd read thousands of times. Logan smiled, 'cause he knew just what it meant. It was the Lord's way of telling him the answer had been right there all along.

BOW NOT BEFORE TYRANTS
FIGHT FOR YOUR FREEDOM
SACRIFICE ALL BUT HONOR
AND DIE WITH DIGNITY

He had to take action. They weren't going to stop with Nathan. Hell, they'd run Randy Sykes out of office just 'cause some bitch claimed he'd fucked her nearly thirty years earlier. No proof, of course, no nothing. Just her word against his. The mayor! And the dust hadn't even settled before the town's two top Karens were battling to take his place. Now they were coming for Augustus Wainwright, for fuck's sake. Those kids claiming to be his descendants—what a steaming pile of horseshit! So they'd given up claiming he was a monster, and now they wanted to be related? There was no point in giving those people what they wanted. In the end, they'd never be satisfied.

The truth was—and not everyone was ready to hear it—the only way to protect what mattered was to wipe all of them off the planet.

A LONE PAIR OF HEADLIGHTS approached the square. Logan stepped out of sight as a car pulled up outside the salon where all the ladies got their hair done. A big man dressed in camo slid out of the passenger side door. Logan recognized him at once as Jeb Sweeney.

When Logan was ten, Jeb coached his Little League team. Every night before he went to sleep, he prayed that Coach Sweeney could be his dad. The coach was fair and patient—and when you did good, he told you he was proud of you. He never yelled at Logan or lost his cool. When he was around, even the parents in the stands were on their best behavior. Then Logan's dad got up in an umpire's face, and Coach Sweeney took him by the collar and escorted him back to his seat. After that game, Jeb invited the team over to his farm to see all his animals. Logan wasn't allowed to go. He worried his dad had discovered his secret plan—to hide under the hay in the barn and stay there forever. He figured if he took good enough care of the animals, Coach Sweeney might just decide to adopt him.

Long after that daydream seemed ridiculous, Logan still looked up to Jeb Sweeney. Every time he drove by the Sweeney farm, he fantasized about pulling into the drive. When one of his horses got sick, Logan saw an opportunity. He paid Jeb to make a house call, figuring he'd show off his compound and maybe find out they shared some interests in common. It may have been a little too hopeful, but it wasn't *insane*. After all, Jeb's brother was a well-known conservative who called attention to the tribulations men faced.

Jeb arrived at his property, and Logan saw him flinch as they passed the shooting range. Then he watched Jeb's face harden when he took in Logan's collection of flags and memorabilia. Jeb didn't ask any questions, and he didn't bother to hide his disgust. He looked at Logan the same way his father had—like there had to be something wrong with him.

It made Logan feel ashamed. When his father had looked at him, Logan had run to his mama. God rest her soul. She'd always done her best to protect him. It wasn't easy, way things were in their home. There were weeks when she was too bruised up to leave the house, so she missed a lot of school events and games. Some kids at school thought he didn't have a mom at all. He would make sure they knew that he had the best mom in the world. She just had to stay home to take care of him and his daddy. And that's the way things were until Logan's senior year of high school. Then he came home one day to find her missing. It wasn't until late the same night that anyone bothered to let him know she was in a coma.

They said it was an accident. But Logan knew better. She'd taken every pill in the bottle. Logan didn't want to be alone with his dad any more than he had when he was still little. Bad things could happen if he and Hollis had the house to themselves.

So the next morning, when his father went hunting, Logan went with him. And as soon as they were way out deep in the woods, he shot Hollis straight through the neck.

In his mind, he'd always imagined his mother would leave the hospital and he'd take real good care of her. But she died of liver failure a few months after his father. At eighteen years old, Logan inherited a fortune. There was more money in his account than he knew what to do with. But Nathan had a few ideas.

LOGAN WALKED OVER TO JEB, who seemed less than thrilled to see him. "What are you doing?"

"Hey, Logan. My brother left his truck here. The doctor says he shouldn't drive tonight, so I'm going to take him home."

"Why didn't he call me?" Logan felt the wound keenly. "He knew I was waiting for him."

"I don't know, Logan," Jeb answered.

"Don't y'all hate each other?"

"Yep. Can't stand the motherfucker. But he's still my brother."

"How are you gonna get home if you drive his truck up to my guest-house?" Logan hated how he sounded. Like a whiny little bitch.

"I think Mitch will be staying with me from here on out. He's in deep shit already. And as you may have noticed, he's not that bright. He'll end up destroying his life if I don't keep an eye on him."

Logan couldn't come up with an argument. Nathan would be livid when he found out Logan had lost custody of their guest. Mitch was their ticket to the mainstream. It was Nathan's first big test, and he was fixing to fail it.

"Everything okay with you?" Jeb asked.

His hands were tingling. Wave after wave of heat washed over him. "It was that fucking doctor, wasn't it?"

"I'm afraid I don't know what you're talking about."

"He turned Mitch against me."

Jeb had that look in his eye again. The *this boy ain't right* look. The look Logan had been getting from people his ENTIRE FUCKING LIFE.

Jeb took a step forward. "Logan, listen to me. Nobody turned anyone against you. Mitch is my brother. It's my job to look after him. You will not go after that doctor. He's the only thing keeping half of the people in this town alive. Do you understand me?"

"Fuck you," Logan said. "And fuck your brother, too."

"Alright, son," Jeb said. "But if I hear about you messing with the doctor, you're going to wish you'd never been born."

JEB DROVE OFF IN MITCH'S truck, leaving Logan alone again with Augustus Wainwright. Then he saw them on the far side of the square. That feminist bitch, Beverly Underwood, and the two little thugs who'd ruined the rally. Everything was falling apart thanks to those three. He saw Beverly Underwood turn his way, and Logan stepped into the dark shadow beside the statue. Looking spooked, she hurried the Wright boys toward her car.

"Y'all can run," Logan said. "But you can't hide."

CHAPTER 23

THE LOST FAMILY: HOW DNA TESTING IS UPENDING WHO WE ARE

So the Wainwright family won't end with me?"

"Sweetheart, you are the tip of one stunted little branch on an otherwise thriving tree," Beverly Underwood told her daughter. She'd been taking a break from cleaning up Jackson Square when Lindsay called.

"Wow." Beverly couldn't see Lindsay on the other side of the phone, but she pictured her searching for words to follow that one up. "I don't know how I should feel about all this," Lindsay finally said.

Beverly looked up at the statue of Augustus Wainwright. "I'm not sure many people have been where we and the Wrights are right now," she said. "But I can promise you one thing, there are a lot of folks headed our way."

THE DAY AFTER HER FATHER passed away, Beverly discovered an envelope on his desk. Written on the front was her name. She thought, briefly, he'd left her a letter. But he hadn't been that kind of father. He'd always loved her—Beverly knew that—but he chose to do so from a distance. Like so many men of his generation, he kept his feelings carefully locked up where they posed no danger to anyone—least of all, him.

Inside the envelope was a single page of monogrammed stationery with eight characters written in her father's shaky hand. *BDW12180*—her initials and birth date. Beverly still kept that slip of paper in her handbag. Wherever she went, it went with her. There was more love in that single gesture than her father could have fit into a fifty-page letter. She knew the moment she saw it that it was the password to his digital family tree.

In the two decades after his wife's death, the tree had been her father's passion. For much of that time, Beverly had avoided all talk of it. Aside from Trip and Lindsay, her father was the only family she had left, and she refused to let Augustus Wainwright come between them.

It was only out of a sense of daughterly duty that Beverly had poured herself a large glass of wine, taken a seat in front of the computer, and typed in the password her father had bequeathed to her. She expected to find a tribute to the Wainwright legacy. Instead, she discovered a fascinating world teeming with characters forgotten by time. Her father had researched dozens of their ancestors, rescuing them from oblivion and adding their stories to the family tree. There was the second son of an English nobleman who became a notorious pirate. A gentleman who'd been kicked out of Plymouth Plantation for having "novel ideas," and a farmer who was likely North America's first axe murderer of European descent.

Beverley was reminded of the advice the town librarian had given her all those years ago. *You get to choose whose footsteps you'll follow,* Jeanette Newman had told the young Beverly. *Find a set that went in the right direction.* She wondered, perhaps, if that's what her father had been looking for all along—someone who could show him a path that led away from Augustus Wainwright.

Unsurprisingly, her father had chosen to research the lives of male ancestors. Beverly found herself captivated by the women on the tree—particularly those who sat alone on a branch, with no husband beside them. They had given birth, but the father of their child remained unknown. Even well into the twentieth century, the life of an unmarried mother would have been impossibly difficult. No woman back then would have chosen that fate for herself. What was the story behind their child's conception? It was easy to assume her great-grandmothers had indulged in illicit or ill-fated romances. It was just as likely—if not more so—that the children were the products of coercion or rape.

Whatever the answer, the sight of those empty brackets made Beverly anxious and angry. Centuries may have passed, but she was determined to force those invisible men to take responsibility for the children they'd sired. But their identities remained stubbornly hidden. Then, a while later, she received an email from the website that hosted her genealogy research. Its new DNA testing service could help fill in blank spots on a family tree. Beverly sent in a swab the very next week.

It took a while, but as more people in America entered their data, Beverly's "matches" began to grow. These were living people to whom she was somehow related. The connection wasn't always obvious. There were several matches who shared none of her known ancestors—which meant they had to be related via an unknown ancestor. One match's family tree listed a man who had lived in a small Scottish village at the same time as a great-great-grandmother who'd given birth to an illegitimate child. Beverly entered the man's name into the empty bracket and the tree lit up. The DNA was a match. Beverly realized she'd uncovered a crime.

Her great-great-grandmother, once a servant in an aristocratic Scottish home, had given birth to a child at age sixteen. Beverly's DNA test revealed the father of the child was none other than the fifty-five-year-old aristocrat who'd employed the girl. A picture of the man revealed a face unlikely to have won over a girl four decades younger. The fact that the girl and her baby spent the next three years in the town poorhouse made it clear that the rich man had done nothing to support her.

Maybe there was an explanation that hadn't occurred to Beverly. But Occam's razor said he'd raped the girl. And by the looks of things, there were other villains lurking in her family tree. Beverly did not want them there, however illustrious their names might have been. Her sympathies lay with their victims. She cringed at the thought that those men's blood might flow through her veins. Then she thought of the women who'd survived. Who'd raised their children against all odds and refused to give in. And she imagined *their* strength inside her. Those were the footsteps she wanted to follow.

Eventually, her thoughts returned to the most famous monster in the Wainwright family tree. Though it had never been proven, Augustus Wainwright was rumored to have raped and impregnated women he enslaved. Beverly realized their descendants would have empty brackets on their family trees as well. She didn't blame them if they weren't interested in filling those spaces. But if they were, she planned to help. Beverly Underwood, one of the two known living descendants of Augustus Wainwright, made her tree and her profile public.

"THEY FOUND YOU. WHAT ARE you going to do?" Lindsay asked her mom.

"The Wright boys are at the doctor's office with Bella Cummings. I'm going to talk to them," Beverly said. "Welcome them to the family."

"Oooh no, Mama." Beverly could hear the cringe in her daughter's voice. "They've always been a part of the family, whether we knew it or not. It's not our place to welcome them."

"Right," Beverly said. "That was silly of me. So what should I say? Should I apologize? You knew Isaac Wright in school, didn't you?"

"Not really," Lindsay said. "He's four years younger."

"Well, what do you think someone his age would want to hear?"

"How 'bout, 'Hi, I'm your cousin Beverly'?"

NOW THEY WERE STANDING IN front of her, looking every bit as nervous as Beverly felt.

"Sorry for dragging you out like that." She held out her hand. "My name is Beverly Underwood. I'm your cousin."

"Yeah, we know." The younger boy broke into a grin as he shook her hand.

"We're Isaac and Elijah Wright," the older brother said.

Beverly had seen these two so many times in the past, walking through town. They made such a fascinating pair. The older brother tall and slender with eyes that seemed focused on something far in the distance, as if he could see what was heading their way. The burly younger brother with the handsome face and mischievous smile. They seemed devoted to each other in a way that made Beverly wish she'd had a sibling.

"You knew about us?" Isaac asked.

"Not exactly," Beverly admitted, "but I knew you might be out there. When I was your age, I found out what kind of man Augustus Wainwright was. I figured it was likely I had cousins in the area, but I didn't know who you were. I made my family tree public just in case you came looking. You must have sent in a DNA swab?"

"I did," Isaac told her. "When I saw your name show up as a match, I knew we shared a common ancestor. I guessed it was Augustus Wainwright. When I plugged his name into my family tree, the whole thing lit up."

Once again, a swab of saliva had exposed a terrible crime. Beverly felt her heart break for the woman Augustus Wainwright had raped. One hundred and fifty years was far too long to wait for a reckoning.

"How did you take the news?" Beverly asked.

"He kept it hidden." Elijah nudged his brother in the side with his elbow. "He didn't even tell *me* until yesterday."

"It was a shock," Isaac admitted. "I knew I had ancestors who were enslaved on the Wainwright plantation, and I thought there might be a chance. But I didn't know how hard the truth would hit me—seeing his name next to a blank space where our great-grandmother's name should have been."

"I can't even imagine," Beverly said. "Your mother owns Fairview Florist. Betsy, am I right?"

"Yes," Elijah confirmed. "And our dad has the repair shop in town."

"James," Isaac said.

"Do they have any idea what you've discovered?" Beverly asked.

Isaac shook his head. "We've been estranged lately."

Beverly thought she knew why, but she didn't dare ask.

"He likes dudes," Elijah volunteered. "And our parents are Christians."

"Really?" Isaac turned to his brother. "Was that necessary?"

"I'm a Christian and my daughter is gay," Beverly told them. "Lindsay Underwood? Maybe you know her? She's a few years older than you."

"She's friends with my best friend," Isaac said. "Bella says she's amazing."

"She is. Watching Lindsay grow into the person she is today has been the highlight of my life. I know that girl is exactly who she was meant to be. If I did one thing right as a parent, it was staying out of her way."

Elijah threw an arm around his brother's shoulder. "So now we know where the gay DNA comes from. Dad can blame Augustus Wainwright."

"I don't think that's how it works," Beverly told him.

"No," Isaac said. "Because if a gay gene came from Augustus Wainwright, half the state of Georgia would be flying rainbow flags on their porches."

"What do you mean?" Beverly asked the boy.

"When was the last time you were on the genealogy site?"

"It's been a while," Beverly confessed. "Things have gotten pretty crazy around here with the book banning and the mayor's race."

"Well, next time you log on, you're in for a surprise," Isaac said. "Looks like we have a lot of relatives in this part of the country."

Beverly didn't answer. Her eyes had been drawn to the statue in the center of the square. Someone was standing just out of sight in the darkness. She felt the hairs on her arms rise. Whoever it was had been watching them.

"How about I give you two a ride home?" She didn't voice her hunch. There was no reason to scare the Wright boys. "I'd like to say hello to your parents if you don't mind."

"Just so you know, I'm not sure how our father will take this news," Isaac warned her.

"Well, you've already told the rest of the town. Your dad's going to find out whether we talk to him tonight or not."

BETSY WRIGHT HURRIED OUT ON the porch to greet them as soon as they arrived. "How's Bella?" she asked.

The Wright boys exchanged a loaded look. "She has a concussion, but she'll recover," Isaac said. Then he cleared his throat. "You were at the rally tonight?"

"Oh yes," Betsy said. It was hard to tell just how angry she was. "You think your father and I would miss out on the big announcement? Even though we were the only people in town who weren't invited?"

"I'm sorry, Mama—" Isaac started.

That was when Mrs. Wright's eyes landed on Beverly.

"We'll talk about this later," she said. "How do you do, Mrs. Underwood?"

"Good evening, Mrs. Wright." Beverly stepped forward. "I drove the boys home just now. Would you mind if I had a quick word with you and your husband?"

Betsy Wright immediately turned to her sons. "There's more to the story? What else did you do?"

"Oh no," Beverly jumped in. "Your boys are wonderful. They were very brave this evening."

"You hear that, Mama?" Elijah said. "Brave and wonderful. We only just met, and yet she knows us so well."

Betsy rolled her eyes. "I better not find out otherwise. Now go get your father for me." When the boys were gone, she turned back to Beverly. "I heard they were planning something for Lula Dean's rally, so James and I went. If I'd known the Cummings girl might get hurt, I'd have stopped the whole thing."

"Your boys did a good job of looking after her. She's with her great-grandma now, and—"

James Wright stepped out the front door. He didn't seem at all surprised to see Beverly. It was almost as if he'd been waiting for her.

"Hello, Mr. Wright." Beverly held out a hand and the man shook it. "My name is Beverly Underwood. I met your sons tonight at the rally by the statue. I thought I should stop by and say hello since it turns out—"

"We're related." Mr. Wright completed the sentence. He didn't sound happy about the fact—and he certainly wasn't surprised.

"Yes," Beverly replied. "How long have you known?"

"Forever," Mr. Wright told her. "The knowledge was passed down through every generation of my family. I was hoping my sons never had to find out. But it seems everyone's secrets are being exposed these days."

"I'm thinking in this case it might turn out for the best," Beverly said. "This town has been hiding too much for too long. Secrets are a disease that eats away at your soul. My grandmother always said the best disinfectant is sunlight."

"She might have learned that from my grandmother—who did your grandmother's laundry."

Beverly's eyes lit up. "Felicity Wright was your grandmother?" she asked. "I remember her well. She was a lovely woman. So funny and sweet. And she made the best cornbread I think I've ever eaten."

"That, she did," James agreed but he wasn't amused. "But you get my point, don't you, Mrs. Underwood?"

No amount of charm was going to smooth things over. There was no way to make that past less painful. "I think I do," Beverly said. "There were two sides of the family. One that prospered and another that suffered. Nothing about that is fair or right."

"And that's why I'm not sure it's possible to bridge the chasm between us."

"To be honest, Mr. Wright, I don't blame you for saying so. I'm still overwhelmed and I don't have all the answers. But I know in my heart that having the statue of Augustus Wainwright pulled down is something we need to do."

That appeared to give James Wright pause. "I have walked by that statue every day of my life, knowing exactly what that man did to my family. As much as I would like to have it removed, I also know how hard it is to convince folks around here that the feelings of someone like me should matter."

"Our two families alone can't convince the town that the statue should come down. But Isaac thinks there may be many more descendants of Augustus Wainwright around here than people realize. There's power in numbers."

"What did you have in mind?"

"Well, I was thinking we might throw a big old family reunion."

CHAPTER 24

THE HEMINGSES OF MONTICELLO

ula slept in the next morning. At ten, she was still in her housecoat, taking her coffee, when an email arrived from James Wright. She almost deleted it right away. It didn't matter how sorry James was. After what his two boys had done, the Wright family was no longer welcome on the Concerned Parents Committee. But Lula was a Christian woman, she reminded herself. At the very least, she should acknowledge James's apology.

When she opened the email, she found no words of contrition—only a link. Assuming it led to an e-card, she clicked, only to find herself faced with a video clip from the morning news.

Mitch Sweeney was bending down to speak into a microphone set up in front of the Troy courthouse. He appeared to be reading from an index card that he held in one hand. *International Movie Star Apologizes to Hometown* screamed the chyron.

"Don't you dare do it, you mouth-breathing moron," Lula warned the digital Mitch as she hit play.

"I want to offer my heartfelt apologies to the Wright family, to Ms. Bella Cummings, who was injured last night at the rally, and to the entire town of Troy. I take full responsibility for my terrible actions, and I hope it's clear to all that violence was not and will never be the answer."

Mitch Sweeney glanced back at a fierce old woman standing directly behind him. Had Lula been chewing her toast at that moment, she would have certainly gagged at the sight of Wilma Jean Cummings looking disturbingly undemented. That's who'd gotten to Mitch. Lord only knew what she'd threatened him with.

"I have consulted with Ms. Cummings's lawyer, and Bella has graciously declined to press charges. In return, I will be sponsoring the upcoming Wainwright family reunion, which will take place right here in Jackson Square next Saturday at noon. Everyone in the state of Georgia is welcome to attend. I will be there, signing autographs and serving pie. Hope to see y'all there."

"Mitch! Mitch!" a reporter called out as he stepped back from the mic. "Does this mean you're no longer opposing the statue's removal?"

Mitch returned to the mic. "Yes, ma'am, that is precisely what it means."

"What made you change your mind?"

Suddenly, the showman seemed to be gone. The man standing at the mic was just an overgrown country boy in overpriced jeans. For a moment, it wasn't clear if he was going to answer. "I see y'all looking at my head wound and thinking my brains must have spilled out on the stage yesterday." He pointed to the long line of stitches on his forehead and the crowd tittered. "Well, I promise, the few brain cells I ever had are still in there. I spent about an hour last night getting stitched up like Frankenstein by a fellow from Queens—that's in New York City, in case you're wondering. But don't go holding that against him. None of us get to decide where we're born. Anyways, Dr. Chokshi told me that this town has a really hard time getting doctors to move here because people take one look at our Confederate statue and figure they aren't welcome. I know there are folks who think that's a bonus, but it made me feel terrible. As far as I'm concerned, it goes against everything the South is supposed to stand for. We're supposed to be the nice people, aren't we? How can we use phrases like *Southern hospitality* if we don't really mean them? If we do, maybe we shouldn't have statues that make people feel scared or unwanted. So all that's just a long way of saying if the people of Troy decide Augustus should go, I will personally pay for his removal. Thank you."

"Traitor!" It was total baloney. Mitch Sweeney was saving his butt and saying what they all wanted to hear. Pretending he cared about hospitality—*please*. The only thing that man cared about was his career.

Lula felt tears coming on. She wasn't going to let this stand. But at that very moment, James Wright and Beverly Underwood appeared together on-screen along with the gay son. Lula's biggest enemies had all joined forces. Adding insult to injury, Beverly looked gorgeous, and her hair was perfect. Lula knew better than to try to make an appointment with Val. None of those former cheerleaders would so much as speak to her. She had to get her hair done at the second-best salon in town.

"Hello, I'm Beverly Underwood." Lula had to pause the video and ask the Lord for strength. The sound of Beverly's prissy voice always drove her to distraction. "I'm a candidate for mayor here in Troy, and I've made it known that if I'm elected, I will have the statue of Augustus Wainwright removed from this park. I also happen to be a direct descendant of the statue's subject. Until recently, a lot of folks thought my daughter and I were the last of the Wainwright line. But just last night more descendants made themselves known. Now I'm proud to be standing here with a couple of them. This is Mr. Isaac Wright, and beside Isaac is his father, Mr. James Wright. I'm proud to call both of them cousins—and I'm thrilled to announce that our family may be much bigger than anyone thought. Isaac was the one who made the discovery, so I'm going to step aside and let him tell you all about it."

The boy approached the mic with no show of nervousness. "I'm Isaac Wright. A while back, I found this book in the library." He held up a copy of *The Hemingses of Monticello*. "For years, people debated whether Thomas Jefferson had fathered six children with an enslaved woman named Sally Hemings. They said it was impossible. A great man like Jefferson would never do such a thing. Then DNA evidence proved with one hundred percent certainty that Hemings's children were also Jefferson's. Now, I don't know about you, but that blew my mind. It called into question everything we've been taught. Not just about the men who founded this country, but also about who has the right to claim America's heritage and history. We've been told that some people built this country, and the rest of us should just be grateful to live here. Those of us whose ancestors *literally* built the South always knew the truth. But after I finished *The Hemingses of Monticello*, I found myself wondering if there was another side of the story that wasn't being told.

"I started doing research into my family tree. DNA testing has allowed us to solve mysteries that have lingered for centuries. And like many Black people in this country, the Wrights have a family tree that is filled with mysteries. All I knew for sure was that many members of my family worked at Avalon, the Wainwright plantation. But I'd heard rumors that we might have a rich, white ancestor, and I had a hunch that I wanted to follow. So I sent in a sample of my DNA, and when the results came back, they were clear as day. Augustus Wainwright, general in the Confederate Army, is my fifth great-grandfather. And if you are a Black person with roots in this county, he may be your grandfather, too."

He looked to Beverly, and she stepped forward to the mic again. "If anyone out there thinks they may be related to us, we are inviting you to come to a family reunion here in Troy on Saturday, June third—"

Lula threw her phone at the wall. Every television station around would be at that reunion. It had all the makings of a *60 Minutes* segment and a PBS documentary. There could even end up being a book.

None of this would have happened if that Neanderthal Logan Walsh hadn't reached for a weapon. If he hadn't dropped to his knee, Lula wouldn't have screamed. Mitch wouldn't have lunged forward and knocked that little busybody off the stage. The two boys would have been escorted out of the square—and everyone in the crowd would have recognized them as the troublemakers they were. There would have been no apology. No press conference. No ridiculous family reunion. No Beverly prancing around in front of the TV cameras like the goddamned queen of Georgia.

Lula took a deep breath. She could get things back on track. She was positive. But someone had to pay for the mistakes so far. So Lula picked up her phone and called Nathan Dugan.

CHAPTER 25

THE CATCHER IN THE RYE

Delvin Crump was in a fine mood. Inside his mailbag was another book bound for Lula Dean's library. It seemed like she'd forgotten all about it, so Delvin had taken over as curator of the collection. It thrilled him to know his books were making it into people's hands. He'd seen that Kelly boy reading one of his titles at the Waffle House on his way out of town that morning.

A couple days earlier, on the morning after the rally, he'd heard Lula screeching as he stopped to deliver her daily bundle of catalogs. He hadn't really intended to eavesdrop, but it wasn't hard to figure out she'd seen the press conference. Delvin got a little giddy just thinking about it. Augustus Wainwright had assumed that statue would be his legacy—and that all his evil deeds would be forgotten in time. Now the descendants of his victims had risen up and joined forces. And they were going to bring that bastard down.

He couldn't have been prouder if Isaac Wright had been his own son. That boy had shown ingenuity and resolve far beyond his years. At seventeen, Isaac not only knew which battles needed to be fought, he was ready to fight them. Delvin remembered being that age like it was yesterday. He hadn't known his ass from a hole in the ground. In fact, it had taken two tours in Afghanistan before he was able to tell them apart.

Delvin felt his smile curdle as he approached the Dugan house. Even though it was working hours, the man's truck was in the drive. When

Delvin had loaded his Jeep that morning, he hadn't been pleased to see the priority delivery box addressed to Nathan Dugan. That evil bastard was the last person on earth he wanted to lay eyes on right now. The post office's motto mentioned snow, sleet, and rain, but it didn't say anything about motherfucking Nazis. Delvin parked his Jeep at the curb and walked down the drive. The box he carried was not particularly heavy. Delvin reflexively glanced at the return address. It had been sent from another part of town. *Holcombe Road*. The name was written in chicken scratch, but he made out the letters that formed the word *Walsh*. There was only one Walsh left in town, Logan Walsh, and Delvin had seen him at the rally, standing right behind Lula and Mitch. For years, he'd heard talk that the Walsh boy had murdered his father. He didn't doubt it. Delvin could tell just looking at Logan that the kid wasn't right. He reminded Delvin of a few guys he'd known in the army—quiet types who seemed perfectly sane until they started talking. Then it would become clear that their reality wasn't one you could recognize. Their earth was flat and run by a shadowy cabal. They always assumed they were under surveillance. Any mark was a symbol and every symbol had a secret meaning. There was a reason for their every action, however bizarre it seemed. Just like there was a reason Logan Walsh had driven three miles out of the way to mail a priority package to a Nazi who lived less than two miles from his house.

Delvin handled the package a little more gingerly. Lord only knew what was in it. He approached the Dugan house with equal care. He'd spent enough time in war zones to know when he'd crossed into dangerous territory. Sure enough, when he reached the front steps, the door opened. Nathan Dugan was standing there, watching Delvin come toward him. He kept his right arm bent at the elbow and his hand hidden behind his back. Dugan had a gun, and he wanted his postman to know it. His thin, colorless lips remained pressed together. Delvin held out the package, and Dugan refused to take it. His eyes flicked down to the floor, as though ordering the postman to set the box at his feet. Delvin laughed and placed it six feet away on the porch banister instead. He caught the sound of a gun barrel sliding out of a holster.

"You sure you want to commit a federal offense this morning, Herr Dugan?" Delvin asked. Dugan didn't respond. "Guess not. Enjoy your day, now," he told the Nazi and chuckled all the way back to the sidewalk.

He was delivering a package to the folks across the street when he saw Nathan Dugan hustle out of his house with an army surplus duffel bag, which he tossed into the bed of his truck. Then he wheeled his trash can out of the garage and to the curb—even though pickup wasn't till the next morning. Within thirty seconds, Nathan Dugan had hopped in his truck and sped off. Delvin had a hunch that he wouldn't be back.

He finished his deliveries on the cul-de-sac and headed back the way he'd come. Along the way, he chugged the last of the Gatorade he'd brought with him. When he reached Nathan Dugan's trash can, he opened it up and made a show of tossing the bottle inside. Lying on top of the other trash was the box he'd just delivered. It had been emptied and its contents tossed into the can as well. Delvin recognized SS lightning bolts. He pulled out his phone and snapped a picture. Then his gut told him that wasn't enough, and he grabbed the box and the two flags that had been folded up inside.

"AIN'T NOTHING ILLEGAL ABOUT OWNING a flag," Sheriff Bradley told Delvin when he called. "Ain't nothing illegal about sending one through the mail, either." Bradley was a good old boy through and through, but he wasn't stupid. If he was acting dense, he was doing it on purpose.

"I know," Delvin told him. "But something feels wrong about this. Dugan gets two flags in the mail, and then he takes off like a bat outta hell?"

"Mighta just gone to the Piggly Wiggly for all we know," said the sheriff. "What were you doing rifling through a man's trash, anyways? Betcha that's illegal if we're looking for crimes to pin on people."

"Look all you want," Delvin said. "I know the law. Once trash is left at the curb, it's public property. Listen, I realize you don't give a damn about

Nazi flags. But something spooked Dugan bad just now. I'd look into it if I were you."

"But you're not me, thank goodness. A sheriff can't go around harassing people for owning flags. Just relax, Mr. Crump. No need to act paranoid. Nathan will be back home by the time you deliver his mail tomorrow morning."

Nathan. Of course.

WHEN THE WORKING DAY ENDED at five o'clock, Delvin drove past the address on Holcombe Road. The house was hidden deep in the woods and the drive was posted. Delvin pulled off the road across from the entrance. His gut was screaming louder than ever that something was wrong. It was the same gut that had kept Delvin alive in Afghanistan, and he'd learned to listen when it spoke to him. The first thing it had taught him was the most lethal creatures on earth were young men with a few bad ideas and nothing to lose. Overseas, Delvin had faced his share of them. Some, but not all, had been Afghans. He'd stared back at one in the mirror every morning.

When Delvin turned eighteen, the army was where young men went when there was nowhere else to go. Some of his fellow soldiers had run away—from abusive homes, bad neighborhoods, poverty and the hopelessness that came with it. A couple kids he knew had come to the forces to find a fight. But most were like Delvin—flailing and lost. The army promised structure and a steady paycheck. Still, Delvin had delayed, spending two full years after high school drinking beer and working dead-end jobs. Then came 9/11, and the recruiters were selling not only escape but a righteous fight. For Delvin, that proved an irresistible combination.

He spent the following years watching boys like him die. Blown up, ambushed, murdered by strangers—or shot by their own hand. He ended the lives of five Afghan fighters. Then one day he realized the war meant nothing to him. He didn't believe in the cause. The Afghans weren't his enemies. The battles that needed to be fought were all back home.

It wasn't until he married Wanda that he finally felt like he was where he needed to be. But Delvin had never forgotten what it was like to be lost, and he knew just how easy it would have been for someone to lead him astray.

A TRUCK PULLED OFF THE road behind him. Jeb Sweeney slid out of the driver's seat. Well over six feet and dressed in army surplus pants, a white T-shirt, and a Braves hat, he looked like a G.I. Joe figure on leave. Delvin didn't know the veterinarian very well, and to be honest, he looked a lot like a man Delvin would rather avoid. But he'd seen Jeb at the CPC's press conferences, holding up signs that made it perfectly clear what he thought of Lula Dean.

Jeb laid a hand on the Jeep's window frame. "Howdy, Mr. Postman," he said. "What brings you out this way?"

"I could ask you the same thing, Doctor," Delvin responded.

Jeb glanced over his shoulder. "I've been concerned about the young man who lives up that drive. I feel like I should pay him a visit, but he's got the property under surveillance and he may not be interested in receiving visitors."

"You think he's dangerous?"

"Yeah," Jeb said. "I do."

Delvin felt a wave of relief. He wasn't the only one. "What tipped you off?"

"He brought me here for a house call a while back. His style of decorating was . . . well, let's just say it was pretty fucked up. Then I had an exchange with him after Lula Dean's rally. He was agitated and angry. Seemed real upset that Mitch had called me to pick him up. I've been trying to keep an eye on the kid since then. Followed him to the post office, but that's the only place he's been."

"He sent Nathan Dugan a box of Nazi flags this morning."

"SS and Gestapo?" Jeb asked, and Delvin nodded. "See, that's a bad fucking sign right there. He's getting rid of prized possessions. He had them in a display case in his den. Along with an arsenal that could take out an army. How'd you find out about the flags?"

"Dugan sped off in his truck as soon as he opened the box. Dumped everything in the trash as he left. I pulled it out."

Jeb bowed his head for a moment then looked up at the trees. "Fuck. Dugan knows something's coming. He doesn't want to stop it, but he doesn't want to be anywhere near when it happens."

"My thought exactly. I tried warning the sheriff—"

"You mean Nathan's second cousin?"

Delvin shook his head at his own stupidity. "Shit."

Jeb chuckled darkly. "Don't give yourself a hard time. As I think we've all learned in recent days, the family trees around here are as tangled as a box of Christmas lights."

"So it's up to us to stop him? I don't suppose you have any thoughts on how to do that?" Delvin asked.

"Well, I doubt he's going to take action tonight. My guess is Logan's prepping for that party Beverly Underwood and the Wrights are throwing. But I'd love to be able to keep a closer eye on him if I could. I got these cameras I use to monitor the feral hogs in my orchard. If I could plant a couple of those up near his house, we would know when he's fixing to make a move. Only problem is, he's not too happy with me right now. And the way things are headed, if he spots someone coming up the drive that he don't want to see, he's liable to shoot first and ask questions later."

Delvin knew Wanda would murder him herself if she heard what he was about to say. "How long do you need to position the cameras?"

"Three minutes," Jeb told him.

"I can give you that," Delvin told him. "Jump in the back. That's the thing about the USPS. Even Nazis need their mail."

"You know what kind of person we're dealing with?" Jeb asked. "I saw a target with Obama's face on it last time I visited. He's not exactly going to welcome either of us with open arms."

Delvin almost laughed. "He's got plenty of company round here. And I deliver the mail to all of them."

LOGAN WALSH WAS NAKED ASIDE from a pair of novelty boxer shorts with little red lobsters on a sea of navy blue. Judging by his rumpled hair and bleary eyes, he'd just dragged himself out of bed. He looked so young, Delvin thought. Not much older than the boys he'd met at boot camp and not a single hair on his chest.

"Hey," Logan said. Just that. *Hey*. Like they were just two regular people who had no reason to hate each other.

Delvin, halfway out of the Jeep, froze at the sight of the gun in the younger man's hand.

Logan glanced down at the gun. "Oh, sorry," he told Delvin. "I just got an alert that someone was coming up the drive. Didn't know it was you."

"That's all right," the postman said. "But I do come bearing bad news, so don't shoot the messenger. We had a package get mangled in the sorter this morning. Couldn't read anything but the return address, which turned out to be yours. Thought I'd bring it up and see if we can get it where it needs to go."

He handed Logan a mangled piece of box and the two flags that had been inside.

"Shit," Logan said. "Y'all really fucked this one up, didn't you?"

"We did. But I don't believe the contents were harmed. If you can write down the right address for me, I'll put it in a brand-new priority box and make sure it gets out this evening."

"Evening?" Logan looked up at the sky and yawned. "Okay," he said. "Pretty sure I have a box in the office. Come in. I'll get it all packed up for ya."

Delvin hadn't expected to be invited inside. He didn't dare glance over his shoulder at the Jeep, but he sure hoped Jeb was watching.

AT SOME POINT IN THE past, it had been a very nice house. Now it resembled the den of a dying beast. The wood floors were hidden beneath mud, filthy clothes, and random detritus. The walls were riddled with bullet holes and the light fixtures had all been shot out.

"Sorry 'bout the mess," Logan said. He walked through the mess in his bare feet.

"I've seen worse," Delvin told him. A kid he'd known in the army had lost it one night and destroyed the barracks. No one had tried to stop him. No one wanted to. Most had felt the same urge at one time or another. That's why they locked the soldiers' guns away every night.

He and Logan reached a room with a desk in the center and ammunition cases lining the walls. Aside from a few guns, the cases had been emptied. Several large army-issue duffel bags had been stuffed to capacity. There was little doubt what was packed inside them.

A hand-drawn map of Jackson Square had been pinned to the wall behind the desk. Symbols indicated an entry point, targets, and an exit. On the desk was a copy of The *Catcher in the Rye*.

"You read that?" Delvin asked as Logan grabbed an empty box off the floor.

"Naw," Logan told him. "I got it out of Lula Dean's library. Had a different cover on it. Was supposed to be the book by that senator—*Manhood*. What about you? You read *The Catcher in the Rye*? It's supposed to be famous, isn't it?"

"Yeah," Delvin said. "You might like it. The hero's a young man who's lost in life. A lot of us feel that way at one point or another. Most of us end up finding our way."

"I'm not a big reader." Logan spread out the SS flag before folding it into a square.

"More of a history buff, I guess?" Delvin asked. "Were the flags part of a collection?"

"Not really," Logan said. "I bought them to make a friend happy, but he says he's done with me, so I'm sending them to him."

There was no emotion in Logan's voice. Not a quiver or a hint of anger. Delvin knew what men looked like when they've been broken. Just do what you're here to do, Delvin ordered himself. Give Jeb enough time to get the cameras in place. Do not get involved.

"Is the friend Nathan Dugan?" *Why the fuck had he gone and done that?* Logan looked up.

"He's not the man you think he is," Delvin told him. "He's a coward who can't feel big unless others feel small. Someone like that doesn't deserve your respect."

"I know," Logan said bluntly. "Nobody does."

"Nobody?"

"People are never who they pretend to be. Everybody thought my daddy was righteous. Judge Walsh is *such* a good man, they'd say. Such a friend of law and order. We're *so* lucky to have him on the bench. They never saw who he really was."

"Who was he?"

"A pig," Logan said. "A filthy disgusting pig who deserved what he got." His voice cracked and Delvin knew he'd broken through. He couldn't tell whether that was a good thing or not.

"I can sense you've been through some serious shit," Delvin said. "You need someone to talk to."

"I had someone," Logan said. "He told me I'm a loser. I pulled a gun at the rally and let Mitch Sweeney get away. Now he says he doesn't want anything to do with me anymore. Says my father was right and I'm totally useless."

"Nathan Dugan is not the person you should be consulting. Maybe we could find you someone who is trained to talk to people in crisis."

Logan looked like he was having trouble making sense of it all. "Why would you want to help me?"

"Because I knew guys like you in the army. They saw too much and they needed help before they hurt themselves or others."

Before he could stop them, his eyes landed on the map of Jackson Square. His host noticed, and it broke the spell. Logan picked the gun up off the desk.

"I'm sorry, Mr. Postman. I believe you mean well, but I can't let you leave now."

"Logan." Delvin tried to keep his voice flat and calm. "I have children who need me."

"They'll survive without a father," Logan said. "I did."

"Did you?" Delvin asked.

"Put the gun down, Logan."

Delvin's head swiveled toward the voice. Jeb had just come around the corner with a pistol in his hand.

"Well, well. Look who's here." Logan's face crumpled, and his lower lip trembled as he spoke. "If it isn't Jeb Sweeney, the fakest motherfucker around. You know I used to pray every night that you were my dad? Then Hollis pulled me out of Little League. Took away the only thing I was ever good at. I thought for sure you'd come save me. But you never asked why I was gone or bothered to come check on me. Do you have any fucking idea what I had to live with?"

"I didn't know—" Jeb said.

"Fuck you."

Logan took aim and pulled the trigger.

CHAPTER 26

THE ART OF CROCHET

Jonathan Bartlett sat at the table in the high school teachers' lounge, sipping his fourth cup of coffee and scrolling through Facebook. Since the town's newspaper had gone belly up three years earlier, Facebook was Troy's sole source of local news—if that's what you wanted to call the gossip, hearsay, wild speculation, conspiracy theories, and general insanity that Jonathan's neighbors tossed with their fact salads. You had to know a person's political leanings, astrological signs, and pharmaceutical history if you wanted to interpret their "news" correctly. Sorting the facts from the fiction was exhausting, confusing, and occasionally hilarious. Like the time Viola Lewis was discovered wandering the beer aisle at Walmart in a thong at six in the morning. Soon the whole town was captivated by a detailed account of her alien abduction. It wasn't till days later that her sister, Violet, popped into the comments to report that Viola had misread the dosage on her Ambien prescription.

It got worse than that, of course. Seemed like somebody was always being accused of Satanism or sleeping around. As a teacher, Jonathan pitied any historian who might one day try to make sense of it all. But like everyone in Troy, he was hooked. Feeling like a junkie, Jonathan refreshed his feed. The talk today was about Logan Walsh. Melody Sykes had just posted a clip from Channel Four.

Reports of Walsh's involvement with a local white nationalist group have not been confirmed and no evidence of any such affiliation was uncovered during a search of his home. Nathan Dugan, a forty-year-old Troy resident whose neo-Nazi sympathies were revealed earlier this spring, was known to many as Walsh's mentor. Reached in San Antonio, where he has been staying with his mother, Dugan told reporters that he believed Walsh was struggling with his sexuality. News Channel Four has not been able to confirm or deny that Walsh was gay. We have, however, confirmed that a copy of *The Catcher in the Rye* was found in his home. As you may recall, John Hinckley was carrying the same book the day he attempted to assassinate President Reagan. Walsh appears to have attempted to hide the book's title by wrapping it in the cover of *Manhood* by Senator Josh Hawley.

Do y'all need any more proof that these gay books are dangerous!!!! Lula had commented below.

Manhood. Jonathan had recently come across a book with that cover. He could see the red and white letters on a red background—and the name of the senator (an Ivy League graduate with a three-hundred-dollar haircut and bespoke suits) who'd written it. Though it wasn't the kind of book that would ordinarily catch his eye, Jonathan knew exactly where he'd seen it. Lula Dean's purple library.

Jonathan set his phone down on the table. He closed his eyes, touched his middle fingers to his thumbs, and began the breathing exercises his therapist had taught him. He needed to calm the hell down. His blood pressure had just shot so high he was watching fireworks on the backs of his eyelids. It was only twelve-thirty and school wasn't over until three. There were still two and a half hours left before he was free to murder Lula Dean.

For the past two years, it had taken a monumental show of self-restraint to keep Lula's (mostly metaphorical) blood off his hands. Jonathan crossed the street when he saw her coming. He turned off the TV whenever Lula showed up on the news. He did give in to temptation one night and drive around collecting lawn signs for her mayoral campaign. He'd taken them home, shot them up with a pellet gun, and set them all ablaze. But so far, that was the worst he'd done.

Sometimes he lay asleep at night, dreaming up horrible fates for her. Eaten by feral hogs was a personal favorite. So was tying her to a bedbug-ridden mattress and watching her slowly sucked dry until there was nothing left but a withered, desiccated husk. Others were a little less fanciful and a few didn't even involve murder. But none of them could be seen through to fruition because he'd promised Elliot he wouldn't.

ELLIOT MINTER WAS JONATHAN'S BEST friend. For years, they'd lived just down the street from each other. They worked at the same school, where Jonathan taught American and European history and Elliot was the beloved musical director. They ate lunch together. They celebrated Christmas at each other's homes. Every Tuesday night, they played Dungeons & Dragons. And after Jonathan's wife died of cancer at age thirty-eight, Elliot Minter kept Jonathan alive.

During the months when Jonathan couldn't find the will to live, Elliot let himself in every morning to make coffee and lure Jonathan out of bed. He made sure Jonathan wore clean clothes and drove him to work. In the evening, Elliot cooked them both dinner. For half a year, Elliot sacrificed his personal life. He kept Jonathan going until he was able to function on his own.

Elliot was a saint. Lula Dean would rot in hell for what she'd done to him.

EVERYONE IN TROY KNEW ELLIOT was gay. He didn't discuss it with most people—because who the hell discusses their private life with a bunch of gossips they barely know? But it wasn't a *secret* and Elliot certainly wasn't ashamed. Under his direction, the music department put on two musicals every year—a feat few heterosexuals could have ever accomplished.

Then, ten years into Elliot's tenure at Troy High School, an email arrived in the principal's inbox. Attached were two pictures of the musical director kissing a handsome, leather-clad man outside a gay bar in Atlanta at three o'clock in the morning. *Elliot Minter is grooming innocent young people to be perverted and promiscuous,* said the note that accompanied the images. The email had been sent from an anonymous address. Later that day, having received no response, the note and pictures began popping up in people's Facebook feeds from an account called Protectors of the Innocent. Most of the early comments were from women gushing over Elliot's incredibly hot lover. Then Nathan Dugan and a couple of other bigots picked up the story and ran with it.

I do not want this pedo anywhere near my son, Nathan wrote.

"Pedo?" Elliot had come carefully to Jonathan's house to strategize over gin and tonics. "The guy I'm kissing in the photos is three years older than me. For fuck's sake, he's in finance."

Is this the lifestyle a high school teacher should be living? Melody Sykes asked, phrasing her comment as a question so she couldn't be called out if the situation ended up going the other way.

"What the hell is this *lifestyle* she's talking about?" Elliot asked. "I was kissing a hedge fund bro. We weren't renovating a historic bed-and-breakfast."

"Nobody's asking why the person sending the pictures was outside a gay bar at three in the morning," Jonathan pointed out. He'd assumed the stalker's identity was as much a mystery to Elliot as anyone else at that point.

"It was Lula Dean," Elliot announced flatly.

"Lula Dean?" Jonathan repeated. "That prissy woman with the little white dog and orange hair?" At that point, Lula hadn't found the dirty cake book that would lead her to fame. "How the hell did you reach *that* conclusion?"

"I know who she was there to see that night." After he told Jonathan the truth—and shared a few pictures—he swore him to secrecy.

"Come on. Those pictures are amazing. You should post them," Jonathan advised.

"No, I shouldn't." Elliot was adamant. "I promised I wouldn't, and I have no interest in being as awful as she is. And please tell me you won't say anything, either. Hopefully this will all pass in time."

IT TOOK A COUPLE OF weeks for the hysteria to build—for harmless stories to be embellished until they were nothing but blatant lies. A video of Elliot showing the cast of his production of *Chicago* how to do a Fosse hip roll was posted online, along with a note of encouragement—You were fabulous today, dahling!—that Elliot had given a sophomore boy. When the school's musical-theater students rallied around Elliot, a group of parents claimed it proved their kids had been brainwashed. Led by Beverly Underwood, the school board came to Elliot's defense and refused to reprimand him. But the damage was done. Elliot's private life was suddenly public. Even a trip to the Piggly Wiggly could be an ordeal. Once, the mother of a high school student had grabbed an egg carton out of his cart and smashed the contents with her fist.

"That's what I'll do to you if I ever catch you talking to Whitney," she'd said.

"Okay," Elliot responded. He had no idea who Whitney was. There had never been a girl by that name in his class.

When the school year ended, Elliot resigned. He left Troy, his dream job, and his best friend behind. And he was fine. He didn't turn to drugs or plunge into the depths of depression. He got a new job in a part of the country where musical directors are assumed to be gay until proven otherwise. He had a nice boyfriend and a cute cat. His apartment was tasteful and located near a big park. But whenever he and Jonathan spoke on the phone, it was clear Elliot was not the same person. He'd lost something that no one should have to lose. No, that wasn't right, Jonathan had to remind himself. Elliot Minter hadn't *lost* anything. His peace of mind, his sense of safety, his belief that most people were good at heart—whatever it was that was no longer there—had been stolen by Lula Dean.

WHEN THE THREE O'CLOCK BELL rang, Jonathan strapped his messenger bag across his chest and rode the wave of rowdy kids out of the school and into the parking lot. He left his car sitting in its spot. His brain was still buzzing with anger, and he needed to walk.

His destination lay on the other side of town. Along the way, he passed Troy's elementary school, which had let out thirty minutes earlier. A woman rushing down the front stairs nearly barreled into him. There was something familiar about her, but he couldn't quite place it.

"Jonathan!"

He stopped and squirmed. "Sorry, I—"

"It's Crystal. Crystal Moore? You and I met at Elliot Minter's house a few times."

There had to be a glitch in the matrix. This was not the Crystal Moore he'd met. That woman wore ballet flats and knee-length skirts. He couldn't remember the color of her hair, but she'd kept it pulled back in a butterfly barrette. This was a black-clad, auburn-haired goddess with a crescent moon pendant dangling from a golden chain around her neck.

"I know." She filled in the silence when he found himself unable to speak. "I've changed since you last saw me. I had the world's best midlife crisis."

"Well, it certainly suits you," Jonathan said. "You look happy and free. Which way are you heading?"

"Across town," Crystal told him. "And you?"

"I'm going that way, too. Mind if I tag along?"

WHEN HIS WIFE, JESS, WAS dying, she'd seen marvelous things. Visions of a past she'd never experienced, and a future she would never visit. On several occasions, Jonathan had entered her hospital room and found her deep in discussion with relatives and ancestors who'd long been dead. They told her things, Jess confided. Most of what she learned she kept to herself. Then, one day when he visited her in the hospital, Jess had announced there would be another woman in Jonathan's life. She described her in detail, down to the color of her dress. Beaming with happiness, she took his hand and said she approved.

"No, you're the only woman I love," Jonathan had told her. "Nothing will ever change that."

"You've let them tell you what love is." Jess pulled him closer and whispered in his ear. "They have *no* idea."

It wasn't what he'd wanted to hear. In fact, it all seemed so ridiculous that he began to question everything Jess had said after they added the palliative drugs to her IV. He knew his life would end when she died. He had no interest in surviving.

After her funeral, he told Elliot as much.

"Jess said you'd say that," Elliot responded. "She had me promise I'd get you through."

He'd made good on that promise. Thanks to Elliot, Jonathan was no longer in danger. But the idea of loving another woman still felt impossible. In the years since Jess had died, no one had caught his eye or captured his interest. Troy was hardly a bachelor's paradise, and Jonathan had gotten used to the loneliness. The person Jess had seen was just a hallucination. This was the South, where ladies loved color. Jess had described a woman in black.

AS THEY APPROACHED LULA DEAN'S library, Jonathan slowed. "This is my destination," he said, though he didn't want the walk to end. Their conversation had felt effortless. His blood pressure had lowered, and his skull was no longer throbbing.

Crystal cocked her head and smiled, and for a moment he was worried she was judging him. "Mine, too," she told him. "Have you visited before?" she asked cautiously.

"I've browsed the shelves, but I've never borrowed anything. But I remembered seeing a particular book, and I wanted to find out if it's still here."

"May I guess which book?" Crystal asked.

"Sure," Jonathan replied.

"Was it *Manhood*?"

She knew. He could see it. They both turned in unison to face the little library. Their eyes scoured each of the shelves.

"Logan Walsh had a copy of *The Catcher in the Rye* wrapped in the cover of *Manhood*—I'm pretty sure he got it from here," Crystal said.

"*The Catcher in the Rye* was on Lula's banned book list."

Crystal looked up at him. Her eyes were the turquoise of bubbling springs and hidden pools. How could he never have noticed before?

"I borrowed a book I thought was *The Rules*," she said. "It turned out to be a banned book about witchcraft that was wrapped in the wrong cover."

Jonathan reached into the library and pulled out *The Art of Crochet*. He opened it up to the title page and showed it to Crystal. "Look at this. *Gender Queer*. Literally, the most banned book in the United States."

"I've read it. It's very sweet," Crystal said. "It's hard to believe we live in a world where parents let their kids beat sex workers in *Grand Theft Auto* and then worry that a graphic novel about a nonbinary person is going to screw them up."

"Do you think Lula did this?" Jonathan asked.

They both laughed at the question.

"Oh, hell no," Crystal said. "Somebody pulled a prank."

Jonathan smirked. "But it's *her* library," he pointed out.

Crystal caught on quickly. "Which means she's responsible for what's in it."

"*Exactly*," Jonathan said.

"A lot of people would think she was in league with Satan if they found out. It wouldn't be very nice to expose her."

"Lula was the reason Elliot had to leave town," Jonathan said.

"I suspected as much," Crystal told him. "That settles it. She deserves whatever she gets."

THAT EVENING OVER MULTIPLE NEGRONIS, Jonathan and Crystal composed a Facebook post.

"Should we create an anonymous account to post it?" Crystal asked when they were finished.

"No." Jonathan was adamant. "We'll use my account. I want her to know that I did it."

Lula Dean says she started the Concerned Parents Committee to protect our town's young people from pornography and propaganda. This morning, I am sad to report that Lula may be the biggest pervert of all. Just last night, I stopped by her library to borrow a wholesome book. I chose *The Art of Crochet*. When I opened it, I couldn't believe my eyes! Inside that perfectly wholesome cover was the book *Gender Queer*. I can only imagine what might have happened if one of the sweet, innocent, impressionable teenagers I teach at Troy High had stumbled across a book about nonbinary people. Of course I immediately checked the other books in Lula's library. Inside the wholesome covers were books about everything from CRT to witchcraft. What was Lula Dean thinking when she did this? When did she start hating children and set out to destroy our town?

They scheduled it to post the following day at 7 a.m.

THE NEXT MORNING, JONATHAN WOKE to the smell of coffee for the first time in years. He could hear Crystal humming, her song growing louder as she approached the bedroom.

"It's a beautiful day," she said, handing him a cup of coffee and planting a kiss on his lips. "Check your phone. All hell is breaking loose."

CHAPTER 27

THE HANDMAID'S TALE

Before she died, Melody Sykes's mother begged her to finish college.

"Do not make the same mistake I did," she pleaded with her daughter. "I placed my trust in a man who wasn't good enough or strong enough to bear the weight. Please promise me that you'll have the tools to look after yourself if anything ever goes wrong."

"I will, Mama," Melody had promised. She would have said anything to be excused from her mother's sickroom.

When lupus made it impossible for her mother to perform her wifely duties, Melody's father decided it was time to move on. Her parents divorced, and her mother settled into a spare room in Melody's grandmother's house. Melody and her siblings went to live with their father, so no child support was awarded. The little bit of alimony her mom received went straight toward medical bills. She had worked as a homemaker for twenty years. She'd never held another job.

It may have looked like bad luck to some folks, but Melody knew better. Her father had informed her and her siblings that their mother had lost God's favor. Terrible things like lupus didn't happen to those who walked the right path. Somewhere along the way, Melody's mother had been led astray. It didn't make sense, but neither did a lot of things. You trusted your father to tell you the truth. If he chose not to, well, he had his reasons.

Melody figured she was perfectly safe. All she had to do was stay righteous and God would reward her. With his protection, no harm could ever befall her. So she spent as little time with her mother as possible. Her father was blessed, and she preferred to stay with him in the light of the Lord. Her dad said Melody's beauty and brains were a sure sign of God's favor. All she had to do was look at her mother to see what happened to women who didn't live as commanded.

Melody had been dating Randy for two years when her mother mercifully passed away. He'd recently graduated from Texas A&M and was eager to return home to Georgia, where a job in the family business was waiting. He promised to pay her mother's funeral expenses if Melody agreed to drop out of school and marry him. If she'd taken any part of her mother's warning to heart, that gesture—along with a three-carat princess-cut diamond set in platinum—set her mind at ease. Once they were married and back in Troy, Melody breathed a sigh of relief. She missed school, but she didn't miss the stress of hiding the fact that she'd always been good at it. Randy couldn't stand it when her grades were better than his.

For the next sixteen years, Melody never questioned whether she'd made the right choice. She and Randy had two sons, a beautiful home with a pool in the backyard, and brand-new cars in the drive. His family was prominent throughout the state, and once Randy became mayor, they were Troy royalty. There wasn't a book club, fundraiser, or women's committee that Melody wasn't asked to join. If there was a list, no one dared leave her off it.

Then, in the course of a single day, the beautiful world Melody had built was blown to smithereens.

Of course, none of it had anything to do with Melody. *Nothing!* She hadn't even been living in the state of Georgia when Randy and his friends allegedly assaulted that girl. *He* certainly never mentioned it. And even though it was now pretty clear that everyone in town knew all about the night in question, no one had ever bothered to tell her. Melody felt like the butt of a very bad joke. The victim of a dark conspiracy. An innocent bystander caught up in a terrible crime. And for the very first time, she understood what her mother had been trying to tell her. Giving a marriage everything you've got means one day you could be left with nothing.

Since Randy resigned and took off to the mountains, her friends' lives had all gotten impossibly busy. No one had time for morning power walks or afternoon coffee anymore. She saw people duck around aisles in the Piggly Wiggly when they spotted her coming. That horrible hypocrite Lula Dean had briefly gone so far as to suggest she was no longer welcome at Concerned Parents Committee meetings. And just to add insult to injury, a frumpy woman at church whose name she'd never bothered to remember informed her their prayer group was holding Melody in the light.

Every evening, Melody got down on her knees to pray for justice. She called out to the Lord and begged him to punish her husband and restore her rightful position in town. But it seemed even Jesus was ignoring her.

SO SHE DECIDED TO TAKE matters into her own hands. It was Lula who'd inspired her plan to poison Randy. Everyone in Troy knew Lula had gotten millions in life insurance when her husband kicked the bucket at a suspiciously young age. One little mushroom could have solved all of Melody's problems in one fell swoop. Then nosy Mara Ocumma had seen her reading that field guide and threatened to rat her out. It wouldn't have been difficult to get rid of Mara, too. She was always eating weird stuff that she'd found in the woods. No one would have suspected a thing if a death cap had found its way into her sandwich. But no matter how angry she was, Melody had to admit that killing off a librarian was a step too far.

She had no choice but to suck it up. She paid Lula a visit, begged for her permission to stay on the CPC, and offered to bake the cupcakes for the Confederate hero rally. She even presented Lula with a sample cupcake complete with hand-piped Dixie flags. Of course Lula had acted as if she was doing Melody a giant favor. Melody had plunged to the bottom of the social ladder, and Lula made it clear she'd be staying there.

Melody went home that afternoon knowing for sure that the good Lord had closed a door on the life she'd once led. Then he decided to open a window.

IT TOOK LESS THAN THREE days for Lula's star to fall. Her rally was an utter disaster. People were suddenly asking questions about her cozy relationship to Logan Walsh and Nathan Dugan. And then a teacher at the high school had accused Lula of filling her little library with the very books she'd banned. People started swarming the little library at eight o'clock in the morning. Standing by her bedroom window across the street, Melody had eavesdropped on the outrage and giggled at the consternation. Lula couldn't have switched the books. Anyone with a functioning brain would have known it was some kid pulling a prank. But that didn't stop the Facebook posts calling for Lula to step down from the mayor's race.

Melody would have had to be blind to miss the opportunity in front of her. She'd been offered a chance to settle every score. To put Lula back in her place. To give that busybody librarian her comeuppance. To get rid of Randy without resorting to murder. To have a career that wouldn't require a college diploma—or any education whatsoever. Melody Sykes was going to run for mayor. It was a job for which she was uniquely suited. She'd already been doing it for years.

Now that Beverly Underwood had gone woke and Lula Dean had been exposed as a Nazi-loving hypocrite, there would be plenty of votes for a compassionate conservative. Someone who wouldn't tear down the town's historical monuments but might add a new plaque to appease the ever-growing Wainwright family. Someone who would protect children from pornography and the gay agenda—without stepping on adults' freedom to read about butt plugs. Someone who would divorce their husband to show solidarity with victims of violence and could lean on her impeccable credentials as a churchgoing mother of two.

IT WAS TIME TO GET to work. Holding her adorable ten-year-old son by the hand, Melody walked across the street to Lula's and took a place beside the little purple library. The crowd that had been gathering all morning in front of the little library fell silent. Melody bit the inside of her lip until she felt tears well in her eyes. She'd discovered the trick back in elementary school. It always worked like a charm.

"I don't know about you, but I feel betrayed," she told her fellow townsfolk. "Even though I didn't agree with all of her choices, I trusted that Lula had this town's best interests in mind."

She squeezed little Beau's hand. "Y'all know that my boys and I have had some trouble. While I was busy trying to save our family, my youngest asked if he could borrow a book from Lula's little library. I didn't see any reason to say no! I trusted her heart and thought I knew her soul. But after her deceptions came to light, I took a closer look at the book Beau had borrowed. This was wrapped in a different cover." She held up *Are You There God? It's Me, Margaret.* "It was on the banned book list, and Lula Dean had it in her library, just waiting for an impressionable child to find it. That child turned out to be my little boy."

"Umm, excuse me, Melody," Crystal Moore interjected. "I think your son has a question."

Melody glanced down and saw Beau standing patiently with his right hand raised. "Yes?" she asked him, feeling a little flustered. This wasn't something they'd planned. In fact, she'd made a point of telling him to stay quiet while she gave her speech.

"Why was the book banned?"

Melody forced herself to smile sweetly. "It deals with subjects that aren't suitable for children your age."

"Have you read it?" Beau wasn't talking back. There was no challenge in the question. He simply wanted to know.

Melody had devoured the book over the course of two summer afternoons when she was eleven years old. She could still remember the blast of cool air that had greeted her when she entered the library. The little Styrofoam beads that popped out of the tiny rip in her beanbag's seams.

The warm, woody smell of the paper as she turned the page. The thrill of reading a book that spoke of serious things and treated her like a person with a brain.

"Who here has read *Are You There God? It's Me, Margaret*?" A voice called out from the crowd. Mara Ocumma stepped forward with her hand held high. A few hands rose behind her, followed by even more, until almost every woman around had her hand in the air.

Beau looked up at Melody. "Does that mean they all read it?" he asked again.

He'd gotten her into a tight spot. Melody could hardly say no. "Yes," she admitted.

"We all read that book when we were your age," Mara told him. "I loved every page of it."

Melody stared daggers at Mara. This was her revenge for their talk at the library.

"Did you read it, too?" Beau asked Melody.

"I did," she admitted.

"What about it isn't good for kids?"

Melody scrambled for an answer. "You're a boy, sweetheart. You don't need to be reading about girls' bodies."

"But I was worried—"

"You see?" Melody called out and the hands in the crowd began to fall. "My son was terrified by what he read in this book. We should be the ones teaching our children what they need to know—not outsourcing it to authors who don't share our values."

"I was worried that those pads under the sink meant you were sick," Beau said. "Nobody would tell me what they were for. I thought you might be dying."

Half the hands that had been held high flew to their owners' hearts. Mara Ocumma seemed stricken and Crystal Moore looked ready to burst into tears.

Melody turned away from the crowd and crouched down in front of her son. Just the thought of her being unwell had drained the blood from his face. It was a fear she knew well—one she'd hidden in the darkest part of her soul. One that often broke free at night and woke her up with a start. She knew what Beau's dad would say if she were to ever get sick— the same thing her father had told her. The two men shared the same values. Women were tolerated as long as they satisfied you and fed you and hid everything about themselves that you might find objectionable. Melody had been walking a tightrope her entire life—the same one she'd seen her own mother fall off. And she'd been on the verge of passing her father's beliefs to a new generation.

"I'm not sick," she assured her son. "I promise you, sweetheart, I'm fine. Having your period is perfectly normal."

"I know," Beau said. "It's just part of being a girl. That's what I learned from the book. I also found out that girls can be funny. Underneath it all, they're just regular people."

Melody heard titters from the crowd, along with a few sniffles. She stood up. It was time to go. She clearly wasn't cut out for politics. Her career had lasted all of five minutes.

"So why was the book banned?" Beau wasn't ready to leave. "Did I miss something?"

The crowd remained silent, waiting for Melody's answer.

"No," she admitted. "You didn't miss anything. If it helped you, I'm glad that you found it."

"It's a wonderful book," Crystal Moore agreed. "Everyone should read it. Girls *and* boys."

"I can't believe the committee had it on their banned books list," said someone in the crowd.

"What the hell were they thinking?"

———

MELODY SYKES TOOK HER SON'S hand and led him back to their house. She'd always assumed most people saw things the way she did. Her father used to say they belonged to a "silent majority" that represented the best of America. Now Melody was beginning to wonder if there might be a much bigger group who'd been holding their tongues—people who minded their own business until push came to shove. It was starting to look like the book-banning business may have shoved them a step too far.

CHAPTER 28

NICKEL AND DIMED

No one had asked Lindsay Underwood to come home. She was supposed to be starting a summer internship that week, but she needed to be with her mom. The shit had hit the fan in Troy—and splattered across the entire country. The reporters camped out in her parents' yard weren't just from Atlanta stations. All the major cable news channels were there as well, along with every freelance journalist, Reddit detective, and TikTok content creator looking for a new spin on the story. Logan Walsh had been plotting a massacre at the time of his death. The Wright-Wainwright reunion—a newsworthy event on its own—had been the target.

Lindsay parked several blocks down the street and cut through a dozen backyards until she reached the one with the wooden swing that her father had built when she was five and her mother still couldn't bear to cut down. The plan was to slip in unseen through the back door. Like all of Lindsay's plans these days, this one went terribly wrong.

"Lindsay!" A reporter popped out from behind the oak, where she'd been waiting to ambush anyone sneaking into the house. She waved at her prey like they were BFFs and it wasn't at all weird she'd been stalking her. "Do you have a sec to chat? Do you have any comment on the death of Logan Walsh?"

She flinched when she got a good look at Lindsay, who'd cried the whole drive down to Troy. "Oh my God. Are you okay?"

The answer was obvious, so Lindsay ignored the question. "Sure, I'll give you a quote," she said. "When I was in elementary school, I used to get bullied because I wasn't like other kids. Logan Walsh was three grades ahead. On several occasions, he stepped in and stood up for me when no one else would. I'm not saying that as proof that Logan was a good person or deserves any sympathy. I think we know how he turned out. I'm saying that all of us should be doing a whole lot of soul-searching these days. What turned a kid who would stick up for an outcast into a man who was planning to kill half of this town—my own mother included? And what are we going to do to stop other disturbed young men from turning into monsters? Even if you don't give a damn about them as people, your safety—all of our safety—depends on the answer."

Lindsay turned her back on the reporter, who clearly hadn't been expecting that kind of answer, and marched into the Underwood home. When the door was closed and locked behind her, she stood inside the mudroom and tried to breathe. According to the *Journal-Constitution,* Logan Walsh had turned a hand-drawn outline of Jackson Square into a tactical battle map. He'd loaded two bags with long rifles and ammunition. He was composing a manifesto on his laptop. Although it remained unfinished, it left no doubt what had been done to him as a child—and what he'd had planned for Jackson Square. And sitting right there on his desk, along with two Nazi flags and a half-full beer, was a copy of *The Catcher in the Rye,* the discarded jacket of *Manhood* folded up beneath it. Logan Walsh had borrowed one of the books that she had left in Lula Dean's library.

Lindsay had fucked up the night she restocked those shelves. She'd kicked over a rock that had long sat undisturbed. Then she'd left town before all the horrible creatures crawled out. Nazis, rapists, and killers—not to mention hypocrites and opportunists. For a while, it felt good to see them exposed. But she should have stepped in when Bella Cummings got hurt. Maybe there would have been time to keep that book out of Logan's hands.

Books don't turn people into murderers. Lindsay knew that. She believed it with all of her heart. But what if Logan had found *The Catcher in the Rye* and remembered that it had been linked to at least three famous shootings? What if that memory had planted the thought of murder in his mind? And what if his plans had succeeded? What if he'd killed the Wright family and her mother and father and God knows how many others? Wouldn't she be at least somewhat responsible?

Lindsay thought of the Logan she knew when they were little. Why hadn't anyone helped him like he'd helped her? How much responsibility did she bear for his death? Or for the pain and suffering of the postman and the veterinarian who'd watched Logan blow his head off?

It was time to come clean. That's why Lindsay had returned to Troy. She'd almost been relieved when she'd driven past Lula's house and seen the crowd outside. Her ruse had been discovered. She was going to confess. But first she needed to apologize to her mother.

BEVERLY UNDERWOOD WAS SITTING ON the living room sofa, surrounded by the entire Wright family. A man with a notepad appeared to be interviewing them as a photographer snapped pictures. Lindsay had almost forgotten the reunion was only ten days away.

"Lindsay!" Beverly cried out. "What on earth? You didn't say you were coming!"

Lindsay tried her best to smile. "I thought I'd surprise you."

"Everybody, this is my wonderful daughter. Lindsay, these are our cousins, the Wrights, and this gentleman is from the *Journal-Constitution*."

Lindsay offered the guests an awkward wave, and they responded in kind.

"Give us a couple minutes, sweetheart. We're just finishing up here. Everything okay?"

"Yeah, Mom," Lindsay assured her. Then she stepped out into the hall and ordered herself to keep it together until the visitors were gone.

"Beverly, when you discovered the connection between the Wainwrights and the Wrights—" she heard the reporter in the living room start to say. Lindsay's mother stopped him.

"Oh no, I didn't discover the connection. Isaac did. He's the reason we're sitting here today."

"Isaac, when you discovered the connection, did you ever worry for the safety of your family?"

There was a pause, then Lindsay heard an older man speak.

"If you don't mind, I'll answer that question," said James Wright.

"Please, by all means," the reporter said.

"Isaac discovered the connection on his own. Apparently one of my brothers let the truth slip a while back. I've known since I was a young boy, but I didn't tell my sons and I had no intention of doing so. When I was growing up, there was nothing we could do with the information. There was no DNA testing back then, so we had no way to prove it. But that was okay, because we didn't *want* to talk about it. Not just because it was horrible, which it was. We knew that telling our story could get us killed. I hear people saying we live in more enlightened times now. Do we? After everything that's happened over the past few days, can anyone look me in the eye and tell me things are all that different?"

"There is one thing that's different." Lindsay peeked around the corner and saw it was the younger boy, Elijah.

"What's that?" James Wright asked.

"There are a whole lot more of us now."

The tilt of Mr. Wright's head suggested he hadn't considered that fact. Then, unable to argue, he nodded.

"That's right," said the reporter, who sounded thrilled to move on. "I've been told that dozens of potential family members have contacted you about the reunion."

"Logan Walsh's suicide has brought a great deal of attention to our cause," Beverly said.

"The Lord works in mysterious ways," Betsy Wright added.

THERE WAS A KNOCK AT the front door just a few feet from where Lindsay stood. She looked through the peephole, expecting to see people with cameras and microphones. Standing on her mother's custom welcome mat were the county sheriff and two deputies.

"Morning, Miss Underwood," Sheriff Bradley said when she opened the door. "May I speak with your parents, please?"

She assumed it was something to do with Logan Walsh. "My father isn't home and Mom is giving an interview right now. Is there something I can do for you?"

"I'm afraid there isn't," said the sheriff. "I'll need to speak to your mother right away."

"Lindsay? Honey? Everything okay?" Beverly Underwood had stepped into the hallway to see what was happening.

"Ma'am, I have a warrant to search the premises." The sheriff held out a sheet of paper while his deputies moved forward into the house. The man kept a straight face, but there was no hiding the fact that he was enjoying his duties.

Lindsay's mother took the page and scanned it. "I don't understand. You're looking for books?"

"Yes, ma'am," the sheriff told her. "I think we're all aware by now that someone removed the books from Mrs. Lula Dean's library and replaced them with titles from the banned books list."

"And you honestly think it was *me*?" Her mother was still smiling. Lindsay could barely hear the conversation over the pounding of her own heart.

"You took the banned books that were removed from the town's libraries and stored them in your home, is that correct?" the sheriff asked.

"Yes, of course. They're still in my basement."

The sheriff gestured for his two men to head down to the basement. "The books have never been in anyone else's possession?"

"Not that I know of," Lindsay's mother said.

"Then you were the only one who could have swapped the titles."

Lindsay's mother stole a glance at her. The look lasted a split second, but it told Lindsay that her mom now knew exactly what had happened. "Even if I was, I don't know how that could possibly be a crime—"

The sheriff cut her off. "Mrs. Dean's library was on her property. The books inside were stolen."

"Stolen?" Lindsay's mom scoffed. "She left them there for people to borrow."

"But they weren't borrowed, ma'am. They were replaced with other titles. Whoever took them had no intention of ever bringing them back."

They heard the sound of footsteps coming up from the basement. The deputies appeared, their arms loaded with books.

"We got *Buffy Halliday Goes to Europe!*, *Chicken Soup for the Soul,* and *101 Cakes to Bake for Your Family,*" said one.

"We also found a bunch of dust jackets," said the other. "They're all from banned books that were removed from the libraries."

"Beverly? You need some help?" Betsy Wright was standing in the doorway to the living room. The reporter who was there for the interview was recording the encounter on his smartphone.

The sheriff kept his eyes focused on Lindsay's mother. "Mrs. Underwood, I'm going to need you to come down to the station."

"It was me." Lindsay finally stepped forward. "I was here a few weeks ago when the library opened. The very first night, I took the books out of Lula's library and switched them. My mother had nothing to do with it."

"That's not true!" Beverly argued. "My daughter is making it all up. I was the one who did it!"

Lindsay pointed at the dust jackets one of the deputies was holding. "Ask my mother to name three of the books that those jackets were taken from."

All eyes turned to Beverly Underwood, who'd clearly drawn a blank.

"Lindsay Underwood, you are under arrest for stealing Lula Dean's little library." The sheriff took Lindsay by the elbow and guided her toward the door.

"What are you talking about?" Beverly gasped. "This is insane!"

Lindsay was walked outside, where two patrol cars were waiting in the drive. Lula Dean watched from the sidewalk with a smug smile while her little white dog finished taking a poop on the Underwoods' lawn. When Winky stood up, Lula offered a little wave, then turned her back to the scene and sashayed away.

WHEN THE UNDERWOOD FAMILY RETURNED home from the station three hours later, they found a tall, scrawny young man in a Metallica T-shirt waiting for them on the front steps. He rose to his feet as Lindsay and her parents approached and took off his Piggly Wiggly hat. "Afternoon," he told Trip and Beverly. "You might not remember me. My name's Ronnie Childers."

"Of course we remember you," Lindsay's mother said, though her husband didn't look quite so certain. "We never forget Lindsay's friends."

"Are you the kid who made the fountain in Jackson Square spray blood?" Trip's eyes lit up momentarily. "That was clever. Wish I'd thought of it myself when I was twelve."

"Thank you, sir," Ronnie said. "I consider that my shining moment. Listen, I'm sorry for ambushing y'all. I just heard about the arrest, and I wanted to come offer my help."

"No!" Lindsay barked. Her cheeks were tearstained, her fingertips black with ink, and her record sullied. "Absolutely not."

She saw her parents exchange surprised looks. "That's very sweet, Ronnie," Beverly said. "But I'm not sure what you could do."

"I was there the night the books were switched," Ronnie said. "My fingerprints are all over them. I'm going to take responsibility."

"You most certainly are not!" Lindsay could have kicked him in the shin. "It was all my idea and you know it. I just hauled you along for the ride."

"I don't understand," Beverly told Ronnie. "Why on earth would you want to get yourself in trouble?"

Ronnie seemed surprised that anyone had to ask. "Because Lindsay has her whole life in front of her. Mine is already ruined."

"Ruined?" Trip asked.

"Yessir. Felony possession of a schedule-one substance," Ronnie informed him.

"Psychedelic mushrooms," Lindsay told her parents. "The same kind that are totally legal in Oregon." She turned back to Ronnie. "I thought we talked about this. Your life isn't ruined. You can go out west and learn how to help people."

Ronnie offered the kind of indulgent smile that's usually reserved for small children. "That was just talk. I can barely pay my rent as it is. I've been saving up for a PS5 for nine months and I'm still nowhere close. There's no way I could ever get to Oregon. I might as well plan a trip to Mars. But that's fine, because you're the one who's going to help people. My good deed will be helping *you*. So let me take the hit for the books. I doubt they'll give me much jail time at all."

For the first time in her existence, Lindsay found herself standing at the edge of despair. She recognized it at once as the deep, dark pit of hopelessness that had almost sucked Ronnie in. She knew there was no way out—and nowhere to go if she ever escaped. Lindsay had cried on the ride down to Troy and again in the police station. But now she broke down and sobbed for Ronnie and Logan and for all the other kids who'd fallen into traps towns like Troy always set for them.

Her father held Lindsay up while he guided her up the stairs and into the house.

"I'm so sorry, Ronnie," she heard her mother say. "Lindsay's having a rough time today. Please don't go to the police. Stop by the house tomorrow if you don't mind. We can talk about all this then."

CHAPTER 29

THE SOUTHERN BELLE'S
GUIDE TO ETIQUETTE

Bella Cummings had been stuck inside for almost a week. She couldn't even get out of bed without her mother acting like she was going to keel over and die.

"Good Lord, Mama, I'm fine!" she argued.

Her mother took Bella's head in her hands and stared pitifully into her eyes. "Baby, you suffered a terrible head injury. Your beautiful brains need time to heal."

"Bella, get back upstairs and get some rest before you give your mother a goddamned stroke!" her father shouted from somewhere in the house.

Bella's brains were the only part of her that hadn't got any rest. She'd been thinking nonstop. Since she was five years old, she'd been plotting her big escape from Troy. She planned to live someplace like San Francisco or New York when she wasn't traveling to far-flung locations. She'd take lots of lovers and turn down all their proposals. Somehow, she'd find a way to make gobs of money while simultaneously saving the world. At the end of the summer, Bella would take the first big step toward that goal. She'd be leaving Troy behind for Brown University in Rhode Island. It was a dream come true. But she didn't want to go.

Something had happened the evening of the rally. She hadn't told anyone about it because there was a good chance they'd just chalk it up to brain damage. But Bella swore she'd felt a powerful new presence in the square that night. According to *The Southern Belle's Guide to Etiquette,* which she kept under her pillow, the ancient god of Justice had been female. The Egyptians called her Maat. The Romans, Justitia. In Greece, she was known as Themis. And when Themis was not obeyed, Nemesis, the goddess of retribution, would show up to kick butt and take names. Bella liked to think that's what had happened. Justice had not been served. Now the woman who'd been wronged all those years earlier had come for Augustus Wainwright's legacy. It was her presence Bella had felt at the rally.

THE SPELL THAT HAD BROUGHT her back was simple. A few strands of DNA. A family Bible. And a collection of books that told the unvarnished truth. It was a spell that would work anywhere in America, and the justice it released could take down criminals who'd gone unpunished for centuries.

VOICES IN THE FOYER DOWNSTAIRS dragged her attention away. Just as she'd been doing since she was little, Bella tiptoed to the stairs to eavesdrop.

"I know y'all are worried about her." It was Wilma's voice. "That's why I brought Dr. Chokshi. If he doesn't give her a clean bill of health, we'll leave her in bed. But if she's good to go, I have use for her."

"But Meemaw—" Bella's dad began to argue.

"You're a grown-up now, hon. You can call me Wilma."

Bella stifled a laugh during the stunned pause that followed.

"Don't make me stand here all day," Wilma added. "It's an emergency, David."

"Okay then, Wilma." Bella's father had given in. "As long as the doctor says she's out of danger."

Bella raced back to her room with a smile on her face and waited for the knock on the door.

"Dr. Chokshi!" She feigned surprise when he stepped into the room.

"Hey, brawler," he said. "How you feeling?"

"Ready for another round," Bella told him.

She passed the neurological exam with flying colors. Dr. Chokshi said he'd never seen pupils dilate and constrict so perfectly.

"You satisfied?" Wilma asked Bella's parents.

"I suppose so," Bella's father said reluctantly.

"Then give me a moment with your girl if you don't mind."

Everyone else left the bedroom and Wilma closed the door. There was a twinkle in the older woman's eye and a spring in her step. Last time Bella had seen her great-grandma so fired up, Wilma had been piping fresh whipped cream into a penis cake.

"Did you know Lindsay Underwood was the one who switched all those books in Lula Dean's library?"

"I did," Bella confessed.

"Well, Lula pressed charges and Lindsay got arrested. Felony theft by taking. That girl did this town a world of good. Get some clothes on. The two of us are going to clear her name."

"I'LL TELL HER YOU'RE HERE to see her," Beverly Underwood said. "But Lindsay hasn't wanted to speak to anyone since it happened. I wouldn't have guessed getting arrested would be such a blow. I've never seen her like this before."

Bella opened her bag and pulled out a book. "Would you mind giving this back to her? Tell her I read it cover to cover, and she needs it more now than I do."

Beverly let out a snort when she lay eyes on the cover. "*The Southern Belle's Guide to Etiquette*? You're saying this belongs to Lindsay? I haven't seen one of these since I threw my mother's old copy in the fireplace when I was thirteen years old."

Wilma wagged a bony finger at Beverly. "That right there just got you my vote for mayor."

"We both know I had your vote anyway, Wilma." Beverly winked at her.

"It's Lindsay's favorite book," Bella told Beverly. "She loaned it to me. Can you tell her it made me the person I am today? Please?"

"Well, alright." Beverly seemed to be questioning Bella's sanity, but she was willing to give it a go. "I'll see what she says."

A few minutes later, Beverly returned down the stairs. "I don't know how you figured it out, Bella, but it seems like that book was the magic charm. Lindsay said to send the both of you up."

WHEN BELLA AND WILMA GOT to Lindsay's room, they found her sitting on the side of her bed wearing pajamas and slippers in three clashing shades of tartan. She had her hair tied in a knot on the top of her head, and black smudges of mascara beneath both eyes.

"Thank you for coming, Bella, but I'm not sure why you're here."

Bella gestured toward the woman beside her. "Lindsay Underwood, I want you to meet your new lawyer. This is Wilma Cummings, my great-grandma. She's a former DA and the best criminal defense attorney Georgia's ever seen. I'll be assisting her with your case."

"You know my dad is a lawyer, right?" Lindsay asked.

"And a good one," Wilma said, stepping forward. "But his specialty is environmental law. You need a defense attorney."

"I'm not planning to mount a defense," Lindsay said in a flat, monotone voice that didn't belong to the person Bella knew. "I did it. I'm guilty."

"Lindsay, you know *The Southern Belle's Guide to Etiquette* says you should never, ever waive your right to a lawyer," Bella reminded her.

"What you did does not merit a felony charge," Wilma added. "And believe me, sweetheart, you do not want a felony on your record."

"Well, I don't know how to avoid it. I'm not going to lie and say I didn't take Lula's books," Lindsay told her.

"You won't have to," Bella assured Lindsay. "Our goal is to make Lula Dean drop the charges."

NOW THAT THEY WERE OFFICIALLY on the case, Bella and Wilma reviewed the charges over coffee and pecan pie.

"Lula's saying Lindsay took twenty-six books valued at twenty dollars each, which puts the total just over the threshold for a felony charge." Wilma looked over her reading glasses. "Five hundred and twenty dollars' worth of books sound right to you?"

Bella nearly choked on her pie. "That woman has no shame. Those books weren't worth twenty dollars when they were brand new."

"Where's the nearest place to buy cheap books?" Wilma asked.

A quick internet search showed the closest thrift store that sold used books was a Goodwill in Macon. Bella was on the road by eleven and pulling into the Goodwill parking lot at twelve-thirty.

The woman behind the counter wasn't sure what to make of Bella at first. "You look awfully young for a private investigator."

"That's what they used to say about Nancy Drew, isn't it? And look how many cases *she* solved." Bella pulled out her phone and pulled up a picture of Lula Dean. "Do you recall seeing this person in your store?"

The woman leaned forward. "Oh sure." She'd only needed a split-second glance. "That's Lula. She used to be a regular. Always looking for dresses and such to turn into costumes for her kids. Hadn't seen her for years until she showed up a few weeks back and bought a bunch of books."

"Do you remember any of the titles?"

The woman's eyes rolled upward as though searching for the answer on the shop's ceiling tiles. "Well, there was *Chicken Soup for the Soul,* I remember that one. And there were a couple I thought we'd never get rid of. One about a girl going to Europe and one on crochet. Can't remember any of the rest off the top of my head. I reckon there were about two dozen in all."

"You happen to remember how much she paid?" Bella asked, though she figured it was a long shot.

"As a matter of fact I do 'cause she demanded a fifty percent discount. Said they smelled musty. I was just glad to get rid of 'em so I gave them to her for seven dollars and seventy-five cents."

"You're sure about that? Seven dollars and seventy-five cents?"

"Oh yes, I'm sure. Had to count it out myself. She paid in dimes, nickels, and pennies."

Outside in the dry, dusty parking lot with the sun beating down on her, Bella phoned Wilma. "I got a woman at a Goodwill in Macon says she sold Lula the books for the library. All of them together cost seven dollars and seventy-five cents. You can't have someone arrested for stealing something that's worth less than ten dollars."

Wilma cackled on the other end of the phone. "What are you talking about? Of course you can, darlin'. This is Georgia. But you just got the charge dropped down to a misdemeanor. And it might be embarrassing enough to make Lula drop the charges as well. I'll reach out to the sheriff's department."

WHEN BELLA GOT TO WILMA'S house, her great-grandmother greeted her at the door with a frown and a shake of her head. "No dice. We're not looking at a felony anymore, but Lula won't budge," she said.

"Can't say I'm surprised," Bella responded. "But I've got another idea I want to explore."

On the drive back from Macon, she'd been thinking about the rally— and the moments right before she'd gotten shoved off the stage. She remembered the Wright brothers unfurling their banner. A couple of reporters down below had called out questions. Then Lula had shouted, "Stop him!" She'd said *him*. Not *them*. Bella was sure of it. Something strange had been happening up on that stage.

Bella cracked open her laptop and searched for news footage of the rally. The professionals' cameras had all been aimed at the two boys and their banner. In each of the videos, Lula shouted, "Stop *him*!" But she hadn't even been facing the Wright boys at the time. *Who was she talking about?* Bella wondered. That was the million-dollar question.

She found the answer on Instagram. Mara Ocumma had posted a video she'd taken from the left side of the stage. You couldn't read the Wrights' banner, but it offered a clear view of Lula and her followers. Bella studied the film frame by frame and found the moment someone caught Lula's eye. The woman wasn't looking at Isaac or Elijah. She was staring in horror at Logan Walsh, who'd dropped to one knee. At first, Bella thought he might be tying a bootlace. But his fingers were on the cuff of his pants. Bella moved forward two frames and saw what she recognized as a gun strapped to Logan's ankle.

Her heart pounding, Bella pressed play. Mitch Sweeney barreled forward, blocking Logan's view of the Wright brothers. Mitch stumbled over a wire and rammed into her. Bella watched her own body fly out over the crowd. Then everyone surged to the front of the stage, and Logan Walsh disappeared in the chaos.

Bella sat back in shock. The Wright brothers could have died that day—and Lula had known all along. She had seen Logan's gun.

"She never called the police," Bella told her great-grandmother. "Logan Walsh could have killed Isaac and Elijah and that bitch didn't call the police."

Never once in her life had she seen Wilma struck speechless. It felt like minutes passed before her great-grandmother cleared her throat. "You were up on that stage, too."

And yet when Bella phoned their client to report their discovery, Lindsay didn't think it was useful.

"You think someone like Lula will ever fess up?" Lindsay sounded tired and resigned to her fate. "She'll just say she didn't see the gun. Doesn't seem like you can prove that she did."

They could try, but Bella knew Lindsay was right. "I don't understand. Why is Lula Dean out to get you?"

"It's not me she wants to destroy," Lindsay said. "It's my mother. She and Lula have hated each other since high school."

Bella grabbed a notebook. "Interesting." She readied her pen. "What's the source of the bad blood?"

"No clue," said Lindsay. "Whenever I ask, my mother just says it's not her story to tell. I know she looks like a sweet little thing, but when Beverly Underwood doesn't want to do something, there's no point in trying to make her. Listen, Bella, I really appreciate all the work you've done, but I'd rather just have this over with."

Bella nearly threw her pen across the room in frustration. "Lindsay, you're acting like you *want* to be punished!"

There was silence on the other end of the phone.

"Oh my God. You do! *Why?*" Bella demanded.

Lindsay sighed. "When Logan Walsh shot himself, there was a copy of *The Catcher in the Rye* on his desk. I think my prank may have given him the inspiration to kill your best friend and my mother."

For a while, they sat in silence on either end of the phone.

It was Bella who finally spoke. "Your mail been delivered yet?"

"What?"

"What time does your mail usually come?"

"Late afternoon? Round this time, usually. Why?"

"Make sure you're dressed. I'll be right over." Bella ended the call and set off across town.

"SHE'S IN HERE."

Bella guided Delvin Crump into the Underwoods' living room. Even at four o'clock, the shorts of his uniform remained perfectly pressed and his socks pulled up all the way to the knee. Sitting on her mama's couch, Lindsay could have been mistaken for a heap of dirty laundry.

"Hello, Mr. Crump." Lindsay stood to greet him.

Delvin Crump took in the girl's smeared mascara and unwashed hair. "Miss Underwood. I hear you're the one who switched out all the books. Were you the one who thought to wrap *Beloved* in the cover of *Our Confederate Heroes*?"

"Yes, sir," Lindsay said with a tremble in her voice. "I'm very sorry for what you saw at Logan Walsh's house."

"I am, too," Delvin said. "Bella tells me you think you're responsible."

Lindsay nodded. "*The Catcher in the Rye* was one of the books I left in Lula's library."

"And you think that book inspired Logan's actions."

Lindsay shrugged and sank down to the sofa. "I think there's a chance."

Delvin took a seat on a chair opposite Lindsay and leaned forward, elbows on his knees. "That was a troubled and tormented young man who'd been used and abused by terrible people all of his life. He had a house filled with weapons and a shooting range with Barack Obama's face pinned to one of the targets. And you think a *book* gave him the idea to kill people?"

Lindsay stayed quiet.

Delvin sat upright. "Sounds ridiculous when I put it that way, doesn't it? But I'm going to go one further for you and put an end to any uncertainty. What I'm about to tell you didn't make any of the news reports. I saw that book sitting on Logan Walsh's desk the day he died. I thought maybe I could use it to get him to open up to me, so I asked him about it. He hadn't read *The Catcher in the Rye*. He didn't know about Hinckley or Mark Chapman or anything else. He wanted to shoot people to prove to Nathan Dugan that he wasn't worthless."

"It wasn't the book that inspired him?"

"It's never the book," Delvin said. "You didn't have anything to do with Logan's life being lost. But I can tell you one thing for sure—you helped make mine joyful again. I'd lost faith in this town. I thought it was filled with people like Lula and Nathan Dugan. But you, Bella, and the Wright boys helped me see that there are plenty of good folks around here. They just haven't been shouting as loud as the others."

All three heads swiveled toward the foyer at the sound of the front door opening and closing. Seconds later, Beverly Underwood appeared in the living room with Ronnie Childers, still wearing his work apron and carrying two bags of groceries.

"Well, hello there," Beverly said, looking somewhat mystified. "Delvin. Bella. To what do we owe the pleasure?"

"They came to give me a pep talk," Lindsay explained.

"Ah." Beverly left it at that for the moment. "Well, look who I found at the Piggly Wiggly!"

"Hey," Ronnie offered awkwardly.

"Ronnie's joining us for dinner tonight and y'all are invited, too. The Wrights will be joining us at six."

"Thank you for the invitation, Beverly, but I got to finish up my route and get back to Wanda," Delvin said, slapping his thighs and lifting up off the chair. "But I'll see you all at the reunion on the third."

"That, you will!" Beverly saw Delvin to the door then came back to Bella. "What about you, honey?"

"I'd love to stay for dinner, Mrs. Underwood," Bella said. "If the Wrights are here, it will save me a trip. There are a few things I need to tell everyone."

"Wonderful!" Then Beverly shot a quick glance at Ronnie Childers. When she looked back at Bella, there was a glimmer of inspiration in her eyes. "You know what? Why don't you do me a favor, hon, and invite your grandma, Wilma, too?"

A FEW HOURS LATER, BELLA was still wondering what Beverly had up her sleeve when their hostess gave Ronnie Childers a spot next to Wilma at the dinner table.

"I think I found your next client, Wilma," Bella heard Beverly say.

"That right?" Wilma asked, her curiosity clearly piqued. "What'd they get you for, young man?"

"Felony possession of a schedule-one substance," Ronnie admitted.

"Oh my!" Betsy Wright, who was sitting close enough to overhear, sounded scandalized.

"Mushrooms." Lindsay's cheeks had regained some of their color, but she still wasn't quite right. "Can you believe that? The same mushrooms that grow in every cow pasture in Georgia. Schedule one—just like heroin."

Wilma shook her head. "Absolutely ridiculous. From what I've read, mushrooms have zero potential for abuse and plenty of recognized medical uses." Wilma patted Ronnie's arm. "Tell me all about it. Start from the beginning, and don't leave anything out."

For the next hour, everyone listened in. Over dessert, Wilma announced her conclusion. "Sounds like unlawful search and seizure to me," she said. "That sheriff is a menace and your public defender must be brain-dead. Come by my house tomorrow morning and we'll get started on your appeal."

The whole table had been so riveted by Ronnie's tale that it wasn't until after the pie plates had been cleared away that Bella had a chance to bring everyone up to speed on her discoveries. She wanted to get the worst bit out of the way first, so she started with what she'd seen on the video of the rally.

"Unfortunately, there's no way to prove that Lula knew Logan had a gun," Lindsay said.

"Maybe in a court of law, but I've seen enough to be sure." James Wright looked like he might explode. "I gave that woman weeks of my spare time, and she couldn't tell me that my sons were in danger?"

His wife reached over and took his hand. "I'm angry, too. But I don't think Lula hid that information on purpose," she said.

Everybody at the table turned their eyes to Betsy.

"I know Lula better than just about anyone," Betsy said. "That woman can't see past her own nose. She's so self-centered that it wouldn't have occurred to her that our boys were at risk. She would have been too busy thinking about her rally being ruined."

"My wife worked with Lula for fifteen years," James explained. "I should have listened when she told me to keep my distance."

"That's right!" Beverly exclaimed. "I forgot Lula used to work at Fairview Florist!"

"So what do you suppose we should do, Mrs. Wright?" Bella asked. "What's the best way to get Lula to drop the charges against Lindsay?"

"Easy," Betsy said with complete confidence. "You want to put an end to Lula's nonsense, you need to find her children."

"That might not be as easy as it sounds," Lindsay said. "I was friendly with Taylor and Talia in school. As far as I know, they haven't been in touch with anyone here since they left."

"I built all the sets for their shows at school." Ronnie spoke up. "I bet I know who can find them. Want me to send a note to Mr. Minter?"

CHAPTER 30

FIFTY SHADES OF GREY

Since Lindsay Underwood's name had appeared at the top of the sheriff's office list of arrests, the people of Troy had been eagerly speculating about what might happen the following Sunday. Would Beverly and Lula both attend services at First Baptist Church? If so, would their showdown take place before the sermon, after the sermon, or (as some clearly hoped) *during* the sermon? If it came to blows (an unlikely outcome but one that could not be dismissed entirely), who would prevail, Lula or Beverly? And—most important—whose side would Jesus take?

When the day finally arrived, the church pews were packed. Beverly Underwood and her family sat in the third row on the right, as always. Some folks started to wonder if Beverly had even been privy to any of the talk around town. Not only was her gorgeous dress not suited for brawling, she didn't appear nervous at all, despite the fact that Lula had two inches and at least thirty pounds on her.

"Bet she's got rocks in her pocketbook," fifteen-year-old Billy Larkin said, pantomiming Lula receiving a wallop upside the head.

"Beverly's tougher than she looks," his mother responded. "If her high kick is half as good as it was back in high school, she won't need to cheat."

Most folks agreed that Lindsay did not seem like the kind of girl who'd steal books for no reason. "I heard she's covering for Ronnie Childers," said Alvin Jones. "By the way—we know for sure she's a lesbian?"

"You're gross," said his sister, who did, indeed, know for certain.

Then Lula arrived, silencing the whispers. All but three sets of eyes followed her from the doors to a spot on the left side of row six, just off the aisle. She wore her orange hair twisted into a tight chignon. Her dress was a flowy layer of peach chiffon over coral silk. Her open-toe shoes were a tasteful nude with kitten heels.

"Smart to wear a tear-away layer," noted ten-year-old Wayne Hodgins, who'd been watching the WWE all morning. "But she better kick off those shoes or she's gonna get whupped."

The preacher stepped up to the pulpit and surveyed his flock. He may have been a man of God, but he wasn't hard of hearing. He'd heard the talk in town, and as always, he'd prepared a sermon custom-tailored to his parishioners' spiritual needs. The morning's theme was "Love Thy Neighbor." It was one of the finest sermons he'd ever delivered, but the preacher wasn't sure anyone heard a word. He felt like a commercial break in the middle of the most riveting drama ever aired on television. Everyone seemed to be counting the minutes until it was over.

WHEN THE WORSHIP SERVICE CONCLUDED, Lula filed out with the rest of the congregation. Beverly exited the church a minute later to find Lula Dean waiting for her on the stairs—along with everyone else. Beverly paid them no mind as she headed down to the street. Waiting below on the sidewalk were two impeccably dressed figures, one short, blond, and rosy-cheeked, the other much taller and veiled. The smaller of the two held a stack of books.

"Must be nice not to care what folks think."

Beverly stopped and turned to face Lula. "I'm sorry. Do you have something you'd like to say to me?"

"Why, yes, I do." Lula not only held her ground, she took a step forward. "Your daughter is a common criminal, and she has no business showing her face in church."

Lindsay started to say something, but her mother held up a finger. Trip Underwood took his daughter by the arm and pulled her back. After two decades of marriage, he knew better than to step into the line of fire.

"I'm surprised a member of the Concerned Parents Committee has a problem with me bringing my daughter to church," Beverly replied. "Isn't that where you'd want her to be?"

Lula ignored the question and turned to face her audience. "It's just like Beverly to go and ruin Sunday worship, isn't it?" she asked the crowd. "First she lets her child destroy my sweet little library. Then she fights to keep filth in our schools. And now she's working with those people to destroy our monuments and insult our heroes. I'm asking y'all—is there anything too low for Beverly Underwood?"

"Well, I wouldn't have a young woman thrown in jail for taking seven dollars' worth of Goodwill books that I passed off as my personal collection," Beverly said.

Beverly's sangfroid seemed to make Lula Dean's blood boil. "So you're okay with her filling my little library with pornography and propaganda? Why are you even running for mayor, Beverly?" she demanded. "It's clear that you hate this town."

"This is ridiculous," Beverly said. "None of the books you banned contain propaganda or pornography. You took them out of the libraries because they told truths people like you and Nathan Dugan don't want told. But I have faith in the people of Troy. I think we are good enough to see where our ancestors went wrong. And we're strong enough to take responsibility for our forefathers' mistakes and make damn sure we never repeat them."

Lula turned to the crowd once again. "What is this woman on about?" she asked. "She's not talking about *slavery,* is she? How many times do we need to have our noses rubbed in that? You think any of us are going to forget slavery was bad? You worried we're gonna slip up someday and start slapping shackles on people?"

"This town's troubles didn't end with slavery. We have to be honest about that."

Lula sighed theatrically. "Dear Lord, I think the woke virus has eaten poor Beverly's brain."

Beverly responded with a knowing smile. "There's still enough of my brain left to remember that your daddy owned a mill that employed half the Black people in Troy. He made his employees work in unsafe conditions and paid them a fraction of what they were owed. The irony is, if he'd treated people fairly, your family might still own the mill. You act like it was stolen out from under you. But the government took it away because your father was a crook."

Lula reared back like she'd been smacked in the face. "How dare you!" she seethed. "My father was just following the accepted practices of his day. He did those people a favor by hiring them. Without him, they would have starved."

"That's true," Beverly conceded. "Those folks wouldn't have been exploited at the Lambert mill if they could have gotten jobs anywhere else in town. Your family isn't the only one that bears responsibility for the way Black citizens were treated."

"Well, look at them now. We've got Black business owners and Black valedictorians. You can't even get a government job in this town if you're white."

"We also have a Confederate general, slaver, and rapist standing in front of our county courthouse—and a group of 'concerned parents' taking books about Black history and slavery out of our schools. What's all that about, anyway?" Beverly asked.

Lula pointed down at two kids, who instantly turned tail and disappeared into the crowd. "The children of Troy do not need to grow up feeling bad about things in the past they had nothing to do with."

"Nobody's saying they're personally responsible. But what's wrong with feeling bad? Isn't that what makes us all try to do better? You worried the next generation might want to improve things around here? Who knows—maybe they'll make sure all people are treated equally and allowed to pursue happiness with those they love. Lord have mercy, wouldn't that be awful? Heaven forbid!"

The crowd knew the gloves were coming off the second they saw Lula's sneer. "You see where she's going with this, don't you?" she asked them. "She starts off talking about slavery and ends up pushing the gay agenda. That's what Beverly Underwood's really after. She wants to shove her daughter's perverted lifestyle down our families' throats."

It felt like the whole town went silent while they all waited for Beverly's response. But Beverly's attention had turned to the dainty blond in an elegant baby-blue dress who'd just climbed the steps to join them.

"Mrs. Underwood." The blond shook Beverly's hand, then waved at someone in the crowd. "Hey, Ronnie!" Then her smile fell as she turned to Lula with a frown. "Oh my, Mama. *Perverted lifestyle*? That was a low blow."

"Talia?" Lula's expression shifted from joy to terror. "What are you doing here, sweetheart?"

Talia leaned forward and gave her mother a peck on the cheek. "I'm real sorry but we're here to stop you before you can cause any more trouble."

"Talia, why don't we—"

Talia had already faced the crowd. "Hey, everyone! My name is Talia Dean. Lula Dean is my mother, and I love her. But you should know she's a world-class hypocrite."

"Talia, please—" Lula was begging.

"I read about Lula's little library and her book banning club. I thought y'all might be interested in seeing what kind of books she had around when her own children were growing up. So I stopped by her house on the way here and gathered a few. I read this one when I was ten." Talia held up a worn copy of *Fifty Shades of Grey*. "Didn't understand a word, but Mama sure spent a lot of time reading it in the bathtub."

There were titters from the crowd.

"I brought a few of her other favorites, too. *Deep Desires. Beyond Shame.*

Pleasure Unbound. Taken by the T-Rex. Satisfying Sasquatch. All the stuff Lula thinks you shouldn't be reading she keeps right on her nightstand. You wouldn't believe what she stores *inside* the nightstand. And she never bothered to keep any of it out of reach of her children. But you know what? Didn't harm us in the slightest. It was the other stuff she did—"

Talia was interrupted by the sound of someone clearing their throat. Everyone turned to see the tall, thin figure in a black fifties-style dress and veil coming up the steps.

"Oops. Looks like Taylor wants to tell this part of the story. Y'all remember my sibling, don't you?"

"Wasn't Taylor a dude?" someone in the crowd whispered a little too loudly.

"A dude? Like a *cowboy*?" Taylor asked. "Oh please. Could a *dude* do this?" Taylor spun around Linda Carter–style. The black dress flared out and then flew away. When she came to a stop, Moxie was wearing a blue spandex uniform with a giant white *M* in the center and thigh-high red boots. She pulled off the hat and veil, revealing a stunning face, gleaming diadem, and lustrous shoulder-length dark curls. The crowd gasped in unison. Kari Kelly clapped with sheer glee and a few others followed suit.

"Ladies and gentlemen, I give you Moxie Laguerre!" Talia cried. "Georgia's favorite drag queen!"

A man nearby couldn't seem to close his mouth, so Moxie placed an elegant finger under his chin and shut it for him. "Buckle up, buttercup, I've got more tricks than that tucked away," Moxie said with a saucy wink. "Sorry it took us so long to get here. We had a governor to deal with down in Florida. Now, gather round, children of all ages! Today's your lucky day! It's drag queen story time!"

A woman pulled her child closer.

"Don't worry," Talia assured her. "This will be family friendly. As y'all will see shortly, *we're* not the ones who hurt children."

"Oh no!" Moxie agreed wholeheartedly. "As a matter of fact, my story today is about two plucky children who triumph against the forces of evil."

"Forces of evil?" Talia repeated. "Come on. Mama's not *that* bad."

"What do you say we leave that up to our audience?" Moxie proposed. Then she clapped her hands together. "Y'all ready?"

They were *so* ready. You could see it. Never before had there been an audience so eager.

"Okay, once upon a time, there was a pair of twins, Taylor and Talia. They lived in a little town with their mother and father, whom they loved very much. Then one day, their daddy died of natural causes. Their mother needed a distraction from her grief and from all the mean things folks in this town were saying about her husband's untimely demise. So she turned to her children. She decided her little girl would be a beauty queen and her little boy would be a famous actor. She signed them up for every kiddie pageant and play in Georgia. And she absolutely loved it! The end." Moxie clapped her hands and smiled broadly.

Talia tapped her shoulder. "Wait, Moxie. How did her children feel about it all?"

Moxie waved off the question. "Oh, *them*? They hated it."

"Why?" Talia pressed.

"Because," Moxie said with a huff, "you did not enjoy being onstage. You did not like fancy dresses and you felt like you were smothering with all that makeup on your face. But no matter how desperately you pleaded, the show always had to go on."

"It was torture," Talia said. "What about you, Taylor?"

"Well, see now, I was the one who wanted to wear the dresses. And when I was twelve, I told my mother."

"And what did Mama say about that?" Talia asked.

"She called me a pervert. Said people in town already treated her like a leper, and she didn't need me giving them something else to gossip about."

Talia winced. "That must have hurt pretty bad," she said.

For a second Moxie broke character. "It did. You know how many twelve-year-old perverts there are in the world, Talia?"

"How many?"

"Exactly *none*," Moxie said, staring straight at Lula. "There are no twelve-year-old perverts. Not a single one. But it took me a few years to figure that out. Then when I was in high school, I met a wonderful teacher who helped me see that there was nothing dirty or depraved about wearing makeup and dresses. It was just *fun*. So I decided I wasn't going to give up my passion so my mom could have the kind of son that *she* wanted."

"Meanwhile," Talia added, "I got tired of pretending to be a beauty queen. So I decided to stop."

Moxie rubbed her hands together eagerly. "I'm sensing an act of rebellion is coming up, Talia."

"That's right, Moxie. And it was *spectacular*. Would you like to tell them?"

"Yes, thank you! Well, one day when we were in our teens, my sister and I decided to switch places. I entered a beauty pageant in Florida under her name. I sang 'The Greatest Love of All' for my talent. And I won. First place. At the end of the show, right after the tiara had been placed on my head, I ripped off my wig and revealed my true identity. It brought down the house, and the entire family was banned from the Florida pageant circuit for life."

"Oh my!" Talia exclaimed. "What did Mama do?"

"She marched up to the high school and accused Mr. Minter, the musical director, of being behind it all. She told him if he didn't stop what he was doing, she'd tell everyone about his *proclivities*."

"That's blackmail!" Talia cried. "Did it work?"

"Not on Mr. Minter. He didn't have anything to do with the beauty pageant. We got the idea from *Victor/Victoria*. But Mama's threat worked on us. We did what she wanted until we turned eighteen and graduated from high school. Then we hit the road."

"I've seen people say on Facebook that we ran away."

Moxie's diadem gleamed as she shook her head from side to side. "Nope," she said. "Despite everything, we still loved our mother. We always planned to come back to see her. But then she went and lost her damn mind."

Talia took a deep breath. "Oh dear. What did she do?"

"She came to one of my first performances in Atlanta, but she was too chicken to go into the club. She must have been sitting outside in the parking lot when she saw Mr. Minter coming out. He was only there to support me, but Lula was so envious that she decided to destroy him."

Talia's eyes went wide. "Ooh, you were right, Moxie. That *is* pretty evil."

"Told you so. Lula started a whisper campaign against the man who'd once saved her son. Made Mr. Minter's life a living hell, from what I've heard. All because she was jealous." Moxie looked around at the crowd. "I sure hope none of y'all got hoodwinked by Mama's lies. I'd hate to think any of you good people played a role in running an innocent man out of town."

Half the crowd looked down at their shoes.

"I didn't think I could ever forgive her after that," Talia admitted.

"Me, either," said Moxie. Then she paused as though confused. "So why did we?"

"Because Mr. Minter called and asked us to."

Several gasps could be heard in the audience.

"You're saying the gay man Lula Dean set out to destroy wants her children to forgive her?" Moxie asked.

"Yep, he told us that people can learn from their mistakes, and we should give Lula a chance to redeem herself."

"What do y'all think?" Moxie asked the crowd. "Should we forgive her?"

"Yes, yes!" cried Kari Kelly. The response from the rest of the crowd was half-hearted at best.

"I was just trying to be a good mother." Lula finally spoke up in her own defense.

"Y'all want to know how to tell if you've been a good parent?" Moxie asked the crowd. "It's real easy. If you have a family that loves each other and children who want to spend time with you, then you've been a good parent."

Talia shook her head at Lula. "Sorry, Mama. Guess that means you failed," she said. "But thanks to Mr. Minter, Taylor and I are willing to give you one more chance."

"But first all this nonsense needs to come to an end," Moxie insisted. "Disband the book committee, bow out of the mayor's race, drop all the charges against Lindsay Underwood, recognize my fabulousness, and never ever utter another homophobic or racist word again."

"Those are our conditions," Talia said. "Either you accept them or we leave right now and you never see either of us again."

"What do you say, Mama?" Moxie asked.

There was a long pause while everyone waited for Lula's answer. For years to come, folks in Troy would wonder if it was Lula's love for her children or the dogeared copy of *Taken by a T-Rex*, which was making its way through the crowd, that finally inspired her to admit defeat.

"Fine," she agreed. "Let's head on home. Y'all want some pie?"

"Lord, no," Talia said. "We've been punished enough."

CHAPTER 31

BATTLING THE BIG LIE

C an we get your names, please?"

"I'm Ken Kelly."

"And I'm Kari Kelly." She giggled. "We are such big fans of yours! We watch you every night!"

"Thank you so much," said Chad Hunter, reporter for the Kellys' favorite news channel. "And thank you for letting us use the video you posted to Instagram."

"It was fun, wasn't it?" Kari said.

"*So* fun," Chad agreed. "You two about ready? I'm just going to record a couple of lines and then ask a few simple questions. Shouldn't take more than a minute or two."

"Ask away!" Ken said.

"Alright then." Chad looked at the camera guy. "You good? Okay, let's do this."

Ken and Kari couldn't have been more thrilled.

"Hi, Brett. I'm here in Troy, Georgia, where citizens received two unwelcome guests after church this past Sunday."

"Oh, I wouldn't say they were *unwelcome*," Kari chimed in. "Unexpected, maybe."

Chad was not amused. "Okay, let's take it again from the top." He shook his head and the annoyance fell from his face. "Hi, Brett. I'm here in Troy, Georgia, where citizens received two unexpected guests after church this past Sunday. I'm standing here with Ken and Kari Kelly, who filmed the bizarre incident." Chad stopped and stood perfectly still for three seconds. "That's where we'll edit in your footage. Ready for the questions?"

"Absolutely!" said Ken.

"What did you make of the performance you witnessed?" Chad asked.

"Oh, it was very impressive," Kari said. "The way Moxie twirled into a whole new outfit!"

"Totally amazing," Ken agreed.

"You know Talia does all the makeup and designs all the costumes? I can't believe the talent on those children! Of course they were always like that—even back in grade school."

"I found the whole thing so inspirational," Ken added. "I got a little teary-eyed watching the Dean kids make up with their mama. Made me think it's time for us to reach out to our son. We've been arguing lately, and—" He had to bite his lower lip before he started blubbering.

"We love you, Keith!" Kari called out, blowing kisses into the camera.

"Your town has been going through some tough times lately, hasn't it?" Chad asked. "It's only been a week since Logan Walsh's suicide. Now there are reports coming out that he may have pulled a gun at a rally?"

The mood turned dark at once. "That was terrible," Ken said.

"And terrifying!" Kari added.

"Something like that happening in a beautiful place like this. Makes you wonder what the world is coming to."

"That kind of thing is not who we are," Kari said. "We're all good, wholesome folks round here."

THAT EVENING, KEN AND KARI raced to the living room and settled into their recliners for the show.

Liberals chuckle when we warn that drag queens are coming for your children. But residents of one small Georgia town have learned the hard way that it's no laughing matter. Let's go to Chad Hunter, who was on the scene earlier today.

"Hi, Brett. I'm here in Troy, Georgia, where citizens received two unwelcome guests after church this past Sunday."

The video cut to Moxie Laguerre calling out to the crowd in Jackson Square.

"Gather round, children of all ages! Today's your lucky day! It's drag queen story time!"

Two drag queens took over the town square, determined to read erotica to the town's children.

The video cut first to Talia holding up a copy of *Fifty Shades of Grey* and then to a woman pulling her child closer.

"I'm standing here with Ken and Kari Kelly, who filmed the bizarre incident. What did you make of the performance you witnessed?"

"That was terrible," Ken said.

"And terrifying!"

"Something like that happening in a beautiful place like this. Makes you wonder what the world is coming to."

"That kind of thing is not who we are," Kari said. "We're all good, wholesome folks round here."

Ken lowered the volume and looked over at his wife, who hadn't eaten a kernel of the popcorn clenched in her fist.

"What the hell just happened?" he asked.

"I don't know, Papa," Kari told him. "But I think we're fake news."

266

CHAPTER 32

THE HEROES OF TROY

ahla Crump!" Betsy Wright called out from her shop door.

The skinny twelve-year-old stopped typing into her phone and ducked behind a Volkswagen.

Mrs. Wright's laugh made Nahla think of apple pie bubbling up through its crust. "I saw you peeping in through my window just now," she said. "Thought maybe you were bored and could use a job."

Nahla stepped out from behind the car. People thought she was shy 'cause she didn't say much. Nahla was not shy in the slightest. When she wanted to be seen, she showed herself. When she had something to say, she said it. "How much does it pay?" she asked.

Betsy Wright seemed to approve of that response. "Five dollars and a red velvet cupcake."

"Three cupcakes," Nahla haggled. "No dollars."

"Only have two cupcakes left. It's been a busy day, and your father took one when he stopped by with the mail this morning."

"Two is fine." Whatever the job was, Nahla would have done it for one. "My dad says your cupcakes are the best he's ever eaten."

"Your daddy ain't wrong," Mrs. Wright said. "Come on in for a moment."

Nahla kept a straight face, but inside, she was beaming. Two cupcakes *and* a chance to check out Fairview Florist? Days didn't get any better than this.

Nahla was eight the first time she visited the shop with her mother. As soon as she left, she constructed a replica in her mind. Whenever Nahla was bored, she'd pay the florist a visit and spend a few hours crafting bouquets like the ones Mrs. Wright made. As soon as she was old enough to wander through Troy on her own, the flowers called to her like sirens. But they weren't the reason she'd been lurking around outside the florist that afternoon. Nahla was investigating. She needed details for the story she was writing about Betsy Wright.

It had been a while since Nahla had been inside the florist's shop, and she was delighted to find it exactly as she remembered. The air inside was cool and layered with fragrance. She picked up top notes of rose, eucalyptus, and lily. Dozens of other scents blended together into a magical perfume. A refrigerated case lined one wall of the shop, and behind its glass doors lay Eden. Lush ferns and flowers of every imaginable color. Clouds of hydrangeas and fluffy pink pillows of peonies. Giant monstera leaves pressed against the windows and vines probed the crevices.

The walls of the shop had been painted a rich forest green. On the white marble counter, Betsy Wright's latest creation was taking shape. It wasn't even half done, but it was already a wonder to behold. Nahla caught a whiff of the giant white magnolias, and they pulled her to them with a heavenly scent.

"How old are you now, Nahla?" she heard Mrs. Wright ask. "Last time I saw you, you dressed up for Halloween like a mini Black Panther princess with your hair in Bantu knots."

"I turned twelve in May."

"You're going to look just like your mama when she was in high school. You know there were boys who'd drive all the way from Alabama just to come watch her cheer?"

Nahla shrugged and continued to examine the arrangement. Besides the flowers, there were saw briars, wild strawberries, moss, and an empty wasp nest. "Being pretty's overrated."

"Is that right?" The way Mrs. Wright said it made Nahla wonder if she'd passed some kind of test. "Then what would you rather be?"

"A force to be reckoned with." She'd once heard her father refer to her mother that way. He'd said it with such awe and respect that Nahla had decided right then and there to follow in her mama's footsteps.

Mrs. Wright chuckled. "Well, you got that in your blood, too." Everyone in Troy knew her mother basically ran the whole courthouse. Nobody dared mess with Wanda Crump.

"Who's this bouquet for?" Nahla asked.

"Bernice Hutton," Mrs. Wright said. "You know her?"

"Nope," said Nahla.

"Well, this is a special commission. Her gentleman friend wants a bouquet that will take her back to the days when they first fell in love."

Nahla turned to face her host. "How is it going to do *that*?" she asked.

"Sam told me a story about their first walk in the woods together. I'm translating his tale into flowers. And that's where you come in." She reached down below the counter and pulled out a wicker basket. "I need you to run over to Jackson Square and gather some supplies for me."

"Supplies?" Nahla asked.

"Leaves, acorns, fallen branches. Don't pick living things. Just grab anything interesting you find on the ground," Mrs. Wright told her. "I'll know what will work when I see it."

IT WAS JUNE FIRST. SCHOOL had just let out for the summer, and kids from all over Troy were making their way to the town pool, beach towels thrown over their shoulders and flip-flops slapping their heels. Nahla shouted hey to a group of girls from her class, but she didn't stop to chat. She'd been given a job, which she took very seriously. When she got to the square, she found the fountain had vanished beneath a tower of glistening soap bubbles. She took a few seconds to admire the prank and then got down to business. There were only so many hours in the day. She wanted to finish her task, watch Mrs. Wright work her magic, and start writing her book all before dinner.

Nahla had come up with the idea for her project in the last week of seventh grade. With summer around the corner, the other kids had been going stir-crazy, but Nahla stuck to her routine. Every day after school, she headed straight for the library, turned in any books she'd finished, and checked out enough to replenish the stack she kept on the nightstand next to her bed. She considered it a terrible omen if the pile ever stood less than three books tall.

With fresh reading material tucked under her arm, she walked to Grandma Martin's house, where there were always freshly baked cookies waiting on the stove. In previous years, her older sister, Jasmine, would have been there, too. But Jasmine was a vegan now and had to keep a safe distance from Grandma's cookies.

"Grandma puts lard in everything," Jasmine told Nahla.

"Good," Nahla said. That just left more treats for her.

She'd eaten at least five cookies the day her epiphany arrived. She was seated at her grandma's kitchen table with a book from a series called The Heroes of Troy open in front of her. Fifty pages in, she slammed the book shut in disgust.

"Something wrong?" Grandma Martin looked up from the sink, where she'd been peeling Yukon Golds to go in her award-winning (and decidedly non-vegan) potato salad.

Nahla held up the book cover for her grandmother to see. "Did you know there was another place called Troy?"

"Mmm-hmm," her grandmother said. "It's the setting for one of the most famous stories of all time. As I recall, it's chock-full of gods and heroes and blood and guts. I would have thought all that would be right up your street."

"Me, too!" Nahla agreed wholeheartedly. "But none of the heroes are girls. Couple of the goddesses. But none of the heroes. Not a single one. Can you believe it?"

Her grandmother wiped her hands on her apron. "I'm gonna let you in on a little secret, sugar. Ain't none of them Black, either."

Nahla sat back in a huff with her arms folded across her chest.

"You really going to get bent out of shape over all that?" Grandma Martin lifted an eyebrow. "Those stories were written by Greek men for other

270

Greek men. We have heroes, too, you know. Difference between ours and theirs is our heroes are real."

Nahla perked up and slid to the edge of her seat. "What's the name of *our* book?" There might be time to run back to the library before she went home.

"Truth is, most of our stories have never been written. But they're out there—tons of them—just waiting for someone to put them down on a page. Maybe you could be the one."

Nahla felt her flesh tingle. "Who are the heroes? Where can I find them?"

"They're all over," her grandmother told her.

"Here in Troy?" Nahla asked.

"Absolutely. Our world isn't all that different from ancient Greece in some ways. We have our big-name goddesses who live up high on the mountain. Those would be your Serena Williamses, Michelle Obamas, and your Beyoncés. Then there are the demigoddesses who walk among the mortals. I'm thinking Stacey Abrams. But even in little towns like Troy, there are heroes all around us, working wonders every day and just waiting for their stories to be told."

"Like who?" Nahla was suddenly skeptical. She couldn't think of anyone in Troy who was capable of working any wonders.

"You don't think your mama has ever fought the forces of evil?"

Nahla shook her head. Her mother was one of a kind. "*Besides* Mama."

"What about your sister? She's working her rump off to save all those whales."

"And getting nowhere." Nahla shook her head again. "A real hero should be clever like Odysseus or invincible like Achilles."

"Invincible?" Grandma Martin pointed at Nahla's book. "You need to finish reading. But listen—why are you letting a bunch of old Greek men tell you what a hero ought to be? They'll have you thinking you got to go to war and kill people to prove yourself. Women have always known better than that. Most of us get what we want without slaughtering anyone. In fact, now that I think of it, the best hero story I ever heard was all about flowers."

"Flowers?" Nahla asked. She had a hunch where the tale was headed.

THERE WAS A REASON TROY had so many Black girl heroes, Nahla's grandmother informed her. "Round these parts, you had to be strong to survive. If you were a woman, didn't hurt to be a genius, too. So every generation got stronger—until it started to become clear that the powers that be couldn't hold us back anymore. That was about the time that Betsy Wright decided she deserved her own shop."

As far as Nahla knew, Betsy Wright had always owned Fairview Florist. But her grandma set her straight. Betsy had spent her first fifteen years out of high school working for a man named Homer Johnson. (At the time, Troy was home to three Homers, two Hectors, a Nestor, and an Ajax.) Like most people, Homer wasn't particularly bad or good. He paid a fair wage and he never got mean or did anything nasty. But he believed in doing things the way they'd always been done. As a florist, he was partial to red roses, pink carnations, and yellow chrysanthemums. As a person, he believed in a world where everyone had their place. White men were meant to lead the way. Black women got to pick up after everyone else. That was the natural order of things, according to Homer Johnson.

Betsy knew that was the order in Troy, too. But there wasn't a damn thing natural about it. *She* was the reason Fairview Florist was thriving. Her ready-made bouquets outsold Mr. Johnson's three to one. There were customers who made a point of coming in on his off days, just so they could be sure Betsy was the one who'd handle their flowers. And she was the one who'd convinced Mr. Johnson to order the new varieties that had proven so popular. In the spring and summertime, she even got up early to pick her own wildflowers.

So when Homer Johnson decided to retire, it seemed perfectly logical that Betsy would buy the business. She and her husband lived frugally, and they had enough saved for a down payment. But they couldn't afford to buy the business outright. They needed a loan from a bank.

Betsy Wright tried all three banks in the county. Only Wachovia would grant her an appointment. The new president, Corey Pruitt, had been quarterback of the football team when she was in high school—and she'd been the tutor responsible for making sure he passed math. When Betsy arrived at the bank, he greeted her warmly at the door. She felt like a VIP when he'd ushered her past all his employees and back to his office.

She'd come prepared with a business plan, a portfolio, updated logos, and sketches of the renovated interior. She laid the documents out on the desk and Corey made a show of looking them over, though he didn't pick any up.

"This is all very impressive," he told her. "I'm sure the next owner will be more than happy to keep you on."

"You're not going to read my materials?"

"I don't need to read anything to know a loan's just too risky. Customer retention could be a serious problem. The people who bought from old Homer might not buy from you."

Because she was Black. That part went without saying.

Betsy stood there, stunned. "I don't understand," she said. "Why would you even see me if you knew you weren't going to help me?"

He looked at her as though it should have been obvious. "For old times' sake!" he said warmly. "It's been fun to catch up!"

IT JUST SO HAPPENED THAT Lula Dean stopped by the shop that afternoon with her twins in tow and found Betsy weeping.

"So you're just gonna take no for an answer?" Lula asked when she heard what had happened.

"What else am I going to do?" Betsy asked.

"Fight like hell!" Lula said. "You knew Corey back in the day, didn't you? Don't you have any dirt you could use?"

"No, and even if I did, I wouldn't resort to blackmail."

Lula shook her head at Betsy's scruples. "That's ridiculous. You know what I'd do? I'd call Angela McGee, the Pruitts' housekeeper. I bet she knows a thing or two you could use."

It was just like Lula to assume all Black women in Troy were friends. Betsy and Angela had never been close. Fortunately, they *were* second cousins. And as it turned out, Angie *did* know a thing or two.

That evening, Betsy had James make the boys dinner while she worked late at the shop. By midnight, she'd completed three bouquets. First thing in the morning, she sent them all out by messenger.

The first bouquet arrived at the home of Pamela Pruitt, Corey Pruitt's mother. Betsy knew from listening to Lula's gossip that Pam had grown up on a horse farm near Newnan. Though she'd married a wealthy man, she'd never been accepted into the rich ladies club. Which appeared to be perfectly fine with Pam. Betsy used every last wildflower she had in Pam Pruitt's bouquet. It was as untamed and colorful as the woman herself. And Betsy made sure the entire arrangement could be fed to a horse.

The second bouquet was delivered to Maisie Pruitt, Corey's devoted wife. Betsy found photos of their wedding on Maisie's Facebook page. She built a stunning arrangement using the same orchids and freesia Maisie had chosen for her bridal bouquet, the white honeysuckle that had decorated the pews in the church, and the purple hydrangeas from the centerpieces at the wedding reception.

The last bouquet arrived later that day at a house in Macon—an address Angela McGee had found on a delivery slip she pulled out of Corey Pruitt's pants before they went in for cleaning. He'd sent a pair of diamond earrings. Betsy chose a dozen bloodred roses. It was completely clichéd—but so was having an affair with your bank's stationery supplier.

None of the bouquets bore a note—just a tag stamped with Fairview Florist's new logo.

The next morning, Betsy got a call from a woman at Wachovia informing her that her business loan had been approved. By the end of the week, the papers were all signed. Fairview Florist was finally hers.

———

"SO MR. PRUITT WAS CHEATING on his wife?" Nahla had asked.

"Maybe I should have started with a G-rated story," her grandmother said.

"*Please.* I'm twelve," Nahla reminded her. "You think I don't know how the world works? I'm just glad Mrs. Wright got the loan she deserved."

"Not only did she get her loan, she also got a contract to supply all the floral arrangements for the bank. Maisie Pruitt made sure she was hired for every fancy wedding in town. And Pam Pruitt is still her best customer."

"*Genius,*" Nahla marveled.

"I'd say Betsy is every bit as clever as Odysseus, wouldn't you?"

"How did she know what to do?" Nahla wanted to know.

Her grandmother shook her head. "Why don't you ask her?"

NAHLA RETURNED TO FAIRVIEW FLORIST with a basketful of beauty. Freshly fallen magnolia leaves, perfectly round acorns, and scarlet magnolia seeds.

"How do you decide what to use?" Nahla asked as Betsy sorted through the basket, picking out all the things she might need.

"I think of every bouquet as a little story," Betsy told her, "and stories are the most powerful things in this world. They can mend broken hearts, bring back good memories, and make people fall in love."

"Or convince them to do the right thing," Nahla added.

Betsy Wright shot Nahla a look. "Sometimes. But the trick is getting to know people well enough to tell their stories. You can't just assume you know what they're like. You have to pay attention. You got to watch and listen."

"I can do that," Nahla said.

"So you think you might grow up to be a florist?" Betsy Wright asked her.

"Maybe. But I'm going to be a writer, too," Nahla told her. "In fact, I'm already working on my very first book."

CHAPTER 33

HUMANKIND

don't know about y'all, but I'm real nervous." Beverly's eyes followed the checkered tablecloth that seemed to go on for miles. There were four kinds of potato salad, a mountain of fried chicken, platters of pulled pork, heaps of hush puppies, and all the other delicacies of the region, along with homemade modak courtesy of Dr. Hank Chokshi. In the center of every picnic table was an arrangement of wildflowers that Betsy Wright had gathered in the fields where the Avalon plantation once stood. "What if no one comes?"

"What if no one comes?" Elijah looked so handsome in his church clothes. You'd never guess that he'd been setting up tables since five in the morning. "Everybody in town is already here!"

He was right. The whole town of Troy had turned out early to help get Jackson Square ready for the Wright-Wainwright family reunion.

"She's talking about cousins," Isaac said as his mother straightened his bow tie.

"Doesn't matter to me if anyone comes," Betsy Wright said. "This day has already been a success in my eyes." She finished fixing her son's tie and nudged her husband. "You got something you wanted to say, James?"

James Wright straightened his spine and cleared his throat. "Yes, I do. Before everyone heads off to help, there's something I need to tell my two boys." Isaac and Elijah stood at attention as their father prepared to address them. "I want you to know that I couldn't have asked for better sons. The two of you are so different, and yet you're both exactly what I always hoped for. Smart, brave, and resilient. You've made me very proud over the past few weeks, and you've given me great hope for the future. I'm very sorry if I ever made you feel like you weren't the finest human beings this world has to offer."

"Does this mean you're okay with me being gay?" Isaac asked.

"I want you to be you," his father said. "I wouldn't change a single thing."

Isaac smiled as he took in his father's words. "Thank you," he said, laying a hand on the older man's shoulder. "That means a lot to me."

"We should thank Lindsay, too," Elijah said.

"*Lindsay?*" James asked.

"My Lindsay?" Beverly looked around at the Wrights, but no one seemed to know what Elijah was talking about. "What does she have to do with any of this?"

"Lindsay switched the books in Lula's library, right? That's where I found *Rivals and Lovers*. When I read it, I knew gay dudes don't go to hell, so I made Mama read it, too, and—"

"You made Mama read that bougie boy romance?" Isaac burst out laughing and couldn't seem to stop.

"Yeah, that's how much we love you, bro," Elijah told him. "I swear, I've never read anything more boring in my entire life."

"Me either," Betsy admitted. "All they did was drink wine and have babies."

"Drink wine and have babies!" Isaac roared, tears streaming down his cheeks.

"Now I feel like I'm missing out," James said. "Maybe I should read it, too."

Isaac laughed even louder and Elijah joined in. "Noooooooo!"

Betsy squeezed her husband's arm. "I don't think it's for you, baby," she told him.

When he finally caught his breath, Isaac planted a kiss on his mother's cheek. "I'm really touched that y'all did that for me."

"We're family," Betsy told him. "There's nothing the four of us can't overcome together. Now let's prove it and go get that damn statue pulled down!"

"Amen to that," said James.

As the Wrights headed off in separate directions, Beverly grabbed the youngest son's arm. "Elijah, you mind giving me a hand for a second?" she asked.

Beverly had just seen Wilma and Bella pull up—very slowly—to the curb. Bella hopped out and opened the back of her SUV. Inside was the seven-tier cake that Wilma had promised as her contribution to the cook-out. Elijah froze at the sight of Bella in a strapless yellow sundress.

"What's the matter?" Beverly asked when she saw his stricken expression.

"She's heading up north for college soon," Elijah said.

"Maybe, but I have a hunch she'll be back," Beverly told him. "Now go show off your muscles and help her carry that cake."

"Alright," Elijah replied with a grin.

"I do hope this cake's G-rated," Beverly joked as she approached the vehicle. "I've heard what Wilma can do with some coconut shavings and whipped cream."

"Don't worry, I made her keep it clean," Bella said.

"Just plain old chocolate with strawberry frosting," said Wilma. "But come on over for the Fourth of July. I got something planned that'll knock your socks off."

"Where'd you get the idea to bake a giant phallus for your birthday, anyway?" asked Beverly.

"You don't know?" Wilma snickered. "Your delinquent daughter put that dirty cake book in Lula Dean's library. Honestly, I can't thank Lindsay enough. It kept me out of the old person's home and made my eighty-fifth birthday one to remember."

"I think you more than paid her back," Beverly said. "I've been meaning to let you know how grateful I am—for everything you two did for Lindsay and for all the help you've given Ronnie Childers. He's such a sweet boy. Did I tell you he was planning to confess to taking Lula's books just to get Lindsay out of trouble?"

"I'm not surprised," Bella said. "Lindsay's changed a lot of lives and earned a lot of goodwill. I wouldn't be the person I am today if she hadn't given me *The Southern Belle's Guide to Etiquette*."

Beverly's brow furrowed. "See, I still don't understand why you keep talking about that horrible guide like it's the greatest book ever written. Is there something I'm missing?"

"It definitely taught *me* a thing or two," Wilma said. "It's got some pictures of lady parts in there that you just got to see for yourself."

Bella cracked up at the sight of Beverly's utter confusion. "It was one of Lindsay's jokes. She put the etiquette guide's jacket on *A Girl's Guide to the Revolution*. That's the book I've been reading."

Elijah came around the back of the vehicle carrying a giant pink cake. "Lindsay's like the town's fairy godmother," he said.

"She's got me inspired, that's for sure," Bella said as Elijah passed by with the cake. "I'm wondering if Troy might be the place I can do the most good. I think I'm gonna take a little time off and see if I can find a school closer to home."

"Oh, I do like the sound of that," Beverly told her. She didn't need to see Elijah's face to know how big his smile was.

"Hey there. Y'all mind if I borrow Ms. Underwood?"

Beverly spun around when she heard the familiar voice. "Darlene!"

The 1996 Troy High School cheerleading squad had reassembled for the first time in twenty years. When Darlene Honeywell pulled Beverly into a hug, Yvette, Wanda, and Val rushed over to join them.

"When did you roll up?" Val asked Darlene.

"Just now." Darlene pointed across the square where Matt and the girls were unloading the car. "I wanted to get here early so I could congratulate the next mayor of Troy."

"Let's not count any chickens," Beverly chided her. "We still have to make it through an election."

"What are you talking about?" Wanda Crump stepped into the conversation. "Lula took off for Atlanta! And you know as well as the rest of us that she ain't coming back after what happened at church. As soon as people saw that T-Rex book, it was over. You won!"

"I still can't believe justice is finally being served," Val said. "First Randy gets the boot, now Augustus. Never thought I'd see the day. And all because of two of the bravest ladies I know."

"You know what, Val, you just reminded me of something," Beverly said. "Darlene, you said your girls gave you the book that inspired you to tell your story. Where did they find it?"

"Lula Dean's library, if you can believe it," Darlene said. "Wrapped in the jacket of that old Nancy Drew book *The Clue in the Diary*."

Wanda grabbed hold of Beverly's shoulder. "What'd I tell you! Y'all thought I was crazy! It was that library making all this stuff happen!"

"Oh *hell*," said Yvette.

Beverly found herself unable to speak.

"I don't get it. What am I missing?" Darlene asked.

"Lindsay took all of Lula's silly-ass books and replaced them with books the committee had banned," Yvette told her. "When the truth came out, Lula even had her arrested—said Lindsay stole the books instead of borrowing them."

Darlene clapped a hand over her mouth. "Lula came to her senses and dropped the charges, I hope?"

"Oh yes," said Val. "And after the party, I'll tell you *why*. It's a heartwarming story with an audiovisual component that's gonna blow your damn mind."

Darlene looked all around the square. "Where is Miss Lindsay?" she asked.

"I sent her and Ronnie Childers to the Piggly Wiggly to pick up more paper plates." Feeling flustered, Beverly fanned herself with her hand. "I got to admit, Darlene, I'm a little choked up by what you just told me. I had no idea Lindsay's prank played a role in your decision."

"Wasn't just Darlene. Lindsay helped Delvin, too." Wanda pointed at her husband, who was happily chatting with Jeb Sweeney as they filled coolers with bottles of water. "You couldn't have lured that man out of the house for nothing this spring. Then he found that library, and suddenly he was Mr. Outgoing. Now look at him with his brand-new bestie. That's a beautiful bromance blooming right there."

"I imagine saving a town together would make you friends for life." Val turned to Wanda with a smirk. "That mean you have to spend time with the movie star?"

"Mitch ain't *that* bad," Wanda tried to tell them. Then she gave up. "Okay, fine. He's a moron. But he's heading back to LA next week."

A whole new can of worms had popped open in Beverly's mind. "Speaking of Mitch, anyone know where he is?" she asked.

"He was stealing hush puppies last I saw," Val said.

Beverly spotted his bald head across the square. He was already scanning the entrances for early arrivals. "Y'all excuse me for a moment. I need to have a word with our favorite movie star."

It was sweet that Mitch was so eager to help with the reunion, but Beverly was a little worried that being met first thing by a giant movie star with a reputation for saying questionable things might be a little much for some folks.

"Beverly, you got a second?" Crystal Moore caught her just as she passed the fountain.

"Hey there, Crystal, thank you so much for coming!" She turned her attention to the gentleman by her side. "Is this the new friend you've been telling me about?"

Crystal beamed. "It is," she confirmed.

The man smiled nervously and held out a hand. "Jonathan Bartlett. I'm a teacher up at the high school, and I'm the one who wrote that Facebook post about Lula Dean's library."

"Oh, that was *so* funny," Beverly said. "I still laugh just thinking about it."

"Thank you. But I know it ended up getting Lindsay in trouble, and I just wanted to apologize."

Beverly dismissed his concerns with a shake of her head. "That had nothing to do with you," she assured him. "Don't waste another thought on it."

"We both feel particularly bad," Crystal chimed in, "because it was books she put in that library that brought the two of us together."

"You don't say," Beverly replied. It was starting to get a bit freaky. "Which books, if you don't mind my asking?"

"*Gender Queer* and *All Women Are Witches.*"

There was no doubt who was responsible for those two classics ending up on Lula's shelves. "Yep, that was definitely my girl," she said.

Just then, Beverly caught sight of her daughter and Ronnie coming back from the store, their arms laden with bags. After Lindsay had been arrested, Beverly tried to plead her case with the sheriff. Her daughter was still so young, she'd reminded him, and it had all been a prank. There was nothing truly dangerous in that little library, or else they would have charged Lindsay with endangerment, too. Nobody had been harmed in the slightest. It had all been a joke.

But that's the thing about jokes, Beverly realized. The fact that they're funny doesn't make them any less serious. Lindsay's little prank had started a chain reaction. The books she'd put in that library had opened eyes, granted courage, and exposed terrible crimes. That's why they were dangerous—why so many people had wanted to hide them. Lindsay had known all along what they could do.

"Beverly?"

She was pulled from her reverie by the sound of Melody Sykes's voice. Beverly wasn't surprised to see the former mayor's wife. She'd personally called to invite her. "Melody, I am so happy you could come."

"Thank you for having me." Melody looked nervous so Beverly laid a hand on her arm.

"Of course! Where are your boys? I hope you brought them. They won't want to miss out on Wilma's cake."

"They're with Mara at the library. She'll bring them over in a few minutes. But I was hoping you might be able to do me a favor before they get here."

"I'll certainly try," Beverly told her. "What do you need?"

Melody took in a breath and seemed to summon her courage. "I'd like you to introduce me to Darlene Honeywell. Randy's never going to apologize, so I figured I should step forward and do it."

"I'd be glad to, Melody. Can I come find you in a couple of minutes? I got a few things I need to take care of first."

"Of course! And would you please tell Lindsay that Beau loved *Are You There God? It's Me, Margaret?*"

"I'll pass that along."

Beverly stepped up on a bench by the fountain.

"Can I get everyone's attention for a moment? It's coming up on noon," she called out. "I want to thank all of you for coming out to help today. Isaac Wright has a few things to say when the day kicks off. But before we start, I was hoping to see a quick show of hands. You all know about Lula Dean's library—that my daughter was the one who switched the books. If you don't know her, that's Lindsay standing over there by the plates."

Lindsay, who'd been unloading boxes of utensils, spun around at the sound of her name and offered a little wave at the people who were now staring at her. Since her chat with Delvin Crump, she'd been getting out of bed in the morning. But she still hadn't quite recovered her old spirit.

"How many of y'all found a book in that library that meant something to you?" Beverly asked the crowd.

Half the hands in the square rose. Beverly's heart swelled. She'd never been more proud of her daughter.

"If you don't mind, would you stop by and let Lindsay know how it made a difference?"

Beverly saw Mr. Stempel making a beeline for her daughter and wondered which book it was that he'd found. Bernice and Sam were right behind him. Crystal and Jonathan. The entire Wright family. Delvin and Jeb. Ken, Kari, and Keith Kelly. She had no idea Lindsay had touched so many lives.

BEVERLY WAS ABOUT TO GO join them when she saw the first reunion guests arrive—a lovely woman in a lemon-colored dress and long braids, looking slightly lost. Mitch Sweeney, acting as official greeter, met her at the curb.

"Welcome to the Wright-Wainwright reunion," he said, offering a meaty arm.

The woman stared up at the giant, her eyes wide. Beverly was hurrying to the rescue when the woman let out a girlish squeal.

"Are you Mitch Sweeney?" she gushed, grabbing hold of him. "I absolutely *loved* you as Roy."

CHAPTER 34

THE GREATEST STORY EVER TOLD

Jeb Sweeney touched his thumb to the biometric lock and quietly pulled his pistol from the safe. It was three-twelve in the morning, and someone was in his house. He'd gotten a few nasty messages on Facebook since the incident at Logan Walsh's house. Nothing that would have worried him a few months back, but now he knew to take trolls more seriously. He crept down the stairs in his bare feet and boxers, fully expecting to come face-to-face with Nathan Dugan or someone just like him.

Instead, he found a giant man in tighty-whities rooting through his kitchen cabinets.

"What the fuck, Mitch." Jeb put the gun down. "You run outta toilet paper or something?"

When Mitch was a teenager, their parents had built him a room with en suite facilities above the garage. Even back then, he'd spent most of his time at the main house. Mitch's room had everything he needed but an audience.

"I'm making coffee. I couldn't sleep. I'm too inspired."

"And you didn't think to put any clothes on before you came over? My wife's upstairs."

Mitch looked down at himself. "What? I got underwear on. Besides, Jenny and I ain't got no secrets." He winked at Jeb.

"You know shit like that is why you keep getting sued." He grabbed a robe from the back of the bathroom door and handed it to his brother.

"Here. Lemme." Jeb nudged Mitch to one side and pulled a can of coffee down from the cupboard.

"Don't you want to know what I'm working on?" Mitch asked.

"That's *exactly* why I came down here with a gun at three o'clock in the morning—to hear about your latest project."

While Jeb scooped coffee into a filter, Mitch sat down at the kitchen table, where a spiral notebook lay open. "I'm sensing some sarcasm, but I'm gonna choose to ignore it. You know how I've been waiting for someone to offer me a role where I play the hero for once?"

After a few seconds, Jeb realized Mitch was waiting for an answer. "Yeah?"

"I'm gonna write a screenplay for myself. Something with a happy ending. Everybody's so fucking angry these days. I wanna see a bunch of people coming together to fix a bad situation instead of bitching and moaning all the fucking time."

"So you want to write about what happened today," Jeb said.

Mitch's jaw dropped like Jeb had just read his mind. "How'd you know?" he asked.

"Wild guess," Jeb told him as he filled the coffeemaker with water.

"I'm telling you. This is the role that's gonna win me an Oscar," Mitch told him. "It's about a guy who gets his DNA done and he finds out he's the descendant of this terrible motherfucker from history who everyone thinks is a hero."

Jeb hit brew and turned around. "Hold up. Are you playing the DNA guy?"

"Of course," Mitch said.

"In this movie, is the hero Black?"

"Well, he's mixed, obviously—"

"Mitch, you cannot play a Black guy."

"Why not?" Mitch asked. "I know it'll be a stretch, but that's how you win awards. Playing gay. Pulling a Christian Bale and getting real fat or real thin. That kind of stuff. The Academy loves it."

Jeb lowered his head and massaged his temples. It was too fucking early for a conversation like this. "Black actors play Black roles. The end. No discussion."

"See?" The chair screeched as Mitch pushed back from the table and folded his beefy arms across his chest. "This shit is so unfair. White men like me can't catch a fucking break these days."

"Mitch?" Mitch was sulking. "Mitch? Look up." Jeb waited until their eyes met. "You are an international movie star, and this is your screenplay. If you want to be in it, write a fucking role for a white guy."

"You think I could make Beverly Underwood a man?" Mitch sounded hopeful.

"Absolutely not," said Jeb.

"Well, shit!" Mitch said. "Who am I supposed to be, then?"

"In this story? Seems to me like you've got three choices. You can play the international movie star who comes to town—"

"That's not a stretch!"

"You could play his brother."

"Fuck that. I'm way too handsome."

Jeb laughed. "Or you could play a Confederate general."

"Another goddamned bad guy," Mitch grumbled.

"But there is one upside. They'd have to create a statue of you for the role. Bet you could take it home when you're done. Something like that might look pretty sweet in your backyard."

"Oh, *hell* yeah." Mitch instantly perked up. "I always wanted a statue."

"I'm sure you did, bubba," Jeb told him.

"You know what? This is great." Freshly inspired, Mitch picked up his pen.

"But before you start, you better reach out to Beverly and the Wrights if you want to tell their story."

Mitch groaned. "What?"

"I know." Jeb patted his brother on the shoulder. "It's a bitch giving people their due. But I promise—you'll get used to it. In time, doing the right thing may even start to come naturally." He poured a cup of coffee and set it down on the table in front of Mitch. "I'm going back to sleep. You wake me up again and I'm gonna come down shooting."

"Hey, before you go, I got something for you." Mitch pulled a document from the back of the spiral notebook and handed it to his brother.

"What is it?" Jeb asked. "I don't have my glasses."

"It's your fucking due," Mitch said. "The house is all yours. All you gotta do is sign."

"You're kidding."

"I'm not a real villain," Mitch said. "I just play them on TV."

CHAPTER 35

HAPPY ENDING

hear I have some big shoes to fill," said Dr. Bamba.

"Oh yes," confirmed Georgia's 2034 Realtor of the Year. Melody loved the chitchat. It was the best part of having her own real estate agency. Talking to folks from other places had given her a lot to think about over the years. "Dr. Chokshi was beloved round here. We sure hate to see him go. But we're absolutely thrilled you're taking over his practice."

"Thank you. Where is Dr. Chokshi going, if you don't mind my asking?"

"Back to Queens—that's in New York City, you know. His parents are getting older, and he wanted to be near them. But we did hold on to him for ten years. Sent him back with a nice Georgia girl, too." Melody slowed the car and pulled to the curb. "Oh no," she said when the doctor reached for her seat belt. "We're not at the listing yet. I just wanted to point out a few of Troy's highlights. That right over there is our new heritage museum. We're real proud of it."

"The big white mansion with the columns?"

"Yes, ma'am. I mean, *Doctor*. One of our finest citizens left the house to the town in her will. Now her great-granddaughter oversees the museum. It tells the story of all the peoples who built Troy and the Muscogee village that came before it. I thought I knew a lot about our history, but every time I go there, I learn something new. A lot of it's tough for people to hear, but it's important, you know? It's like finding out you were born with a health condition. Maybe you didn't do anything to deserve it. But if you ignore it, nothing's going to get better. You gotta look at the problem before you can fix it."

Melody took her foot off the brake and guided the car back onto the road.

"The mayor mentioned there's an educational fund?"

"Yep, Bella oversees that as well. Her great-grandma, Wilma, was a wealthy woman. Before she died, Ms. Cummings established a fund that would help put all the kids round here through school. They get a bonus if they come back to Troy when they're done. Oh, look over there. That's our library."

"*That's* the town library?" A beautiful modern structure sat between a 1980s-era bank and the local post office. It looked less like civic architecture than a temple to books.

"Yes, well, we had an unfortunate incident a while back. I only bring it up so you won't be surprised when you hear. There was a young man in town who got involved with some nefarious types. He was plotting a massacre when two local heroes stopped him. He ended up shooting himself."

"Oh no!"

"Yes, it was a terrible time. He'd gotten a lot of bad ideas in his head. So, after that, we wanted to make sure people here always have access to the best information. The young man had inherited a fortune and he had no living kin. When the state eventually took the money, the governor directed it be used to help stop the spread of disinformation and hate. And that's how the library got built."

"Was that Governor Underwood?"

"Yes, we're proud to say Beverly Underwood is one of our own. As is our congressional representative, Isaac Wright. He's one of the youngest members of the House of Representatives. I personally think he'll be president someday."

Dr. Bamba watched the picturesque buildings on Main Street scroll by as Melody continued the tour.

"They're relatives, are they not?" she asked. "I remember seeing an interview with the two of them."

"Distant cousins," said Melody. "But the Wright-Wainwright families are very close. They hold a big reunion in our town square every summer.

People come from around the country, and everyone in Troy is invited. That's where it takes place, right over there."

"That's a beautiful statue in the square." Dr. Bamba gazed at the bronze image of a woman of African descent, clothed in a simple dress, her hair tucked beneath a scarf. In one hand she held a set of scales, in the other a sword. She appeared in motion, one foot in front of the other, her skirt rippling in the wind. Her face was a portrait of determination and courage. Her eyes were wide open and looking forward.

"We had a statue of a Confederate general standing there for a long time. He's in the museum now. Part of the Hall of Shame, as some folks call it. Mitch Sweeney, the international movie star, personally paid for the statue to be removed and replaced."

"Didn't Sweeney win an Oscar for playing a Confederate general?"

"Same general. Augustus Wainwright. Mitch spared no expense when we chose the sculptor. We had a town vote to see who would replace the general. As I recall, there was one vote for Little Richard, one vote for Mitch Sweeney, and all the rest went to the lady right there in front of our courthouse."

"Who is she?" Dr. Bamba asked.

"We don't know her name. She was the start of the Wright family line, and the Wrights have tried everything they can to find out who she was. But we know it was her descendants who helped us all see the truth. So we just call her *Justice*."

Melody continued a couple blocks before she slowed and pointed out the window at a building on Main Street.

"Look at that, they've got the sign up!"

"*Healing Journeys*?"

"Beverly Underwood's daughter and her friend Ronnie Childers are opening a therapeutic-psilocybin clinic. They already have a bunch out west, but this will be the first one since Georgia legalized psychedelic mushrooms. We're expecting the clinic to bring a lot of business to the town. Believe it or not, those little fungi can work wonders. Once my kids were off to college, I went out to Oregon and dealt with some terrible stuff I'd never been able to process."

"Psilocybin can be very effective," Dr. Bamba said. "I'm glad Georgia's seen the light."

"Amen to that," said Melody Sykes.

The tour came to an end in front of a pretty house with a white picket fence. Melody pulled over and put the car in park.

"Alright now, here's the property. As you can see, it's very centrally located. And the exterior is one of the best examples of Victorian architecture in the South."

"It's gorgeous! I can't believe it's been on the market so long," Dr. Bamba exclaimed. "And at such a reasonable price!"

"Well, when you get inside, you'll see why. The interior isn't to everyone's liking. You ever heard of Moxie Laguerre?"

"Of course!" Dr. Bamba lit up. "I love her show. And her sister's so talented."

"Well, it's their mama's house, and let's just say those apples didn't fall too far from that tree. Lula's living up in Atlanta with her children now. That's why they're selling the house. But the place is a little over the top, to say the least."

"That's not a problem. I've been looking forward to doing some interior decorating."

"Well, who knows, this might just be the place for you! But there is one thing I need to mention. There's something on the property that is very important to the town of Troy. If you buy the house, we're willing to move it, but we're real big on heritage and history here, and we'd be thrilled if the next owner allowed it to stay."

"What is it?" the doctor asked.

"Come over here and I'll show you," Melody said.

"*Lula's Little Library*?" Dr. Bamba read, and opened the door and trailed a finger across the spines until it came to a stop at a little book that appeared to be hand-bound. The title had faded, but she could decipher *The Heroes of Troy, Georgia by Nahla Crump.*

"Help yourself," Melody told her. "You'll be one of us soon."

MY LITTLE FREE LIBRARY
OF BANNED BOOKS

grew up in a small town in rural North Carolina and no matter where I live, I will always consider myself a Southerner. My complicated relationship with the South is something I think about every day. There is so much to love about the Southeastern states—and so much that hurts my soul. But I want to make it perfectly clear that the issues addressed in this novel—book banning, white nationalism, anti-Semitism, etc.—are by no means unique to the South. These are *American* problems. Pretending they only occur in the South has allowed them to flourish unchecked elsewhere in the United States.

My childhood in the South couldn't have been more idyllic. Looking back, I realize just how fortunate I was. My family never faced prejudice for our beliefs, our background, or the color of our skin. We weren't rich, but we had enough of everything. Perhaps my greatest stroke of luck, however, was the parents I was blessed with. My mother and father had both traveled extensively and lived among other peoples. Before they started their own business, my parents were teachers. My father was a lifelong lover of history. My mother was a passionate defender of underdogs who relished nothing more than a righteous cause. In short, my parents knew the truth and they were determined to pass it along to their children.

I grew up with many kids who shared the same advantage. Contrary to popular belief, the rural South is home to countless principled, well-informed people. But I also knew kids who were far less fortunate. Some simply had no access to the truth and grew up in a vacuum that would eventually be filled with disinformation and conspiracies. A tiny but notable minority were fed a diet of hatred and lies from an early age. My heart breaks for those kids. How can you come to know what's right when all the information you're ever given is wrong?

The fact that I grew up being told the truth did not make me superior to those children. It made me *luckier*. Some of the people I admire most today are those who did not share my privilege. Denied the truth, they were forced to educate themselves. Think of the determination that took. Consider the *time*. How on earth did they manage to do it? The answer is simple: *books*. Even now in the digital age, the written word remains the bedrock of all learning. Books and the libraries that house them are among our most precious resources. As we all know, these days, they are both under threat.

I suspect most of the book banners we read about are opportunists who see a chance to grab attention and power. The *Tampa Bay Times* published an investigative piece in August 2023 that showed that hundreds of the complaints made against books in Florida schools were lodged by the same two people. Though I had already written most of this book by then, that revelation confirmed that Lula Dean wasn't just a figment of my imagination.

But I fear there are more sinister elements at work behind the scenes. They know keeping people scared and ignorant is an effective means of controlling them. Removing books about the Holocaust makes it easier to use Jewish people as scapegoats. Banning works on the subject of slavery prevents conversations about what we owe the people this country so grievously injured. Convincing parents that novels featuring LGBTQ+ heroes can turn their kids gay will distract them from the fact that American children keep dying from gun violence and our schools are woefully underfunded.

In early 2023, my brilliant editor (and fellow Southerner) Rachel Kahan visited Texas, where book banning has become all too common, and saw neighborhood activists pushing back on the bans. When she returned to work, she sent me a question. *What do you think about a novel featuring a little free library filled with banned books?* After her note, I couldn't *stop* thinking about it. I spent hours pondering the books I'd choose. My imaginary little free library is at the heart of this novel. Most of the books mentioned are real. A few are made up and some are mentioned only for comic effect. The ones I recommend most are listed below. Those with an asterisk have been banned in parts of the United States. You'll find no pornography. No communist propaganda. Just the truth.

Beloved by Toni Morrison
Anne Frank: The Diary of a Young Girl by Anne Frank
Maus by Art Spiegelman
The Hemingses of Monticello* by Annette Gordon-Reed
How the Word Is Passed by Clint Smith
Speak by Laurie Halse Anderson
Are You There God? It's Me, Margaret by Judy Blume
All Boys Aren't Blue by George M. Johnson
Gender Queer by Maia Kobabe
All That She Carried by Tiya Miles
The Handmaid's Tale by Margaret Atwood
Nickel and Dimed by Barbara Ehrenreich
Battling the Big Lie by Dan Pfeiffer
Humankind by Rutger Bregman

With regard to the long-lost cousins featured in this novel: the advances in DNA technology and genealogy I've described are very real. As I write, *The Lost Family* by Libby Copeland is one of the few books available on the subject. I encourage everyone to explore your own family history. If you're an American, this new technology may change your understanding of our country's history.

And finally: *A Girl's Guide to the Revolution* does not exist—but it should. I hope one of you will write it.

Kirsten Miller

ACKNOWLEDGMENTS

This book would not exist were it not for my editor, Rachel Kahan. She provided the first spark of inspiration, fanned the flames as the book took form, and added a lick of gasoline here and there as the mood struck. I am forever in her debt.

I would not be writing today were it not for my agent, the incomparable Suzanne Gluck, who has championed all my best ideas and swiftly killed the crappy ones for the past two decades.

Over those same twenty years, Steven Daly has been the first to read every one of my books. I couldn't ask for a finer editor or better sounding board. It doesn't hurt that he laughs at my jokes.

My eternal gratitude to the librarians in Sylva, North Carolina. The public library was the Miller kids' second home throughout the 1980s. My passions and interests can all be traced back to books, movies, computer games, and music I discovered there.

A big shout-out to my always entertaining siblings and siblings-in-law. (Guess which one of y'all inspired the Sweeney family dialogue and the feral hog jokes.)

And finally, this book is a loving tribute to my childhood best friend, Erica Waldrop. For years, Erica fought like hell to have the Confederate statue in our hometown removed. When she died tragically in 2021, I promised myself I would do whatever I could to keep up the fight. I hope I've done you proud, Erica.

**Turn the page for an exclusive extract
from Kirsten Miller's brand-new
empowering feminist novel**

The Women of Wild Hill

*It's always three, isn't it? Three furies, three fates, three
graces. Science still has no explanation for the number
three, but women instinctively feel its power. We don't
know why three works, but we know it does. Three is
the number that gets the job done.*

**Blending witchcraft, magic, and family legacy,
The Women of Wild Hill is a modern-day
novel about witches and sisterhood that will
make everyone believe the power to change
the world is in their hands.**

BLOOD

*E*very morning when I was a wee girl, women would come knocking at our cottage door. They came to see my mother, who was known far and wide for her tonics and potions. In the iron cauldron over our fire, she would cook up whatever was needed. A remedy for persistent fever, a salve for bothersome rash. If she deemed her guest trustworthy, she might fashion a philter to entice a reluctant suitor, a draught that could empty the womb, or a poison to rid the woman's house of a troublesome pest.

Even as a child, I knew what could happen to women like my mother. Her very own sister had been put to death by order of the king. When it came time to begin my training, my mother told me what made us different. A powerful elixir flowed through our veins. By then, I knew blood was essential for life to flourish. Spill too much and death would follow. My mother pricked her finger and showed me the drop. Inside were thousands of years of our family history, she told me. It held our treasures and secrets and fatal flaws. All of it was passed from mother to infant, in an exchange so perilous it often proved fatal. But if the child lived, it would inherit a unique set of gifts. If it were a girl, she would learn our ways.

I wanted nothing more than to follow in my mother's footsteps. But she knew from the moment I was born that I was meant for something different. My gifts would carry me far away, to a land we hardly knew existed, to place called Wild Hill. The Old One had chosen me for a special mission. I was to watch over six generations of Duncans—and wait for the bloodline to produce the most powerful of our kind.

QUEEN OF THE DARK

Brigid Laguerre was halfway to drunk and all the way stoned. When she was working, she never dabbled. The business required every ounce of her focus. But on her few idle days, she liked to maintain a state of inebriation. If her mind was free to wander, it was prone to go places she didn't want it to go.

At the moment, it was captivated by the ripples on the swimming pool. They shifted direction whenever the devil winds changed course, the water seeking a way out of the box that trapped it. She needed another drink to maintain her buzz, but she couldn't bear to slide her legs off the chaise lounge or leave the shade of her umbrella. The walk to the wet bar might be short, but the sun felt fierce. She briefly regretted giving her staff the day off. Then she remembered the mood she'd woken up to. There were days when it was dangerous for her to be near another living soul. This was definitely one of them.

Brigid's foul moods usually came with obvious causes, but the previous day had been a delight. Production had wrapped on her latest movie. She and her favorite lover had eaten excellent tacos from a roadside stand and enjoyed some of the raunchiest sex of her life. Then she'd gone to sleep all alone, just the way she liked. Nine hours later, she opened her eyes to find herself stuck in a very dark place. She could only hope it was due to a shift in her hormones or a nightmare she couldn't recall. She didn't want to consider the other options.

Brigid reached out for the joint she'd left on the side table. The lighter was already in her other hand. Before the two had a chance to meet, she caught a whiff of smoke in the air. She pulled off her sunglasses and squinted through the sunshine at the mountains that surrounded the valley. Four decades earlier, when her mother first pinned her fire map to their wall, California wildfire season had lasted a few months of the year. Now, entire communities went up in flames every day. *They've been building homes where the Old One doesn't want them* she could hear Aunt Ivy say. And while there was a great deal of truth in that statement, according to the news, most of the latest fires had been arson.

Brigid could see no sign of smoke in the sky and the stench didn't linger. Satisfied that her house wasn't in danger, she lit her joint, just as the phone wedged under her right butt check vibrated with an alert. She picked it up, certain she'd put the goddamn thing on do not disturb mode. The day was determined to fuck with her vibe.

Calum Geddes dead at 75.

Brigid stared at the phone. Out of hundreds of texts and notifications, somehow that one had made it past her defenses. If that was what the universe was desperate to tell her, it could have saved its energy. Brigid scrolled through her other notifications.

Meet the Queen of the Dark's latest lover!
Toxic plume envelops Salt Lake City
Tornado touches down outside Manhattan
Queen of the Dark gets her groove back in Jamaica!

Brigid tucked the phone under her butt cheek and slid her sunglasses back on. Was she supposed to give a fuck that Calum Geddes was dead? If so, maybe someone could tell her why. Brigid hadn't spoken to her mother's last boyfriend in thirty years. Nor had she possessed any desire to do so. Brigid had always suspected Calum went out of his way to avoid her. They both knew what her mother would have thought of the man he'd become. Maybe he'd been that way from the very beginning. If Brigid had learned two things over the past thirty years, it was people are fucking full of surprises. And she'd inherited her mother's shitty taste in men.

Though she knew she shouldn't, Brigid took another long drag on her joint before tapping it out. Then she lay back with her eyes closed, all the bad memories swirling around in her head. Brigid needed a drink to stop thinking. She opened her eyes to find two more staring back at her. A raven stood between her bare feet at the end of the chaise lounge. One enormous black bird might be a coincidence. But there were two more perched on a neighboring chair. She didn't need anyone to tell her that three birds staring straight at you were a sign.

"What?" she demanded, sounding ruder than she wanted.

The ravens didn't need to respond. Brigid knew what they had come to tell her. Someone was going to die.

"Who?" she asked, and the ravens flew off over the trees. Brigid let her eyes pan the remains of the orchard her mother had loved. After a decade-long drought, only a few trees still fruited. The animals that had once made their home in the branches had long-since passed away of old age.

She spotted the man half hidden behind a dead orange tree, his phone camera aimed in her direction. If her employees had been at the house, Brigid might have worried for their sake. But she and the intruder were alone on the property, and Brigid knew for a fact she'd be just fine. If she was going to kick the bucket, she'd have already seen it. That was her gift. She knew how people were going to die.

Sitting perfectly still, Brigid waited to witness the man's demise. She'd stopped fighting the visions years earlier. Instead, she'd learned to use them as fodder for her work. Critics called her movies inventive, original, and (more than once) the product of a diseased mind. She wondered what they would say if they knew how much she'd stolen from real people's lives. There wasn't a single species of death she hadn't witnessed at some point over the years. She still marveled that no two had ever been the same.

The vast majority of the dead were strangers—people who'd accidentally passed through the range of her sight. But Brigid had seen loved one's deaths as well. After her mother's suicide, she'd attempted to stop a few, just to prove to herself that she was utterly helpless. And she was. Her efforts never amounted to anything. So she'd decided long ago not to have any loved ones.

All she could do was refuse to take part. In her youth, she'd helped dispatch men the Old One marked for death. In the three decades that had passed since her mother's death, Brigid hadn't murdered a single soul. She'd wanted to. Oh how she'd wanted to. But she hadn't—and wouldn't. She refused to play the Old One's game.

*

Now, as she watched the intruder, she wondered how he would die. He seemed to be too far away for her gift to work, but the presence of the ravens could only mean one thing. Growing impatient, she decided to bring him closer. As soon as the thought passed through her head, the lead raven hopped to the side of the chaise longue and out of her way. Brigid rose and put on a black silk robe but didn't bother to tie it. He'd already seen everything she had.

"So how much do naked pictures of me go for these days?" she called out.

The intruder ducked back behind the orange tree.

"You're about two feet wider than the trunk," Brigid pointed out, leaving the *you fucking moron* part unsaid. "I was just about to make myself a drink. Do you want one?"

Brigid winced as she stepped out of a shadow and into the sunshine. She really did need that drink. When her eyes adjusted to the light, she could see the intruder peeking out from behind the trunk again. Tall and pale with dyed black hair, just like every one of her stalkers for the last twenty-five years. He didn't look very dangerous. None of them ever did. Even the ones with arrest records as long as her arm. Though this one did seem much younger than most. She was almost sorry he was going to die.

"Suit yourself," she said when he didn't budge. "But you might as well come say hello. There's nobody around here but me."

Brigid made her way to the wet bar on the other side of the pool. She could hear the crunch of his sneakers on the parched ground, followed by silence when he reached the patio. Brigid had spent hundreds of thousands of dollars on walls, cameras and razor wire to avoid moments like this. But that didn't mean she wasn't prepared for those defenses to fail. She opened the wet bar, mixed herself a Dark 'n Stormy and drank half of it down in one gulp.

"Now. What can I make for you?" she asked the man who was standing nearby.

"Your eyes really are icy."

Same thing they all said. "Yep. Always have been."

"And your figure is gorgeous. You haven't aged a day."

That was new. "Thanks," she managed to muster.

As foul as it was, she was glad he'd said it. This way she wouldn't feel an ounce of pity when it was over. His dirty black jeans were ripped at the knees and his t-shirt bore the title of Brigid's first horror flick—a movie she'd shot before he was born. In those twenty-five years since the release, she had climbed ladders that had long been off limits to anyone with two X chromosomes. Now she was a Tony short of an EGOT. Yet this motherfucker felt free to trespass on her private property, snap pictures of her in the nude and comment on the state of her body.

"You look like a whiskey man to me." Brigid dropped some ice in a tumbler and filled the glass with amber liquid from a special bottle no one else was allowed to touch. The powerful sleeping solution she'd mixed in was undetectable to the eye or tongue.

He took several steps toward her. "I can't believe you're real."

He was so close now. It seemed impossible that the vision hadn't yet come.

"Oh I'm very real." Brigid reached out and playfully pinched him as he picked up the tumbler.

Nothing happened. Brigid glanced down at her hand and rubbed her fingers together. Maybe they hadn't made contact with his flesh. She reached out and pinched the man again, this time hard enough to make him yelp. Nothing. The motherfucker wasn't meant to perish.

"What the hell? I believed you the first time." He rubbed his injured arm then lifted the glass to his lips.

"Sorry, darling," she said. "That whisky will make it all better."

Once he'd passed out in a heap, Brigid phoned the cops. Then she frisked the intruder before the police arrived. In his backpack, she found syringes filled with a pale blue fluid and zip ties. He wasn't the first psycho to come for her—and he probably would not be the last. She often wondered if the Old One was testing her—seeing how much Brigid could take before she succumbed to the urge to take a life.

The policemen who arrived performed the same search and was far less sanguine about the contents of the backpack.

One took her aside while his colleagues marched the intruder away. He was at least ten years younger, but his muscles and masculinity gave him the confidence to talk down to her. "You live on your own?" he asked as though that made Brigid strange.

Overcome by a vision, Brigid didn't answer right away. She saw the police officer writhing around on the ground, his hands on his cock as a snake emerged from the leg of his pants. That was new and different. She made a mental note of his death. It would work well in her next movie.

"Ma'am? Do you live alone?"

"Yes." Brigid snapped out of it. "Always have, always will."

"A woman as famous as you should have better security," the cop told her. "This guy could have killed you."

Brigid just nodded and walked away. Why bother to argue? The poor bastard would be dead soon. And as always, Brigid Laguerre would be just fine.

*

That night, long after the sun had disappeared over the ocean, Brigid sat beside the pool. She had barely budged since the police left. There was no one inside to turn the lights on, and her beautiful Spanish colonial looked completely deserted.

Her phone hadn't stopped buzzing all evening. Every media organization in the country was reaching out for a comment on the death of Calum Geddes. Brigid glanced down at the screen and saw the latest call was coming from a New York number. She ignored the call and clicked on a CNN link.

Calum Geddes, the billionaire media mogul, died today at the age of seventy-five. Raised in the Bronx by a single mother who often struggled to keep food on the table, Geddes' rise to fame and fortune has often been cited as proof that the American dream hasn't died. Ironically, Geddes dedicated his career to ensuring that fewer Americans are able to witness their own dreams come true. The country he leaves behind bears little resemblance to the one in which he was born. Our people are divided, our lands have been ravaged by climate change and our children live in fear of the future. No single person bears more responsibility for the current state of America than Calum Geddes.

And yet it wasn't that long ago that Geddes was ridiculed by his rivals as a washout. Then, in 1994, personal tragedy struck when the love of his life took her own. Flora Duncan was an heiress and mother of two teenage girls—one of them actress and producer, Brigid Laguerre. After Flora's death, friends and associates say, Geddes was never the same again.

Brigid snarled at the screen. "Calum turns out to be evil incarnate, and it must be a woman's fault." Then she drunkenly hurled the phone into the pool. "Fuck you. Fuck all of you. And fuck you for bringing my name into it."

She felt eyes on her and looked up to find one of the ravens standing on the railing. This time, it held a piece of metal in its beak.

"You again?"

The bird opened its beak and the metal object fell with a clang at Brigid's feet. She picked it up and twirled it between her fingers. It was a cast iron skeleton key.

"What is this?" Nothing on her property was anywhere as old as the key.

The bird flapped its wings. Then it hopped off the balcony. Brigid stood up and peered over the railing. The bird was looking up at her from the patio below. It was waiting for her to come down.

"Guess we're going for a walk," Brigid muttered. She stuck the key, an unlit joint and a lighter into her bra and polished off her drink.

*

The moon overhead, looking full to bursting, cast a silvery light over the landscape. No cinematographer could compete with nature. Brigid admired the moon's beauty, but she didn't need the illumination. She had always been able to see in the dark. She made her way through golden grass and effortlessly wove around the brittle skeletons of lavender bushes that hadn't survived the long drought. A snake hiding beneath a pile of rocks shook its rattle at Brigid when she passed. Up ahead, the raven stood, still and stoic, on a low hanging tree branch, waiting for her to catch up. As soon as she arrived, it flapped its wings and glided to a boulder on the top of a hill. Brigid climbed up to meet it. This time, it stayed put. Brigid had reached her destination.

"Okay, bird. What is it I'm supposed to see?" She turned around to gauge just how far she'd come. Below sat her beautiful white stucco house, with its red Spanish tiles and turquoise pool surrounded by dying orange trees. "What do you want from me?"

And then, as if the Old One had been waiting for Brigid to ask, she saw an ocean on the opposite side of the continent. Her sister was standing beside her in a black dress. She remembered the day well. It had been her last on the Island. In thirty years, she'd never once gone back. The Old One was telling her the time had come for a family reunion.

"You can show me anything you want. You know I'm not the one you've got to convince." She felt it only fair to point that out. "All I ever did was tell that bitch the truth. She's the one who cut me off."

Brigid stopped. Movement had caught her eye. There was a figure down below. She watched him dart from one hiding spot to the next, moving ever closer toward her house. There was no doubt it was a man. At first, she thought it might be the intruder from that afternoon. Could they have released him so quickly? She dug in her robe's pockets for her phone before she remembered tossing it into the pool. She looked around for the bird who'd guided her to safety, but the raven had left her to her own devices. "I don't give a fuck what he steals. I'm not going to kill him," she informed the Old One. She'd just have to wait it out.

Then a light flared in the darkness. Just a spot of orange on black, like the flame of a cigarette lighter. A dry bush near the house went up like a pile of kindling. She saw the man take a step back and put his hands in his pockets as he watched the inferno build. It wasn't the intruder from earlier. It was the police officer who'd asked if she lived alone.

The fire climbed the back wall of the house. The home Brigid and her sister had grown up in. Her final connection to the mother who'd abandoned her. The place where three decades of designer gowns were stored. She wondered if, somewhere, Flora was adding another orange pin to her map.

Brigid knew she was too far away to save her home. But unless she could place a call, the fire could take the entire valley with it. There was only one way to get back to the house fast enough to do any good—the same way she'd come. That meant going right past the arsonist. She'd have to kill him. Even as she thought it, she was moving.

She didn't go out of her way to be quiet, but he never heard her. As she drew closer, she could see him in profile as he watched the flames scale the wall and overtake the bedrooms. From the ecstatic look on his face, she could tell that it wasn't the first fire he'd set. Far from it. And she already knew what she needed to do.

When she heard the rattle coming from the same bush she'd passed,

Brigid reached inside and grabbed the snake. It writhed in her hand and whipped at her legs, but she knew it wouldn't bite. The ravens had decreed that someone would die that day, but it wasn't going to be her.

"Hey there," she said when she was on him. She held the snake behind her back.

If an actor in one of her films had ever shrieked the way he did, she'd have demanded another take. Too over the top, she'd have told them.

"Ms. Laguerre! I'm so glad you're not in there. I came back to check in on you, and found the house on fire. I've called it in, and the fire department should be here shortly." His eyes were drawn to the furious rattlesnake whipping Brigid's legs. "Are you okay?" The cop took a step back as he tried to make sense of it all.

"No," Brigid told him. "I'm very upset. You're the first motherfucker I've killed in thirty years."

"I don't . . ."

He got it when Brigid pulled back the waistband of his jogging pants and dropped the snake inside. She didn't bother to watch what happened next. There was no need to see his death twice. Instead, Brigid walked into her beloved childhood home for the very last time and dialed 911.

*

The fire crews saved the canyon, but the house wasn't spared. They found the arsonist's corpse with his pants down around his thighs and a nasty snakebite to the scrotum.

Brigid was taken to the hospital and treated for shock. At eight am the next morning, she was released into the care of her personal assistant. Within hours, she was spotted boarding a plane all alone, looking somber and chic in her trademark head-to-toe black. Tucked inside her breast pocket was a cast iron key.

311

Don't miss Kirsten Miller's gripping debut feminist thriller,

The Change . . .

**Nessa: The Seeker
Jo: The Protector
Harriett: The Punisher**

With newfound powers the time has come to take matters into their own hands...
Widowed Nessa lives alone in her house near the ocean. In the quiet hours,
she hears voices belonging to the dead – who will only speak to her.

On the cusp of fifty Harriett's marriage and career imploded, but her life is far
from over – in fact, she's undergone a stunning metamorphosis.

Jo spent years at war with her body. The rage that arrived with menopause felt
like the last straw – until she discovers she's able to channel it.

Guided by voices only Nessa can hear, the trio discover the abandoned body
of a teenage girl. The police have written off the victim. But the women have
not. Their own investigations lead to more bodies, and a world of wealth
where the rules don't apply – and the realisation that laws are designed to
protect villains, not the vulnerable.

**Now three women will avenge the innocent and punish the guilty.
IT'S TIME.**

ONE PLACE. MANY STORIES

Bold, innovative and
empowering publishing.

FOLLOW US ON:

@HQStories